BEAUTIFUL LIES

BEAUTIFUL SOULS
BOOK 1

PAULA DOMBROWIAK

beautiful LIES

PAULA DOMBROWIAK

Dark Angel Publishing

beautiful LIES

By: Paula Dombrowiak
Copyright © 2023 Paula Dombrowiak
First Edition, 2023
All rights reserved. No part of this publication may be reproduced, stored in any retrieval system, or transmitted in any form or by any means, including electronic, mechanical, photocopy, recording, or otherwise, without the prior written permission of the above copyright owner of this book.

This is a work of fiction. Names, characters, places, brands, media, and incidents are either the products of the author's imagination or are used fictitiously.

Cover Design: Paula Dombrowiak
Editor: Katy Nielsen

www.pauladombrowiak.com

To the over forty club, this book is for you.

AUTHOR'S NOTE

This story takes place in the Phoenix Metro area of Arizona. You might recognize some of the landmarks described in this book and while some of the places and names are accurate, others have been embellished or changed for the sake of the story.

For example, the Yucca Tap Room where Lake first meets Adrian, is a real place in Danelle Plaza in Tempe on the corner of Mill and Southern Avenue. It has been in business for over forty years. When the monsoon hits and it starts to rain, Adrian pulls Lake into the alcove of a record store. There is no such record store and was created to provide shelter for these two lovers.

The Salt River Wild Horses, featured in a pivotal scene in the book, are very much real. If you ever get a chance to visit Arizona, tubing down the Salt River is an absolute must. If you would like to learn more about the Salt River Wild Horses, you can visit the Salt River Wild Horse Management Group.

I hope when you read this book, you recognize places you've been or may want to visit because Arizona is a diverse ecosystem of untamed beauty that will capture your heart and invade your soul.

CONTENTS

Playlist	xiii
Prologue	1
1. Don't Be A Drama Queen	5
2. I Smell Rain	21
3. The Tap Room	31
4. Let it Burn	39
5. Old Enough to Drink	51
6. Bride or Bride?	61
7. Jake Ryan	71
8. Earth to Lake	81
9. It's a Family Name	85
10. We Have Your Father	99
11. Now it's Your Turn	113
12. It's a Great Ass	123
13. The Best I've Ever Had	131
14. You Kept Me Waiting	141
15. Beautiful Lies	151
16. The Third Button	157
17. So Goddamn Pretty	167
18. Too Old for Nicknames	181
19. Still Having Fun?	191
20. I Remember Everything	203
21. Turn it Up	217
22. Annual Potluck	235
23. So, You're the Reason	243
24. Moral Compass	247
25. Expiration Date	255
26. Playing Dirty	261
27. Big Shoes to Fill	269
28. Wingman	279
Five Months Later	
29. Graceland	287
30. Since You Asked Nicely	297
Epilogue	305
King of Nothing Blurb	313
King of Nothing Excerpt	315

Also by Paula Dombrowiak — 323
About the Author — 325
Acknowledgments — 327

PLAYLIST

Album

This book contains interactive chapters with song titles and links so you can listen while you read. The songs are listed in order of when they appear in the book.

Prologue: This is How a Heart Breaks by *Rob Thomas*

1. Only Happy When it Rains by *Garbage*
2. A Change Would Do You Good by *Sheryl Crow*
3. The Pusher by *Steppenwolf*
4. In the Air Tonight by *In This Moment*
5. Girls Talk Boys by *5 Seconds of Summer*
6. Polyester Bride by *Liz Phair*
7. Reasons I Drink by *Alanis Morissette*
8. How you Feel by *Wargirl*
9. My Favorite Mistake by *Sheryl Crow* and For Your Love by *Måneskin*
10. Wouldn't Want to Be Like You by *Sheryl Crow, St. Vincent* and Criminal by *Fiona Apple*

11. Rolling Stone by *Lainey Wilson*
12. Never Say Never (with Lainey Wilson) by *Cole Swindell and Stone by Whiskey Myers*
13. Lie to Me by *Tate McRae and Ali Gatie*
14. Medicine Man by *Charlotte OC*
15. House Fire by *Tyler Childers*
16. Tear Me to Pieces by *MEG MYERS*
17. Take Me Away by *Morgan Wade* and Crazy by *Aerosmith*
18. Strong Enough by *Sheryl Crow* and Bird by *Billie Marten*
19. Given the Dog a Bone by *AC/DC* and Thrills by *Donna Missal*
20. You Put a Spell on Me by *Austin Giorgio*
21. Kashmir by *Samvel Ayrapetyan* and Heat Waves by *Glass Animals*
22. Immortale (feat. Vegas Jones) by *Måneskin*
23. Starfire by *Caitlyn Smith*
24. Tell Me When It's Over by *Sheryl Crow* and *Chris Stapleton*
25. Lie to Me by *Jonny Lang*
26. World On Fire by *Sarah McLachlan*
27. Sex & Stardust by ZZ Ward
28. Stars by *The Cranberries*
29. Pain of Love by *Whissell*
30. Lovesick by *BANKS* and If You Were Here by *Thompson Twins*

Epilogue: Never Loved a Girl by *Aerosmith*

PROLOGUE

THIS IS HOW A HEART BREAKS BY ROB THOMAS

There are times in your life when you choose to stay stagnant, as if you're a voyeur watching it pass you by, but the problem is you think you're a part of it, not realizing you've made any choice at all. You think you're living but you're not – until someone crashes into your life, turns it upside down, and shows you a different angle. That's when muted colors turn vibrant and you begin to notice the beat of your own heart, each one thumping against your ribcage as if it's trying to break free. You notice the air pressing down and suddenly you're aware of gravity, because that's all that's keeping you grounded.

That's what happened to me, one year ago, on the eve of my forty-third birthday.

But I was too stubborn, too stuck in the past; unable to recognize what was right in front of me.

Now I'm in a race against time to get to him. Each mile is an endless void, taking up space, and taking up time.

Time that I'm running out of...

I can almost hear his dirty whispers in my ear. "You've made me wait far too long, Lake."

The image of him takes up all the space in my mind… so perfect, so pretty that it hurts.

Pushing my Porsche past the speed limit, I drive South on the 101 towards Tempe. Lightning flashes in the distance illuminating the McDowell Mountain range, outlining its formidable peak against the backdrop of night. The low rumble of thunder follows in its wake and strong winds rattle the car.

The monsoon.

Even with all the windows up I can still smell the impending rain, and with every shaky breath, I feel the dust enter my lungs. When the rain finally comes, it hits my windshield hard, amplified by the car moving above the speed limit. Every drop forces me to remember the night we met a year ago. What I remember the most and what is the hardest to escape my mind are his eyes, a soft brown with secret green flecks that you wouldn't notice unless they were trained on you. It's been too long since I last laid eyes on him, but his every feature is locked in my mind forever. Dark hair resting over his ears, barely skimming his shoulders, that felt like silk between my fingers, and feathered along my chest, between my breasts, and teased my stomach as he made me forget about the world around us. Beautiful tattoos adorned his arm, snaking over his chest and along his ribcage, and the way his skin felt as my finger traced each one, committing them to memory.

My heart hammers in my chest as I merge onto 60, getting closer, but still not close enough. Even at this late hour traffic is still heavy, because Friday night is when downtown Tempe comes to life. The rain pours down on the city, like it's washing away its sins and beginning again.

My sins are not so easily washed away.

Gripping the steering wheel I curse in frustration, because I've never been a patient woman. When I want something, I want it now, and I'm no closer to him than I was ten minutes ago.

A bolt of nervous energy runs through me like the lightning that divides the sky as soon as I find a parking spot. Heavy rains soaks me the minute I exit the car. Only adrenaline carries me forward as I take off running down Mill Avenue towards Southern.

Towards *him*.

The street fills with electricity as another bolt of lightning illuminates the sky, raising the hairs on my arm. My *Graceland* shirt is plastered to my body, and my hair is dripping wet. When I get to the *Tap Room*, everything stops, except my heart. Every beat against my chest is amplified like a drum filling my ears. Standing in front of the bar where I first laid eyes on Adrian Corvin nearly one year ago, on the eve of my forty-third birthday, I'm suddenly unable to move. He was the guy on the stage with the velvet voice and the soulful eyes that saw past my walls to the broken woman beneath.

I'd like to say he fixed me.

That his hands and his heart pieced me back together.

But I wouldn't let him.

If I could tell the younger me not to go to this bar a year ago, I still wouldn't have listened.

Jolting back to reality when the door crashes open, the bouncer looks out at the storm and sees me standing there in the pouring rain looking like a very sad version of myself, but in reality, I've never felt more myself. People huddle under the awning looking at the rain collecting near the curb, running along like a river with nowhere to go. Sheets of water are pushed onto the sidewalk as cars pass.

Stepping over the threshold and into the bar, the pounding of the rain stops but it's overtaken by the noise coming from inside the bar. Water drips from my clothes onto the floor and people stare as they walk by. I can only imagine what I look like, but I don't care.

An Aerosmith song pours from the speakers inside the bar, but it doesn't fill me with the joy I had been anticipating, not like it used to. The *Tap Room* had consumed my Friday nights where I would watch him play, entranced by how much fun he had on stage, the smile that came so easy to him, and the way the crowd responded. Looking around the bar, whispers of his words come back to haunt me. I can almost feel his lips brush my ear, and his breath tease the hairs on my neck when he said, *I will never be able to listen to another Aerosmith song without thinking of your sweet fucking pussy.*

My heart drops into my belly like a sinking rock because I know I'm too late, but I wander further into the bar anyway, taking the same steps I did a year ago, and I'm an idiot if I think it will yield the same results… because when I look up at the stage, he's not there. In his place is Finlay, and he doesn't look happy to see me.

1

DON'T BE A DRAMA QUEEN

Only Happy When It Rains by Garbage

My office is filled with the early morning light, overlooking the Scottsdale riverfront. It's a trendy part of town with professional buildings, coffee shops, restaurants, and boutiques. Chewing on the cap of a pen, I stare at my laptop, reviewing the same set of financial statements I was last night.

The only person allowed to barge into my office, besides Glen the CEO, is my direct assistant, Miles. From my desk, I see Miles making his way through the maze of cubicles with a determined stride, tablet clutched to his chest, and a mischievous wink in his eye.

Miles's curly mop of brown hair is temporarily blown off his forehead as he pushes my door further open with a whimsical whoosh. "The applicants for the intern position are waiting in the lobby," he reminds me.

Holding a finger up to shush me, he says, "And I picked up your favorite." He sets down an iced coffee in front of me.

Miles is wearing his signature bowtie, a red plaid print shirt, and brown suspenders that match his stylish shoes. He's the one that keeps me on task, runs my schedule and probably knows me better than my best friend, Georgie. Well, not quite, but he's the one that schedules my bikini waxes and pap smears, so I'd say he knows me pretty damn well.

"That's today?" I sigh, slumping back in my chair and scooping up my coffee. Fitting my feet back in my heels under my desk which I'd kicked off earlier, I sigh. "I don't have the energy for that today."

"It's only nine o'clock in the morning," Miles sighs, but he knows I've been here for a couple of hours already, as well as staying late last night. This prospective acquisition has me on edge lately, and more than a little stressed out.

"Your point?" I glare at him while taking a sip of my coffee.

"I emailed the résumés to you last week," Miles continues, ignoring my comment.

"Yes, I know."

"Did you look at them?" he asks, hand on his hip with an accusing stare aimed my way.

"Skimmed," I say, casually. "Top of their classes, stellar backgrounds, blah, blah, blah," I recite, waving my hand in the air dismissively.

"Should I start bringing them in?" he asks.

"Do I have a choice?" I ask, sarcasm evident in my tone as I blink innocently at him.

"Be nice," he warns.

"What? I'm always nice," I say, offended.

"I'm serious," he points at me. "I'm the one that has to hand them tissues when they exit."

I wave him away. "Let's not be dramatic."

"Did you forget about Aspen Holloway last year?" Miles asks.

"Who names their kid Aspen?" I ask, opening my email to pull up the résumés.

"Umm, have you looked at your birth certificate, *Lake*?" Miles retorts, clutching his tablet to his chest.

I laugh. "I'm sure *you* have. Lake is a family name, and I reserve the right to hire whomever I want."

Miles has been dealing with me long enough to know when I'm joking, although I like to trip him up occasionally.

"That's not the point! You can't *not* hire someone because of their name," he reminds me.

"Michael Clark was an excellent intern last year," I remind him, "and a good strong name, too," I tease.

"You're impossible," Miles gripes while shaking his head, making a point of grabbing the box of tissues off the side table and looking at me pointedly as he exits. I don't know how I got so lucky to find an assistant as great as Miles, but he gets bonus points for putting up with me.

A few moments pass before Miles brings in the first candidate.

"Blaine Robertson, this is Lake Kennedy," Miles introduces us, directing Blaine into my office.

He's a young man with short blonde hair, a nice smile, and cunning blue eyes. He's wearing a tailored dark suit with a red tie. I remember his résumé, top of his class, glowing recommendations from his professors and his previous internship.

When he walks in, it's not the confident stride I notice but it's the briefcase he's carrying in his right hand. On the side of the briefcase are his initials, BR, embroidered into the leather. Before he can even set it down to shake my hand I say, "Next!"

"What?" he says, clearly confused, looking from me to Miles who discretely hands him a tissue and escorts him from my office.

Miles glares over his shoulder at me, and I say, "A briefcase, Miles. He's twenty. Come on!"

The next four candidates have everything on paper you could want; great GPA's, stellar experience at previous internships and glowing recommendations, but they aren't any different from Blaine who graced my office earlier with his tailored suit and custom briefcase. I could pick from any of them and I'm sure they would do a great job. In an industry that is dominated by men with fancy educations, I'm looking for something different.

"Wyatt Bloom, this is Lake Kennedy," Miles introduces me to the young woman who extends her hand to shake mine before sitting.

"Wyatt?" I ask. "As in Wyatt Earp?" I peer at her over my reading glasses.

"I guess my parents took to Arizona a bit too much," she says nervously, and I try to give her a comforting smile.

Her suit jacket is draped over her arm, exposing a satiny camisole underneath with sweat stains evident under her armpits. Her blonde hair is pulled back into a low bun, and she gazes at me with nervous brown eyes.

She notices my scrutiny and says, "Sorry, it's just so hot outside and I hate wearing these things."

I hold up my hand to stop her from putting the jacket back on. "Not necessary," I say.

She takes a seat, crossing her legs demurely, and fanning out her pleated skirt.

"So, Wyatt, why are you here?" I sit back in my chair, pulling my glasses off and playing with the arm.

She looks confused. "Oh, um, isn't this the interview for the internship in the Finance department?"

"You're quick, but I asked you *why* you're here."

She straightens up, as if she's trying to get her bearings. "I'll be starting my last year at Barrett Honors at ASU in Finance, and…"

I hold my hand up for her to stop. Her mouth remains open, but no sound comes out.

"Let's start over," I say, standing up and walking to the front of my desk. I lean on the corner and grip the edge. "Why finance, and why *this* internship?"

I've read her résumé which tells me nothing of her character or her personality. Not that you need *personality* in Finance, which is proved by some of the men I work with, namely Lewis in legal. If I must spend time with someone for the better part of my day, then I reserve the right to be particular about whom I choose.

She looks at me confused, as if she's trying to figure out what it is she thinks I want to hear.

"There's no right or wrong answer here," I reassure her.

Furrowing her eyebrows, she blurts, "That's not true." I tilt my head urging her to continue, intrigued. "If I say I want this internship at Zentech because Finance is my passion and I want to be a part of a growing business so that I can grow along with it, well, then," she stops to take a breath, "I'm just like every other candidate telling you what it is you want to hear."

"Then what's the real answer?" I ask, giving her a comforting smile. "The one they train you *not* to say in interviews."

"I grew up in a middle-class family in Glendale. My mom is an elementary school teacher, and my dad sells cars," Wyatt explains, her brows furrowed in concentration as if she's contemplating what it is she's willing to admit. "I don't want to be middle class."

I move from my spot on the edge of the desk and re-take my seat, crossing my legs as I lean back.

"You can make a lot of money in this business," I agree.

"Look, Zentech would be a great company to intern at. I have a feeling I could learn a lot from you," she says coyly. "Not to mention you're a woman."

"I am."

"What I mean is, I know there's a disparaging number of women executives, especially in Finance. I'd rather work here than at a company who doesn't value me."

"And you think at Zentech you'd be valued?" I ask, picking up my pen and twirling it in my hand.

"I hope so," she crosses and uncrosses her legs, playing nervously with the pleating of her skirt.

"Do you have a boyfriend?" I ask.

She pinches her eyebrows together in confusion. "I don't think…"

"Interns do the work that no one else wants to do. You work when I work, and you do exactly what I tell you to do. If you last the next nine months, and if you're lucky, you'd get offered a full-time position," I explain, and Wyatt nods. "Boyfriends get in the way. I hope you're not the type of girl to let a guy get in the way of your ambition."

"That's a pretty cynical way of thinking," Wyatt says.

Hearing everything I need to hear, I pick up my phone, not looking directly at Wyatt. "Miles," I say into the receiver. "Can you please come in?"

Wyatt leans forward, placing her hands on the desk. "I should have just told you what you wanted to hear." She shakes her head and stands up, gathering her jacket.

I look up from the phone. "You did," I reply kindly.

Miles enters the room, tablet in hand. Looking between us, he reaches for the box of tissues, and I shake my head.

"And that's why you got the internship," I tell her.

Wyatt's eyes widen, a smile breaking out on her face. "Really?"

"Miles will take you to HR to get all your paperwork completed," I say, looking at Miles as he nods. "You can start on Monday."

I stand up and extend my hand to her as she shakes it, still in disbelief.

"You won't regret this," she says, excitedly.

"Let's hope not." I take a seat while Miles escorts her out of my office.

Before the door closes, he sticks his head back in.

"Put her on the Waterman acquisition and get her access to all the files," I tell him.

"On it," Miles says as he closes the door behind him with a big smile on his face.

"WELL, THAT WAS PAINFUL," Miles groans, walking beside me as we head back to my office. Looking at my watch, I'm happy the day is almost over and I can take these heels off. I'd been walking to and from meetings all day with barely a break in between.

"Oh, the new intern's not that bad. I'm sure she'll grow on you," I tease.

"Not the intern." Miles glares at me. "I was talking about the Asa Waterman meeting," Miles clarifies. He usually accompanies me in meetings to take notes while I present, and this time he was witness to me complaining about Waterman's CFO being unresponsive to sending over the files we'd asked for weeks ago.

"Painful for Waterman I'm sure," I say, about to push my office door open when Glen, our CEO, catches me.

"Have a minute?" he asks, looking from me to Miles.

I hold up my finger. "One minute," I say kindly and enter my office while Miles scurries over to Glen, working out my schedule to allow for a few minutes.

In the meantime, I check my emails and start a draft to the team detailing a list of items we need to go over next week.

Glen sticks his head inside my office, and I wave him through. "I heard you're giving Waterman hell," he says, motioning down the hall to the conference room I just left.

"Nothing he can't handle." It's mostly true.

Glen is in his sixties, tall and lean with hair that has almost completely turned gray – except for the pieces of dark brown that peak through on the sides. He's been good to me which is why I've given him so many years of my life, but lately, the pressure is wearing on me. I started working for him back in college to earn extra cash when the company was small and only had a handful of employees. There was no plan to stay here for nearly twenty years, but when I got pregnant with Noelle, I quickly had to get my shit together, and Glen was very flexible with my time.

He picks up a picture of Noelle from my desk, smiling as he looks at it.

"I still can't get over how much the two of you look alike." He sets the picture back down and sits on the edge of my desk.

"I remember when she used to raid the break room back when she was this tall." Glen gestures with his hand just below his hip as he chuckles. That was back when it was a family company; less employees meant less rules. Over the years Glen has become less about family and more about leaving behind a legacy.

Looking over at the picture he was holding, I remember the day at the San Diego Zoo, one of those silly photos where you stick your head through a cardboard cutout of an animal. Noelle was a zebra, and I was a monkey. We share the same dark brown hair and blue eyes.

"Seventeen," I answer. "It's her last year of high school," I say wistfully.

"I have a cubicle for her if she wants it. We could use another Kennedy with your killer instinct," Glen says jokingly, but I know the small talk is only a ruse for what he really wants to say, so I bide my time.

"She has a killer instinct, but it's for music not business, Glen, so you're out of luck," I tell him.

"That's too bad. Speaking of killer instincts, Waterman might be a bit cocky,"

"A bit?" I ask, cutting him off.

"But I need this deal to go smoothly, Lake," he says, ignoring my comment and looking at me pointedly. His kind eyes turn dark, taking on a professional demeanor.

Legacy is at the top of his mind this last year, ever since the heart attack. It's aged him, when before he was perpetually the youthful forty-something man who started a company in his garage that grew to be one of the top point of sale manufacturers in the valley. Without Waterman, it will stay in the valley, and that's not what Glen wants to leave behind to his kids.

"I know how much you want this," I tell him. "But you put *me* on it..."

"I didn't say *want*; I said *need*," he cuts me off, his eyebrows pinched together.

Placing my palms on the shiny wood desk between us I lean towards him, looking him directly in the eye.

"Just because it comes with pretty wrapping paper doesn't mean there isn't a viper waiting inside, Glen," I warn and straighten my shirt, smoothing down the wrinkles. "My job is to unwrap it, layer by layer." I shrug, straightening up and crossing my arms over my chest.

Glen knows exactly who I am and what my job is, and that's why he nods in agreement, shoving his hands in his pockets, satisfied. "Well, unwrap it without the claws," he says, and exits my office without a goodbye.

As soon as Glen leaves, Miles pokes his head back in and I wave him off. Slumping back in my chair, I kick off my heels and let out a big breath when I get a text from Noelle.

I can stare down an angry auditor or give bad news to a boardroom full of executives, but my seventeen-year-old daughter has the power to break me with the roll of her eyes. When she wants to hang out with me, I take every chance I can get – which is why I feel crestfallen when

I get a text that she wants to spend the night at her friend, Sofia's, house tonight instead of watching movies with me.

> L: Ditching me for your friend on my birthday? I see how you are.

I text back, teasing.

> N: Don't be a drama queen; your birthday isn't until Sunday.

She types back and I send her a smiley face with the tongue out.

> N: Did you know The Breakfast Club was made in 1985?

She adds, referring to the movie she's ditching.

> L: Yes, I know how old I am. Thanks for reminding me.

Movie nights are my favorite, and spending my birthday with Noelle, with some popcorn, pizza, and John Hughes is all I need.

"You have a fitting appointment with your sister this afternoon." Miles interrupts, poking his head back into my office.

I stare back at him with disdain.

"If you don't go, your sister will call me," Miles says. "Please don't put me through that," he begs.

"And people say I'm the mean sister," I grumble, giving him a playful smile.

"Normally you are, but she has the whole bridezilla thing going on right now," Miles retorts, handing me a black and gold wrapped present.

"I thought I told you not to give me any more presents after the last birthday present you gave me," I growl and narrow my eyes at him.

"I mixed up the boxes," he says, haughtily. "How many times do I have to explain?" His cheeks turn red as he remembers the mistake. "And besides, this isn't for your birthday," he pulls it away from me. "It's for your sister's bridal shower this weekend."

I snatch the present from him. "You bought it off the registry, I hope?" I ask him. "And personally checked the box before wrapping it?" I look at him pointedly.

"Yes," he scoffs.

"Because if my sister opens fish slippers…" I warn, but I'm cut off.

"For the last time, it was a gag gift for Patricia's retirement party!" he says, rather loudly, and I have to suppress a smile.

"Thank you, Miles." I take it from him, giving it a little shake.

"I still can't believe your sister would have a bridal shower on your birthday," Miles scoffs, shaking his head.

"Yeah, well, that's my sister," I tell him, but honestly, I couldn't care less about my birthday.

"And who has a wedding in August?" Miles asks. "In Arizona?" he adds, as if I don't already know how excruciatingly hot it is.

My phone vibrates with another text, and this time it's from my friend Georgie.

> G: Meet for dinner in Tempe after work?

Normally I would decline, opting for a quiet night at home and a glass of wine, but after the day I've had and the fact that I have to spend part of the afternoon trying on gowns with my sister, dinner with Georgie sounds great, especially since my kid ditched me.

> L: Will there be drinks involved?

I can almost see her eyes roll.

> G: Is this a serious question? Have you finally lost your marbles?

> L: Diablo's?

I suggest a great Italian place close to the college that I haven't been to in ages.

> G: Deal, and do not cancel on me!

"You're late," Beth snipes, turning around in her wedding dress from her spot on the podium.

Momentarily I stop, admiring how stunning she would look if she didn't have such a sour face. Beth is three years younger than me, and although we look alike, that's where the similarities end.

"I had to go home and change first," I explain, setting my purse down on the nearest chair.

"Into an *Aerosmith* t-shirt?" she asks, looking at my choice of attire disdainfully.

"Only the best for you, Beth," I say sarcastically, plastering a smile on my face as one of the associates makes her way over to us.

"You must be Lake, Beth's sister," she says, extending her hand for me to shake, with her beaming white teeth, severe blonde ponytail, and tight pencil skirt.

"The one and only," I reply, shaking her hand.

"I can see the family resemblance," she says, nodding her head as she looks from Beth to me.

"Thanks, considering she's adopted," I tease, squinting my eyes at Beth.

"Wasn't funny when I was a little kid, still isn't," Beth says, annoyed.

The woman looks at us, confused. "I'll get the dress ready for you to try on in the dressing room. I'm Sabrina, if you need anything," she says, ignoring our sniping. "Would you like a glass of Cham…"

"Yes," I interrupt, not giving her a chance to finish.

"pagne, while you wait?" she finishes anyway and I give her a pointed look.

"Before she dehydrates," Beth says, sarcastically, turning back around to admire herself in the mirror.

"I work, Beth. I'm sorry I was late," I tell her, trying to smooth things over.

"We all know how hard you work," she takes a jab at me while looking over her shoulder. "Can you help me?" She motions for me to grab the bottom of her dress so she can step down.

"By the way, you look really beautiful," I say, letting the lace of her dress fall back to the floor.

"Thank you." Her expression softens as she smooths down the material of her dress.

"Where's the rest of the bridal party?" I ask, looking around to see if they're lurking in the dressing rooms somewhere.

"They all had their fittings weeks ago," she explains, her expression softening. "I thought it would be nice if it was just you and I." She looks down and adjusts the top of her dress.

What she really means is that she wanted to make sure I got my fitting done in time so I didn't have an excuse to back out. I'm happy for my sister, but being a bridesmaid was excruciating the first time I did it for Beth, and that was nearly fifteen years ago, and I was chasing around a toddler.

Before we can finish our conversation, Sabrina makes her way back over, handing me a glass of champagne. "Fitting room number twelve is all set up for you whenever you're ready," she says.

"I think I'm going to need some help to get out of this," Beth says nervously, looking down at her dress and trying to figure out how to get ahold of the zipper.

Sabrina laughs. "Of course, that's what I'm here for."

While Sabrina helps Beth out of her dress, I make my way through the store admiring the dresses, before reaching the fitting rooms. Close behind is Sabrina, her heels catching on the Berber carpeting announcing her arrival.

"I can hold that for you." Sabrina says, reaching for my drink, but I move it out of her reach, narrowing my eyes at her while I slip inside fitting room number twelve.

A cushioned bench seat lines the back wall with a decorative mirror. Hanging on the back of the door is my dress – still inside the bag. I brace myself to unzip and unleash the horror trapped inside when there's a knock on my door.

"Do you need help in there?" Sabrina's voice filters through the thin dressing room door.

"I've been dressing myself since I was five, but thanks," I say, and unzip the bag as if ripping off a Band-Aid.

When I step out of the dressing room Beth examines me, a sappy expression on her face as she admires the dress.

"This is punishment, isn't it, Beth?" I ask, turning around to face her because I can't look at myself in the mirror.

"What are you talking about? It looks gorgeous on you." She spins me back to face the mirror, looking at me from behind. The chiffon skirt flows all the way to the floor with a slit that opens when I walk. It cinches at the waist, the material criss-crossing at the top, with thin spaghetti straps. The dress itself is better than the first bridesmaid dress I wore, but it's her color choice that I don't like.

"It's pink," I say. "I don't remember it being so *pink* before." I scrunch up my nose, scrutinizing it in the mirror.

"Yes," she says, clearly annoyed, "because that's the color scheme of my wedding; *pink*."

Sabrina gathers the chiffon at the back rather tightly and sticks a couple of pins through the material, making it fit snug enough so we can keep the wedding PG13. She looks in the mirror at me and drops her eyes to my cleavage. "We have some products in the back to give you a little more oomph," she gestures with her own cleavage, lifting it up higher to make a point.

Beth laughs while I spin around and say, "I'm forty-two,"

"Three," Beth interjects, and I glare at her.

"Two," I say sternly, "and I've had a kid. Plus, I'm not wearing a bra," I spin back around and try to push my boobs up higher. "This is not a true measurement of their potential," I explain to Sabrina.

She clears her throat. "I can have this ready to pick up next week," Sabrina says, leaving Beth and I alone.

"Just don't, Beth," I hold my finger up as she snickers while I walk back into the dressing room to change.

Once inside, I take another look in the mirror and hold each boob up, taking a better look. They're definitely not what they used to be, but I'm proud to say they've held up well over the years. "Pretty fucking good for a forty-two-year-old," I whisper.

After changing, I zip up the bag and hang it on the outside of the door for Sabrina.

Taking my glass of champagne with me, I follow Beth through the store. We pass by racks of white wedding dresses, and my fingers skim as I pass, feeling the different materials of silk and lace.

"Do you think you'll ever get married?" she asks, noticing my fingers lingering on one of the dresses.

I laugh. "Probably not," I say, following her to the display of shoes at the far wall.

"You just have to find the right person," she says.

"The only age-appropriate men for me are old, divorced, or if they've never been married, then something's wrong with them," I explain.

"*You've* never been married," Beth points out.

"Exactly my point," I say, raising an eyebrow as she picks up a beautiful jewel encrusted heel.

Beth shakes her head and laughs.

"Looks very uncomfortable," I say and Beth sighs, placing it back on the rack.

She turns toward me. "I didn't mean to plan the bridal shower on your birthday; it's just that Laura's family was only able to…"

"I'm not five, Beth," I cut her off. "It's just a birthday." Which is true, and I'd rather not celebrate it. Her bridal shower falling on my birthday is actually a welcomed distraction.

"I don't know why I'm looking at shoes, I already have a pair," she says, flopping her arms at her sides.

"You know I'm happy for you, right?" I say, grabbing onto her arms, holding her in front of me.

"I know," she sighs. Her expression turns solemn, and I know we're both thinking the same thing.

"I wish mom were here, too." We both feel her absence, especially during big moments like this. As the years go by, the gap in her presence gets bigger instead of smaller.

"What do you think she would say?" Beth asks, tilting her head, her brown hair falling down her shoulder. She has mom's heart shaped face and wide eyes, while I take more after our dad's angular, sharp jaw.

"About you marrying a woman?" I ask, confused, and Beth nods. "Mom wouldn't care if you were marrying the Loch Ness Monster, as long as it made you happy," I confirm.

Beth laughs, her posture easing, and she pulls her purse further up her shoulder. "I'm sorry if I've been a bit bridezilla lately," she apologizes as we make our way to the entrance.

"A bit?" I tease, eyeing her.

"Okay, a lot, but I promise to rein it in," Beth laughs.

We stop in front of the double doors and Beth looks at me expectantly. "Are you bringing Noelle to the shower? I haven't seen her in a while, and Ashley will be so excited."

Already feeling the heat through the glass, I brace myself.

"She's looking forward to it," I say with a smile, knowing I passed on my penchant for social gatherings to her.

"She is not, and neither are you," Beth laughs, knowing us better than I thought. "But you better be there and on your best behavior. Eric is picking up Ashley after the shower," she warns.

"Who, me?" I feign innocence, giving her an overly sweet look but I can't be responsible for my behavior around her dick of an ex-husband.

"I don't need any more problems with Eric," Beth says, referring to the last time he and I came in contact at Ashley's birthday party when he wasn't willing to let her stay later.

"He tripped, Beth." I roll my eyes. "I can't be held responsible for his clumsiness."

Beth holds back a smile while opening the door, unleashing a wave of hot air. "Do not forget to pick up your dress," she reminds me, pointing at me with an accusatory finger.

"What if I accidentally pick up a blue one instead?" I tease, while walking backwards to my car through the parking lot.

"Lake," she warns, narrowing her eyes at me while I slip on my sunglasses.

"Sabrina seems like the type to mix things up," I say, while shimmying my hips, eliciting just a hint of a smile from Beth.

"If you show up in anything but a pink dress, so help me God, Lake," Beth yells jokingly across the parking lot and I laugh, sliding in the driver's seat of my car.

2

I SMELL RAIN

A Change Would Do You Good by Sheryl Crow

The drive to Tempe isn't so bad being opposite of rush hour traffic. The problem is finding parking in a college town that's meant for walking or biking. I must admit that I'm looking forward to having a nice dinner with Georgie. After the week I've had, and that dress, I deserve a nice evening out.

The restaurant is a few blocks over, and even with the setting sun, the heat is oppressive, like a thick blanket, and I can already feel sweat collecting at the small of my back. In the distance, heat rises from the asphalt causing bright wavy lines like a mirage.

The clouds behind the high rises are an unnaturally vibrant mix of pinks and oranges, casting reflections in the windows of nearby office buildings as the sun sets. Mill Avenue is teeming with college students back from the summer. Music filters onto the street from nearby restaurants and local music venues. By the time I get to Diablo's I'm already sticky with sweat. When I pull open the door, the cranked a/c hits me, feeling like heaven.

Looking around for Georgie, I notice she's not here yet, so I settle for a seat at the bar and order a drink while I wait. ASU colors of deep maroon and brilliant gold adorn the walls. Sun Devils merchandise and framed jerseys hang on the wall, along with pictures of the football stadium when it was first being built.

All of the TVs in the restaurant are tuned to various sports games, but I have no idea who they are, nor do I care. Although the rest of the patrons in the restaurant seem to care when I hear loud cheering from a few tables nearby.

The place isn't that crowded yet since it's still early, and it doesn't take long for the bartender to set the martini I ordered in front of me.

"Ever get to see them in concert?" he asks over the noise. He's a nice-looking man, a little younger than me, with dark hair slicked back. When he smiles, the lines next to his eyes crinkle.

For a moment I'm confused until he points to the t-shirt I'm wearing. Looking down, I remember what I'm wearing. It's a vintage *Aerosmith* t-shirt from the *Toys In The Attic* era, way before my time, but I'm still able to appreciate it. I hate to wash it, because one of these days it'll disintegrate in the machine.

"Long time ago," I say, taking a sip of my drink, not really interested in making small talk with him, but he seems nice.

"Great band in their prime," he says while making another drink, his attention still clearly on me.

I honestly can't remember the last time I saw a concert; probably before Noelle was born and I was still in my early twenties.

"Still are," I say, cocking my head to the side. He smiles disbelievingly and I take another sip of my drink. If he thinks he's going to win me over by taking shots at my favorite band, he's mistaken.

"If you like music, you should check out the *Tap Room* down the street. They have a great cover band that plays on the weekends," he offers while pouring tequila in a margarita glass.

"I am well aware of the *Tap Room*," I say, crossing my legs and resting my arm on the bar top as I check the door for Georgie.

"You've been?" he asks, still trying to make conversation.

"Long time ago," I say, leaving it at that.

I haven't been to the *Tap Room* since I graduated college. This area keeps reinventing itself every few years, and places I used to go to are all gone, but not the *Tap Room*. The low-key brick building has stayed the same and stands strong even back to when my dad went to ASU in the seventies. It has a reputation – an infamous one at that. A lot of great bands have played there, but I've lost touch over the years while raising my daughter and nurturing my career.

As soon as the bartender is done delivering a drink a few seats down, he settles back in front of me, resting his forearms against the wood, sleeves rolled up.

"Maybe one of these weekends when I'm off, you'd want to check it out with me?" he asks expectantly.

I take a drink of my martini and level my eyes on him. "I said I was aware of it, not that I'd want to go there," I say, then add, "with you".

Scoffing, he seems to think I'm trying to play hard to get, but it's actually the opposite. Before he can protest, Georgie interrupts by giving me a hug.

"I've missed you," she says, all smiles, still in her multi-colored animal print scrubs.

Sensing that she's interrupted something when she lets go, she looks between me and the bartender.

"I'll let the hostess know to get your table ready," he says and walks away.

"Are you scaring off men already?" she teases, looking down at the watch on her wrist. "It's only seven o'clock."

"The night is young, Georgie, just wait," I say teasingly, lifting my martini glass in front of her before taking a lavish sip.

Her thick blonde hair is pulled back into a low ponytail, showing off her high cheekbones and lovely green eyes. She's much shorter than me, so when we stand together it makes me look like a giant. I'm glad I'm sitting down right now.

"What was that all about?" she asks suspiciously with her hand on her hip.

The hostess approaches us. "Your table's ready," she says, and leads us over to a booth near the bar.

"He was telling me about a band that plays on the weekend at the *Tap Room*," I tell her as we take our seats.

"He was flirting with you," she retorts and picks up her menu.

"He was not," I reply, hiding behind my own menu.

"Of course, he was." She pushes my menu down. "Why wouldn't he? Look at you. Even in that band t-shirt, you're gorgeous," Georgie says. "And you're successful," she adds.

"Why is everyone obsessed with my t-shirt today?" I ask, disgruntled. "And men don't care about accomplishments. They care about waist and bra size."

"Not true," she says, shaking her menu. "And you have nothing to worry about in that department." She looks at me pointedly.

"Oh yeah? Who's the flavor of the week for Dr. Stickuphisass?" I ask, referring to Georgie's boss at the veterinary office she works at. "Did she cure cancer, win a Nobel peace prize?" I smirk, knowing I'm right.

"He doesn't count," she grumbles. "And I didn't say anything was wrong with your shirt. You look cute in it," she replies.

"I wear high heels and skirts all week," I say, feeling the need to defend my attire. "I get home, and all I want to do is wear something comfortable. What's wrong with that?" I ask her.

"Nothing's wrong with that," Georgie says, sincerely. "Look at me," she motions to her attire, "scrubs are oh so sexy, aren't they?"

Then she lifts her foot up. "And of course, don't forget the crocs."

I laugh. "At least your work clothes are comfortable. Can you see Glen's face if I showed up at work in jeans and a t-shirt?"

"I think he would pass out," Georgie says, "and not because he's a tight ass, but because he's never seen you in casual clothes before."

"Not true. Remember that time we had a team building event at the golf club?" I remind her. "I wore a golf shirt and khakis."

Georgie belts out a laugh while I look across the room to the bartender. He's chatting with a pretty college age girl who took my seat, leaning onto the bar with the same sexy, bashful smile he gave me.

"Look," I motion for Georgie to turn around, "how easily I'm replaced." I raise an eyebrow.

Georgie scoffs.

"You're just mad that he proved my point." I pull my menu back up.

"He's a bartender. Short attention span," she says. "What about any of the guys at work?"

"I'm not looking to date anyone. I'm busy. I don't have time for anything other than work and Noelle."

"Noelle's going to fly the coop soon, and then what are you gonna do? Sit at home with your 80s movies?" she asks accusatorially.

"Hey!" I scold her. "I still have a whole year left with her."

I pick up my menu, and before Georgie can comment, the waitress approaches our table to take our order. I've had a rough week, and clearly the alcohol hasn't taken off the edge, so I order carbs in the form of a creamy pasta dish.

"Can we get a nice bottle of Moscato?" Georgie asks the waitress, and I raise an eyebrow because she usually snubs her nose at my unsophisticated taste for sweet wines.

"It's hot as fuck outside, and besides, it's your birthday," she says, placing her forearms on the table.

"Oh, it's your birthday?" the waitress asks excitedly.

"If you sing to me, I will stab someone with a fork," I warn, picking up the utensil from the table.

"We don't sing," the waitress says nervously, "but we do have a free dessert."

"I can get on board with that," I say, placing the fork down and handing her my menu.

Georgie props her chin up on the back of her hand and looks at me.

"What's that look for?" I ask.

"You know I love you," she says.

"Don't be sappy; you know how I hate that." I drain the last of my martini, knowing I'm gonna need it.

"But you gotta get back out there or it's gonna dry up like a raisin," Georgie says, and then she leans in. "It might have already happened. Have you looked at it lately?" she asks, raising an eyebrow.

"You're disgusting, you know that?" I say and Georgie leans back in the booth laughing. "Okay, what about you? I don't see you dating anyone," I say, crossing my arms over my chest with satisfaction.

"Dating and fucking are two very different things."

The waitress drops off our bottle of wine just in time to hear Georgie's eloquent explanation.

"Working in a bar, I've heard worse. You ladies enjoy your evening." She winks at Georgie and leaves us to pour the bottle ourselves.

"I like her," Georgie admits, pointing a finger in her direction.

"Look, all I'm saying is that if anyone deserves to be happy, it's you," she says, lifting her glass. "Happy birthday."

I clink my glass with hers and take a sip.

"Just wait until *your* birthday," I tease.

"Ugh, don't remind me," Georgie sneers, setting her wine glass back on the table.

"Welcome to the forty club," I say, smiling.

"Not yet," she reminds me with stern eyes.

"Let's just enjoy dinner, and you can fill me in on your afternoon with Beth," Georgie suggests and settles in.

"I want to be able to eat my dinner, Georgie," I say, shaking out the napkin and placing it in my lap.

"That bad?" she asks.

"Not really, but I'll be glad when all this wedding stuff is over and I can have my life back," I say.

"Oh, come on now, we all know your sister can be a pain in the ass, but aren't you happy for her?" Georgie asks.

"Of course, I am," I tell her. "It's just been a stressful week, and Beth was the target I got to take it out on." I raise my eyebrows conspiratorially. "That was just a bonus," I wink.

Georgie laughs. "You know what's good for stress?"

"Chocolate and wine?" I raise my glass as proof, cutting her off, just as when our food arrives.

"And pasta," Georgie says, staring at her big plate of manicotti. She picks up her fork, and before she takes a bite, she looks at me and says, "And sex, Lake. Sex is good for stress." She places a forkful in her mouth while I shake my head and laugh.

I can barely finish half my pasta, but when I look over at Georgie's plate, I see she's almost eaten all of it.

"How someone as small as you can fit all of that in your stomach, I'll never know," I say, draining the last of my glass.

"You have no idea what I can fit in here," Georgie teases, raising an eyebrow and patting her stomach.

I laugh, causing my own stomach to ache. It's been way too long since I've had a night like this. We don't find the time often enough to hang out, and I don't want to go home to an empty house.

"Do you want to go over to the *Tap Room*?" I ask Georgie, leaning forward. "I was told they have a good band on the weekends." I smile, raising my eyebrows.

She looks down at her scrubs and frowns.

"Forget it, it's okay. I was just thinking since we're close by," I say, throwing my napkin over my plate.

The waitress makes her way back to our table, and before she has a chance to speak, I say, "Just the check."

"You don't want your dessert?" she asks.

I pat my stomach. "I don't think I could eat it."

"Really?" Georgie protests.

"Do you have a hollow leg I don't know about?" I joke.

"I'll box it up for you," the waitress says, and clears our plates.

As soon as she leaves, Georgie says, "You should go."

"Go where?" I ask, confused.

"To the *Tap Room*."

"It's fine, we can go another weekend." I wave her suggestion away.

"You say that, but then we'll never go," Georgie says, and it's true. "Plus, you'll be busy with your sister's wedding, and the next time either of us is free will be pushing next month."

"You're still coming, right?" I ask, expectantly.

"Miss the wedding of the century? Never," she quips.

I look out the window to the crowded street and watch as people walk by. This is my life, putting things off another day, another week, another month, until they're completely forgotten. The fact that I happened to be free for dinner tonight was a miracle, and Noelle is spending the night at Sofia's.

As if she can see right through me, Georgie says, "Ah hell, who cares if I'm in my scrubs? Let's go."

"Really? You don't have to," I say. "Now I feel like I've guilted you into it."

"You didn't guilt me," she says sternly. "It'll be fun."

As soon as the check arrives, Georgie grabs it.

"I got it," she says, snatching it before I have a chance to.

"Stop, you don't have to do that. Let me give you half." I reach in my purse to grab my wallet.

"It's your birthday, let me pay." She places money in the checkbook and closes it.

Once we step outside, I stop and close my eyes, inhaling deeply. It smells like rain. I look up at the clouds in the dark sky and feel the wind pick up.

"You're doing that weird thing again," Georgie says, checking to make sure she has everything.

I level my eyes to Georgie's. "It's going to rain," I tell her.

"Thank fuck." She pulls her large bag further up her shoulder after pulling her phone out to check it. "Shit!" she says.

"Hang on." She motions for me to wait while she turns for some privacy.

"I thought the meds were helping him," I hear her say. "I know, but..." her voice trails off and any excitement I had about going to the *Tap Room* with Georgie is crushed when she turns to me and says, "I'm sorry."

"You have to go," I say, trying to keep a smile on my face so she doesn't know how disappointed I am.

"Yeah, Charlie isn't responding to the meds anymore and Mrs. Hampton's bringing him in to be put down. Dr. Stickuphisass needs me to assist," she says.

"He can't run that place without you, huh?" I ask.

Georgie and I used to work together until about five years ago when she quit, went back to school, and started her second life, as she calls it, as a vet tech. The minute she made the decision to leave corporate life I could sense a shift in her, as if the pressure weighing her down was lifting. She seems happier now.

"He's lacking in the emotional department, if you know what I mean, and Mrs. Hampton will be crushed."

"It's okay."

"Dr. Stickuphisass is a jerk sometimes, but when he does things like this after hours for his customers, it reminds me he does have a heart in there somewhere," Georgie says with a slight chuckle. "I really am sorry." Her expression turns remorseful as she leans in for a hug.

"You should still go," she says into my hair.

"No." I shrug, pulling away.

"Why not? Enjoy some music, live a little," she says.

"I live."

"You're going to go home and watch John Hughes films all weekend, aren't you?"

I give her an appalled look. "No, smart ass," I say. "Noelle ditched me to sleep over at Sofia's."

"Lake, go," Georgie says with a stern expression. She might be short, but she can be intimidating when she wants to be. "This is your sign."

I nod, pacifying her. "Go take care of Charlie."

"Love you," Georgie concedes, giving me a hug.

I watch as she crosses the street and then look in the direction of where my car is parked. Maybe it's the impending rain or the music on the breeze taunting me, but instead of walking to my car, I walk in the opposite direction.

3

THE TAP ROOM

The Pusher by Steppenwolf

The electricity in the air from the impending storm crackles against my skin as I walk down to the corner. When I reach the end of the block, I take a turn onto Southern, following a group of college students to Danelle Plaza. Each step feels like I'm moving back in time because the plaza is exactly the same – even if the businesses that have taken up residence have changed. Everything is new; the auto parts store, a smoke shop, and thrift store... but not the *Tap Room*.

The same white brick facade and weathered aluminum awning with the distinct white lettering, *Yucca Tap Room* remain. The entrance is still covered in bold, bright artwork with arrows leading you in, as if you could ever miss it. The bouncer takes one look at me and waves me through, not even bothering to card me. I'm not twenty anymore, which is the last time I was here.

Everything looks the same, and yet so different. Maybe it's because I'm looking at it through different eyes – older eyes.

It's dark and loud, with people moving from one room to the next. The same L shaped bar with a stained wooden counter sits in the corner. Mirrors line the wall with shelves of liquor illuminated by backlighting, and the TV screens above the bar list all the local beers on tap. I manage to squeeze my way through the crowd and get the attention of the bartender.

He's a young guy, nice looking, with a dark beard shaved close and a black t-shirt with the bar's emblem on it – a green mountain with gold lettering, *Yucca*, across it, and the words *Tap Room* below it.

"What can I get you, sweetheart?" he calls out over the noise.

This isn't the kind of place you order a martini in.

Looking over the list of beers displayed on the TV screen above, it feels a bit overwhelming.

"Blueberry blonde?" he asks, raising an eyebrow at me.

"Excuse me?" I ask, confused by what he means. I'm not a beer drinker, so I don't know the terms.

"That's what she's drinking," he points to a young blonde woman wearing a pretty sundress at the end of the bar holding a beer glass with something purple in it.

I slide my eyes back to him. "Do I look like I drink grape juice…" I pause, looking for a name tag.

"Gael," he says, looking me up and down and then cocks his head to the side with a smile. "You look like you could put Putin in his place," Gael laughs and turns around, leaving me even more confused.

A few moments later, he returns with a tall glass of dark ale and slides it in front of me. Although I'm not a beer drinker, the way he's looking at me, it's as if he's challenging me to drink it.

"Not Today, Putin," he says, pointing at the beer and I raise a questioning eyebrow. "Russian Imperial," he clarifies.

I laugh. "Oh, Gael, you're good," I say, and take a tentative sip. "Whew." It's a heavy mix of dark chocolate, coffee, and *very* ripe fruit that makes my lips pucker. I wipe my mouth with the back of my hand.

"You like?" Gael asks as he leans against the bar top with a smug expression.

"This'll definitely put some hair on *your* chest, Gael," I say, making him laugh.

Placing a couple of bills on the bar top, I take my beer with me as I leave to explore the rest of the bar.

The restaurant is busy with every table now taken, and a line forming to get drinks. It's not just a college bar like it was back in my day. There are young professionals from the nearby businesses that have sprouted up over the years, older folks that probably live in the nearby neighborhoods, and I suppose people like me who are looking for a little nostalgia.

The arcade at the back has been expanded. Pinball machines and other vintage games line the wall. The retro sounds of buttons and levers fill the space, mixing with the music from next door and people talking. I don't feel so out of place in my t-shirt, cut off shorts, and sneakers. It's too hot for anything more, and everyone else is just as casual. Georgie would have been right at home in her scrubs, but in a way I'm glad she didn't come. It gives me time to explore and contemplate the girl I was before I had Noelle.

On the other side of the restaurant, I wander into the bar's live music venue. A sultry *Steppenwolf* song seeps into the bar as the singer's deep voice sings into the mic. Making my way closer to see the band on the riser, I see a thick crowd standing at the front of the stage. Tables frame the room but none are empty, so I lean against one of the wooden columns at the back, content to watch life teeming around me as if I'm in the center of a tornado just waiting to be swept up.

The *Tap Room* is the kind of place you can lose yourself in, and that's exactly what I intend to do.

I can't help the smile on my face as I take a drink of my beer, letting the perfect mix of sweet and bitter coat my throat. Remembering this place like it was yesterday, my college roommates and I would sneak in with our fake IDs, often staying until last call. Rules were a little looser back then, but I imagine some still get away with it. We were young; we owned the dance floor and held court at one of these very tables. In fact, I think these are the same fucking tables from twenty years ago.

Now I own the *boardroom* instead of owning the dance floor. I may have grown up, but that same girl is still inside.

The humidity curls the hairs at the nape of my neck, and I wish I had a hair tie to offer some relief. Trying to cool myself off, I settle for leaning my cheek against the cold glass of beer.

Scanning the crowd, I look up towards the stage and lock eyes with the singer, a pretty face to go with that pretty voice. The venue is so small I can make out pieces of dark brown hair sticking to the sweat on his forehead, and watch with rapt attention as his mouth practically swallows the mic with lush lips that are perfectly kissable.

What is it about musicians that make them so goddamn sexy? I wonder to myself. Is it the tortured artist persona writing poetic lyrics? The vulnerability it takes to perform on stage? Or the romantic notion of being untouchable?

Maybe it's the prospect of so much passion on stage being transferred to the bedroom.

This guy is made of jagged edges, tattoos, ripped jeans, and definitely not age appropriate for me. Old enough to drink, but just young enough to make it hurt. My whole body feels hot as he continues to stare at me. The crowd loves it when he emphasizes certain lyrics of *The Pusher*, shaking the hair from his face, and using his hands to draw them in. Admittedly, I haven't been to a concert in a long time, but there's something about him that is authentic and exciting.

Maybe it's the beer or the stifling heat, but his eyes seem to follow as I make my way around the room. Caught staring back, it's as if he sees my thoughts when the corner of his lip tugs into a knowing smile. It's impossible for him to know that I'm imagining what kind of lover he would be – selfish or generous, relentless or fleeting, but his smile says otherwise. That smile could knock a girl right out of her panties. Maybe for one night I can be someone else, and that makes the prospects endless.

Finishing the rest of my beer, I set the empty glass on a nearby table before slipping into the restroom so that I can breathe. While waiting in the short line, I look at all the writing on the walls and on the sides of the stalls. It's a typical dive bar bathroom, with bad lighting, leaky faucets, and sticky floors.

As I wash my hands and look at myself in the mirror, I notice my hair has gone limp, and any makeup I had on has long since melted off. I run my fingers through my hair trying to salvage the volume, but it's no use. The brown waves hang just at the tops of my shoulders, and I sweep it to the side. As soon as I reach over to grab a paper towel from the dispenser, I see it... written in black sharpie, is something I had almost forgotten existed.

Twenty fucking years and they couldn't have repainted the walls? I shake my head and drop the used paper towel into the garbage can.

Questioning why I came here, I wonder was it to relive some part of me that has been buried twenty years deep? I'm forty-three years old for fucks sake.

This isn't me.

I don't look back.

And I don't have regrets.

Every decision I've made in my life since *him* has brought me here, to the person I am today. I'm successful, whether or not my hair is styled or my makeup is perfect. Better yet, I'm successful because *he* isn't in my life anymore.

Pushing open the bathroom door I walk through the bar, slipping between the crowd and find myself on the street. A gust of wind travels down the long strip mall. Everything is dark, all the other stores closed for the night. Closing my eyes, I inhale deeply and smell the rain.

It's coming.

The city hibernates all year waiting for the rain to penetrate the hard-shelled soil, breaking it open, and once it does, everything comes to life.

A lightning bolt stretches across the sky just as the wind picks up, blowing the hair from my neck and cooling it. I start to walk down the block on the way back to my car, passing a darkened record store when I hear a voice call out behind me. "Hey!"

Without even turning around, I know it's him, the singer with the velvet voice and the kissable lips. The wind continues to blow like a freight train down the block, picking up the edges of my shirt and blowing my hair across my face. Turning around, I see he's standing on the sidewalk, looking every bit as delicious as he did on stage. I wait for him to look around me, to the person whose attention he was really trying to get, but he just stares at me the same way he did in the bar, like he's trying to unearth my secrets.

Caught in the spider's web of his soulful eyes, I'm unable to move.

The silence is broken when the sky opens and dumps heavy sheets of rain, plastering my hair to my face and my shirt against my body in less than a minute. Moving towards me, each step closing the distance between us, the bashful smile on his face causes my pulse to quicken, and the blood rushing in my ears becomes the only sound I can hear. When he reaches me, I can see the pulse in his neck as his hand grips my waist, guiding me into the alcove of the darkened record store, taking us out of the rain. With his hand still on my waist, the heat from it makes me shiver.

His close proximity takes the breath out of me, and I watch as the water drips from his hair onto his full lips, leaving a trail down his chin. In the dim light of the alcove with only the streetlamp to illuminate his face, I see the green flecks in his brown eyes as he searches mine. They pull me in like a magnet; intense and beautiful. My palms press against his chest slowly gathering his shirt between my fingers, all while my heart pounds in my chest, because this stranger drew me in the minute I laid eyes on him in the bar. It's as if he is a tiny piece of my past buried long ago now being unearthed.

Maybe it's the wind, the way it wraps itself around us, pushing us together rather than pulling us apart, but I feel as though this is a chance I need to take. How many times in the last eighteen years had I truly taken something just for myself? And how many more times in my lifetime will I get a chance to choose something for myself?

In the small space between us, a question lingers in the air.

Can I kiss you?

Wanting it and doing it are two different things, because once I cross that line, will I be taking a step backwards? Looking at his beautiful rain-soaked face, I know the answer.

The reach is slow and tantalizing as his lips move dangerously close to mine. Hesitant and seductive, heady, and dangerous, I brush my nose along his, feeling his breath against my lips before taking a taste. His kiss is like a shot of bourbon, sweet and smooth with hints of caramel and vanilla, with no burn, and no regret. My back hits the wall of the record store as he steps forward, deepening the kiss, a moan escaping between us. This kiss causes my body to come alive like the desert reacting to the rain.

His hands slip underneath my shirt, skimming along my stomach before drawing my leg around his waist. Pressing his hips further into me causes an ache deep in my belly that spreads between my thighs. It's the kind of ache that draws out all reason, collapses any hesitation, and makes you feral for more.

I don't know this man.

I've never seen him before in my life.

But there's a long dormant beast inside of me that stretches and unfurls, awakened by his kiss.

It's wild and reckless like the monsoon happening around us, but I can't seem to stop myself.

If I feel this way with just a kiss…

I can only imagine what it would be like to take this further.

The problem is, I don't want to just imagine it.

In this little dark corner of Mill Avenue, hidden in the alcove of the record store safe from the rain, I feel more alive than I have in a very long time.

4

LET IT BURN

IN THE AIR TONIGHT BY IN THIS MOMENT

"Where do you live?" I ask breathlessly, holding him back with just a press of my palm to his chest.

His hands grip my hair as he whispers, "Just a couple of blocks over."

Swallowing hard, I bite my lip as I nod. Feeling as if I'm holding onto a lightning bolt, I'm equally afraid to let go as I am of being burned.

Looking out towards the street, the pavement glistens with rain, cars splash puddles of water as they drive by, and I can hear the nearby chatter of people running down the sidewalk. The rain has woken up the city and it's teeming with life.

"It's still raining," he says, turning back to me, and I notice the dimples on his cheeks as he smiles.

"I like the rain," I say, swallowing down any residual nervousness.

Slipping his hand through mine, he pulls me into the rain and we run down the sidewalk together. The steady drip cools my heated skin and soothes my nerves. Running my tongue along my swollen lips, I taste the remnants of bourbon from his kiss, and feel tingles spread as he runs a thumb along the top of my hand.

If I don't get to his apartment soon, I may back out. In the alcove I didn't have time to think, I just felt, and now I'm starting to get inside my head, wondering what he's thinking. Is this something he does often? I slide my eyes to him.

He's young and pretty with an edge just under the surface.

Tattoos line his left arm and peek out above the collar of his shirt.

His beautiful head of dark hair feels like silk, even when wet, and he plays guitar.

Of course, he's done this before.

There's a large grassy area and a sidewalk that winds in between the two-story trendy apartment buildings. They look pricey, definitely above the pay grade of a struggling musician. When we turn the corner, there's a large pool, the water lit up with underwater lights. The rain breaks the surface causing ripples of light to reflect on the side of the building.

My palm is wet inside his, but he doesn't let go until we get to the concrete stairwell on the outside of his building. Stopping on the first step, I grip the railing as I search his brown eyes looking for a sign. I'm smarter than this, an educated woman with a lot more years on him, and yet I feel like a reckless teenager.

Maybe desire has clouded my mind, but when I look at him, I see a man who makes promises to wreck me in the best possible way. When his hand circles my waist possessively and his thumb digs deliciously into my hip, I know there is no way I'm leaving here unsatisfied.

His voice is a breathless whisper. "I don't usually…" he tries to explain but I place my finger against his lips to silence him.

"Don't lie." A slow smile spreads on my face. "Of course, you have," I whisper.

His lips curve into a sexy smirk, and then he bites down gently on my finger before taking my hand again and leading me up the stairs. We stop in front of his door, and I stand against the brick of the building while he digs the keys out of his pocket. He leans in to take my mouth again before unlocking the door, only reaffirming how much I want this.

How much I *need* this.

God, I need this.

"You are the sexiest woman I have ever met," he says against my lips.

Another lie, but I don't mind.

We both know why we're here. There are no promises, no expectations, and no truths.

Only lies.

And I love the way he lies.

He captures my lips again, his tongue slipping inside, causing me to moan. When he palms my ass bringing me closer to him, we tumble into his apartment. As soon as we enter, I pull away to get a look at this stranger's home for the first time.

Flicking on the light the small entryway is illuminated, calling attention to a black metal table lining the wall where he tosses his keys into a glass bowl sitting on top.

"I'll be right back." He squeezes my hand before letting go and heads down the hallway, leaving me to admire a framed poster of graffiti art that hangs in the entryway. Colorful feathers fall from an angel's wing and turn black when they hit the ground. Walking past it, my hand reaches out to touch it, expecting to feel the feathers. It's so beautiful.

My wet shoes squeak on the flooring as I walk further inside to a small living room. The cold air from the a/c hits my wet skin, and I can feel my nipples pebble under my shirt when I hear bare feet pad through the apartment behind me. When I turn around, I see he has two towels and he hands one to me. I use it to squeeze the water from the ends of my hair and try to pat my shirt dry with no use.

Turning towards the entryway, I ask, "Where did you get that poster?"

"A record store in Santa Monica. It's a photo of a graffiti artists work in L.A. The artist is Gabriel Guzman. Have you heard of him?" he asks, using the towel to dry his face.

Shaking my head, no, I look around the apartment some more. A fireplace is built into the wall, with a gray masculine couch in front of it. Through the patio door and past the small balcony, I can see the pool in the center of the complex, with its glittery water calm now that the storm has passed.

"Do you want something to drink?" he asks, tossing the towel on the counter.

"Water, please," I say, as I follow him into the small kitchen, walking past two tall shelves full of record albums and books.

Using my finger to trace them and try to make out the titles, wondering what kind of music he likes, but the light from the hallway doesn't stretch this far. Nervous energy flutters over my skin like phantom wings as I take him in – shirt sticking to his chest, and jeans sitting low on his hips. He leans against the counter holding the water out to me. Twisting off the cap, I don't realize how thirsty I am until I take a sip, almost drinking the whole bottle at once. In my haste, droplets of water escape my lips and fall down my chin. Before I can wipe them away, he leans in and captures them with his tongue.

I've never had someone lick water from my chin before, but it sends a pulse straight down my chest which settles between my legs. He takes the almost empty water bottle from my hand and sets it on the counter, looking at me with questioning eyes. I wish I knew what he was thinking, but it's best I don't.

With his raspy voice, he starts to ask, "What's your..." But I stop him from finishing by pressing my lips to his with a kiss that deepens by the second.

I didn't come here to talk or to get to know him.

I came here for one thing and one thing only.

Feeling his erection press against me, I can't help but lean further into him, seeking out the delicious ache that's building inside me. In response, he turns me around quickly and pushes me against the counter. Kissing him is like a slow dance that I never want to end. It's as if he has all the time in the world to explore my mouth with his tongue.

He doesn't try to say anything else but he speaks to me with his eyes. And his eyes tell me a story of a man on fire.

He understands the assignment.

No names, only this.

Cupping my ass with his large hands, he lifts me onto the counter, spreading my thighs wide as his body settles between them. The heels of my shoes hit the cabinet beneath me, and it's the only sound in the room aside from the hum of the air conditioner kicking on.

While kissing him, I use my hands to explore his body, skimming across his waist and making my way up his back to finally settle in his hair. Even wet it feels lush, the perfect length to grip and pull as he causes everything inside of me to light up as if I've been plugged into an electric socket. Every so often he pulls away to look at me, gripping the side of my face and breathing me in. Deciding he hasn't had enough, he kisses me once more before kneeling in front of me to take my wet shoe in his hand, untying the laces. Slipping each one off until my feet are bare, he runs his hands over the top to warm them.

Looking up at me from between my thighs through thick black lashes, I feel my heart bang against my chest, aching for him to run his hands up my legs and thinking about what he will do to me next. Rising before me, I gather the material of his shirt in my hands, lifting it off his body and tossing it to the floor. He allows me to slowly explore the tattoos that span across his chest and down his rib cage, ending at the smooth flatness of his stomach that innocently tightens under my touch. The dim light only gives me a partial view of the black ink that looks like wings or scales, I can't tell which, but I find them incredibly sexy.

I'm only offered a few moments to explore before his patience runs out and he gathers my hair in his fist, pulling me to him and crashing his mouth against mine. Hot kisses turn into hungry nips as he takes the nubs of my erect nipples between his teeth through the material of my wet shirt. I whimper helplessly as my body vibrates with equal parts nervous energy and excitement. I've felt attraction before but never like this, and never in a way that threatens to pull me apart from the inside out.

I wasn't prepared for tonight.

I wasn't prepared for *him*.

He runs his hands under my shirt, and lifts it effortlessly over my head. Shaking out my hair, I'm acutely aware of the simple black cotton bra I'm wearing as my chest heaves. Not that I should be embarrassed about my bra, because it only seems a nuisance for what he's really after, and he couldn't care less if it's made of silk or cotton. Running his hand over my shoulder, he slips his finger under the strap, he pushes it down my arm, trailing behind it with kisses, and leaving goosebumps in his wake.

While his eyes hold me captive, he reaches behind me, unclasping my bra like a master, letting the material fall away, leaving me bare and vulnerable. He looks into my eyes for a moment longer as if he's waiting for permission, while his callused fingers follow the length of my spine to the small of my back.

My nipples harden into tight points giving me away, the skin at the base pulling so taut I can feel them ache to be touched. When he runs his thumb over the nub, it leaves me breathless. A pulse shoots down my body and lands directly between my thighs, as if he's pulled on an invisible thread the moment he takes my nipple between his lips. My fingers sink further into his hair, holding him to me.

My breath hitches, mouth open as if ready to speak, but there are no words meaningful enough to audibly express my emotions. This man knows exactly what he's doing – and he's doing it *very* well.

The swirl of his tongue is like a narcotic injected deep under my skin and running through my veins like wildfire. Closing my eyes, I can feel an impending storm building inside, threatening to unravel me. It has been way too long since I've been touched like this, making me raw and extra sensitive. I'm a live wire ready to explode. If I'm already close to the edge with just his mouth on me, I can only imagine how it will feel when he fucks me. Just thinking about it makes me pulse.

"Fuck," he groans against my breast, and the sound of his voice fills the silent space between us, bringing me ever so closer. I feel everything through his touch, the desperate vibration of his voice and the nervous twitch of his fingers as they dig possessively into my tender flesh.

I don't have control over my actions in this moment as my body squirms, eager for more contact, chasing that all-consuming friction to satisfy the ache. It's a feral instinct, something so deeply hidden I don't recognize it until a moan escapes my lips. This feeling is a high to be chased, and a need that washes over me like a tidal wave.

Capturing his lips, I kiss him with desperate nips and caress him with greedy hands. Sensing what I need, he grabs both my hips and lifts me off the counter, carrying me through the apartment. He smiles against my lips as I tug on his hair until I feel the strands stretch, making him groan.

Strong hands grip my ass while I kiss him deep and needy, not caring in the least if I seem too aggressive because I know exactly what I want. He sets me down on the bed, crawling over me as we kiss. When he pulls away, I writhe as I watch him rise before me.

In the darkened room, all I feel are the soft cool sheets against my bare back as I prop myself up on my elbows to watch him unbutton his jeans. The clank of his belt being freed rings through my chest, settling in the pit of my stomach. Each rise and fall of his chest grabs my attention until I venture to let my eyes travel down to the small pattering of hair on his smooth, flat stomach. The zipper yawns open, giving me a tease of what to expect, seeing the hardness under his boxers. I can feel the wetness pool in my panties.

There's an energy coursing through my body.

Something foreign... and frightening.

I am past the point of no return when he lowers his head to my stomach, running his tongue along my skin as he hooks his fingers under the waistband of my shorts, gently pulling them down my legs, leaving my panties intact. My heart hammers in my chest, and every breath is drawn like it will be my last. His smile is sexy and captivating, just like it was on stage at the bar, and I'm reminded why I came home with him in the first place. It calms my nerves even though my thighs shake as he slowly crawls up my body, spreading my legs, pressing kisses against my quivering belly, flicking my nipples with his tongue, palming my breast while his cock slides over the material of my panties.

"Ohhh," I moan, a sigh escaping my lips as my body involuntarily bucks against his. He teases me with a kiss, pulling on my lower lip before he makes his way back down my body.

All that stands between him and I is my white cotton panties that don't even match the bra that is long forgotten on the floor of his kitchen. He groans his approval as his thumb brushes along the center of my panties, revealing just how wet I am for him.

If I'm being honest, no one has ever made me feel this out of control and spiraling with need. Maybe it's because I haven't had sex in nearly eight long years, but I have a feeling that it's because of him. The way he looked at me when he was on stage, and the way his voice called to me on the street, no one had ever made me *feel*.

My breath hitches as he kisses my inner thigh. He slips his fingers under the sides of my panties, teasing the edges before pulling them down my thighs. Sitting back on his heels, he brings them to his nose and inhales as I watch the look of pure lust cross over his face, making my stomach tighten.

His eyes flick open, trained on mine when he says, "If you taste half as good as you smell..." he pauses, tossing my panties to the side, "then *fuck*," he whispers before gripping my hips and pulling me to his mouth.

Running his tongue up my seam, the moment it hits my already throbbing clit I buck against his mouth, gasping for air. The sensation is too intense, and my thighs instinctively try to close, squirming to get out of his grip as I whimper.

The combination of his tongue and fingers has me unraveling, like I'm in the first car of a roller coaster slowly being pulled to the crest, and when I look down, I don't see the tracks. The sight of him between my thighs has me undone. Bringing his eyes to meet mine, they flutter with a drunken haze, and I realize he's drunk on *me*. *I* did this to him, and there are no lies buried in the brown hues of his eyes.

When he latches onto my clit, he detonates the grenade.

"Oh, God!" The words escape my mouth with force as my body shakes. If I knew his name, I'd be screaming *it* right now instead of God's.

He moves his mouth from me and places a palm over my sensitive clit, the pressure deepening the orgasm but giving me the space I need to process everything. It's embarrassing how quickly he made me come. It's too much, too soon, and my chest heaves trying to suck in air.

"Relax," he says, his voice smooth like satin in the darkness of his bedroom.

But I can't relax; not when his head is between my thighs and he's looking at me like he wants to eat me alive.

Gripping the sheets, I ball them in my palms, using them as an anchor as I come down from my orgasm. Dark hair falls over his eyes and his face is in shadow, but I can see his glistening mouth tilt into a sexy smile.

"Do you want me to fuck you?" he asks, but the parting of his lips make me believe that inside he's saying, *please let me fuck you.*

Little seeds of embarrassment sprout inside of me, and I nod as my thighs continue to shake, the anticipation heightened as I see his glistening cock peak above the waistband of his boxers. I've never been as fascinated with a man's cock like I am with his.

I want to wrap my hand around it, feel its silky smooth skin pulse under my touch. My attention is diverted back to him when he speaks.

"I need you to say it," he whispers, with his deep voice as he hovers above me, forearms tense, muscles tight, shaking under the strain of his weight, and it's then that I see the pulse in his neck. He wants me badly, and the power has shifted with that tiny movement.

My eyes flick up to his, noticing his dilated pupils begging me to say it. "I want you to fuck me," I whisper, the words feeling foreign on my tongue because I have never uttered them before tonight.

He sits back on his heels, stretching his body to reach the nightstand so he can pull out a condom and I watch as he quickly rips it open with his teeth and expertly rolling it down his cock while ridding himself of his boxers.

Reaching for him, I snake my arms around his neck and feel his cock press against me as I crawl into his lap while kissing him. Rolling my hips against him, I practically beg for it.

"I need you to say it again." His voice is strained and needy as he grabs onto my hips to stop me from moving, but I can't help it as I fight against his hold, needing to feel him. His breath comes out shaky against my lips as he tries to control himself when I know all he wants to do is sink into me.

I want him so badly my body aches, and I reach up, slipping my fingers into his hair and pulling him to me, but he resists, keeping my ass firm against his thighs.

"Say it," he commands, keeping his lips out of my reach.

My eyes snap open to find him staring at me intently and the smell of his cologne swirls between us making me lightheaded with need. "Fuck me," I beg, desperately.

He complies by lifting my hips, and I can feel the head of his cock at my entrance right before he slams into me from below. The force pushes me back onto the bed where he fucks me fast and hard like the rhythm of a heavy metal song until a sheen of sweat breaks out on both our bodies, causing a second orgasm to rip through me with record speed.

It's a desperate, feral fuck, like nothing I've ever had before; reckless, and out of control. Lips, teeth, and tongues collide in an attempt to climb inside each other. I don't even try to silence the cries coming from my mouth, feeling the freedom they provide as each one is released into the darkened space of his bedroom, and like the hungry man he is, he swallows them whole.

He started a fire inside of me that spreads to every limb and I let it burn.

In the darkness his hand finds mine, linking them together above my head. Closing his eyes, his body shakes, and his cock pulses inside me as I come down from the high just as his begins. The adrenaline seeping from my body leaves me breathless and weak.

"Holy fuck." His voice cracks as he slows his pace, riding out his own orgasm before he captures my lips.

Opening his eyes, he looks down at me with unabashed tenderness, hair falling in his face, and that bashful smile. "I can usually go all night, but *fuck*, you..." I bite his lip, pulling the soft, velvety skin between my teeth and slipping my tongue inside, effectively stopping him from finishing lie number three.

Laughing against his lips, I feel them pull into a smile. Resting his forehead against mine, he plants a chaste kiss on my mouth before pulling out, and collapsing to the mattress next to me as if he spent his last bit of energy on that kiss. Grabbing onto my hand, he rests it against his chest that moves with the cadence of his breaths. Even on the back of my hand I can feel his heart pounding like the beat of a drum.

We lie next to each other, our chests heaving as I stare up at the ceiling, watching the fan slowly rotate, casting long shadows in the darkened room.

Turning my head to look at him, I make out his strong jaw, full lips, and gentle slope of his nose. He brushes his thumb over the top of my hand just like he did on the walk over, and I pinch my brows together. Closing my eyes, I take a deep shuddering breath.

With just one taste... I'm an addict, and I'll want him again and again until there is nothing left of him.

And that's why I can never see him again.

5

OLD ENOUGH TO DRINK

Girls Talk Boys by 5 Seconds of Summer

Looking at the clock next to the bed, I realize it's almost two a.m.

Time has slipped by, and I don't remember when I fell asleep.

Gently untangling myself from the sheets, I slip out from under his arm that's stretched across my stomach. A soft moan escapes his lips, but his eyes remain closed, and I can still hear his steady breathing. His thick, dark hair is tousled against the pillow with pieces falling over his face, soft eyes, and lush lips. The sheets are pooled at his waist, and I stare at his chest, my eyes wandering down to the flat of his stomach, and I wet my lips at the sight.

Resting my feet against the floor, I sit for a moment, running my fingers through my hair. My whole body aches having used muscles that even yoga didn't prepare me for, but in a good way. Smiling, I stuff my face in the palm of my hands, shaking my head just to get my bearings and my mind wanders.

While the first time was rushed and exciting, the second time he fucked me slow, taking his time to touch and taste every part of my body. The rush was gone, but the ache remained. Thinking about how his skin felt under my touch as I ran my hands over his smooth stomach, appreciated the hard, youthful lines of his body, tasted him, inhaled him, and rode him until we both came, taking everything he was willing to give, and I still hadn't had enough of him.

Feeling as though I've been living inside this fairytale for far too long, I know it's time for me to leave.

The room is still bathed in darkness, but streams of moonlight filter in through the bedroom window giving me patches of visibility to find my clothes.

My foot brushes against an article of clothing and I reach down to find my shorts. Sliding onto all fours to search for my underwear, I lift the sheet so I can see under the bed when I spot the outline of a skateboard.

A fucking skateboard. I slap my hand over my mouth to stop from laughing.

Unable to find my underwear, I resolve to slip my shorts on without them, remembering my shirt and bra are still in the kitchen, along with my shoes.

Shirtless and barefoot, I silently walk down the hallway and into the living room, taking a moment to look around his apartment one more time. Above the fireplace is a framed poster, and on the mantel are what look like family pictures, but it's too dark to make them out. The patio blinds that look out over the now darkened pool are still open, and the outside lights of nearby apartments illuminate the deserted walkway. Everything is still and serene, the storm having passed long ago. Seeing my reflection in the patio door glass, bare breasts and hair tousled, I wonder, *who is this woman?*

Feeling like a thief in the night, I pad into the kitchen to retrieve the rest of my clothes, remembering the way he lifted me onto the counter with ease, settled his hips between my legs, and kissed me with as much passion as he sang with on stage. Even after everything we did, and now that my mind isn't clouded, I realize he's still a stranger to me.

Peering down the dark hall that leads to his bedroom, I listen for any sounds that let me know he's woken up, and hearing nothing but silence. There's no need for awkward goodbyes, exchanging of false information, and promises that will only be broken.

Quickly finding my shirt, I slip it over my head, not bothering to put my bra on. Instead, I stuff it in the pocket of my shorts and grab my shoes. I collect my purse that I'd left on the table under the poster in the hallway, and set the strap over my shoulder.

Taking one last look around the apartment before slipping silently out the front door, I'm careful to close it quietly. Feeling bad that I can't lock it because I don't want to leave him vulnerable, I stand there at a loss, but there's nothing I can do about it. On the stairs I take a moment to sit down and slip my shoes on. The rain has long since passed, the sidewalk's dry, and the night air has been left warm and humid. A cat runs down the steps, startling me, and slips into a patch of bushes; reminding me how desolate the apartment complex is as I look around.

My limbs feel like Jell-O, and muscles I didn't know I had ache with exertion. As I walk down the steps, I am well aware that I don't have panties on as the friction rubs against my sore and sensitive areas.

Everything is quiet except for the faint sound of a car passing on the nearby road, and air conditioners kicking on – even in the middle of the night. Passing between the apartment buildings I make it out to the street, fully aware that I'm not wearing a bra, and wished I'd taken the extra few minutes to put it on. Hugging myself, I push on towards Mill Avenue. Every restaurant, bar, and store I pass is dark, closed for the night. Even the once lively *Tap Room* is ominously silent, only a few drunken stragglers on the sidewalk across the street remain.

My car is parked a couple blocks over, and when the group of people turn the corner and I can no longer hear them, fear settles into my belly. Feeling a lump of tears rise to my throat, I swallow them down.

All thoughts of leaving my car several blocks away were tampered down in a lust filled haze when I decided to leave the bar and go home with a stranger. I'm smarter than this, and I don't know what possessed me to go home with him.

But that's a lie.

I do know what possessed me.

Him.

He could have been a murderer, a serial killer, someone who likes to hurt women.

But he wasn't any of those things.

He was gentle until I asked him not to be, and even then, he had to ask me twice, to tell him exactly what I wanted. He didn't say much, but only because I wouldn't let him. I didn't want his name to accidentally slip past his lips.

If I knew his name, he wouldn't have been a stranger anymore.

When I get to my car, I slam the door shut and hit the lock. I suck in a big, shaky breath before turning over the ignition and putting the car in gear. When I turn onto the empty street, I head in the opposite direction of my house.

As soon as I pull in front of Georgie's house, I realize it's nearly three a.m. I should just go home, but my hands have been shaking on the wheel ever since I left the parking lot. A light turns on in her living room, and a few moments later the curtain pulls open. My car idling in front of her house probably woke her up.

Resolving to shut the engine off, I walk up to the front door where she's waiting for me with a concerned expression on her face.

"What happened? Is it Noelle?" she asks.

I love that she loves my daughter and it's the first thing she asks when she sees me, shaken, on her front doorstep. After reassuring her it's not Noelle, I step into her arms, needing the comfort of someone familiar. The buoyancy of my emotions comes to the surface, and as much as I try to stop them, I can't.

Georgie lets me use her shower and lends me a pair of her underwear, telling me to keep them.

With my hair still damp, I explain what happened after she left me at the Italian restaurant last night. As I explain, she doesn't judge, and she doesn't state the obvious.

I'm adult enough to know the risk I took, and the recklessness in which I did it. Thinking about Noelle is what left me apprehensive and shaken, because I knew the gravity of my actions and what it could have cost me.

I recount every detail, from entering the *Tap Room*, making out with a stranger in a record store alcove, to letting him take me back to his apartment where he carried me to his bedroom and fucked me so hard he left bruises where his fingers dug into my hips.

When I'm finished, she gets up from the kitchen table, digs around in the cabinet and produces a bottle of Baileys. She pours a hearty amount in her coffee mug and tops mine off, too. When she's taken a couple of sips, she looks me in the eye and says, "Well, that was one hell of a birthday present."

Placing my hand over my mouth, I break down into laughter. When Georgie snort-giggles, I laugh even harder. She pounds her fist on the table and squirms in her seat, having trouble catching her breath because she's laughing so hard. I have to clench my thighs together so I don't piss my pants and have to borrow another pair of underwear from her.

In between fits of laughter she asks, "How young did you say he was?"

I think about the skateboard under his bed and roll my eyes. "Old enough to drink and young enough to fuck me three times in one night," I say, holding up three fingers and bite my lip.

Georgie almost spits out her coffee while I clutch my tender stomach from laughing so hard.

Pressing my face into my palms, I confess, "I don't even know his name, Georgie." Straightening up in my chair, I square my shoulders because I know I'm being ridiculous. "I didn't want to know his name."

It's nearly five a.m., and the Bailey's in my coffee is not helping my exhaustion. Georgie gives me a sympathetic look.

"You should go take a nap," Georgie says. "You'll be no good for Noelle if you don't get some sleep."

She'll be home sometime this morning, and she'll see how much of a wreck I am if I don't get at least a few hours of sleep. There aren't any secrets between us, and I pride myself on being honest with her so that she would do the same with me, but I don't think I can look her in the eye and make this confession.

Georgie walks with me into her living room, setting me up on the couch with a spare blanket and pillow because I refused to use her guest room to just take a nap.

The truth is, once I sink into that mattress, it'll be hell waking up. I'd much rather hang out in her living room, talking for as long as my weary eyes will let me.

Setting my mug on the coffee table, I feel the Baileys sitting nice and warm in my belly. Georgie always knows how to make things better, and it usually involves alcohol. Laying my head on the pillow, I pull the blanket around my shoulders nice and tight.

Georgie curls up in the chair opposite me, holding her mug with a thoughtful expression. Her hair is in a messy bun and she's wearing pajama bottoms with little dogs printed on them, making me smile. We've been friends for a long time, meeting at work nearly fifteen years ago, and she's seen me go through a lot of tough times since then. She's like a sister to me and an aunt to Noelle, which I appreciate more than she knows. Thinking about how she reacted when I showed up on her doorstep makes me wonder.

"Do you regret not having any kids?" I ask.

"I have my fur babies," she says without actually answering, but I understand what she means. Georgie is the kind of person who lives in the moment, no time for regrets, and always thankful for what she has in the present.

"Tell me about Charlie," I say sleepily, thinking about the dog she had to help put to sleep last night.

"He had a tumor around his heart and the medication wasn't working," she explains. "He was having a hard time breathing, and we couldn't make her wait until Monday morning." Georgie pulls her legs under her body, propping her chin up with her palm. "I stayed in the room with Mrs. Hampton until he was gone." Her voice is quiet but strong.

"I don't know how you do it," I say, my eyes beginning to flutter shut.

I can hear her sigh. "It's hard, but in a way it's a privilege to give an animal a peaceful way to cross over the rainbow bridge," she says, her voice trailing away.

Her living room is quiet, and this couch is very comfortable.

When I wake up, the chair across from me is empty, and the sun filters through the front windows. I have a headache from lack of sleep, and search for my phone to see what time it is. My eyes pop open when I discover it's nearly nine a.m. Noelle will be home soon, and if I'm not there she'll worry, and I don't want to have to explain why I wasn't.

Shuffling into the bathroom I try to comb through my messy hair, made worse by having fallen asleep while it was still wet. Poking my head out of the bathroom, knowing Georgie is up because I can smell fresh coffee brewing, I yell down the hall, "Mind if I use your toothbrush?" My mouth feels dry and gross.

"There's an extra one in the cabinet," she yells back.

Pulling it open, I sift through deodorant tubes, perfumes, floss, and finally find a couple of brand-new toothbrushes with her dentist's name printed on them.

With the toothbrush stuck in my mouth, Georgie enters the bathroom, hugging a tiny white kitten close to her chest. It mewls incessantly, and I wonder why I didn't hear it earlier, only now realizing it's probably the reason why Georgie was up at three a.m. when she noticed my car parked outside.

"Who is this little guy?" I melt at the sight of him, petting his soft fur with my finger.

"It's a she, and I'm fostering these little guys until they're big enough to be adopted," Georgie says, looking down at the kitten who paws at her shirt, mouth open as if she's looking for food.

"I thought you were a dog person," I comment, turning back to the sink and spitting out the toothpaste.

"I am now an equal opportunity animal person," she says. "Hamsters are growing on me, even the ones that bite."

"Don't let Noelle see this one. She'll hound me for eternity to take one home." I give her one last scratch on the head.

"Take one, it's yours. I'll even let you skip the adoption paperwork," Georgie says, seriously.

"Clearly you're never allowed to talk to Noelle again," I reply sarcastically, following her back into the kitchen where I pour myself a cup of fresh coffee.

"Seriously, you need a pet," she says, leaning against the counter, now dressed in a pair of shorts and a t-shirt.

"I'm not home enough to take care of a pet," I tell her.

"For Noelle," Georgie counters, while preparing kitten food.

"She's going to be leaving for college in a year, and then I'll be stuck with it." I take a sip of my coffee, savoring the caffeine now flowing through my system.

"Would that be so bad?" Georgie asks as she pushes the laundry room door open further, exposing a crate.

"Yes," I grumble, noticing three more kittens in the crate mewling for food. I watch as she feeds them with a syringe. When their tummies are full, the mewling subsides, and they all curl up together in the corner of the crate.

"I'm surprised you don't have a houseful of kittens." I smile at her over the steam in my coffee cup while taking a seat at her kitchen table.

"They're cute but a lot of work. By the time they're old enough to be adopted, I've had my fill. Besides, then I get to open my home to another set that needs help," she says, taking the seat opposite me and crossing her legs.

"You're really enjoying your second life, huh?" That's what she called it when she made the decision to leave corporate life behind and pursue something that made her feel fulfilled.

"It has its difficulties," she says, pressing her lips together.

Checking the time on her microwave, I realize how late it is. "Shit, I should get going," I say and take another sip of my coffee before dumping the rest in the sink.

When I turn around, Georgie is leaning against the counter looking at me thoughtfully. I know that look and she might not have passed judgment on me last night when I was emotional, but I am fully recovered this morning.

"You know that I only want happiness for you, right?" she asks.

"But..." I continue for her.

"I wish you would open yourself to someone, let them in for real, and not just a random one-night stand."

Taking a deep breath, I know what she says is true. I haven't let many people into my life, and that's by choice. It's not just me that I have to think about, it's Noelle too.

"By the way, I don't plan on having anymore random hook-ups," I say, and instead of telling me what I already know, she steps forward, pulling me into a hug.

"Love you," she whispers into my hair.

"I know," I say, giving her a squeeze before letting go.

IT TAKES thirty minutes to get home, and Noelle's red VW Bug is already parked in the garage when I pull in. She's sitting in one of the stools at the kitchen island when I enter the house.

With a concerned expression she begins, "I was just about to call you. Where were you?"

Before I can answer, she points to my *Aerosmith* shirt, tilting her head and asks, "Weren't you wearing that last night?"

Looking down at my shirt momentarily, I shrug, "Yes. I stayed at Georgie's."

It's not a lie, but I feel it in the pit of my stomach. Looking at her big blue eyes staring back at me, I decide to change the subject.

"Did you eat breakfast already?" I ask, chugging a bottle of water that I grabbed from the fridge.

"Skittles," Noelle says smiling, and I shake my head.

I'm not known for my cooking skills, but my kid does eat better than Skittles for breakfast.

"It was left over from Halloween last year and we wanted to see if it was still good," she laughs.

"*Berdena's* or *Alo's*?" I ask, naming off her two favorite cafes for breakfast.

"I'm feeling French Toast this morning," Noelle replies, gathering her hair into a bun.

"*Berdena's* it is." I toss the empty water bottle in the trash. "Let me go change and we can go. I'm starving."

Running down the hall to my bedroom, I pull off my shirt, noticing how it smells like him, a mixture of masculine cologne and sweet liquor. Bringing it to my nose, I inhale slowly, allowing myself a few scandalous thoughts about the young musician with the pretty face and the kissable lips.

Tossing my shirt in the hamper, I exchange Georgie's underwear for my own before heading into the bathroom to grab some lip gloss and use my finger to spread it over my chapped lips. My thoughts are interrupted when Noelle enters my bedroom and plops down on the bed.

"Did you hear the monsoon storm last night?" she asks, unaware that I was at the center of it.

"Yeah." I throw the lip gloss back in the drawer and walk out to my bedroom. The king size bed sits in the center of the wall opposite the bathroom, adorned with decorative pillows. An oversized chair sits in the corner by the window.

"It was wicked. One of the umbrellas in Sofia's back yard fell in the pool. We helped her dad fish it out," Noelle says with a smile.

"I bet you did."

"What did you and Georgie do last night?" she asks while I grab a shirt from my closet and slip it on.

"Got into a whole lotta trouble," I tease, wiggling my brows.

Noelle laughs. "I don't doubt that," she says. "I bet sitting at home watching movies with me will be boring in comparison."

Sitting down on the bed next to her, I drape my arm over her shoulders. "I'd rather watch movies with you any day of the week then raise hell with Georgie," I tell her.

6

BRIDE OR BRIDE?

Polyester Bride by Liz Phair

Slipping on my heels, I rush into the kitchen. As usual, I'm running late.

Noelle sits on the kitchen island, her feet dangling as she smiles while taking a sip of her coffee. I give her a disapproving look.

"Addiction is hereditary, so you only have yourself to blame," she quips, peering at me through the steam.

"So is incontinence. Have fun with that when you're older," I tease, and she rolls her eyes.

"Something to look forward to, thanks," Noelle replies sarcastically.

Stopping for a moment, I take in my kid who is just on the verge of no longer being a kid. Somewhere along the years her face has lost its roundness, and now has a sharper edge. She's always liked her hair long and refused to let me cut it. Anytime she dresses up, she looks much older than seventeen which worries me, but Noelle has developed a sharp tongue and a quick wit.

Reaching out to touch her dark waves, I ask, "How did you get to be so beautiful?"

"I take after my mama," she says sweetly, batting her eyelashes dramatically which makes me laugh.

"You're staring at me with that sappy way that says you're thinking about me leaving home for college, again," Noelle teases, moving out of my grasp.

I love her sharp tongue and quick wit – but not when it's directed at me.

Putting my hand on my hip, I say, "You don't know everything."

She gives me a disbelieving look and I tell her, "I can look at you any way I want. I made you, kid." Raising a challenging eyebrow, I grab my keys from the hook by the kitchen door.

"Are you gonna look at me like that for a whole year?" she asks, jumping down from the chair and dumping her leftover coffee in the sink.

"If I want to."

She sticks her tongue out at me while I check to make sure I have everything.

"I forgot the present," I say, and in my haste, I catch my heel in the damaged tile, almost face planting, but managing to grab onto the edge of the counter just in time to save myself from a hip replacement.

"Shit!" I gasp.

"I'll get it," Noelle says, running past me down the hallway. "Where is it?" she calls over her shoulder.

"In my office," I yell back, checking to make sure my heel isn't damaged. Noelle reappears into the hall with the black and gold wrapped wedding present.

"Miles wrapped this, didn't he?" Noelle asks as she turns it around in her hands, inspecting it.

Taking the present from her, I admit, "Of course he did. If I wrapped it, it would look like a toddler taped it together."

"Does that mean Miles wraps my Christmas presents?" Noelle asks, horrified.

Shutting my mouth, I look away guiltily. "Hurry up, we'll be late," I order to deflect the question.

We head towards the garage, and Noelle says, "By the way, I thought we were getting new flooring."

"We are," I reassure her. "I haven't had time to find someone yet," I admit, "although I'm putting it at the top of my list now." I lift my heel again, re-checking for damage.

"You said that the last time you almost bit the dust," she teases.

"Well, if someone hadn't ruined the tile by roller skating through the house nonstop when they were younger..." I tease and look at her pointedly. The large open floorplan was just begging to be turned into a roller derby rink, especially with the pillar in the middle where she would launch herself off of to make a figure eight through the house.

"You never told me to stop!" she argues.

"How could I when you were so goddamn cute in those lighted skates and a tutu?" I justify, grabbing her cheek as she pulls away, clearly annoyed with me.

Laughing, I lock the garage door behind me.

Noelle hits the opener and looks at me with a megawatt smile, blinking those big blue eyes of hers. "You look *really* pretty," she compliments me, but I've been raising this kid for seventeen years and my radar just pinged.

"What do you want?" I ask hesitantly as I place a hand on my hip, because she knows I have a hard time saying no to her.

"Can I drive the Porsche?" she asks.

"No." The word slips out effortlessly. There are a lot of things I can never say no to when she asks, but driving my Porsche isn't one of them.

As soon as we pull up to my sister, Beth's, house, I notice the pink and gold streamers with balloons on either side of the front door.

"Looks like we're at the right place," I say, surveying the house.

Cars line the street so I pass the house, unnecessarily parking half a block away.

"Are you trying to get in your steps for the day?" Noelle asks, unbuckling her seatbelt.

"It's so we don't get blocked in and can't leave," I explain, shifting the car into park. It's not that I don't want to celebrate my sister, but I'm not much for crowds and parties. When I've had my fill, I don't want any issues stopping me from leaving.

"Who needs school when your mother is your teacher?" She makes an exaggerated bow as we get out of the car.

I put my arm around her shoulder as we walk down the sidewalk. "Stick with me, kid, and soon you'll be learning how to pick locks," I tease.

The front door is unlocked, and as soon as we enter, it's an assault of pink everywhere. Pink streamers, pink balloons, pink plates with pink utensils…

Noelle curls her lip. "There's a lot of pink," she states the obvious, looking around, horrified.

"Be glad you weren't asked to be a flower girl," I retort, and shove her further into the house.

Beth greets us before we reach the living room. She's a ball of nervous energy in her pink spaghetti strap dress with a flared skirt and bare feet.

Looking around at all the other guests wearing some form of pastel, I feel a bit out of place in my copper-colored blouse and black skirt. "Was there a dress code?" I ask.

Beth gives me an annoyed look. "On time as usual." She ignores my question and then turns her attention to Noelle, smiling. "You look beautiful," she says, squeezing her shoulders and pulling her in for a hug.

"So do you, Aunt Beth," Noelle says.

"Your kid has better manners than you," she says teasingly, but I know Beth and she likes to get in her little digs.

Looking across the room, I see her fiancée, Laura, with her younger sister, Ianna. Those are about the only two people I know here.

Beth scans the house. "Ashley's here somewhere," she tells Noelle, who then trots off in the direction of her cousin's room.

"How's Ashley doing?" I ask.

"She's fine," Beth says quietly, while walking me into the house.

Stopping her, I place my hand on her arm and pin her with a look. "What?" I prod.

She turns to look at me, crossing her arms over her chest. "Eric's being difficult about letting me have Ashley for the whole weekend of the wedding, and he's picking her up later today," she admits.

"He's just pissed because Laura has a bigger dick than him and actually knows how to use it," I say, tersely.

"Really, Lake?" Beth scoffs.

"What?" I shrug. "He's your ex-husband, Beth," I say. "Who cares what he thinks anyway?"

"Easy for you to say because you don't have to share your kid with an ex-husband," she says, maybe not realizing how insensitive she's being.

"Yeah, real fucking lucky," I say, cocking my head to the side.

"Come on, let me introduce you to everyone," Beth says, closing the conversation and dragging me into the kitchen.

It's a melee of arms and hands dishing out food and speaking in a language I don't understand. The presence of Laura's large family is overwhelming, and the fact that not all of them speak English well makes it hard to have small talk.

"Lake, you remember my soon to be mother-in-law, Florina," Beth says, beaming.

Laura's mother is short and round with a kind face but she doesn't speak English very well, and I've always found it hard to communicate with her. She takes my hand smiling and says, "Lake?" as if she doesn't remember my name, which is completely reasonable. She motions with her hands like she's paddling a canoe, and I look to Beth for assistance but she's useless because she doesn't speak Romanian either.

"*Acesta este numele ei,*" *That's her name,* Ianna explains in Romanian.

"Ah, nice to meet you," Florina says in her best English, cupping my hand in hers.

"It's really good to see you again." I remind her that we've met before, but she looks at me with a confused expression so I just go with it.

Holding out the present I brought, I thought it was wrapped stylishly until I notice all of the other presents are wrapped in some form of pink. Florina smiles and takes the package from me, ambling over to place it on the pile where it sticks out like a sore thumb.

While Beth is whisked away by other guests, Ianna visits with me in the kitchen.

"Help yourself to some food," she says, gesturing to plates of hamburgers and hotdogs, along with all kinds of sides and desserts.

"Thank you," I say politely, but I don't mention that I'm vegetarian, so I grab a plate of salad.

"Is Noelle with you?" she asks.

"Yeah, she's with Ashley somewhere," I say, looking around the party but not finding them. Laura moved in with Beth months ago, and even though her home is a little small, it was so they didn't have to uproot Ashley from her friends and school.

"They're probably hiding from my little monsters. They adore Ashley," she says, scooping potato salad onto a plate – and with good timing – because two of her kids come tearing through the kitchen. "She's like the big sister they never knew they wanted," Ianna laughs, grabbing one of the kids to slow them down.

Remembering how Ashley was with Noelle, following her around because she was the older one, a little twinge of jealousy bubbles from deep within me, but I try to tamp it down. Ianna's kids aren't family, at least not in the same way Noelle is, and yet they look more comfortable in Beth's home than I do.

"How's Noelle doing? She composes music, right?" Ianna asks, and I'm surprised she remembers. It was a couple months ago that I mentioned it to her.

"Good," I say, smiling. "She's been busy working on this winter recital for school."

She looks like she wants me to invite her, but I wouldn't do that without Noelle being okay with it, so I don't say anything.

"Winter," Ianna says, pulling at her top to let some air in, "seems so far off. Feels like summer just started," she says.

"I used to hate the summers growing up," I admit.

Ianna smiles, setting her plate down. "And now?" she asks.

I pick up a carrot stick. "Now they just never end," I reply before taking a bite and Ianna laughs.

"Ain't that the truth," she says.

I poke at the little pink bells made of crepe paper in the center of the island. "Everything looks beautiful," I say, looking around at the rest of the decorations.

"Thanks. I had so much fun at the party store picking everything out. I was so excited to finally plan my sister's wedding I may have gone a little overboard," she says, and I shift uncomfortably.

"And of course, I know you're busy with work and the single mom thing. I honestly don't know how you do it," she says, trying to make me feel better.

"Well, I only have one kid which is a lot easier than managing three," I say, already wishing I were home in my pajamas watching a movie.

"I should have asked if you wanted to help," Ianna says sweetly, but it just makes me feel worse, which I know she didn't intend.

"My work schedule is crazy, but you did a much better job than I would have," I admit, which is true. I don't know where Noelle got her creativity, because it certainly wasn't from me.

We stand in awkward silence, and to fill the void, I shove a forkful of lettuce in my mouth.

"You know, we're so excited to have Beth as part of the family. Ugh, Laura went through a bunch of duds before finding Beth. She really is the sweetest," Ianna says, squeezing my arm.

I choke on the lettuce I just shoved into my mouth and Ianna smacks my back, ready to give me the Heimlich maneuver. I hold my hand up for her to stand down as I gather myself.

"I'm fine," I say, still choking a little.

"Here's some water," she says, handing me a bottle of water from the fridge.

"Do you have anything stronger?" I clear my throat.

"We have some Prosecco and orange juice over there." She points to the counter behind me with the champagne bottles lined up and orange juice on ice.

"Perfect." I pour myself a glass and drop in a few raspberries because I still need to get in my daily serving of fruit, and if anyone says this doesn't count, I will cut them.

Setting my half-eaten plate of lettuce on the counter, I excuse myself making my way down the hallway toward my niece, Ashley's, room. It's been a while since I've checked in on her.

Poking my head in, Ashley looks up from Noelle's phone as they sit heads together, laughing about something. "Hi, Aunt Lake," she smiles.

"You got braces," I say, noticing the newly minted metal in her mouth.

"Last week," she grumbles. "They're not so bad though."

Ashley takes after her dad, with her long thick blonde hair and hazel eyes. Her and Noelle look like two sides of a coin, one dark and one light.

Just when I'm about to ask how she's been doing, Ianna interrupts letting us know the games are about to start.

Games, I mouth to Noelle with my eyebrows up in mock excitement. She scrunches her nose in distaste. I'm afraid Noelle got her anti-social behavior from me.

Ashley jumps off the bed. "Are you coming?" she asks Noelle who stares back blankly. "It'll be fun," Ashley begs. "Come on."

There's nothing like peer pressure to get you off your ass and do something you hate.

Reluctantly, Noelle slides off the bed and I follow them down the hall into the living room where Laura's family and both her and my sister's friends are gathered on the couch. Ana, Laura's younger sister who must be in her mid-thirties, and a very noticeable baby bump, starts passing out paper and giving everyone instructions.

There's an empty folding chair next to the couch so I take it, crossing my legs and placing my hands in my lap while Noelle sits on the floor next to Ashley, who has her hands full with all the younger kids fighting each other to sit on her lap. Next to me is a pretty young woman I've never met before, so she must be one of Laura's friends.

She leans over and whispers, "You didn't get the memo either?"

Looking at her I'm confused for a moment, and then I realize we're both wearing dark colors. She has on a heather gray tank top and jean shorts. Her dark hair is pulled up in a messy bun, revealing a row of trendy ear piercings.

"I'm not much of a pastel girl," I admit.

"Me neither," she laughs. "Taylor," she introduces herself.

"Lake," I reply, extending my hand.

"Bride or," she falters, "Bride?" she laughs, not sure what to say.

"Bride," I say, with a smile. "I'm Beth's older sister," I explain.

"And you?"

"I'm Adrian's girlfriend," she says.

"Adrian?" I ask, confused.

"Laura's younger brother," she explains further.

"There are more of them?" I say aloud, not meaning for it to sound negative, but how many fucking kids are there in this family? I knew of Laura, Ianna, and Ana, but I didn't know there was a brother.

"It's a big family. Hard to keep straight," Taylor says.

Ana stands at the front getting everyone's attention to start the game, in which we're supposed to divide into teams and try to make the best wedding dress using tissue and toilet paper.

The older woman sitting next to me turns, looking at me expectantly. "Not going to happen," I say, and she turns to the group of ladies on the other side.

"You don't like games?" Taylor asks.

"I'm not really much of a joiner," I reply, causing Taylor to laugh.

Noelle has reluctantly teamed up with Ashley and the little kids. Watching as they use her as a mannequin, they race around in circles with toilet paper making her look more like a mummy than a bride. She catches my eye, giving me a distressed expression. I'm sure to hear all about this later.

"Here's your tissue paper," Ana says, shoving a package into my hands and then delivering some to the group next to us.

"I could use a drink right now," I sigh, "a real drink, not the Prosecco in the kitchen." I set my glass down somewhere and now I can't remember where I left it.

Taylor takes the tissue from my hands and places it on the empty couch cushion. "I know where they stashed the good stuff." She motions for me to follow her onto the patio where the cooler sits. The misters are on full blast, but even with that, the air is suffocating. I'll endure this over making a tissue paper wedding dress any day though.

She pops the top off the cooler and motions for me to take my pick. There are cans of beer and hard seltzer.

"This is the good stuff?" I ask, looking at Taylor. "I was thinking more like a vodka martini."

Taylor laughs, lifting the top further. "It's either this or a Mimosa." She raises her eyebrows, so I grab a seltzer.

Taylor pulls the tab on hers and looks inside the house at all the women laughing with their monstrosity of mummy dresses.

"Your sister is really lucky. She's marrying into a great family," Taylor says. There's a hint of jealousy in her tone that grabs my attention, and I watch her as she watches them as if she's on the outside, and not just on the patio.

Turning to look inside the house, I see Beth laughing hysterically while she tries to walk in her tissue paper dress. The smile on her face is infectious, and it's been a long time since I've seen her truly happy.

"Yeah, I guess so," I say, holding my can of hard seltzer and heading back into the house.

Pulling out my phone, I can't help but take a picture of Noelle wrapped up in toilet paper with a tissue paper veil. When she catches me, she shoots me an evil glare.

7

JAKE RYAN

Reasons I Drink by Alanis Morissette

"I'm sorry," I say behind my palm, trying to contain the laughter.

"This is not funny," Noelle demands, trying to stomp her foot but the toilet paper prevents her.

The little kids giggle and throw toilet paper in the air, and I'm glad I don't have to clean up this mess. Shoving my phone protectively back inside my bra strap, I stop Noelle from grabbing it to erase the evidence.

"Can we leave?" she begs.

"We haven't even had cake yet," I say, smiling, and look over at Ashley who is trying to contain her laughter.

"I have to leave soon anyway. My dad's coming to pick me up," Ashley says, sounding a little upset that she can't stay longer because she actually likes this kind of thing. Divorce is never a good thing, but when parents can't put their kids' happiness first, it's a shame. Eric wasn't exactly a stellar guy to begin with, but I like him even less now.

Helping to pull the toilet paper from her body, Noelle finally breaks free, sighing as if she can finally breathe.

"What am I supposed to tell everyone?" I whisper to her.

"Tell them I have a stomachache," Noelle offers, shrugging. "It's the excuse you used to get out of staying longer at holiday dinners," she winks.

"Hey, those were dire situations," I remind her.

I must still look non-committal because she shoves a finger to my chest. "You owe me," she says, with her blue eyes narrowed at me.

Putting my arm around her shoulder conspiratorially, I give Ashley's arm a little squeeze goodbye, trying to be covert as we make our way out of the living room.

Not making it out of the living room in time for Ianna to catch us, she rushes over and pins Noelle with a cartoonish 1st place medal. "For the best wedding dress," she says, excitedly.

The little kids jump around excited, and Ianna holds out a pouch with prizes in it full of candy and little trinkets.

"Are you sure that's a good idea?" I tease Ianna, seeing they all pulled out some Fun Dip which is basically colored sugar.

"Probably not, but then there's always the sugar crash. They'll sleep the whole way home," Ianna laughs.

She holds the bag to Noelle, but she shakes her head and Ianna shrugs.

"I always knew you were a winner," I tease Noelle.

The minute Ianna leaves, Noelle yanks the pin off and one of the little kids runs off with it.

"You're loving this, aren't you?" Noelle seethes, her plump lips morphed into a thin line as she glares at me.

"Every minute, kid," I say. "Here, let me help you." I yank on a few more stubborn pieces of tissue. "Hmm," I inspect the toilet paper. "This is a two-ply house, fancy," I joke and pull the remaining pieces off her.

"Can we go now before they start passing around diapers with melted candy in them?" she demands grumpily.

"That's a baby shower game," I correct her. "And yes."

Using your kid to lie your way out of a party so you can leave early is a bit unethical, but I'm not above doing it. Besides, I have a ton of work to get ahead on, and Noelle and I have our movie night. "I just have to grab my purse and say goodbye to Beth at least."

Noelle follows me into the bedroom where I stashed my purse as if she thinks I'm going to leave without her.

"I always knew you were attached to me, but this is a bit much," I say, teasingly.

"I'm not taking any chances," Noelle says. "They might try to rope me into another game."

In the kitchen, Florina is packing up the leftover food, but I don't see Beth or Laura anywhere.

"It was so nice to see you, but we have to leave," I explain, as she rearranges the plates of food on the island.

"No, no, take some." She tries to shove paper plates of food wrapped in plastic at me.

"I'm fine really," I say, "but thank you."

"Have you seen the food in our fridge?" Noelle asks, nudging me with her elbow.

"What food?" I ask.

"Exactly," Noelle says, taking one of the plates from Florina and smiling thankfully.

When she insists that I take a piece of cake, I can't refuse that. It hasn't even been cut into yet when she hacks it with the serving knife and plops a big piece on a plate for me. The middle is strawberries and cream and looks heavenly. I look to Noelle who is thinking the same thing – birthday cake. She gives me a sympathetic smile.

"You're not leaving, are you?" Laura catches us before we exit the kitchen, our arms guiltily loaded with cake and food.

"Yeah, Noelle has a bit of a stomachache and I have to find someone to redo the flooring in my house. It's a mess, you know," I say, because it's not a lie. I was going to start researching installers.

"This is perfect, my dad owns a flooring company!" she says excitedly. "He'll give you the family discount."

"That's so nice of you," I say, feeling a bit awkward, "but you don't have to do that."

"Of course I do, you're gonna be family," Laura says. "He did our house." She points to the flooring in the hallway that extends into the kitchen. It's a beautiful dark wood that I hadn't noticed before. "It looks like real wood, doesn't it? You wouldn't know it's laminate planks," she says proudly.

"It's really beautiful." As far as I can tell, he did a great job putting it in.

"I'll pass on your information to him," she says.

She's trying to be nice, but I don't want to take advantage. "If you're sure," I say.

"Sure about what?" Beth interjects, putting her arm around Laura's waist as she joins us.

I'm struck by how much of a beautiful couple they make. Laura is demure and willowy with bleached-blonde hair and wide brown eyes. The beauty mark adjacent to her lip is strategically placed, giving her an eighties model vibe. She's much too sweet and happy for *our* family, especially after meeting her sisters and parents. Not that Beth and I are overly jaded, but we know what it's like to have a close family only to have it taken from us when our mother died. Family gatherings became a source of sadness, and we began to dread them because watching other people find joy can be painful.

After years of being in an unhappy marriage, it's nice to see Beth finally in a place where she can start to enjoy holidays and family gatherings again, no matter how much it might sting a bit for me. I think losing our mother so young – even if our father tried hard to make up for our loss – we sought out the wrong kind of love, Beth with her ex-husband, and me with Noelle's father.

"I'm going to give my dad your sister's information so he can give her an estimate on new flooring," Laura explains.

"He did our house," Beth confirms.

Our house.

"Great, it's settled," Laura beams.

"Thank you. That's really nice of you," I tell her. "Saves me having to try and find someone."

"It was really good to see you." Laura unlinks her arm from around Beth's waist to give me a hug.

When she pulls away, she looks at Noelle. "Ugh, such a beauty," she says, patting the side of her face before walking back to the party, leaving us with Beth.

Noelle looks like she's withering beside me. "We better get going."

"Thanks for coming," Beth says and then leans in. "I see you got some birthday cake," she teases, squeezing my arm.

Holding the plate of cake in the air I smile, hesitating for a moment as I take a good look at my sister. Finally, I say, "You look really happy, Beth."

Her expression softens, the angular shape of her face changing. "I am."

"If you need anything, let me know," I remind her.

Holding the door for Noelle, she passes through, and my sister calls out behind us. "Don't forget to be at the hotel on Friday at five for the rehearsal dinner. You are staying at the hotel, aren't you?" she asks, expectantly.

I turn around and smile. "We'll be there," I say, walking backwards, the sun on my back.

"On time," Beth adds sternly, looking at me pointedly.

"Yes, Mother," I tease, cringing a little bit as I say it, but Beth doesn't notice my little slip as she closes the front door.

Noelle and I walk down the sidewalk toward my car, and in the distance, I see Eric, Beth's ex-husband, walking towards us. The sight of him irritates me, and so does how he tries to use Ashley to get back at Beth. He sidesteps into the street when he notices me, probably remembering the last time we ran into each other.

"Eric," I acknowledge him. "I see you still intimidate easily."

He looks at me cautiously. "You know, Lake, I used to wonder why you didn't have a husband, but I get it now." Before he continues, he slides his eyes to Noelle, hesitating on what he really wants to say. "You could scare a Javelina with that attitude," he says.

"Just the ones that don't have balls," I say with a sarcastic smile, and saunter down the sidewalk.

Noelle chuckles beside me until we reach the car and then she really lets loose.

"If I were a good mother, I would have just ignored him and gone on my way," I say, regretting parking so far down, because the afternoon sun beating on us is unpleasant.

Noelle knits her eyebrows. "Don't say that. You were just being honest."

"Well, I shouldn't be *so* honest around you," I explain. "It's just that Eric really gets on my nerves," I admit as I turn towards her.

"He doesn't like that Aunt Beth is marrying a woman?" Noelle asks, her lips pressed into a thin line and her brows pinched in obvious annoyance.

"Men get their egos bruised easily," I explain. "He doesn't like that she's marrying anyone that isn't him," I explain.

"Even though he doesn't love her anymore?" Noelle asks innocently.

"A man with an ego and something to prove is the most dangerous kind."

We reach the car and Noelle places her hand on my arm to stop me.

"You and Aunt Beth aren't close," she says, "but you defend her."

I take a deep breath. "We love each other, but it's complicated," I say. "You'd understand if you had a sister."

Noelle narrows her eyes at me, unsatisfied with my explanation, so I continue. "Think of it this way – no one else is allowed to pick on Beth but me. It's what older sisters do."

She doesn't seem particularly happy about my explanation, but she doesn't protest.

"I don't think I'd like having a sister," Noelle says, shaking her head.

"You just want me all to yourself," I say, knocking into her with my hip.

Noelle laughs and I hold up the car keys in front of her.

"Really?" she beams.

"Consider it your wedding present. You were a toilet paper bride after all," I say, laughing.

Technically, I had a drink, even if I didn't finish it, but I don't take chances where my daughter is concerned.

"Makes it all worth it," Noelle says as I drop the keys into her eager palm.

"No speeding," I warn her.

"So don't take your example then?" Noelle teases as she slides into the driver's seat of my Porsche. I'm not a flashy person, but I do like speed and comfort. After all the hard work I put in to be where I'm at in my career, I earned this one tiny pleasure.

She starts the engine, adjusting her seat and mirror.

"I'm never getting married," Noelle says, pulling away from the curb.

I buckle my seatbelt and smile.

Kicking off my shoes, I prop my feet onto the coffee table. Noelle carries a bowl of popcorn into the living room and sets it down between us on the couch. She curls her legs underneath herself and digs into the bowl before grabbing the remote.

"What are we watching?" I ask hesitantly.

She looks at me and I remind her, "I owe you, so it's your pick."

"But you let me drive the Porsche," she says, confused.

"Because I had a drink, not because you got roped into being the toilet paper bride," I confess, guiltily.

"I feel used," she deadpans, and I roll my eyes.

"Just pick a movie, but please don't let it be one of your weird Anime shows," I beg, teasingly.

Noelle smiles and rubs her palms together maniacally.

"They are *not* weird," she says, offended. "And that's not what I was going to pick."

She tips the remote towards the TV and queues up the movie. As soon as the opening song plays, I turn towards her equal parts confused and excited. She smiles sweetly, resting her head on my shoulder.

"I know *Sixteen Candles* is your favorite," she says before shoveling popcorn in her mouth, "and it's fitting because today's your birthday." She tilts her head towards me so I can see her eyes and I lean down, planting a kiss on her forehead.

"Thanks, kid."

Settling into the couch a little further, I pop a few kernels in my mouth. I think I have the best kid in the world.

We watch the movie in silence, aside from a few grunts and laughs from Noelle who finds the inappropriateness funny.

"This is so wrong on so many levels," Noelle says.

"It was the eighties," I say, shrugging.

"Why do you like this movie so much?" she asks, laughing.

"It's romantic," I reply.

"How is giving some nerdy kid your underwear, romantic?" she asks in disgust.

"Not that part," I give her a little tap on the leg. "The *Jake* part."

"Jake is a jerk. He basically leaves his girlfriend with some oversexed high school kids and runs off to find Samantha," Noelle says, clearly offended.

She has a bit of a point there that I can't argue with. "Okay, true, but it's because he realizes who he really wants." I turn towards her and cross my legs. "He picks her up in his Porsche, takes her back to his house, and they sit on his table with a birthday cake that he got just for her," I say, and Noelle narrows her eyes at me.

"Come on, now that's romantic," I plead, moving the bowl of devoured popcorn onto the coffee table and brushing some of the crumbs into my hand before heading into the kitchen to throw them in the trash.

"Since when are you romantic?" she asks, disbelievingly.

"Way deep down in here." I tap at my heart and laugh.

Noelle follows me into the kitchen and leans against the counter. "Did you ever have that with Steven?" She never refers to him as her dad, because he never really was one.

Letting the top of the garbage can slam shut, I sigh. Noelle was five when Steven left, and she remembers very little about him. I've never sugarcoated my relationship with Steven to her, but I've also tried hard not to villainize him either, even though he is the villain of my story. But that's *my* story, not hers. She just got caught up in our dysfunction.

"In the beginning maybe, but that's a movie, not reality." I shake my head and walk past her back into the living room to finish cleaning up. Remembering falling head over heels in love with Steven… it feels tainted now, and I can see that me being younger and less experienced was exactly why I appealed to him. The thought sits heavy in the pit of my stomach. Even though it's been twelve years, what I recognize now as trauma is still very much my present, even if I try to deny it.

"Why can't that be a reality?" Noelle asks.

"I don't know. I guess guys like that don't exist in real life," I explain while grabbing the bowl and holding it out for her to take the last few kernels before throwing it in the sink. "Besides, have you ever thought about what happens after the birthday cake?" I ask. "That's when everything goes to shit." I realize how cynical I'm being a little too late, and I don't want to put my pain onto her, but love is an illusion that most people will never be able to grasp. It's the smoke and mirrors that fool you.

"Now there's the cynical mother I know and love," Noelle teases, lightening the mood.

Giving her a kiss on the forehead, I thank her.

"What if he did exist?" Noelle persists.

"What are you getting at, Elle?" I walk back into the kitchen, using the nickname I gave her when she was little. I dump the remaining popcorn in the trash and set the bowl in the sink.

"Why didn't you ever get married?"

Leaning against the counter, I look at her lovingly. "Because *you* are the love of my life."

"I'm being serious," she says, crossing her arms over her chest.

"You wanna know the truth?" I ask, her expression becoming serious as she nods.

"I didn't want to share you with anyone. I didn't want someone else having a say in *our* life," I explain honestly. "Because when you get married, that's what happens. You have to think of someone else other than just yourself," I explain.

I can see the wheels turning in her head as she knits her brows together. "Is it wrong to say that I'm glad you never got married?" she asks.

"It's not wrong to feel how you feel," I answer honestly, reaching out to touch her hair.

"But I feel bad because I want you to be happy."

Pulling her into my arms, I say, "Don't feel bad. These are my choices." But I don't say that these are my *consequences* too. The decisions I made in my past have affected her, but I've done everything since to make up for it.

"But I'm the reason you don't have someone," she frets and looks up at me with her big blue eyes.

"Don't need anyone but you, kid." I kiss the top of her head.

"You *could* see someone," she says, "if you wanted to."

Sighing heavily, I can't help but think about the other night and the man that caused me to abandon all reason. He stripped me bare with his eyes and his hands, pulling things from me I didn't even know I still had. Do I regret it? In theory, maybe, because I'm incapable of separating feelings from necessity, and now I've opened myself up to the knowledge of what I've been missing. It's a fine line to walk, being a woman made of flesh and blood and being a mother. The two shouldn't contradict each other, but nature demands it.

"Have you ever?" she asks when I don't respond.

"Have I ever what?" I ask while finishing the dishes.

"Seen someone?" she answers. "Like a boyfriend?" Her big blue eyes look to me for answers. "It's okay if you have and never told me. I get it."

I never lie to my kid.

I've never had to.

"Yes." She waits for me to finish, but I don't elaborate.

"What happened to them?"

I lean my hip against the counter, drying my hands on a towel and slinging it over my shoulder. Noelle and I are a package deal. That doesn't end when she turns eighteen. It's for life. Even when she doesn't live with me anymore, our relationship doesn't change, but it would if I brought someone into our life in any serious manner.

"None of them were Jake Ryan," I say simply, and then look her directly in the eye, tilting my mouth into a small smirk. "Besides, I have my own Porsche."

8

EARTH TO LAKE

How you Feel by Wargirl

Tapping a pen to my lip, I stare down at the joggers on the Scottsdale waterfront trail getting in an early morning run before the triple digit temperatures make it unbearable. It's a clear day, the clouds burned away by the hot summer sun, and I can see the golden brown and red hues of the McDowell Mountain range in the distance. At least I get a pretty view from my office, especially if I have to spend so much time here.

Large wooden bookcases line the wall behind my desk, various binders containing historical data, but mostly it's there for show. A glass plaque that I received only this past year celebrating my twenty years with the company sits on one of the shelves. I've put so much of my energy into building this company, which was once small with only a handful of employees, and that plaque is really all I have as a reminder. Raising Noelle on my own had its challenges, even without trying to work my way up in a company and in an industry that is male dominated. In technology, it's so much harder to be taken seriously as a woman.

In these few quiet moments before the office fills with employees and the emails demand attention, I allow myself a few scandalous thoughts. The memory of calloused fingers skimming over my bare skin, gripping my legs, and brown eyes looking up at me from under thick black lashes from between my thighs, causes heat to prickle up my neck.

When I close my eyes, I can almost feel his tongue circling my nipple, and the sweet burn of his…

"Earth to Lake!" Miles yells as if he's called my name a few times before grabbing my attention.

With his tablet in hand, he stands in the doorway in his pressed linen pants, shiny loafers, and smiling face.

"I asked if you had a nice weekend," he says, as I round my desk and take a seat in the soft leather high back chair. "How was the shower?"

I squeeze my thighs together. "Fine. It was like a Disney princess threw up glitter all over the place." I clear my throat. "Oh, by the way, black and gold wrapping paper?" I shake my head and when I look up at him, I notice he swallows hard. "An excellent choice," I say, smiling.

Miles continues to stand in my doorway as if he's waiting for something, so I pull my glasses from my face and ask, "How was *your* weekend, Miles?"

"Well, since you asked…" He eagerly takes the seat across from me, crossing his ankle over his opposite thigh. "Edmund took me to the Monet immersion. Have you been?" He doesn't wait for me to answer before continuing. "You have to go, it's an experience. Anyway," Miles continues, shaking his head and switching gears, "I sent you an email with a link to the Waterman financials they sent over."

"Did they provide an org chart too?" I ask, and look up to see Miles's worried expression. Acquisitions always lead to redundancy, and Miles is well aware of this.

"It's in the folder," he says, smoothing down his pants.

"Let's put Wyatt on the financials."

A confused expression crosses Miles's face. "Are you sure?"

"She needs something to do, doesn't she?" I ask, looking up from my laptop, pointedly.

"Yes, but," he hesitates, "it's just so high profile," Miles states.

"I want to see what she finds," I explain.

"You really don't like Waterman, do you?"

Asa Waterman is a man with an ego and something to prove. I've been around long enough to understand what makes people tick, and I trust my instincts.

"What I think about Waterman is irrelevant. This is what Glen wants, but I'm still doing my job," I explain.

Miles settles further into his seat, pulling the tablet in front of him, ready to go down the list of meetings and items on our to-do list when Wyatt taps on my open office door.

"Good morning," she says, brightly. "I hope I'm not interrupting anything, but I brought donuts," she says as she enters, holding the box.

"Bosa?" I peer over at the box and then narrow my eyes at Miles. He looks back at me guiltily, letting Wyatt in on the secret to get on my good side.

Wyatt looks at Miles conspiratorially before opening the box and offering one to me. Pulling out a chocolate sprinkled donut, Wyatt hands me a napkin and I place it on my desk.

"You should put that out for the staff, they'll love you for it," I say, and Wyatt beams.

She starts to make her exit, but I stop her. "Stay. Miles can put that out for you."

Miles rises from his seat, letting Wyatt take it. She hands him the donuts and he leaves us alone in my office.

Wyatt's blonde hair is pulled back in a low bun and she's wearing navy blue trimmed ankle length pants, paired with navy blue heels. Instead of a suit jacket, she has a lovely cream-colored button up blouse.

"How are you settling in?" I ask, crossing my legs and smoothing out my pin striped skirt.

"Everyone has been so welcoming," Wyatt says. "The guys in IT have been super helpful getting my laptop set up and passwords." She blushes, and I know exactly why.

"Ah," I say, tapping my pen against the desk. "Stay away from Mark in IT," I warn.

"Oh, Mark and I, we aren't... I mean, I wasn't..." she pinches her brows together.

"Yes, you were," I say. "I get it, he's pretty." I set the pen down and lean forward. "Many young interns have walked out of here crying over Mark."

"Well, that hardly seems fair. Shouldn't he be reprimanded?" Wyatt speaks up.

"Consider yourself warned." I don't answer her question directly. Everything Mark does is not on company time, but it's an example of why it's not a good idea to start an office affair. It evidently bleeds into work and no good will come of that when things go wrong, which they usually do.

"While we're at it, stay away from Marcia's potluck dip," I warn, making a face.

Wyatt lifts her eyebrows.

I shake my head. "It's just like Mark – looks good on the outside but once you have a taste, it doesn't go down so well."

Wyatt covers her mouth, suppressing a smile. "Good to know," she says.

"Look, Wyatt," I say in a serious tone, "everything I do and say is for a reason, not because I want to make your time here difficult," I explain.

"I don't think you're being difficult," Wyatt says, surprised.

"You will, and when you do, just know it's not because I enjoy making people cry or feel bad about themselves; so, unless you do something stupid, which I hope you don't, that's not my intention."

"You've been here a long time." It's not a question, and I track her eyes to the plaque behind me.

"I have," I say, leaning back in my chair.

"I trust that you know what you're doing," Wyatt says.

9

IT'S A FAMILY NAME

My Favorite Mistake by Sheryl Crow

"Hurry up!" I yell down the hall. "We're going to be late."

Noelle wheels her bag across the tile and we both head out to the garage, flinging our luggage in the back seat like two college girls heading off for Spring break. It's nearly four-thirty p.m. and it'll take at least forty minutes to get to the hotel. Beth is gonna be pissed because the rehearsal dinner starts at five p.m.

"Don't speed," Noelle reminds as she buckles her seatbelt.

"I don't speed," I scoff.

Noelle chuckles, shaking her head.

"Did you remember your dress?" I ask before backing all the way out of the driveway.

"Of course," she says.

Checking my mirror, I make sure my bridesmaid dress is still in its bag, draped over the backseat.

"Georgie is meeting us there later," I remind Noelle.

Noelle groans.

"What?" I ask, signaling to merge onto the freeway. "You like Georgie," I remind her.

"This is going to be an interesting weekend," Noelle says, settling further into the seat and pulling her phone out while I laugh.

Between my family, Laura's family, rehearsal dinners, and wedding preparations, Noelle is right. This will be an interesting weekend.

Forty-five minutes later I pull up to the resort using the circular driveway and stop under the portico. The valet takes my keys, and another man grabs the luggage from the backseat while we hurry into the lobby. For a moment, I stop to admire the rich reds and browns of the velvety couches and chairs that match the colors of the surrounding mountains. A picture of a cowboy hangs above the fireplace and antlers adorn the walls, giving it a warm mountain lodge feel.

"Where is the Saguaro banquet hall?" I ask, "for the Kennedy/Corvin rehearsal dinner?" Looking at my watch, I realize we're now almost fifteen minutes late.

"I'm gonna need you to run interference with Aunt Beth," I say to Noelle. "You know, bat those big blue eyes at her and she'll forget how late we are."

Noelle shakes her head at me.

"The rehearsal dinner is in the private dining room of the Compass restaurant on the property," the clerk says, handing me a map and pointing to the restaurant nestled into the side of the mountain.

"I'll have your bags taken to your room." She hands me our room card, and Noelle and I rush through a courtyard and down a long hallway in the direction of the restaurant.

My heels click on the polished flooring until we hit the hallway lined with an antique looking rug. My father stands outside the restaurant, looking relieved to see us. He's a large man in his seventies with silver hair, blue eyes, and looks quite dapper in his dark suit, but his tie looks like it's from the seventies.

"Grandpa," Noelle says, being engulfed into a hug once we reach him.

He smiles at me, reaching over Noelle to give my arm a squeeze.

"What are you doing out here?" I ask. "Shouldn't you be inside?"

"Waiting for my two girls," he says.

"You didn't want to be in there alone, huh?" I ask, looping my arm through his while Noelle does the same on his other side.

"No one speaks English in there," he grumbles. "I have no idea what they're saying."

I laugh. "Well, we're here now, so you can talk to us."

"Oh, by the way, I read that book you told me about last time."

"Which one?" Noelle asks excitedly.

"Scum Villain something," he says, struggling with the name.

"You mean Scum Villain Self-Saving System?"

"That's the one," he says.

"You have him reading your comics?" I ask, amused.

"It's not a comic, Mom," she corrects me. "It's a light novel."

"Oh, excuse me," I say, rolling my eyes.

"Yes, Lake," my dad says, sarcastically. "Don't you know anything?" he teases.

We walk further into the restaurant and I ask, "How upset is she?"

"Somewhere between politely angry and postal," he says, using his hand to demonstrate.

"Good to know."

In the back of the restaurant is a private dining room hidden behind a pair of glass doors. We stop and my dad turns to me before opening the door.

"Brace yourselves," he warns, ominously.

When he opens the door, it's nothing but chaos as everyone at the table speaks at once, English and Romanian mixing together. Momentarily, the noise is silenced by curiosity as to who is entering as heads swivel in our direction. The table is full of drinks and half eaten appetizers. All of Laura's family is there, and a few of Beth's friends who are in the bridal party. Aside from that, us three are the only family members of Beth's.

"Come on, kid, you can sit next to me so we can discuss Scum Villain," my dad says as he veers Noelle towards the other end of the table, and I look after her wistfully because the only other seat open is across from my sister. It doesn't give me a good vantage point to avoid being yelled at by her for being late. As soon as I sit down, everyone resumes their chatter and my sister turns her attention to me.

"Nice of you to join," she says with a sarcastic tone.

"Sorry," I reply guiltily, taking my seat and not bothering to bore her with an excuse. She knows me well enough to know that I'm terrible with time management at home.

The waiter enters and takes my drink order as I take a few scraps of leftover food from one of the plates lining the middle of the table. It's a delicious rice croquet.

"Well, I bet he's glad he finally has someone to talk to," Beth says, motioning down to the end of the table where our dad and Noelle have their heads together.

"Where's Ashley?" I ask, looking around.

"Eric is dropping her off later," Beth sighs taking a sip of her wine, and I can tell the stress is more than just caused by the wedding.

I can't help admiring how beautiful Beth looks with her dark hair pulled back, and a lovely strapless flowered sundress that shows off her slim figure and glowing tan.

Beside her, Laura turns her attention to us. "Lake, you look gorgeous in blue," Laura compliments, admiring my royal blue wrap-around dress. "I tried talking Beth into blue for our wedding colors to match her eyes, but she insisted on pink," Laura says innocently, resting her hand on Beth's shoulder.

Cocking my head to the side I glare at Beth, but she covertly avoids eye contact.

"Oh really, well that's a shame," I say sarcastically, taking a sip of my martini.

The private dining room is a large enough space to accommodate the more than twenty people I've been able to mentally count in my head, but the frosted, dimly lit sconces adorning the rich wood paneled walls creates an intimate atmosphere. Everyone talks at once, and I'm surprised I can hear a word Laura is saying. When the doors open, the room falls silent once again as everyone turns to see who's entering. I nearly drop my martini glass as I follow suit to see the man standing in the doorway is the same man I had a one-night stand with two weeks ago.

For Your Love by Måneskin

"Addy!" Laura bolts out of her seat and both her sisters, Ianna and Ana, rush forward, engulfing him in hugs. Surveying the room I see there is nowhere to hide, and I can feel my palms start to sweat.

Crossing and uncrossing my legs, I try to find a comfortable position, but there isn't one. As much as I want to look away, I can't. I did something in my past life that I'm paying for now, because of all the people for him to be related to, my sister's fiancée is the worst possible outcome.

The guy I had a one-night stand with is my future sister-in-law's *little brother*.

When his sisters move, I lock eyes with *him*. There's a flicker of shock in his eyes too which is both amusing and satisfying. It's clear he wasn't expecting to see me either.

But here he stands with that dark ruffled hair, those piercing brown eyes, and a helmet tucked under his arm.

"Did you ride your bike here?" Ianna asks, giving him a playful shove. "You better not have gotten your suit wrinkled," she warns.

With a bashful smile, he leans in to say something I'm not privy to.

Florina rounds the table, grabbing his face, "Adrian," she says, before giving her son a peck on the cheek as a way of greeting.

Adrian.

That's his name.

The name I didn't want to hear, the name I didn't want to know, because it would make him real. Then I remember meeting his *girlfriend*, Taylor, at the bridal shower last week.

And all I can think of is what a *fucking* liar.

He looks in my direction again, and I want to either crawl under the table or climb over it and punch him. My chest prickles with heat that travels up my neck and into my cheeks.

Looking around for the waiter, I am desperate for another martini. When I chance a glance in his direction again, I hear him ask Laura something in Romanian, *Cine este*? Laura slides her eyes in my direction, smiling, and I see her mouth form the word, *Lake*.

Turning away, I try to focus on something else when Laura's cousin, who I was sitting next to, stands up and scoots her chair over loudly. When the waiter pushes an extra chair next to me, I'm certain this is karmic payback.

As Adrian takes the seat next to me I get a whiff of his cologne, taking me back to his apartment that night. I cross my legs under the table away from him and when the waiter drops off another martini, I take it gladly.

"Thank God," I say, taking a hearty sip.

"Adrian, have you met my sister, Lake?" Beth asks from across the table, and if she wasn't so far away, I would kick her.

I don't know what I expect him to say, that yes, we met me when he cheated on his girlfriend with me during a one-night stand, but we never got around to getting each other's names because he was too busy fucking me so hard I woke up the neighbors with my screams?

Not daring to look at him, I don't know who I'm going to see – the young man in front of that bar who captivated me, or the little brother to my soon to be sister-in-law?

"No," Adrian replies with his velvety voice, and I press my thighs together under the table.

Beth shoots me a disapproving look from across the table because I'm being rude, so I turn to him with a fake smile. "Lake," I say, introducing myself.

He smirks as if this is all a game and he's leading in points. "Lake," he says. "That's different."

I narrow my eyes at him. "It's a family name," I say, holding my martini. "My dead mother's maiden name, actually. Where did you get yours from?" I ask, tilting my head as if waiting for an answer.

"Lake," Beth warns, her eyes wide in shock. "Sorry," she addresses Adrian. "My sister can have a mouth on her," she apologizes for me.

"Oh," Adrian turns towards me, "I'm well aware," he winks, causing me to choke and spit out my martini.

"Lake, are you okay?" Beth asks, concerned.

Holding my hand up I manage to compose myself, and lean

towards the person sitting next to me, realizing its Marius, Adrian's father, who speaks even less English than Florina.

Spending the rest of the evening trying to avoid Adrian, I attempt to make conversation with Marius, but I am well aware of him next to me, making it hard to concentrate. Most of the time I nod and smile while mentally comparing his features to Adrian's, and wondering how I didn't make the connection before. They have the same brown eyes that crinkle at the sides when they smile, but where Marius has an angular jaw, Adrian's is softer and more rounded.

"You have pretty eyes," Adrian whispers in my ear, causing the hairs on my neck to stand up.

"Excuse me?" I ask quickly, turning around to see him smiling at me. The fine dark hairs along his jaw and chin are a little longer than I remembered. What once could be construed as missing a shave has now turned into something deliberate, and I have to say that I like it.

"My dad, he says you have pretty eyes," Adrian clarifies, pulling my attention back to him. I can't help but watch as his lips touch the glass of bourbon when he takes a sip. The way he casually drapes his arm over the back of the chair and his easy smile tells me that I don't make him as uncomfortable as he makes me. Clearly this is not an awkward situation for him until his dad leans over saying something in Romanian that causes Adrian's cheeks to redden.

"What was he saying?" I ask curiously. "So I can make sure he's not roping me into an arranged marriage or something," I explain, teasingly.

Adrian's laugh is a deep rumble that travels through the small space between us, and I can't help but lean in a little closer so that I can hear him over the loud chatter in the dining room. "He was telling you a Romanian fairytale about *The Princess and the Fisherman*."

Marius leans over me, using his hands to encourage Adrian to continue. Leaning my elbow on the table, I tilt my head. "Do tell," I prod him to continue.

He doesn't hesitate. "It's about a princess who goes to the market to buy a fish and ends up falling in love with the fisherman," he says simply and without any romantic details, but I get the feeling he's leaving something out.

"I remind him of someone who would buy fish?" I tease, intrigued. "Clearly he doesn't know me," I laugh, taking a sip of my drink. My second martini is definitely making it easier for me to be in the same room as him.

"Why's that?" Adrian asks.

"Well, for one, I don't eat anything that has fucking eyes, and besides, I wouldn't know how to cook a fish even if I did eat one," I tell him, raising my martini glass as if toasting to a dead fish.

Adrian laughs, and when he leans around me, he says something to his father in Romanian, *Ea nu mănâncăn carne*. The words roll off his tongue easily, beautifully, and poetically.

Marius scoffs and throws his hands in the air, clearly disgruntled about something.

"What did you say to him?" I narrow my eyes suspiciously.

Adrian laughs again, shaking his thick head of hair. "I told him you don't eat anything with fucking eyes." His smile throws me off kilter, and he looks at me as if he's replaying our night together in his head.

Marius laughs, reaching around to smack his son in the arm.

"What else did he say?" I ask, but Adrian hides behind his drink, taking a slow sip, which just makes me more curious. "Tell me," I urge him further.

Adrian clears his throat, looking at his father embarrassed, and then back at me. Reluctantly he says, "He told me to stop messing around with girls my own age because this one will make a man out of me."

He looks like he's bracing for me to slap him, but all I can do is laugh. Just when I'm about to say something, Laura interrupts.

"I see you met my little brother," Laura says from beside Adrian as she rests her hand on his shoulder. The action jolts me back into reality, and I'm reminded that not only is Adrian Laura's little brother, but tomorrow he will be Beth's brother-in-law.

"I sure did," I say, smiling at Laura.

"Well, good," she says, leaning down between us, her cheeks red and her eyes bright. "Now," she demands with a ruffle to Adrian's hair, "make sure you treat her like family, Addy."

Florina squeezes her short, round body between us and asks, "What's this?"

"Dad and Adrian are going to do Lake's flooring," Laura explains to her, and my eyes go wide because at no point did I realize that Adrian would be involved in replacing my flooring.

"Oh, *lay*," Florina uses her hands to demonstrate. "Get laid," she says and smiles innocently, nodding her head, and I spit out my martini for the second time tonight.

Adrian chuckles next to me, obviously used to his mother's mispronunciation of English words, but he doesn't correct her. We're interrupted by Ianna's loud voice from the other end of the table, getting everyone's attention. "A toast!"

The chatter quickly quiets down to a low enough decibel, and chairs and bodies shuffle in her direction. Ianna raises her glass and looks across the table to her sister, Laura, who takes her place next to Beth across the table from me. "To my sister, Laura, and her soon to be wife, Beth." Ianna's voice cracks and she takes a moment to regain her composure. "We couldn't be happier about the joining of our families." Ianna looks around the table and her eyes linger on me. "I wish you a long and happy life together."

Adrian stands with his glass in hand and yells, "*Noroc!*" Everyone else follows, the room soon booming with cheers.

Raising my glass, I clink it with others around me, seeing Noelle's bright face doing the same with her ginger ale. Leaning over the table, I tip mine to both Beth and Laura, their smiles infectious, marking the happy occasion. Turning around, I'm met with Adrian's brown eyes, holding his glass up to meet mine. Hesitating for only a minute, I touch my glass to his, and we both take a sip, peering at each other over the rim.

"Well, I don't know about you guys, but I've got a busy day tomorrow," Beth jokes, and everyone erupts into laughter, noise once again filling the small room.

Feeling my phone vibrate next to me on the table, I pick it up, noticing a text from Georgie that she's almost here. Grabbing my purse, I walk over to where my dad and Noelle sit together.

"Georgie's almost here. I'm going to meet her at the lobby," I say, motioning for Noelle to come with me.

"Is it okay if I go back to Aunt Beth's room and hang out with Ashley?" Noelle asks. "Her dad is dropping her off in a little bit." She looks at me expectantly.

"I can walk her there," my dad says. "My room is a few doors down." He stands up from the table, stretching out his legs.

"Let me know when you want me to come get you," I tell her.

"Mom," she rolls her eyes. "I'm seventeen. I think I can find my way to our room."

"Remember what I told you," I say, pointing a finger at her. "Being polite is what gets you killed."

"Don't be a drama queen," Noelle says, laughing.

"Why do you think I'm still around?" I wink, playfully.

Bending down, I give my dad a kiss on the cheek. "Love you, Daddy."

Making my way past Laura's family still lingering in the dining room, I slip out into the hallway towards the lobby when I hear that familiar voice behind me, "Hey."

That one word lingers in the air like a promise, and I slowly turn to see Adrian standing there with his leather jacket and helmet tucked under his arm. Guests exit the dining room and pass around us as we stare at each other until reality kicks in.

I don't know what he expects from me. We spent one night together under the illusion that we would never see each other again, but here he is in a cruel twist of fate, and I can't forget the fact that it's possible he has a girlfriend.

Turning around, I head down the hallway again to meet Georgie at the lobby, when Adrian grabs my arm and hauls me into a small room off the main corridor that's used as a business center.

"What are you doing?" I yank my arm from his grasp and move towards the door intent on yanking it open, but Adrian steps in front of me, blocking my exit. Even with his leather jacket and tattoo snaking above the collar of his shirt, he doesn't look threatening. It's quite the opposite as the room fills with the scent of his cologne, and I step back hitting the table behind me.

"Well, at least I know you're not a serial killer," I say angrily, crossing my arms over my chest. "You're just a fucking cheater."

"Is that why you're so hostile towards me?" Adrian's mouth turns into a cocky smile as his eyes drop to my heaving chest. "You think I'm a cheater?" He takes a step closer, his tall frame hovering above me.

"I met your girlfriend, Taylor," I reply, and his eyes widen in curiosity. "At the bridal shower – *after* you fucked me," I clarify in a crude way, just to bring my point home.

He rubs his chin. "She's not my girlfriend," he says. Before I can protest, he finishes, "anymore."

"But she *was* the night we met," I remind him.

"It's complicated."

I bark out a laugh while rolling my eyes. "It's a yes or no answer."

"Yes, but…" he starts to say.

"But what?" I ask, because there's nothing he can say that will change the fact that he fucked me while he still had a girlfriend.

When he doesn't answer, I push off from the desk. "You're all the same," I scoff, shaking my head but as soon as I pass him, he touches my wrist and leans into my hair.

"I wasn't expecting to meet *you*," he admits, his breath tickling my cheek.

Turning my head to meet his eyes, he looks at me through thick black lashes. "You mean you weren't expecting to meet me *again*," I clarify.

Adrian runs a hand through his hair, causing pieces to fall into his face and covering his eyes. He lets out a long sigh. "We'd been on again off again for months," he tries to explain, "trying to decide if we could make it work."

"I think you made a decision the minute you took me home."

At least Adrian has the good sense to look remorseful.

"I made that decision the moment you walked in the bar," he says, jarring me. I don't know if I can believe him but he's very convincing, making me wonder if it even really matters.

"Why should I believe you?"

"Because I'm not that guy," he says with frustration, and then he stands in front of me, feet apart, with those eyes that never waver. "I meant what I said that night. That's not something I usually do."

"And I do?" I cock my head to the side, offended.

"That's not how I meant it," Adrian explains and shakes his head. "I have sisters."

I can see the sincerity in his eyes, not to mention witnessing how much his sisters adore him, but there's just one thing.

"None of this really matters anyway," I explain, shaking my head. "One-night stands are just that, one night," I clarify, but here he is, the guy that kissed me in the rain, the stranger that made me feel – for one night – that I was something more than just someone's mother, someone's boss, or even someone's sister.

Adrian relaxes, leaning against the door jamb. "Did you really think I could be a serial killer?" he asks, the corners of his mouth lifting into a smile.

"You still could be," I say, lifting my chin. "Just because you're Laura's brother doesn't mean anything. I've seen true crime dramas."

He moves imperceptibly closer to me, the scent of his cologne becoming stronger, his eyes pinning me when he says, "If I were a serial killer, you probably wouldn't have been allowed to sneak out of my apartment in the middle of the night."

The room feels hot as I let my eyes travel down his sharp jawline to the tattoo snaking up his neck and knowing that it curves around his broad shoulder, down his back and over his ribs. He steps forward, capturing me with his eyes and pinning me with his body.

"Do I make you nervous, Lake?" he asks, making me swallow hard. "You were hoping you'd never see me again? Is that it?"

"Exactly."

"And why is that." His finger gently travels down my arm, leaving goosebumps in its wake, "when you seemed to enjoy your birthday present so much?" Adrian's lip pulls up at the corner.

"How did you…" I pinch my eyebrows together.

"My sister," he explains.

"Of course," I grumble. "Well, don't act so fucking smug about it," I say, annoyed that he's able to get under my skin.

"Tell me you haven't been thinking about me." His eyes travel to the pulse in my neck.

I *have* been thinking about him.

A bead of sweat forms in the hollow, and his eyes follow as it falls below the neckline of my dress. He licks his lips, and the action causes my stomach to tighten. "Because I sure as *fuck* have been thinking about you."

That's lie number four.

With hooded eyes he stares down at me, his lips hovering close to mine, and I suck in a breath the minute his hip presses into me; knowing exactly how it would feel to kiss him, to sink into those soft lips, to feel the dominant way he slips his tongue into my mouth, scares me.

And I don't scare easily.

My phone vibrates between us, causing me to come to my senses. I slide away from him, putting the phone to my ear.

"Where are you?" Georgie's shrill voice says on the other end. "I'm in the lobby."

"I'll be there in a few minutes," I say, my eyes never leaving his.

Hanging up the phone, I notice he's still blocking my exit.

"What do you want from me?" I ask.

"A lot more than you're willing to give." He moves away from the door, smiling as he rubs at the scruff on his chin.

Shaking my head I slip through the door, letting it close behind me and I lean against the wall to catch my breath. The restaurant is now cleared out, the hall is empty, and I'm struck by a thought. Yanking the door back open, I lean in and ask, "How old are you?"

"Thirty-one," he smirks.

"Jesus fucking Christ," I say, annoyed by his cocky grin. Before I let the door go, I lean in and say, "Oh, by the way, nice fucking skateboard under your bed." I let the door go and walk down the hallway.

"I haven't used that skateboard in a long time!" he yells in amusement at my back as I turn the corner in a huff.

10

WE HAVE YOUR FATHER

Wouldn't Want to Be Like You by Sheryl Crow, St. Vincent

Georgie taps her foot at the front desk, her blonde ponytail swinging behind her as soon as she sees me. Predictably, she has a huge smile on her face and a bottle of wine in her hand.

"You do know they sell alcohol on the premises? This isn't Amish country," I tell her as I approach, my heels clicking on the tile floor of the lobby.

"I don't travel well without my favorite red," Georgie says, holding the bottle in front of her.

"God, am I glad to see *you*," I pluck the bottle of wine from her hand, "and this wine." I give her a hug.

"That bad, huh?" she asks, as she follows me through the lobby. We cross through the open courtyard, the sun setting and the clouds coloring the sky with beautiful pinks and oranges. The bridal party is staying in the bungalows at the back of the property, a long stretch of rooms with doors that open to the courtyard, and beautiful palms and bird of paradise lining the walkways.

"You have no idea," I say ominously as we reach the room.

"Do tell all of the dinner gossip," Georgie says, excitedly. "Did your dad make an inappropriate joke?" She grabs onto my arm, laughing, "Or did Beth lose her shit because you were late?"

"Hey, who says I was late?" I ask, cradling the wine in my arm as I dig for the room key.

"Lake, come on," Georgie states, raising an eyebrow.

We burst into laughter as I open the door to my room, and we practically fall in. Mine and Noelle's luggage is sitting at the end of the nearest bed. The room is decorated in a cozy western style, the duvet a bold pattern with orange and brown colors.

Plopping down on the mattress, I kick my shoes off while Georgie wheels her luggage to the opposite bed.

As soon as she sits down, I turn towards her and say, "He's here."

Momentarily looking confused, Georgie puckers her lips but then I see it dawn in her eyes. She doesn't say anything as she walks over to the mini bar, grabs two plastic cups, and then plops down on the bed next to me.

"I think we're gonna need wine before you explain that further," she says, holding a cup out to me.

It takes two and half glasses each to drain the bottle while I fill her in on everything, as we settle comfortably into the room. Georgie hangs her dress in the closet next to mine and begins to rifle through her suitcase for options of shoes to go with it.

"You may wear heels all week, but I'm getting tired of crocs and scrubs, so when I get a chance to dress up, I like to make it count," she says when she catches me rolling my eyes.

Comfortable in bare feet, a tank top, and my sleep shorts, I lean over the bed towards the mini bar, riffling through the tiny bottles.

"If you had brought more than one bottle of wine we wouldn't have had to break into the mini bar," I say, unscrewing the top to a tiny bottle of gin and mixing it with a bottle of coke Georgie got from the vending machine.

"Geez, these are expensive," Georgie says, eyeing the price tag as I hand one to her.

"Then it's a good thing you're not paying for the room," I reply.

"Who is?" Georgie asks.

"My sister." I laugh into the palm of my hand as I lay on my stomach sprawled across the bed.

"What?" Georgie's eyes go wide. "She's gonna kill *me* and then *you*," she says in a panic.

Empty chip bags lay crumpled all over the bed, and I toss one out of the way so I can stuff my face into the mattress to muffle the laughter.

"I don't want to be around when she gets the bill," Georgie says, collapsing onto the bed next to me.

"I wasn't going to let her pay for it anyway." I sit up, crossing my legs and grabbing one of the pillows to hold in my lap.

Georgie crosses her legs and sits opposite me.

"So are we not gonna talk about the elephant in the room?" she asks slyly.

"What elephant?" I ask, knowing full well what elephant she's talking about.

"Come on, you can hold your liquor, I've seen worse," she teases. "You know damn well what elephant," she says, eyeing me.

The mention of him sobers me right up.

"You make me sound like a lush," I say, offended.

Georgie tosses a half-eaten bag of ten-dollar cookies at me which I catch and toss to the side.

"It sounded like he was pretty into you," Georgie says.

I pick at the fringe on the decorative pillow in my lap. "As of tomorrow, he'll be my sister-in-law's 'little' brother, Georgie." The thought gives me an uneasy feeling because I shouldn't be thinking about him the way I have.

"Technically your co-brother-in-law," Georgie confirms.

"Don't ever say that again, it sounds gross." I smack her.

"Sorry," she shrugs, shuffling through the carnage on the bed. "I wish I hadn't thrown those cookies at you because now I'm hungry."

"It was a one-time thing. I got it out of my system. That's all there is to say." I lean over and toss the bag of cookies to her.

There's a knock at the door and both Georgie and I look at each other – me, clutching the pillow in front of me, and Georgie mid bite of a cookie.

Slowly, I get off the bed, aware that I'm not wearing a bra and my shorts aren't doing a very good job of covering my ass. Georgie slides off the bed after me and we tiptoe to the door. Peering through the security hole, I rear back, hitting Georgie in the nose. She gives a high pitch squeal.

Ouch!" she whines while she holds her nose.

"Well, if you weren't so fucking short!" I whisper shout.

"Hey," Georgie says, offended. "Is it him?" Georgie asks excitedly.

"Worse," I say opening the door, and Georgie's face falls.

Beth steps into the room wearing a veil and her pajamas.

"It looks like a frat party in here," she says, looking around. "Is that from the minibar?" She points to the bed and I race over to start picking up the evidence, eyeing Georgie to help.

"I was going to pay for all of this," Georgie explains, quickly tossing the empty bottles and chip bags in the trash.

"I thought you started the party without me," Beth says, and both Georgie and I look at each other, confused.

Pressing my lips together, I try to think of something to say. Turning to Georgie, I mouth, "Was I supposed to throw a bachelorette party?" I ask, but Georgie's no help because she just stares at me like a deer in headlights.

"Fuck," I whisper while turning back to Beth.

She starts laughing. "I'm just messing with you, but seriously, the look on your face," Beth says before plopping down on the bed.

"Jesus, Beth." I give her a little push.

"I swear, the two of you are like Laverne and Shirley." She laughs even harder when I look at Georgie, giving her my *what the fuck?* face.

"Am I Laverne in this scenario?" Georgie asks.

"Obviously not. I'm Laverne," I say.

"But I have blonde hair," Georgie protests.

"Shirley was the short one," I counter.

"How drunk are the two of you?" Beth asks, clutching one of the pillows to her chest.

"Did Beth make a joke?" Georgie asks.

"Holy shit, pigs do fly!" I say loudly and flop down on the bed next to Beth.

"I'm not that terrible, am I?" Beth turns to me, tucking her hand under her cheek.

My sister can be an asshole, but she's the only sister I have.

"Just a little bridezilla-ish lately," I say.

"I'm getting married tomorrow," she says, puckering her lips.

"Yeah, you are," I tell her, "so what are you doing in my room? Shouldn't you be with Laura?" I ask.

"No!" Beth shrieks, sitting up. "It's the night before the wedding, that's bad luck. We have separate rooms."

"Is that really a thing? Are you 'saving' yourself until the wedding night?" I tease.

Beth rolls her eyes. "It's tradition."

"You *have* tasted the goods, right?" I raise my eyebrows, suddenly feeling all those mini bar liquor bottles make their way through my veins right to my mouth.

Beth groans. "You're disturbing," she gripes as she pushes me over.

"I think it's very sweet," Georgie pipes up.

Suddenly aware that Beth is in my room and Noelle is not, I ask, "Hey, where's my kid? She's supposed to be in your room with Ashley." I ask.

"Oh my God, the Youtube videos, the weird Japanese death metal, I had to take a break," Beth sighs, grabbing a bag of chips and popping them open.

"Where did you get those?" Georgie says, looking at the chips longingly as Beth shrugs.

"Do you have fucking worms?" I ask Georgie, annoyed, but don't wait for an answer before turning back to Beth.

"Welcome to my world." I roll my eyes and then look at her, the alcohol making me sappy. "I really like Laura, and her family is wonderful."

"Oh, I know you do," Georgie mumbles and I shoot her a glare.

"I'm just saying that I'm very happy for you, Beth." I put my arm around her, and she lays her head on my shoulder. For a moment it feels like we're kids again, back when things weren't so complicated.

A loud ringing interrupts the moment, and we all look around for the source.

"Is that the fire alarm? Did someone set a fire?" Beth sits up quickly, looking around the room nervously.

I look in Georgie's direction.

"Why are you looking at me?" Georgie asks angrily, her blonde hair having fallen out of its ponytail.

"Puerta Vallarta?" I say, triggering her memory.

"I'd never smoked a cigar before," she shouts. "Besides, it's not like the hotel burned down."

"Only the hotel rug," I say.

"Should I be worried?" Beth looks at both of us and I say "Yes," at the same time Georgie says "No".

Beth shakes her head, the veil falling over her eyes.

"I think it's the room phone," Georgie points to the nightstand.

"They still have those?" I ask.

"Of course they still have those. This isn't the year twenty-four hundred where everyone communicates telepathically," Beth says sarcastically.

I raise my eyebrows and shake my head at her while leaning over to grab the phone.

"Hello?"

"Ms. Kennedy, this is the front desk," the woman says. "We have your father here. It seems he got a little lost and wouldn't let any of us help him back to his room."

"I'll be right there," I say, hanging up the phone.

"What is it?" Georgie asks.

"I gotta put a bra on for this." I get up from the bed and rifle through my bag. "We have to go pick dad up at the front desk," I tell her.

"What is he doing at the front desk?" Beth asks, pulling the veil from her head.

I stare at her. "How am I supposed to know?" I pull a bra from my suitcase. "Turn around," I motion.

"Oh please, you didn't have boobs in high school, and you still don't," Beth says.

"Because God gave them all to you," I say sarcastically.

Georgie starts giggling. I slip on my bra under my shirt and grab both Beth and Georgie by the arm. "Let's go get Dad."

"Why do I have to go? He's not my dad," Georgie whines.

"You wanna miss this?" I ask her.

"Good point." She lets the door close behind us and we walk across the courtyard towards the front lobby to pick up my father like he's a lost toddler at the mall.

Criminal by Fiona Apple

Sliding my sunglasses further up my nose to block out the blaring sun, I walk across the courtyard to the dining room intent on getting myself some coffee before having to deal with the craziness of Beth's wedding. The cloud cover does little to give reprieve from the heat, and even though there is a chance of rain, it will only make it worse.

Entering the dining hall, I notice Adrian and Laura near the door in a heated exchange. I'm not usually one for gossip, but I can't help but linger a little longer wanting to overhear their conversation.

"Why did you invite her?" Adrian asks. His back is to me so I can't see his face, but his voice is a little more than annoyed.

"She was my friend first before the two of you ever started dating and I wanted her here." Laura states.

Adrian sighs deeply and runs a hand through his hair.

"It's awkward," he says.

"That's the problem with dating one of my friends, Addy," Laura says, clearly annoyed.

"Dating?" Adrian replies, equally annoyed. "You know it was more than just dating." He pauses long enough for Laura to interject.

"The two of you were on again, off again. How am I supposed to keep up?"

"We're done."

With her hand on her hip, Laura gives Adrian a disbelieving look as if she's heard this before.

"For good," he says definitively.

Laura places a hand on her brother's shoulder and looks at him thoughtfully. "I don't want to get in the middle. You know I love you both, so don't tell me something that will make me hate Taylor."

Feeling as though I have violated their privacy long enough, I leave them to finish the rest of their conversation and get in line for coffee. My head hurts and the aspirin hasn't kicked in yet.

"Rough night?" Adrian asks from close to my ear.

Turning, I see his dark hair is ruffled from him running his hand through it, a few stray pieces settling against his forehead. Looking perfect in a plain white t-shirt, stretched tight across his lean chest in a way I can't help but admire, thankfully safely unnoticed behind my sunglasses still covering my eyes.

"Have you ever slept with my sister?" I lower my glasses just enough to look him in the eye.

"Excuse me?" he asks, slightly horrified.

"Be glad because she snores, and I think I actually have bruises from her elbowing me in her sleep." Turning over my arm, I look for proof.

Adrian laughs. "You're very funny," he says with a smile that brings out his dimples.

"I've been called worse," I quip, turning back around to find the line has moved up a little bit.

Adrian leans close, placing his chin over my shoulder. "You're wearing that same *Aerosmith* shirt," he says, almost with a groan.

Turning around, I ask, "Is that all it took for you to take me home? My shirt?"

His lip curves into a smile as he rubs the stubble on his chin. "It wasn't the shirt."

The way he says things with such certainty and meaning is unnerving and causes my stomach to tighten. My bravado waning, I turn away so I don't have to meet his eyes.

"It was dark that night," I whisper, remembering the rain covered street, and the dim light in the alcove of the record store.

"I saw you just fine," he says clearly.

Beads of sweat form on my brow, and the room becomes way too warm. It could be the room full of bodies standing in a line so close to one another; or it could be just the one standing so close to me.

"Why is this line so fucking slow?" I complain, using my key card to try and cool myself down but it doesn't help. "And who in their right mind gets married in August?" I ask stubbornly. "In Phoenix," I add.

"That's when they met," Adrian says in a serious tone, just as the line moves up and the coffee machine becomes free.

My hand falters while reaching to grab a Styrofoam cup. I never thought to ask my sister why she chose to get married in August, but Adrian knew. I know we've grown apart over the years, having different lives, but it was never more noticeable until now.

"Of course," I fib, finally grabbing two cups so I can bring one to Noelle. "I'm just a little hungover and it's so hot. I'm sorry if I was rude," I explain, feeling bad about complaining.

"It's a valid complaint," he offers. "Do you think I'm looking forward to wearing a suit in a hundred-ten-degree weather?"

He's not, but maybe I am. Picturing his dark hair resting atop a black suit jacket, a crisp white collared shirt barely able to contain the beautiful tattoo peaking over the top… Shaking my head, I take both cups of coffee and don't look behind me before exiting into the courtyard. Noticing the clouds have gotten thicker in such a short amount of time, I stop to look up at the sky. I have never hated a day of rain in my life, and I don't hate it now. The grounds are cast in shadow, and I begin to feel drops of water on my arms.

Feeling his presence beside me, I say, "My sister's gonna be pissed." I let a laugh escape my lips knowing it won't be funny to her at all.

"Rain is a sign of good luck on your wedding day in Romanian culture," Adrian says in a deep throaty voice.

The rain slowly flattens his unruly locks, dampening his shirt and causing it to mold to the muscles of his chest. All I can think of is that night, how he grabbed onto my waist, pulling me into the alcove to keep me safe from the rain, and his fingers burning a hole right through my shirt… the exact same shirt I'm wearing right now. As the rain comes down, the same wild and destructive feeling courses through me, and the ache between my thighs betrays what I know is going to bring me down or break me in half.

In the soft brown hues of his eyes I can see myself being reflected back, because with him, I'm free to be whomever I want. There are no expectations, no pressure – just freedom.

There is a respectable distance between us, but the space feels crowded and the air heavy when he says, "You like to be in control." It's as if he sees right through me.

I just stare at him, unblinking. He tilts his head to the side with a cocky grin and asks, "Wouldn't it be nice to just let go?"

Wouldn't it be nice to just let go? That sentence hangs like a dangling carrot in the space between us. Every aspect of my life is controlled by obligation and responsibility which I have wholeheartedly accepted, and the only time I have ever strayed is when I was with him. For once, I don't want to be the one in control, or the person everyone counts on. The pressure can be stifling, just like summer in Phoenix.

The rain falls harder as big fat drops land on my face and arms, plastering my shirt further to my body. His eyes travel from the rain falling off my chin to my hardening nipples under my shirt from the cool rain. Maybe I want to lose control, but I will make him work for it.

Leaning towards him so I can whisper in his ear, I say, "I don't think you'd know what to do with me, little boy, if I really let go."

When I pull away I notice the heat in his eyes, the piece of him that wants to find out if it's true, right here in this courtyard. My skin prickles with excitement at the chase, even if I'm flirting with danger. One night with him wasn't enough.

There's a squeal in the distance that pulls my attention away from him, and I look across the courtyard to see my sister running towards us as if she's trying to dodge the rain.

"Why are you just standing in the rain, Lake?" she asks, holding a jacket over her head. If she's suddenly aware that Adrian is standing next to me, she looks between the two of us, faltering. "I'm getting married today!" she yells.

Adrian chuckles while running a hand through his damp hair, and I leave him in the courtyard while I follow my sister towards her room.

When I glance over my shoulder at him, he's still standing in the rain, watching me leave.

Florina walks towards us down the long row of rooms under the overhang. Her cheeks are red, as she raises her arms to give Beth a kiss on the cheek. "It's good luck," she says, pointing to the rain.

Beth looks out at the courtyard and sighs. "It's going to ruin my hair."

"I'm sure it'll be fine, Beth," I try to reassure her.

When we enter the room, Noelle is sitting on the bed opposite of Ashley. She perks up when I hand her the cup of coffee which is no longer piping hot.

"You look like a drowned rat," Noelle says, taking the cup from me.

"Thanks," I say mockingly while leaning down to give Ashley a kiss on the top of her head. "Hey, sweetie," I say, and she smiles up at me. Both girls are still in their pajamas, but their hair and makeup are done.

The room is loud and obnoxious as it fills up with Beth's friends and some of Laura's family who are no doubt making their way back and forth from Laura's room.

"How was your night?" I ask Noelle, plopping down on the bed next to her. Reaching out, I pull a piece of her long brown hair over her shoulder, admiring the beautiful curls.

"I'm now fluent in Romanian," she jokes and Ashley sniggers.

My phone vibrates and I pull it from my wet pocket, trying to dry it off with the edge of my shirt but it's no use.

> G: Um, did you forget someone?

> L: Shit

"I'll be right back, I need to grab Georgie and get the rest of my stuff from the room," I explain to Noelle and pass Beth on my way out. "I'll be right back," I say to her.

"I missed you, kid." I blow a kiss to Noelle and then look teasingly at Beth adding, "I had to sleep next to your aunt and it was not pleasant," I say, giving my sister the evil eye but she's not paying attention to me.

Exiting the room, I get only a few feet from the room when Beth calls my name. She lets the door close behind her, a serious expression on her face. She's pissed at me about something, and I know I'm in for a lecture, I just don't know what for.

"He's going to be my brother-in-law," she says in an ominous tone, causing my stomach to drop. Finding it hard to believe Adrian would tell his sister about me, the fact remains that I don't really know him.

My lack of response prompts her to continue. "I saw the two of you in the courtyard," Beth says.

"We were just talking. You wanted me to be friendly," I say jokingly.

"It didn't look like just talking," she accuses. Now's my chance to come clean, to explain to her I had a one-night stand with some guy that turned out to be Laura's brother. Maybe we'd have a big laugh and move on, but I know that's not how this is going to go down. I don't think Beth would find it funny, especially not hours before she's about to get married.

At work and with my kid I'm very direct, sometimes to a fault, but anything to do with my emotions makes me uncomfortable. I haven't been as forthcoming with Beth about things that matter. As much as I want to be open and honest with her, it's just more than I can handle, and that's why I don't tell her about Adrian.

The truth is I like having a secret that only Adrian and I share, something that is just mine, even if it was only for one night.

So I tell her, "It was nothing, Beth." Shaking my head, even I can feel the lie has taken up the oxygen from the space between us. Whenever Adrian's near, there is always *something* between us.

"I love Laura, and her family has been nothing but welcoming," Beth says, "so, please don't do anything that would jeopardize that."

"I would never do anything to hurt you or Laura," I say, eyes wide, but I fear the guilty look on my face makes it obvious I already have.

"Then stay away from him," she pleads. Maybe she doesn't get the reaction she wants out of me, but then she adds, "Besides, he's like ten years younger than you."

"That's out of line, Beth," I warn her, ready to stand my ground, but I've already had reservations about that. Beth just dug the knife in a little deeper.

"This is my wedding day. Let's not do this right now," she sighs as if I'm the one causing problems. I know Beth has been stressed about the wedding and this is terrible timing, so I let it go.

All I can do is nod because the words are stuck in my throat. Beth turns back towards the room leaving me standing there alone. Having an overwhelming need for my kid right now, I grab the door before it closes. "Noelle," I say, a little too sternly. She swivels towards me, her smile instantly faltering as she sees the look on my face. "Let's go."

Noelle slides off the bed and waves to Ashley as she exits the room. Hugging her as soon as the door closes, Noelle asks, "Mom, what's wrong?"

Putting my arm around her shoulder, I steer her through the courtyard and back to our room. "I just missed you," I say, pushing out my bottom lip, because it's the truth.

"You and Aunt Beth are fighting, aren't you?" she asks, stopping me before we open the door.

"Yeah, but it's okay. We'll be okay." I give her a small comforting smile, because that's what I do, I make things better.

As soon as I open the door, Georgie flaps her arms in the air. "I know I'm short but I'm not invisible," she huffs, gathering her stuff.

"God, what happened here? It looks like bridesmaids gone wild." Noelle scrunches up her nose while picking up an empty wine bottle from the dresser.

"We're getting ready in here," I tell Georgie, ignoring Noelle's question.

By the look on Georgie's face, she knows something's wrong but she lets it go, knowing I'll tell her about it later and not in front of Noelle.

Starting the shower, I pull my dress out of the bag and hang it up on the outside of the bathroom door. The steam should help with any wrinkles.

Georgie runs her fingers over the soft pink chiffon material. "Too bad it's not blue," she says.

"Don't get me started," I say, before closing the door.

11

NOW IT'S YOUR TURN

Rolling Stone by Lainey Wilson

"**D**o I look okay?" Laura asks for the hundredth time as she looks at her reflection in the mirror.

"You look stunning," I say, standing behind her.

She's wearing a mermaid style silk dress with an open back. Her blonde hair is piled on top with curls that fall down her neck. Florina is constantly fussing with the dress, pulling the material out so it doesn't wrinkle. Her sister, Ianna, is taking pictures with her phone while her kids race around the room, and Ana waddles around the room, her baby bump looking beautiful in the pale pink bridesmaid dress.

Even though the a/c is cranked up, I'm already sweating. The afternoon sun on the walk over to the church across the street from the hotel was uncomfortable.

"Where's Noelle?" Ianna asks, taking a break from pictures as she fluffs her hair in the mirror.

"She's with Ashley checking on things in the church," I reply. "Teenagers." I shrug.

Her three kids race by – the oldest one in a beautiful pink tulle dress with flowers in her hair, the other two in a miniature version – as Ianna yells at them to settle down. "Tell me teenagers are easier," she sighs, exasperated. I can tell it's been a stressful morning for her already.

"I lucked out in the teenager department," I admit, "but I think she's an anomaly."

"Don't say that," Ianna laughs as she smooths the wrinkles out of her pink strapless dress. She stops fussing with her hair and stares at me through the mirror's reflection, her face softening. "You look beautiful in pink," she says. "I can't believe you're forty. You and your sister defy time," she says sweetly.

Looking at myself in the mirror over Ianna's shoulder, I must admit the dress is beautiful, even if it's pink. On the outside I'm a forty-three-year-old mom with a few more lines around her eyes, a few stretch marks, and scars inside and out, but I still feel like the twenty-year-old girl who fell in love with the wrong person.

"We need a picture," Ianna says, gathering everyone together.

Ianna smiles at me, snaking her arm around my waist and making sure I get in the picture. She hasn't asked why I'm in here and not with Beth which I appreciate more than she'll ever know. Beth and I never had a big family, and all of this is overwhelming. All we had was each other, and I guess I never knew what I was missing, but I'm not marrying into Laura's family; Beth is.

"I should go check on Beth," I tell Ianna, slipping out of her grasp and gathering the bottom of my dress so I don't trip on the ends. My heels have caught on the material more than once already.

"Wait!" Laura shouts, rushing over and giving me a hug. "Thank you," she says, but I don't know why.

"It's going to be a beautiful wedding," I reassure her.

Before leaving the room, I watch as Ianna walks over to Laura, looking at her with so much love and happiness my stomach feels like it's in knots.

In the lobby of the church, guests are still entering and taking their seats. Noelle meets me in front of Beth's dressing room to wait until everyone gets seated. Wearing a beautiful blue dress that flares at the waist, she definitely looks older than her seventeen years.

Inside the small dressing room, there are only a few bridesmaids. Beth is wearing a beautiful white silk strapless dress that pushes her breasts up and cinches at the waist. The skirt is made of tulle and fans out behind her, covering the floor like a waterfall. Seeing it on her in the bridal shop was one thing, but seeing her in it at the church just minutes from getting married takes my breath away for more reasons than I'm willing to admit.

"You look," I start to say but get choked up. Even after everything, I'm still happy for her. "Stunning," I finish.

Beth smiles at me, barely able to contain her nervous excitement. "Thanks," she says, and I can tell she might want to say something else, but now is not the time to get into it. "It wasn't like this the first time," she admits, turning to look at herself in the mirror one last time.

"Because this is the real thing," I say looking over her shoulder, seeing all the differences between us, but all of the similarities too.

"Where's Dad?" Beth asks, pinching her eyebrows together.

"Shit," I say.

"Are you serious, Lake?"

"I'm joking, Beth. He needed to sit down so I left him with Georgie in one of the church pews."

"Now I'm even more worried," Beth says, her eyes wide, and planting her hands on her hips.

I nudge Noelle. "Go check on your grandpa," I whisper to her.

Noelle leaves us to enter the church while we gather outside the doors waiting for the music to start when Laura arrives. Her dad, Marius, is holding her arm, and I'm guessing this is the first time they have seen each other in their wedding dresses because they both tear up.

"Makeup, oh no, *ruina*," Florina fusses, shoving tissues at them.

The doors open, and my dad and Noelle approach us. He looks so handsome in his tux. He takes one look at Beth and his eyes tear up. Florina shoves tissues at him too.

"Look at you, Beth," he says, giving her a kiss on the cheek while holding onto her with shaky hands. "Your mom would have been so happy for you," he whispers into her ear.

My sister looks absolutely radiant, like a piece of glass sharp enough to cut through anything. Ianna wrangles the wedding party to stand together for a group photo. I take my place in the middle of the group as the music inside the church starts up.

In the melee of the crowd, I feel someone next to me, a hand lightly touching the small of my back, and a thumb gently brushing across the material of my dress. It feels like an electric pulse is humming through my body, excitement rising from the depths of my belly, and I turn my head slightly, raising my eyes to meet his, and the scent of his cologne filling the space between us.

His freshly shaven jaw, slicked back hair, and tailored suit – meant to give the illusion of a gentleman on the surface – does little to hide the smoldering musician with the dirty mouth underneath. His brown eyes peer down at me, his lip pulling up at the corner with a hint of a smile, causes me to swallow hard, while his hand on my back slowly moves up. When his fingers make contact with my bare skin, it's like a live wire coursing through me. My lip's part while the camera flashes again and the group disperses, pulling us apart.

It's as if I was just on the teacups at Disneyland when the ride stops, and I have to find something that's not moving or I'd fall over. Grabbing my bouquet of pink and white roses from the table, we line up in front of the door, the bridesmaids entering first while both Beth and Laura wait at the back to walk down the aisle together.

The doors open and the music filters out into the front of the church. Everyone in the pews stands to watch as we walk down the aisle. There is no formal order, and when I look to my right, it's Adrian who walks next to me down the aisle. Just as I imagined, the crisp white collar of his dress shirt barely contains the tips of the tattoo on his neck. His wavy dark hair rests gently at the tops of the black suit jacket that stretches across his shoulders. In the pocket of his suit jacket is a familiar white cotton that would appear to anyone else as a pocket square, but I know are my fucking underwear.

He looks devastatingly handsome in a suit, but nothing will ever compare to how untamed and beautiful he looked the night we first met.

Such a pretty boy with a filthy mouth.

My eyes drop to his hands noticing how he rubs them together nervously; those same hands that gripped my hips as he fucked me from behind, shattering every last bit of doubt that I would not be able to go the rest of my life without ever feeling like that again. I can feel it now, like a tether between us, drawing tight across the aisle as we walk together, then I veer to the left and Adrian veers to the right, taking our places on our respective sisters' sides.

The music changes, and while everyone is looking to the back of the church where both Beth and Laura are escorted up the aisle by their fathers, Adrian and I are looking at each other.

"You have to hold it with both hands. Massage it a little, not man handle it, and it'll feel like it's getting bigger but that's impossible, so you wait, squeezing your eyes shut until the pressure from the inside makes the top blow and everything spills out," Georgie says to a crowd of guests as she holds a bottle of champagne in her hands.

Sure enough, with a little massaging and less manhandling, the cork pops open and champagne fizzes to the top, spilling over as everyone laughs. She hands the bottle of champagne back to the bartender and he pours the drinks while shaking his head.

"Are you trying to steal my job?" he teases.

Georgie props her elbow on the bar and flirtatiously bats her eyelashes. "Only if I get to keep the tips," she says, causing the bartender to laugh.

Sipping my champagne, thanks to Georgie, I watch as Laura and Beth dance together in the middle of the crowd. The two of them fit together like missing puzzle pieces finally united. The sound of glasses clinking together rings through the banquet hall like a harp, getting their attention. Even from this distance, Beth's smile lights up the room as she pulls Laura in for a kiss while the whole room cheers.

Ianna's three little girls race through the crowd, and I watch as Adrian picks up the youngest one who was straggling behind, and lifts her into his arms. She giggles while he tickles her and then holds her hand out pretending to dance which she seems to love.

"Thanks for popping my lesbian wedding cherry," Georgie says, all smiles, while shimmying in her little black dress and perfect leopard print strappy heels. "I'm having a great time."

"You're welcome." I clink my champagne glass with hers.

"But seriously, it really is a beautiful wedding," Georgie says, and I look at my sister and Laura making their way around the room to greet guests.

Ianna's two other girls have made their way over to Adrian, having found their little sister having fun without them. Like jealous little girls, they climb all over Adrian as he tries to dance. He seems so at ease and unbothered by their relentless pursuit to gain his attention.

Leaning over the bar, I twist the glass of champagne around in my hands. The DJ makes an announcement that I don't pay attention to. A live band starts up, and then I hear Adrian's voice, the deep timbre cutting through the chatter of the wedding guests and the room becomes quiet. The song needs no translation even though it's in Romanian, because of how he cradles the guitar to his body like a lover, and the way the notes are elongated as if he wants to hold onto each one. Clearly it's a love song, and a popular one, as Laura's family begins to sing along with him.

Beth rests her head on Laura's shoulder, as they stand at the edge of the crowd while Adrian steps down from the riser. His hair has fallen loose, dark hair covering the tops of his ears, the suit jacket long discarded, and his tie pulled loose with the top button of his shirt now open. He's so comfortable in front of a mic with a guitar strapped to his body and an easy smile on his face.

"I can see the appeal," Georgie says in my ear, as we both watch with rapt attention.

Taking a sip of my champagne, I lean against the bar. Georgie rests her shoulder against mine. "There's nothing wrong with having a little fun," she says.

"Until someone gets hurt." I look across the room at Adrian and watch as Taylor, in her tight-fitting red dress, makes her way over to him and his expression turns tense.

THE GROUND IS DRY, not a hint of evidence that it had been raining earlier, aside from the thick and muggy air, as we walk across the dimly lit courtyard.

"I am perfectly capable of getting to my room by myself," my dad says.

Raising my eyebrows at him, he waves me off. "I told them I could find my way back just fine," he says, referring to last night's adventure.

"Of course," I say, using his key card to open his door.

Sitting on the end of the bed, he pulls the tie from around his neck and lets it drape over his palm as he stares down at it.

"Do you know where I got this tie from?" he asks, holding it up for me to see.

"No," I reply and take a seat next to him. The brown and orange paisley pattern doesn't match anything he's wearing, and looks like something out of the seventies, but he wears it for almost every formal occasion.

"I had finally gotten the courage to ask your mother on a date, but I didn't have anything nice to wear so I borrowed a dress shirt from your Uncle Dennis," he tells me. I like the way my dad's blue eyes shine when he smiles, the lines pulling at the edges becoming more prominent.

"I was walking across campus on my way to your mother's dorm. Back then, there was only the Science building and the Herberger." He refers to the old ASU campus in Tempe. "She was in Manzanita Hall, and on my way over I ran into Professor Talbert, my engineering teacher."

"He took one look at me and said I couldn't go to Winnie Lake's dorm looking like I wasn't a serious man with prospects." My dad laughs as he remembers the moment. "He let me borrow his tie to go with Dennis's dress shirt." Letting go of the tie, it drapes over his lap. "Because of that, I was late picking her up and she was angry. She told me she'd go on a date with me once I was on time," he laughs, the sound comforting.

His expression turns somber. "I never got to return the tie to Professor Talbert though, because he was struck by a car and killed the next day while walking across the street in front of the engineering building."

I place my hand on his shoulder. "You never told me that," I say, placing my hand over his.

He's told a lot of stories over the years but never this one, and I like hearing stories about my mother when she was younger.

"It's not something I like to remember," he says, peering over at me. "We had a vigil for him on campus. Lots of students liked him; he was very popular," he sighs. "I wore his tie and saw Winnie from across the crowd. She was so beautiful; I couldn't take my eyes off her." He grabs hold of my hand.

"We went to the Devils Den and had a bite to eat after the vigil. Of course, it's not there anymore, turned into a Pita Jungle or something now. That was our first date." He nods proudly, smiling at the memory. "I didn't know how to return the tie so I kept it, but it reminds me of your mother now more than Professor Talbert because she said it was ugly and I should never wear it again," he laughs. "We'd get into an argument over wearing this tie, but I wore it on purpose because, God, she was beautiful when she was angry."

Thinking about my mother I smile, because she *was* beautiful, and kind, but she had a temper... and dad loved to test her patience.

"That is quite a story," I tell him. "And the fact that you kept the tie this long is amazing."

"I wanted to bring a little piece of her with me today," he admits, patting my hand and then pulling away.

"All this time, I just thought you had bad taste," I tease, making him laugh.

"I miss her, Lake," he says, and I can feel it all the way down to my bones. "You have a lot of your mother in you – especially her stubbornness." He turns to look at me and I sniff, shaking my head.

"I'm not gonna be around much longer," he says.

"Don't say that, Dad," I tell him.

"It's inevitable I'm afraid." He pats my hand. "I want both of my girls to be happy."

"I am…"

"Did you see Beth tonight?" he asks, and I nod thinking of how happy Beth looked.

"She's found it."

"Found what?" I ask, confused.

"*It*, Lake," he says, pointing to my chest. "Now it's your turn."

12

IT'S A GREAT ASS

Never Say Never (with Lainey Wilson) by Cole Swindell

Taking the long way back to my room, I enjoy the quiet of the resort. It's late into the evening; all the guests are tucked safely in their rooms. There's only the sound of the waterfall from the pool in the distance to keep me company.

Slipping the heels off my feet, I hook my finger under the straps, slinging them over my shoulder. There's a little bit of a breeze but not enough to cool me off; the air is still balmy. The hotel is made up of Spanish style stucco buildings, dark wood grained doors, with pineapple palms and bird of paradise lining the walkways. Palo Verde trees provide little cover, but their branches fold over the sidewalk creating the illusion of a tunnel.

The lights from the hotel shimmer across the pool as I hold onto the metal bar of the gate wishing I could slip through and submerge myself in the water, dress and all, but the gate is locked.

"Has anyone told you how great your ass looks in that dress?" I don't have to turn around to know who it is, but I do anyway, catching a glimpse of him over my shoulder as he approaches.

Adrian.

"Your father might have but I could be wrong. I'm not fluent in Romanian," I say, lifting an eyebrow.

Adrian's deep laugh washes over my skin. "I wouldn't put it past him," he jokes. "It's a great fucking ass." He tilts his head, the hint of a smirk on his face.

That's lie number five.

His knuckles drag down the open back of my dress and he grabs a handful of my ass in his palm, causing me to tip my head back against his shoulder. Taking the heels from my hand, he lets them fall to the ground, clattering as they hit the pavement.

I shouldn't want this, but I do.

His hands on me are better than any martini I've ever tasted, causing me to forget my sister's warning.

Hot, sweet breath caresses my neck. "You made me wait *far* too long," he says, while his hand moves purposefully to the front of my dress.

Like an expert, he easily parts the fabric of my dress and slips his hand between the folds of pink chiffon. His fingers glide over the silk material of my panties, causing my breath to hitch. One touch has me on edge already, and I forget that I'm in public.

That's a lie.

I know I'm in public.

I just don't care.

Sighing audibly, I grip the bars of the fence as his fingers slide under the edges of my panties, his breath hot against my neck. Teasing, he slides back to front, gripping my thigh before slipping his finger into the crease feeling how wet I am.

"Fuck, you're wet," he groans, pressing a kiss to my neck while I grind my ass further into his already growing erection. His other hand presses against my stomach, holding me to him before moving freely up my dress to cup my breast.

Lush oleander bushes hide us from the general walkway, but anyone could walk by and see us. My dress might be able to hide his hand, but it does nothing to stifle the moans escaping my lips.

There is a dark part of me that wants to be caught and put an end to this just as much as I never want it to stop. Grinding against his erection, I move to the cadence of his fingers slipping in and out, teasing and circling my already sensitive clit.

Gripping the bars tighter, my moans get increasingly louder as my orgasm builds. Biting the bottom of my lip, I try to be quiet but I can't, and the waterfall can only drown out so much noise.

"Oh, God," I whimper, and he covers my mouth with his hand.

"Shhhh," he whispers, covering my mouth with his hand which only increases the ache. His fingers grip my cheek, and his palm collects my cries.

He pumps his fingers into me faster, running the slickness over my clit and increasing the speed until I am completely lost. The feeling of falling off a cliff, not caring when or if I hit the bottom scares me, but I can't stop it. I want him inside me, bending me to the point of breaking.

"Just let go," he groans, and I can hear the ache in his voice, how much he wants to bend me over and take me against the fence.

My eyes spring open and I watch as the water cascades over the rocks. There's no sound except for the blood pumping in my ears, and everything pulses like the hum of a refrigerator fighting against the heat. Biting down on his finger to suppress my scream, it comes out like a muffled cry. His fingers slowly circle my clit as I pulse around him, pressing my thighs together to stop the burn and he removes his hand from my mouth.

"Fuck," he says, inspecting it. "You fucking drew blood." He looks at me with feral eyes.

He's so pretty, it hurts.

Leaning against the fence, I'm not even close to being satisfied. He grabs me by the back of the neck and crashes his mouth to mine.

Fingers pull at my hair, bending my neck to open for him, letting his tongue slip inside. Wrapping my leg around his waist, he pushes me into the fence, grinding his hard cock into my pelvis.

"If I don't fuck you right now, I might just come in my pants," he groans, breathing heavily.

Smiling against his mouth, I know that wasn't a lie. He really will come in his pants.

"Let me take you back to my room," he pleads between kisses.

"No," I say.

I can't go back to his room when my kid is waiting for me in mine.

"Don't say no," he begs. I never thought I was the kind of woman who liked to hear a man beg, but I get off on it, like a hit of something potent and reckless.

Holding my face with both hands, his eyes are hooded, and I can feel the desperation coming off him in waves.

"Come here," I say, pulling him across the walkway to the entrance of the hotel, spotting a sign for the ladies' room.

We hit the door, tumbling inside without breaking the kiss. Dipping his hand in the front of my dress, he pulls my breast free from its constraint. With my hands in his hair, I pull him to me. His mouth is hot, pulling at my nipple while desperately trying to find the slit hidden within the material of my dress.

"The door," I whisper, bringing him back to reality.

He reaches behind and turns the lock on the door while I step back further into the bathroom, aware that my dress is hanging off one shoulder and my lipstick is smeared. Reaching for his jacket, I tug at the pocket square and ask, "Do you keep souvenirs from all the women you fuck?"

His lip pulls up at the corner, tucking my panties further into the pocket before pulling the jacket off and laying it on the counter behind me. "Only yours," he says, before lifting me up.

His tall, lean body settles between my legs spreading them open further, and I wrap myself around him. Kissing me, his lips move over my jaw and down my neck, pulling my nipple into his mouth again. Fumbling through the layers of my dress in search of my panties, he can't seem to get them off fast enough.

Done playing around, I tell him. "Just rip them." He yanks hard, the material digging into my flesh before coming apart.

He grabs a condom from his pocket before unbuckling his belt, letting his pants fall to his ankles. Reaching for his cock I fist it in my hand, trying to guide it to me, and I hear his breath hitch, but he stops me. Then he kneels before me, bunching the pale pink chiffon around my waist as he raises my legs over his shoulder. "I need to taste you first," he says, pulling me to him.

I'm forced back against the bathroom mirror, arching my back as my fingers desperately search for something to grip onto as his head disappears under the material of my dress, tongue teasing until he has me writhing on the bathroom counter, pulling at his hair. My whole body tenses as I whimper and moan, feeling the building storm that gathers inside me.

"Ah, oh, God," I cry, slapping my palm to the wall.

He pulls his mouth away momentarily, long enough to peer up at me from between my thighs through thick black lashes. "Now you know my name," he rasps. "If you want something to scream, don't let it be God's." His head disappears beneath the chiffon, and I suck in a breath as his tongue swirls along the sensitive nub of my clit, and I rock against him, fucking his mouth.

I'm so close, standing on the edge, waiting for him to give me that final push, and when he does, I scream his name until he slams into me with relentless force.

Each thrust is more desperate than the last, as if he's trying to climb his way inside me. Gripping his back, I can feel every muscle as he drives into me, fucking me through the orgasm, making my thighs shake, and causing every muscle in my body to pulse. His mouth desperately seeks out mine, and when we connect, it's achingly slow. My heart bangs against my ribcage as I fight for air, desperate to not give up this feeling, because once it ends, reality will sink in

"Jesus Christ," he whispers, heart pounding through his wrinkled white dress shirt.

Dragging the palms of his hands down the sides of my hair, the rough pads of his thumbs brush against my cheek softly. Leaning his forehead against mine with his eyes still closed and breathing heavy, he whispers, "I've never fucked anyone in a bathroom before." And then he laughs while trying to catch his breath, and places a gentle kiss on my forehead.

That's lie number six.

Smoothing down the skirt of my dress, I tuck my breast back into the top, and slip the strap back onto my shoulder. Adrian helps me down from the sink and I run a hand through my hair, not wanting to look like I just got fucked in a bathroom, but I'm afraid it's a lost cause.

I can't explain the draw I have to him or what it is he sees in me, but it's visceral and I can't deny it.

He collects his jacket, draping it over his arm, and looks at me. "What is this, Lake?" he asks, running a hand through his unruly hair.

"Something that shouldn't have happened," I say, trying to gain back some composure.

Instead of protesting, he kisses me.

Stone by Whiskey Myers

Slipping out of the shower, I pat my hair dry and wrap the towel around me. The bathroom is dark because I couldn't bear to turn the light on. It doesn't matter though, because I can still see myself through the fog and darkness.

I can say this isn't me, that I don't know who this person is staring back at me, but I'd be lying. I've been pretending for the last seventeen years that I'm someone else. This version of me has been suppressed for so long that I didn't remember she existed, until I looked up on that stage and locked eyes with Adrian Corvin and my world tilted.

This life I have carefully constructed for myself and my daughter doesn't have room for a man like Adrian – a younger man who has a vastly different path than me, not to mention that my sister just married into his family.

While slipping on a night shirt and underwear, it only now dawns on me that my shredded panties are probably lying on that bathroom floor for some unsuspecting maid to find in the morning. Or worse, a guest. Unless Adrian took them. The thought thrills me more than it should.

Gently, I slip between the covers beside Noelle. She stirs, turning over to face me. Her brown hair covers part of her face and I push it aside.

"I fell asleep," she says groggily.

"Yeah, you did," I whisper.

"It was a really fun wedding," she says with her eyes closed and her lips puckered.

"It was," I say, and tuck the blankets further around her.

Looking over at the other bed, I know it's empty because I don't hear Georgie snoring. She must have stayed at the reception after I took my dad back to his room. The door opens, a stream of light from the outside lamp streaks across the darkened room, and the door crashes into the wall.

"Shit, sorry," Georgie whispers, as she closes the door gently behind her while she tiptoes into the room.

Noelle sits up, looking at me. "Can you tell your friend this isn't a sorority house?" she says, annoyed.

"Look, kid," Georgie says as she plops down on her bed. "Us adults," she motions to me, "don't have a curfew."

Noelle scoffs and flops back onto her pillow.

"Maybe you need to live a little, Noelle. You're gonna be an adult soon." I hear her shoes hit the floor.

"Don't give my kid advice when you're drunk," I scold, jokingly.

"I'm not drunk," Georgie argues as she unzips her dress, letting it fall to the floor while she crawls into bed in just her bra and underwear.

I snort laugh.

"Okay, maybe a little." I hear her fluff the pillow.

"Just go to sleep. We have to check out in the morning," I warn her.

"I can't just fall asleep on command," Georgie says, and I can hear her shuffling around in the bed, trying to find a comfortable position.

Noelle turns over and pulls the blanket over her head, groaning. Georgie hooks her thumb in Noelle's direction. "Lightweight," she whispers as I laugh.

Noelle rips the blanket from over her head. "I'm seventeen and I'm more mature than you," she yells back.

In the shadowy darkness of the room, I can see Georgie mocking her. "I swear sometimes I feel like I have two kids instead of one," I grumble.

"Hey!" Georgie complains and pops her head up.

"Just go to sleep," Noelle demands, and the room becomes eerily quiet.

Muffled voices outside the room fade away as guests pass through the courtyard, and I settle into the bed further, even though I'm not tired. My mind won't shut off as I go through the events of the evening, Adrian's hand palming my ass, pushing my dress around my waist, and fucking me in the bathroom. Maybe I should regret it because this is leading nowhere, but I don't.

I had sex in a fucking bathroom, and it was good.

Really good.

From the other side of the room I hear Georgie snoring, so I turn over on my back, shoving the extra pillow over my face.

13

THE BEST I'VE EVER HAD

Lie to Me by Tate McRae & Ali Gatie

"Those mattresses are really comfortable," Georgie says, as she reaches over me to grab the creamer.

"I'm glad *someone* slept well," I grumble, taking my cup back to the table.

Unable to fall asleep because of her snoring, when I finally did I was restless, and now I'm paying for it. Taking a seat next to Noelle who is effectively blocking us out by having her earbuds in, she's engrossed in watching something on her phone. She crosses her long legs and dangles her flip flop precariously from her toe as she wiggles her foot.

"Maybe you should have drunk more, it would have knocked you out," Georgie laughs, spreading cream cheese on her bagel.

"Drinking is not always the answer, Georgie," I say, shaking my head while dumping creamer into my coffee.

"It's always the answer." She eyes me while taking a bite of her bagel. "By the way, where are the happy couple?" Georgie looks around the dining room, ignoring my comment.

"They had to catch an early flight to Hawaii," I explain.

"Jealous," Georgie groans.

Feeling the tightness in my stomach when I think about going back to work tomorrow, I sigh. Usually I try to get ahead of the week by checking email and getting organized over the weekend, but with the wedding, I couldn't do that. Tomorrow will be a long day.

"There are my beautiful girls," my dad says, grabbing my attention as he approaches the table.

"Aw shucks, Benjamin, you spoil me." Georgie waves at him bashfully while I palm my face. Georgie looks at me offended. "What?" she says, pretending outrage. "I'm part of the family."

"Right you are, Georgie." My dad smiles at Georgie who gives me a smug look. "I'm heading out. Gotta pick up Fritz from the sitter."

"Are you okay to get home yourself?" I ask.

"I'm not an invalid, Lake," he says, glaring at me, and Noelle laughs.

"Oh look, she can hear us. Glad I didn't say anything inappropriate," Georgie gripes and narrows her eyes at Noelle.

"As if that's stopped you before," Noelle quips, rolling her eyes at Georgie.

"You come visit me soon," my dad says to Noelle. "I want to know what classes you're going to pick for freshman year."

"That's a year away," Noelle grumbles, setting down her phone.

"First year of college is important. Got to start off on the right foot. It's never too early to start planning, or you won't get the good professors," he says sharply.

"I'll come by soon," Noelle says sweetly.

"You save all the sweets for him, and I just get all the sass," I say jokingly to Noelle.

"That's how it's supposed to work, Lake," my dad teases before waving goodbye. Watching as he leaves, I spot Adrian entering the dining room with ruffled hair, and back in his jeans and t-shirt. The suit was very nice, but it doesn't fit him as well as casual does. He catches my eye from across the room, stopping momentarily, a slow smile spreading on his face before walking over to the table where

Ianna and her kids are sitting. Immediately, the younger one jumps in his lap and gives her older siblings a very satisfied smirk. Ianna leans over and whispers something in his ear that makes him laugh.

I think about what my dad said to me last night; *Beth found 'it', now it's your turn.* I don't have hopes for that because I know people, and all they do is disappoint. It's a risk that doesn't have a high percentage of return.

"We need to get going soon, too," I say, taking a sip of my coffee. "Are you all packed?" I ask, pulling an earbud from Noelle's ear to get her attention.

She rolls her eyes, snatching the earbud from me.

"You better get to it," I say. "We have to check out in an hour."

She grumbles while getting up from the table and acts like her legs are made of lead.

"I'm asking you to pack, not solve world hunger," I say to her back as she drags her feet towards the exit of the dining room.

"Gen Z," Georgie gripes as she hooks her thumb in Noelle's direction, shaking her head.

"Are *you* finished packing?" I ask Georgie pointedly.

She looks down at the table guiltily and sighs. "Vacation's over."

"I need more coffee before we head out." I grab the leftover food and plates from the table. "I'll meet you back at the room."

Getting in line there are a few people ahead of me, and I tap my foot impatiently as they peruse through the complimentary breakfast. I'm staring at one of the paintings that line the wall, the back of a horse as it walks away, its owner, a cowboy, holding the lead rope. All I can think of is how that horse doesn't know where it's going. I don't know why I focus so much on it. Maybe it's because of everything that's happened in the last couple of weeks, or maybe it's because of everything that's happened in the last twenty years.

The couple behind me starts whispering, and it pulls my attention away from the painting. I hear the woman say, "I was on my way back to the room last night and I heard moaning."

"From someone's room?" the man asks.

"Near the pool in the bushes," she says quietly.

Staring straight ahead, I focus back on the painting again when a hand rests against the small of my back just as the line moves up.

"Morning," Adrian's rough but gentle voice whispers in my ear.

Looking around the dining room, I whisper back tersely, "Is this a game to you?"

"I don't like games, Lake," he says in a tone so serious that I almost believe him.

The couple behind us keep whispering and I dip my head slightly, turning my ear towards them while catching Adrian's eye. The sun creeping through the windows casts rays of light that cut right through the room slicing it in half, causing the green flecks in his eyes to shimmer.

"In the bushes?" I hear the man behind me say with a slightly raised voice in shock.

"Yes," she hisses, trying to keep her voice down, unaware that I am fully trained on them now.

"Did you see anything?" the man asks curiously.

Both Adrian and I are quiet, looking anywhere but at the couple behind us – whom I don't recognize – but could be friends of either Laura or Beth. My cheeks feel as if they're on fire, knowing full well they're talking about me. Hoping the woman didn't see anything and recognize me, I keep my face forward, acutely aware of Adrian beside me, his hand at his side brushing purposefully against my bare thigh, sending a shiver up my body. I don't remember anyone passing by us last night, but then again, if they had, I wasn't paying attention. A grand piano could have fallen from a second story balcony, and I wouldn't have noticed.

"No," she says with an embarrassed lilt. "I'm not a voyeur." But then she leans in closer to whom I assume is her husband. "It sounded pretty hot though."

Shifting uncomfortably, I slide my eyes to Adrian who is looking down at me with a smirk on his face, and I roll my eyes at him.

"Hmm," her husband says. "Where was I last night while this was going on?"

"You fell asleep in the room." She sounds irritated. "How come we don't do things like that?" she asks.

"You want to be *fucked*," he lowers his voice probably realizing he's speaking too loudly, "in a bush instead of a bed?" he hisses.

"Maybe," she answers coyly.

Adrian leans in close to my ear and whispers, "They wish they were us." All I can smell is his cologne, and my whole body feels like it's on fire just thinking about last night. When I dare to look at him, he's wearing a smug smile on his face as if he's won a prize for dirtiest fuck.

The line moves up and I grab the coffee pot and turn towards him.

"You're very cocky, you know that?" I say, topping off my cup.

Adrian shrugs with a smile, leaning against the counter looking like a wolf in sheep's clothing. "Neither I nor God heard any complaints last night."

Moving out of ear shot from the other people in line, I pull him to the side, laughing. "You're delusional if you think I'm dickmatized," I say, while my eyes can't help but wander down to his crotch. "In fact," I lean in further, hovering my lips near his ear, feeling the air shift between us while his lips part. "You're the one that keeps following me around, so I'd say you might be a little pussy whipped."

Instead of retreating, he leans over me casually, as if he's going to grab something off the table, causing the backs of my thighs to hit the counter. "A little?" he groans lifting an eyebrow, and my pulse quickens. The room is full of wedding guests, and anyone could interpret this as something more than casual, but I am transfixed on his lips when he says, "It's the best pussy I've ever had."

Momentarily immobilized, I process lie number seven as those words move down my body, along with his eyes, settling between my thighs and searing a hole right through my panties.

He rattles me, and I don't get rattled.

Regaining my composure, I clear my throat as Adrian chuckles, knowing he's affected me. Sweat collects at the small of my back, as I slide out of his hold. The room is hot, and not just because it's August in Arizona. I'm determined to gain back some of my upper hand because I'm not about to be bested by a thirty-one-year-old guy with a skateboard under his bed.

Before leaving, I look over my shoulder at him and say, "You bet your ass it is." Strutting across the dining room towards the exit, I don't look behind me, but I will bet anything he's staring at my ass. Through the reflection in the glass doors, I see him leaning against the counter, raising the cup of coffee to his lips as he watches me leave.

As soon as I get outside, I lean against the stucco building, pushing the hair off my face and suck in a deep breath before continuing back to my room. When I get to the door, I can hear Georgie and Noelle playfully arguing inside.

"I'm just asking you to look under the bed." Georgie's voice carries through the door.

"Why would it be under *my* bed?" asks Noelle.

"Do you question your mother like this?" I hear Georgie ask.

"My mother doesn't ask stupid questions." Noelle places her hand on her hips, and I can't help but laugh at the look on Georgie's face.

"Do you hear this?" Georgie gestures to me.

"I heard." Groaning, I close the door behind me.

All of the garbage has been picked up, but there are still items on the bed that have yet to be packed.

"My luggage is all ready and waiting by the door. Meanwhile, you two are still messing around," I say, while heading into the bathroom to make sure I grabbed everything.

"What are you trying to say?" Noelle asks from behind me.

"To move your ass or Georgie can drive you home," I threaten.

When I re-enter the room, Georgie has a satisfied expression on her face as she looks at Noelle.

"God, no," Noelle pleads, grabbing the last of her clothes and stuffing them in her bag without folding them, half of which she didn't even wear. The rest of my Sunday will be spent doing laundry.

"What's wrong with me driving you home?" Georgie says, offended.

"You listen to talk radio," Noelle says, zipping up her bag.

"I like to know what's happening in the world," Georgie says, zipping up her own bag and pulling out the handle.

Holding the door until both of them are out, I let it slam shut while I follow them to the lobby.

"I just need to check out," I say to them as I stop by the front lobby.

"Wait here until they bring the car around," I tell Noelle, pointing to the plush oversized chairs in the lobby. Georgie follows me to the front desk and says, "Your kid…" she pauses while I glare at her, waiting for what's going to come out of her mouth next, "Is magnificent." I laugh while placing the key card on the counter.

"How was everything?" the clerk asks.

"Wonderful, thanks," I say, digging in my purse for my wallet.

"The room has already been taken care of by the Kennedy/Corvin party," the clerk says, smiling.

I *was* going to pay for the mini bar, but thinking back on what an ass Beth was to me, I place my wallet back in my purse and smile at Georgie who raises a questioning eyebrow.

"I'm telling you, Lake, your kid is going to be a force to be reckoned with. I feel sorry for whoever falls for her because she is going to break a lot of hearts," Georgie says, while I look over my shoulder at Noelle who's draping her legs over the arm of the chair. Everything Georgie says is true, and that's what scares me the most about letting her go. Here I can keep a watchful eye on her, but out there, in the real world, my scope is a bit smaller.

"That's what worries me," I say, turning towards Georgie and cocking my head to the side.

"And you," Georgie points an accusatory finger at me, "need to spill the tea."

Laughing, I say, "I think you've been hanging around Noelle too much this weekend."

When we exit the hotel's double doors to the portico, I hand the valet my ticket.

"It's too fucking hot out," Georgie says, fanning herself with one of the hotel brochures.

Without any preamble, I blurt, "I had sex in the hotel bathroom last night."

Georgie's mouth drops open. "With the dirty-mouthed, hot musician?" she asks.

"No, the bartender," I say, sneering at Georgie. "Of course, the dirty-mouthed, hot musician. Who do you think I am?" As soon as it comes out of my mouth I roll my eyes, because after having a one-night stand with a stranger, and then having sex with him in the hotel bathroom at my sister's wedding, it's a reasonable assumption that I have finally lost my mind.

Georgie narrows her eyes at me.

"But it's not happening again." I shake my head. "I wasn't thinking straight. It was like this spontaneous thing and I don't really understand why I did it, but oh God, Georgie," I grab onto her arms, "It was good." The words spill from my mouth a mile a minute. "Like *really* fucking good."

"Good to know you're feeding the kitty," she winks. "But you know exactly why you did it," Georgie says, and this is why I regret telling her because she's gonna give me a big dose of the truth. "He's hot, and he's obviously got it bad for you."

"I don't do things like that." I let go of her. "This isn't me. I have a kid."

"You're a woman." Georgie forces me to look at her. "A very *sexy* woman, and the fact that you have a kid is irrelevant," she says. "You deserve to have some fun. God knows you earned it."

"This isn't right," I tell her, shaking my head.

"Why, because he's younger?" She gives me the evil eye. "There's nothing wrong with that. Hat's off to you my friend," she says, as if I'm her hero. "You bagged a hot, younger musician who obviously knows how to fuck you right, and that is a rare find."

"It's not just that," I admit. "He's *family*," I say with distaste.

"He's not *family*, Lake," Georgie chastises me. "He happens to be related to your sister's wife." She puckers her lips, looking around before continuing, "Far removed from being family."

"Well, when you say it like that," I roll my eyes, "it doesn't make it any better," I protest.

"What are you so afraid of?" Georgie asks.

So many things.

"Making a fool of myself, all the things that can go wrong, not to mention my kid," I tell her because Georgie doesn't get it. She doesn't have a kid or a sister, and she's never had to think of anyone else but herself. I would never say that to her because I think it would come across as insensitive, but it's the truth.

"That kid," she points to the lobby, "is going to be an adult in less than a year, Lake. And making a fool of yourself is not possible."

"And then there's Beth," I say, causing Georgie to square her shoulders.

"What about Beth?" Georgie asks.

"She saw us," I start to say and see Georgie's expression change to horror. "Not having sex, God," I roll my eyes. "She saw us talking the morning of her wedding. We were in the courtyard, and it was raining." How can I explain this draw I have to him when even I don't understand it? "She didn't like it." I don't go into it further because I don't feel like talking about Beth.

"Since when do you care what Beth likes?" Georgie asks, and it's a legitimate question. Normally I wouldn't, but this is so much more personal.

"I just want her to be happy," I say, squinting my eyes to the sun that streams in over Georgie's shoulder.

"And she is," Georgie says. "She had a fabulous lesbian wedding, the best I've ever been to."

"This is the only one you've ever been to," I point out.

"And I will compare Beth's lesbian wedding to every other lesbian wedding I attend in the future," she says, grabbing me by the shoulders and making me look at her. "Don't let her take up all the happiness. There's plenty to go around."

My car pulls up along the curb, the valet revving the engine a little too vigorously, and I text Noelle that we're ready to leave.

The young valet exits the driver's seat and says, "I love my job," to himself, while eyeing my car enviously.

He drops the keys into the palm of my hand, and I give him a nice tip.

"Thanks," he says, and runs off to get the next car.

"You have all the young ones eating out of your hand, don't you?" Georgie teases and knocks her hip into me.

"Huh?" Noelle asks, sidling up next to us, the wheels of her luggage catching in the grout of the clay tiles that make up the front of the hotel.

"Tell your mom to live a little," Georgie says, winking.

I grab Noelle's luggage and place it in my trunk. "You have weird friends," Noelle says, buckling her seatbelt.

"Yeah." I look in the rearview mirror and watch as Georgie waves goodbye to us, her own car pulling up to the curb. "But weird is good."

14

YOU KEPT ME WAITING

MEDICINE MAN BY CHARLOTTE OC

Saturdays are my favorite. It's the one day of the week where I can wake up and not think about work. As I pad past Noelle's room, I see she's already up and practicing her violin. The sound filters from her room, down the hallway, and into the kitchen where I sit at the island eating leftover pizza from last night. Somehow the classical music she's playing makes it feel like I'm eating a gourmet meal.

Staring across the living room through the glass patio doors, I look at the mountain preserve our house backs up to. Through the view fence I can see the sagebrush that still flourishes even in the middle of a dry summer; a deep green against the rich browns of the mountain terrain.

"Is that from last night?" Noelle asks as she pads into the kitchen, passing by me on her way to the refrigerator.

"Don't judge," I admonish, taking a bite. "Here, look at your Aunt Beth trying to parasail." I shove the phone at her.

Noelle takes it and laughs. "She looks like she's constipated." We both laugh.

"She's been torturing me with honeymoon pictures for the last two weeks," I complain, laying the phone back down.

"When will they be back?"

"Tomorrow."

Noelle sifts through the refrigerator and sighs when she doesn't find what she's looking for. Her brown ponytail sways across her back as she lifts herself up on one of the barstools, helping herself to a piece of my cold pizza.

"Do you want to go to *Berdena's*?" I ask, feeling guilty that I'm not much of a cook and rely on eating out most of the time.

"Can't. I'm giving a lesson today," she says.

"You know, this work thing is getting in the way of our quality time," I pout.

"It *would* be work if I were getting paid for it." She takes a bite. "School requires it, but I really like working with the kids. They don't have access to music programs, so it's really cool to see how excited they are when we come."

My phone vibrates again on the island and I'm reluctant to pick it up because I don't want to see another photo of Beth eating a Dole whip or drinking something fruity from a coconut. When I pick it up, it's a number I don't recognize.

> Unknown: I'm in the area. I can stop by.

I stare at the phone confused, thinking this must be a wrong number, so I text back.

> L: Wrong number.

> Unknown: I need to measure.

Setting the phone back on the table Noelle asks, "Who is it?"

"I think it's Laura's dad coming to measure the rooms for the flooring," I say. The language barrier is a bit of an issue both ways.

"Oh, thank God, because I swear, if you fall and break your neck on that tile, I'm not changing your diapers," Noelle teases, slipping her feet into a pair of random flip flops lying near the front door.

"Change my diapers?" I swivel around in the kitchen stool. "What are you talking about?" I leave the phone upside down on the counter.

"Because you'll break a hip and can't get to the toilet," she explains.

"Well, thanks. I see how much you love me," I tease, as she retreats towards the garage. "I changed *your* diapers!" I yell after her, and she waves me off.

Peeking around the corner, she points at me. "No parties, and no boys," she teases, grabbing her violin case from the table by the door.

"Aw, but, Mom, I won't be the popular girl at school if I don't let him go all the way," I say, sarcastically as she leaves through the garage door.

Looking over at the cracked tile in the kitchen, I scoff. *She won't change my diapers.* I shake my head. It's a good thing I have a healthy 401K to pay for my elderly care. *Someone* is changing my diapers, no matter what.

The doorbell rings and I know it's not Noelle, so it must be Marius. As I get up to answer the door, through the double frosted panes I can see a shadow that is definitely not Marius. Tall and lean with a halo of hair that I have sunk my fingers into and know exactly how it feels, Adrian stands on my front porch with his feet apart and hands stuffed into the pockets of his jeans as he waits for me to answer.

Hesitating, I know he sees me through the doors, so pretending I'm not home is not an option. Reluctantly I open the door, and there he stands, hair tied back, wearing a gray t-shirt, jeans, and tan carpenter boots.

"Seriously?" I rest my hand on my hip, my other arm blocking his entry. "How did you get my number?" I pause, "And my address?"

"My sister," he explains with a cocky grin. "She told me to give you the family discount." He raises his eyebrows.

"Why does everything that comes out of your mouth sound sexual?" I ask.

"Might be because you're hoping it is." He gives me a cocky smirk, and I roll my eyes.

"Some might call this stalking," I point out.

"And some might call this doing you a favor for my sister," Adrian counters.

"She said your dad owned the company," I glare at him.

"He does, but I'm the installer," he says, shifting his weight. "Would you rather my dad be the one here?" he asks, playfully.

Ignoring his question, I say, "This is strictly professional, got it?" I don't want there to be any misunderstanding about him being in my home. Going to his apartment that night at the bar was a mistake, and having sex with him at my sister's wedding was an even bigger mistake. So why am I imagining my legs wrapped around his waist while he fucks me on the kitchen island?

"Yes, ma'am," he says, jolting me from my daydream. Ma'am is a sure-fire way to kill any sexuality looming around between my legs.

"Excuse me?" I ask disdainfully.

He holds his hands in the air. "Clearly the wrong choice of words," he apologizes, raising an eyebrow. "What would you like me to call you?" he asks, the tone of his voice low and deep.

"Lake is fine," I say, shifting uncomfortably.

"Lake," he says in a deep sexy voice, and I like the way my name sounds coming from his lips. "Are you going to let me in?"

Finally realizing I'm standing in the heat and letting all the cold air out, I move my hand from the doorframe so he can enter. As he stands in my foyer, I convince myself that it's perfectly innocent. His sister gave him my information before I realized who he was or even before he knew who I was. He's just fulfilling an obligation because Laura asked him to be kind.

Of course, she didn't ask him to give me oral sex in the bathroom at her wedding either, but he did.

Adrian looks around my home, his eyes going wide as he surveys the expansive living room and kitchen. "Jesus, what do you do for a living?" he asks, walking further into the house.

I have a chef's kitchen with a double oven, but neither I nor Noelle cooks. There are four bedrooms, one of which I use as my office and the other as a guest room, although I've never had a guest. The house is more than what Noelle and I need, but when I bought it, I was in a different place in life. If I could tell my younger self that I would never need that extra room, or that double oven, because I wasn't going to fill it with children or home cooked meals, I would have saved myself the constant reminder.

This has been our home since Noelle was five, and the sound of her violin has been ingrained in these walls and in these floors ever since.

"I work in finance," I reply, trailing after him into my kitchen while he toes the broken tile with his boot. Pieces of dark hair fall loose over his face as he kneels down to inspect the damaged area.

"This is pretty old tile," he says, and his eyes trail over my bare feet and legs as he rises, meeting my eyes.

"It's original to the home. I've never had the flooring replaced," I explain.

"I can see that," he says and looks around critically. "Finance, huh?" He circles back. "What exactly do you do?"

I could say that currently I'm going through the company's organizational chart to eliminate redundant jobs preparing for an acquisition, or that I'm contending with some condescending asshole who looks more at my chest than my face when I speak to him, but I don't. Instead I give my standard answer. "It's pretty boring."

Adrian stands to his full height, filling up the space of my kitchen. He's not a large man, but he has a big presence. "I doubt anything you do is boring," he says, and then notices the plate of half eaten pizza on the island next to him.

"Is that your breakfast?" he asks, pointing to the pizza.

"Don't judge," I say, grabbing the plate and tossing it in the garbage.

"I wasn't judging." He holds his hands in the air, a sexy smirk on his face.

"Yes, you were," I say, shaking my head.

"I was thinking that someone needs to feed you properly." He leans against the island with his eyes trained on me, causing me to conjure an inappropriate image in my mind.

Realizing that I'm only wearing a thin tank top and shorts, I cross my arms over my chest.

"I eat just fine," I protest.

"I doubt that," he muses, stepping over to my refrigerator and taking a peek inside.

There are a few yogurt containers, eggs that I'll probably never cook but thought about, and almond milk for my coffee.

Adrian laughs, shaking his head, and I push the refrigerator door closed. Standing mere inches from him, I can feel the heat emanating from his body. "Is this how you treat all your customers? Go through their fridge and judge their eating habits?" I ask.

He leans against the refrigerator door, casually crossing his ankle over the other while raking his eyes over my body. "Only the ones I fuck."

I should be used to it by now, but his dirty words still shock me. If I had taken a sip of my coffee, I would have spit it out all over his t-shirt.

He makes my heartbeat flutter rapidly against my chest and heat skitter across my skin. "Wow, you're pretty fucking forward. What happened to keeping things professional?" I ask, crossing my arms over my chest.

"Your rules not mine, and that means you shouldn't be eye fucking me," he says, leaning towards me. "But don't stop, I like it." His cocky smile infuriates and turns me on at the same time.

"I wasn't eye fucking you," I lie, taking a step back, because obviously being in the same space as him is dangerous.

Adrian chuckles disbelievingly.

"Pretend," I warn, moving to the kitchen island, creating an even bigger distance between us. "You're here to do my flooring, nothing else."

Adrian stands with his feet apart, his thumbs hooked into his jeans causing them to sit low on his hips. He gives me an amused expression as if he's only humoring me by getting down to business. "So what were you thinking of doing?"

Squaring my shoulders, I meet his eyes. "Get rid of all of it," I say, picturing the ugly tile and carpet gone, replaced with something fresh and new. It feels like it's time to make some changes.

Adrian gestures to the living room and I follow. "Pulling up the carpeting won't be a problem," he says. "But it's the tile that's going to be messy," he explains, walking back into the kitchen and looking down the hall towards the bedroom as I follow him. "I'd have to use a jack hammer," he demonstrates using an imaginary jack hammer, "to break it open," he finishes, winking at me.

Picturing him in my home, jack hammering tile, is an image that I may have to take with me to bed tonight. My eyes travel down his tanned arm, the muscular cords in his forearms stretching, and the tattoos covering the entirety, even the one's etched below his knuckles. He is so different from any other man I've been with, and maybe that's what is so attractive about him.

"Do you know what you want?" he asks, pulling my attention back to meet his eyes, and by the smirk on his face, he knows I was checking him out again.

Leaning over the island, I play with the decorative bowl that sits near the center, rearranging its contents as I contemplate. Finally, looking around the room, I push my hair to the side.

"Something light to brighten up the space, don't you think?" I ask, turning towards him, noticing how his eyes are fixated on my shoulder. I realize the strap of my tank top has fallen, hanging loosely against my arm. I pull it back up, his eyes tracking my movements as he swallows hard. Afraid what I'll see when I meet his eyes, I turn away.

"Good choice," he clears his throat.

Pulling a tool from his pocket, he kneels down and positions the laser to get an accurate measurement of the kitchen.

"Coffee?" I offer while he works, looking for something other than him to focus on.

"Sure," he says, straightening up and looking at me over his shoulder.

"How do you take it?" I ask, feeling the side of the pot to test if it's still warm and then pouring him a cup.

"Black is fine," he says, and I slide it across the island towards him.

Adrian takes it, holding it in his hands, peering at me over the steam before taking a sip. Holding my own, I follow him into the living room where he stops at the pile of DVDs sitting on the end table, stopping to check out the titles.

"Your kids?" he asks, picking up my well used copy of *Sixteen Candles*.

Noelle and I had watched it weeks ago; the same weekend I'd first met Adrian at the *Tap Room*. Not embarrassed by my choice of movies, I take it from him and say, "It's my favorite."

He nods without judgment, walking towards the back patio and stopping to admire the view. Water cascades over the stone shelf that drops into the Roman style pool. It looks very inviting now as the room begins to heat up, even though my a/c is turned low.

Adrian turns as if he can feel me staring at him. "Nice pool," he says.

Nodding, I think about how little we got to use it over the summer. Noelle has gotten increasingly busy, especially since this is her last year of high school. What with her preparing for her school's winter recital and the volunteer obligations, I see her less and less these days.

Adrian finishes measuring the living room and points down the hallway. "Should I follow you into the bedroom?"

"Excuse me?" I ask, wishing I had something to fan myself with.

"You said you wanted to do the entire house. I assume that means the bedrooms too?" He lifts an eyebrow waiting for me to answer.

"O-Oh," I stammer, "yes." I walk down the hallway and scan my bedroom for anything out of place.

Adrian follows close behind and stands in the middle of my bedroom, the view jarring. I watch as he looks around assessing my bedroom while he takes measurements, clearly trying to figure me out.

"You don't like me in your bedroom?" he asks, using the velvety tone that pulls me under and makes me forget important things. He watches me closely, paying attention to my reaction to his question.

"I don't mind," I reply, carefully choosing my words.

Satisfied, he walks into my closet making a low whistle while I follow behind him, stopping at the entrance. Organized with shelves and an island in the middle where I keep my jewelry and other intimate items, the closet, like the rest of the house, is a bit much, especially just for me. A quarter of it is filled with shoes, all colors and styles, mostly for work or formal functions.

One section holds designer dresses I've worn to past Christmas parties and other work events. Entering further into the closet, I watch as he moves to the section where I keep all my casual clothes. Noelle and I have a thing for buying silly t-shirts from every place we've visited, and I've kept all of my vintage concert t-shirts from when I was younger. His hand lingers on the *Aerosmith* shirt I wore to the *Tap Room* that night, but then picks up a pair of gold high heels with a strap that goes around the ankles, looking at me as if he's imagining me in them.

"Next time, you should wear these," he says, and the closer he moves towards me, the more I step back.

"You're very presumptuous," I say, grabbing the shoes and placing them back on the shelf.

"Past experience would say the odds are in my favor," he winks, towering over me as my body reacts in ways I can't control. He's very perceptive, and his eyes on me aren't just for admiring, they're assessing. "Do I make you nervous, Lake?" His question makes my cheeks heat.

"No," I say too quickly.

He steps a little closer, placing his boot between my feet, effectively wedging his leg between my thighs. "Then why are you trembling?" He runs a finger across my shoulder, playing with the strap of my tank top, and I like the gentle way he handles me.

"There are a lot of reasons why I'm trembling, but none of them are because I'm nervous," I challenge, looking him right in the eye.

Years of working in Corporate America, especially with men who think they can take advantage of a woman, has toughened me. I don't intimidate easily, no matter how many orgasms he's given me.

His face is inches from mine and the scent of his cologne fills my closet. Watching as he licks his lips, they inch towards mine like the pull of a magnet. His hand wraps around the back of my head while his thumb holds me in place, pressing into my cheek. My heart thunders in my chest and the ache between my legs increases.

"Two weeks, Lake," he groans. "You kept me waiting two weeks."

Without hesitation, he crashes his mouth to mine, gathering my hair in his fist, forcing my head back. I kiss him back, parting my lips and letting his tongue slip inside.

When he pulls my leg up and slips his hand under my shorts to cup my ass, dangerously close to the edge of my panties, my brain threatens to short-circuit.

15

BEAUTIFUL LIES

House Fire by Tyler Childers

Not here. The words invade my brain.

Not in the room that is just across the hall from where my daughter sleeps. Placing my hand to his chest, it effectively causes him to release me even though he looks like he doesn't want to.

Resting his forehead against mine, he breathes heavily before pushing himself away, showing great restraint.

"Not here," I tell him breathlessly.

Pushing back the pieces of my tousled hair, I try to regain my composure.

He doesn't look like he agrees with it, but he moves away from me anyway, running a hand through his hair in frustration. Feeling like I've drawn a box around myself for the past seventeen years, I forgot it was even there – until him. Adrian makes me want to cut ties with this self-imposed prison I've locked myself into. It's a dangerous thought, but it makes me feel alive.

"If you want me to stay away from you right now then you need to stop doing that," Adrian's deep voice causes my eyes to flick up to his.

"Stop doing what?" I ask, nervously.

"Biting your lip," he all but growled, and I immediately let go of my lip that I hadn't even known I was biting.

It's very apparent by the strain in his jeans that I affect him in the same way he affects me. I've only ever experienced the type of push and pull with someone that has never been equal. Being with him feels like sitting on a grenade, and any moment the pin could be pulled and we both go up in flames. The problem with a flame that burns hot and fast is that it will burn out at some point, and there'll be nothing left.

Staring at all that lush hair, dreamy eyes, and those abs I know are hiding under his gray t-shirt, my judgment isn't so clouded that I'm remiss about what exactly he wants with me. I'm a forty-three year old mom with a teenage daughter, and years of baggage that has prevented me from getting close to anyone.

I have to know. "What do you think you're doing?" I ask him.

His once playful demeanor turns serious, and I don't give him a chance to answer.

"I'm forty-three years old," I say, pinching my eyebrows together.

"I know how old you are, Lake." He levels his gaze on me and when I don't continue, he asks, "What does that matter?"

"You're thirty-one." Frustrated that he doesn't seem to get it, I pivot against the doorframe, heading out to the hallway before he catches up, and grabs my arm to stop me.

"You want my *statistics*, Lake?" He asks but doesn't wait for me to answer. "I've worked hard all my life. I'm not under the delusion that I'm going to make it as a professional musician, and I even went to college." He must see the shock cross my face no matter how hard I try to suppress it because he explains further. "Yes, Lake, I'm not just some rock star wannabe, I have a business degree so I could make sure Corvin & Son is sustainable because my family depends on it."

"Despite what you think," I say as I look around my home, "I'm not a snob." I shake my head, embarrassed. I never wanted to make Adrian feel as if I'm looking down on him.

"I didn't tell you all of that to make you feel bad," he explains. "I just want you to know who I am."

Despite all of that, there is this barrier inside of me that I won't cross. "None of that matters." I shrug, searching his eyes.

"You're using our age difference as an excuse," he says in frustration.

"There's more to it than just age, Adrian," I say, walking away because it's too much, too soon. In my haste to create distance from him I forget to look out for the broken tile and stub my toe. "Fuck!" I yell, hopping on one foot, and stumbling to the kitchen stool.

Adrian kneels in front of me, taking my foot in his hand and inspecting my toe for damage. The only thing that seems to be bruised at the moment is my ego. His fingers wrap around my ankle, holding my foot flat on his thigh as he leans down to plant a kiss on the tip of my toe. Looking down at him, it's hard to deny that I have feelings. It's hard not to when he does things like this, but my reservations are valid.

"I don't want to be made a fool of," I whisper, pulling my foot from his grasp, and he rises in front of me with a serious expression.

"I would *never* make a fool of you," he says with such sincerity that I almost believe him. I *want* to believe him, but in my head, I'm cataloging this as lie number seven, but it still doesn't stop me from wanting it, wanting *him*.

"If this were a thing," I pause to take a breath because I feel as though I'm assuming what he wants rather than what I want, "I'm in a different place in life than you, and I have more to worry about than just myself," I explain as I look up him, so fucking pretty and so fucking willing to give me anything I want. The conversation I had with Georgie circles like a helicopter around in my brain. There is no reason I can't have fun, especially if it's in the form of Adrian Corvin.

He waits for me to continue with his arms crossed over his chest, the black lines of his tattoo straining along with his muscles. "What I mean is," I stand up from the chair, so we are at least on somewhat equal level even though my toe is throbbing, "if you're going to fuck me," I say, noticing his Adam's apple bob with a tight swallow, "then you fuck *only* me." Images of Taylor in her red dress at the wedding keep crossing my mind. Adrian made it clear that he and Taylor are done. Although I don't want anything serious with him, I don't want to be made a fool of.

"Those are the terms?" Adrian asks, caging me in with his arm stretched over to rest on the kitchen island behind me. His close proximity makes my head spin, but I hold my own.

"This doesn't need to be anything more than what it is," I tell him, the small of my back digging into the counter behind me.

"And what is this?" he asks, gesturing between us.

It's hard to explain what's happening, but I'm not willing to give more... but I also don't want it to end. "Casual," I say. "Nothing serious."

"Just fun," he confirms, pulling away and rubbing the hair on his chin pensively.

He should be excited that I'm not looking for a relationship. Isn't that every guy's ideal relationship? To fuck without commitment?

"You can't tell your family about us," I say, firmly.

"I'm not in the habit of telling my sisters who I fuck," Adrian says as he licks his lips, and the word 'fuck' coming from his mouth causes my stomach to tighten, "but I don't like lying to them either."

Rounding the island I put more distance between us and bite my fingernail nervously. "Understood." I grab the discarded coffee cup and dump the contents in the sink to give myself something to do. It doesn't stop me from sneaking secret looks at him. At least I don't have to wonder what he's thinking because he seems to have no problem voicing what he wants. The way he's looking at me... it's *me* he wants.

"Is there a timeframe to this *arrangement*?" He can't help but smile, and I'm sure it's because he knows he makes me uncomfortable.

I'm making things up as I go along because I've never had an *arrangement* with anyone before. It was either a relationship or it wasn't, and it's been a very long time since I've had to figure things out with someone.

"Until it's not fun anymore," I say somberly, resting my hip against the counter, drying my hands with the towel.

Adrian stands with his feet apart and crosses his arms over his chest. I can't help but stare at him. "And I can't touch you in your home?" he asks.

Shaking my head, no, I want to close my eyes because looking at him makes my brain clouded, but I need to stand firm. He's like this delicious piece of cake and I've made a commitment to follow a horrendous diet fad that I'm only allowed to cheat on the weekends with… but it's only Tuesday.

"Okay," he says, nodding, then swivels on the heel of his carpenter boots and walks towards the door.

My mouth drops open in confusion. Maybe he finally realized that I'm too complicated for him. When I hear the front door shut my body jolts at the noise, and I step into the foyer to see him gone. There's not even an outline of his shadow through the frosted double pane doors.

What the fuck just happened?

Standing at the door I feel my phone vibrate in my back pocket. Slowly I pull it out and look at the message on the screen from the same unknown number that texted me earlier.

> A: Can you come out front please?

Confused, I wait a minute before opening the front door to see Adrian on the side of my front porch. As soon as I step out, he grabs the back of my neck, pulling me to him and crashing his mouth to mine with such force that I stumble. Holding me in place, he saves me from falling in the oleander bushes and I wrap my arms around his shoulders, sinking my fingers into his hair as I lean into the kiss.

"What are you doing?" I ask breathlessly between kisses.

He backs me up to the post, placing his hand above me like a cage. "You said I couldn't touch you in the house," he rasps, while I run my thumb over one of his dimples and press my body further into him. "You're tempting me to fuck you on this front porch, but I'll settle for this." He smiles, capturing my mouth again, and I feel it all the way down to my toes.

"You have a thing for bushes," I laugh against his mouth as I look to the oleander bushes we almost fell into that line my front window.

He doesn't miss a beat, staring at me with hooded eyes, and says, "I have a thing for *you*."

This was only supposed to be one night, but here he is on my front porch, kissing me and telling me things I have no business believing. Our arrangement means no expectations, and no truths – only lies.

And he tells beautiful lies.

16

THE THIRD BUTTON

Tear me to Pieces by MEG MYERS

My phone vibrates against the polished wood conference table, shaking the projector that Lewis, the Chief Legal Officer's laptop is plugged into, causing his PowerPoint presentation to shake on the screen.

From across the table, Lewis narrows his eyes at me in annoyance, and I purse my lips in response.

Discreetly, I turn my phone over to look at the text.

> A: Can I see you?

My heart accelerates as if I'm in the passenger seat of a race car sitting at the starting line anticipating the green light.

> L: I'm in a board meeting.

Placing the phone back on the table, I try to focus on Lewis who bores us with the latest updates on consumer harm. He sits in front of his laptop across from me, bald head reflecting the light from the projector while sweat accumulates. Papers shuffle and someone clears their throat. From outside the large conference room, people pass by the glass doors, some stop and chat with each other. Everything is the same, except it isn't, because *I'm* different.

I have a secret.

Something that occupies my mind and distracts me from paying attention.

> A: I bet every man in that room wishes they were fucking you on top of that conference table right now.

My pulse quickens and heat floods between my thighs. Nervously looking around the room, I quickly shove the phone into my lap as if they can all see my texts. It's silly, I know, but I can feel my cheeks already burning.

And so it begins.

> L: You have a very dirty mouth.

When my phone vibrates in my lap, Miles darts his eyes in my direction, lifting an eyebrow. Next to him is Wyatt who seems unaffected and oddly riveted by Lewis's presentation while she takes notes. Usually, I'm never distracted during meetings, even ones where Lewis drones on with his regulatory legal jargon that no one can understand.

Discreetly, I turn the phone over to read the next text while it's still in my lap.

> A: I happen to know that you like my dirty mouth.

Raising a pen to my lips, I begin chewing on the cap while images of Adrian invade my mind – dark hair falling in his face, brown eyes peering at me through impossibly long lashes, and those soft lips that pinned me to the post on my front porch while his hands gripped my hair.

Narrowing my eyes at the phone as if he could see me, I type my response.

> L: I'm a grown woman. I don't sext, or whatever this is.

> A: Tell me you don't want me to bend you over that table.

Pressing my lips together, I try to suppress a smile by bringing my fist to my mouth and coughing softly. Letting the strap of my shoe fall past my ankle, it swings freely as I shake my foot nervously.

> L: Adrian, I'm serious.

> A: While I slowly push your skirt up over your perfect ass.

> L: Someone could see my phone!

Getting more nervous I look around the room, but no one is paying attention to me and they are oblivious to the fact that my flooring contractor is *sexting* me.

> A: And press your face to that shiny wood table while slipping my fingers under your panties.

While he continues I squirm in my chair, looking to the empty space between me and Lewis that is slowly filling up with the image of Adrian pushing my skirt up, and pressing my face into the wood.

> A: Feel how wet you are for me...

> L: I'm putting my phone away.

Seeing the ellipses, there is no way I can turn my phone off now and I'm sure he knows it.

Twirling the pen between my fingers, my attention is drawn back to the room when Asa Waterman, the man whose business we're acquiring, speaks up asking Lewis to elaborate on our regulatory change management process to be able to identify international consumer laws. Feeling the groan that threatens to erupt from my throat I suppress it as best I can, tilting my head in Asa's direction to give him a dirty look.

I was never very fond of him in the first place and the feeling is mutual, except when he's staring at my cleavage. He's a fifty-something year old man who's going to make a lot of money, but instead of retiring, he wants a seat on the Board. Men like him want one thing; all the control with little responsibility.

In my lap I feel the phone vibrate against the already growing ache between my legs, and I press them together as I turn my phone over discreetly.

> A: Before I fuck you so hard you scream my name.

Running a hand through my hair, I let it fall over my face and press my knuckles to my mouth as I read his words over again, suppressing a smile.

Crossing and uncrossing my legs under the table, I try desperately to relieve the ache as the room becomes hotter. As if that weren't enough, he continues to text.

> A: And I'm not even done with you yet because I want those fucking expensive gold heels wrapped around my neck.

"Lake!"

Startled and already rattled by the message I just read, my phone slips out of my hand and into the air. As I scramble to grab it, praying to the Holy Spirit that it doesn't land upright for someone to see, the phone bangs on the table getting the attention of everyone in the room. Before Miles can grab it, I snatch it up, switching it off before tossing it in my laptop bag. Miles purses his lips, obviously wanting to say something but he can't.

"Yes, sorry," I say, diverting my attention to Glen.

"I thought you could give us an update on the project you're working on," Glen says, careful not to say any specifics because of Miles and Wyatt being in the room.

Reaching over the table to take the projector connection from Lewis, I look down at Asa who seems to be distracted by the gap in my blouse created by my reach. As soon as I get the projector hooked up, I turn to Miles and Wyatt.

"Some of these findings are sensitive, so I'll ask you to please excuse yourselves," I say.

Miles, used to this when he attends Board meetings with me, gathers his things and takes Wyatt with him outside the room.

"Findings?" Asa pipes up angrily from the end of the table.

Opening up the PowerPoint I created, I place a hand to my hip as I look at him.

"Don't worry, Asa, if we'd found anything illegal, you'd probably be in handcuffs right now," I joke, but Asa doesn't find it funny, although half the Board members chuckle in their seats.

"What is this?" Asa demands, turning to face Glen. "Are you running a circus?" he asks, and I know he's referring to my juggling act with the phone which stings a little. He looks at me as if he wants him to give me a spanking for having the audacity to make a joke at his expense.

"Lake may be a little rough around the edges, but she's someone you want on your side." Glen, at least, has my back, although I couldn't care less what Asa thinks of me.

I take them through some of the redundancies I've uncovered, and when I'm done, Glen looks pleased although it still needs to be run by the Board for approval once I can get everything finalized. Unplugging my laptop, I gather the rest of my things while the room clears.

Before exiting, Glen calls me over to him. "Lake," he says, and I wait until the room is empty, even Asa Waterman, who gives me a dirty look before leaving.

"If he can't take a joke, that's not my problem," I say before he has the chance to chastise me.

Glen has always been a fair man, giving me many opportunities in my career over the years, but this acquisition has given him amnesia to everything I've done in the past.

"I know how much you want to be respected and God knows you earned this position, but you don't have to piss off Asa just to prove a point," Glen says.

"Do you know why the other Board members laugh at your bad jokes?" I ask him.

"They're not that bad" he laughs, waving me off.

"Because you're a man," I say, demanding his attention.

Glen furrows his brows, now suddenly interested, but I can tell he doesn't like where this is going.

"Lake, I don't think…"

"I make the same joke and they look to you for a signal that it's okay to laugh," I point out. "I can understand that, Glen, because you're the boss, the one they should respect the most, but what you fail to see or maybe you succeed at ignoring is that when you walk into a room, they look at you to see how they should react. When I walk into a room, the first thing they do is check to see how low my blouse is buttoned today." Hoisting my laptop bag further up my shoulder, I look at him pointedly.

Glen has the decency to look embarrassed for them. "They're not all like that." He tries but fails to make an excuse.

"I'll let you in on a little secret. While men like Asa Waterman are distracted by that third button, they never see me coming, and *that*, Glen," I say, poking him playfully in the chest, "is more powerful than a bunch of old men laughing at a dumb joke."

Opening the door to the conference room, I don't wait for a reply because I know I won't get the one I deserve. My suspicion that Miles was waiting for me outside is confirmed when he matches my stride as I strut down the long row of cubicles on the way to my office.

"What was all that about?" he asks, following me down the hallway. Glass offices line the outer wall while the cubicles fill in the center space like a rat maze. Passing by the name plates stamped on the doors, Barry Engles, Jude Singleton, Robert Franklin, and Lewis McBride, I scoff.

"Third buttons, Miles," I say, sliding my eyes to him with a sly smile, and Miles shakes his head in confusion but he knows better than to ask for an explanation.

When we get to my office I pause at the door, resting my hand on the frame. "I'm going home for the day," I say.

"Do you need anything?" he asks, in a kind voice.

"I'm good, thanks," I say, leaving him outside of my office as I walk over to my desk to gather the rest of my things.

As soon as Miles leaves, I place my palms to the desk, taking a moment to gather my thoughts. It's not easy being the only woman in the Boardroom, especially when I just acted like a fool. Thinking about Asa's smug expression and Glen's pitiful excuses does little to calm my heart rate. Angrily, I shove a pile of papers onto the floor just as Wyatt barges into my office, startling me.

"I know it's Arizona, Wyatt, but this isn't the Wild West," I say, clearly irritated. "People knock before they enter."

"Sorry," Wyatt says timidly, her blonde hair falling over her shoulder as she bends to gather the papers that fell off my desk.

"You don't have to do that," I say, grabbing a few that peek out from under my desk.

Wyatt stands, gathering the papers in her hands and uses my desk to shuffle them before placing them back in a pile.

"Is there something I can help you with?" I try to stop my voice from sounding annoyed, but I'd really like to just go home.

"I just wanted to let you know that I'm almost finished with the Accounts Receivable reconciliation, and I'll have it to you probably by the end of the week," Wyatt says.

"If anything stands out, I'll add it to the findings," I say, rounding my desk.

"What do you want me to do with all the pending questions? Compile everything so we can go over it with Waterman's CFO?" Wyatt asks with an eager expression. She's been here a few weeks; working on the days she doesn't have class, and staying late to get through her workload. College teaches you the mechanics of business, the nature of debits and credits, how to understand a balance sheet, calculate earnings per share, but it does nothing to teach you about human nature.

"There's something you need to learn, Wyatt," I say, throwing the strap of my laptop bag over my shoulder as I head for my door. "Never ask questions that you don't already have the answers to."

"So what do you want me to do?" she asks.

Waiting by the door, I gesture for her to exit. Once in the hall, I shut my door and turn to her.

"Find the answers, and then I will ask the questions." I give her a wink and then walk down the hallway towards the elevator.

Pulling out my phone while I wait, I see the last of Adrian's texts making my cheeks heat. Visibly rolling my eyes, I can't believe I let myself get so flustered in a meeting. I tap out a reply.

> L: I hate you.

> A: Already?

> L: I was in a meeting and you...

> A: I what?

> L: Distracted me.

Seeing the ellipses appear and disappear angers me because I imagine he's pretty pleased with himself for rattling me.

> A: Let me distract you more tonight.

The nerve.

The elevator doors open and I get on, shaking my head. Usually when I leave the elevator is empty, but today it's half full, so I shift to the back and lean against the railing.

> L: It's a weeknight.

> A: Do you have a curfew?

> L: No, I have a job.

> A: Then come to the Tap Room Friday night and watch me play.

> L: I'm not a fucking groupie.

    Exiting the elevator I head to my car, and it's not until I get behind the driver's seat that I check my phone again.

> A: I'll make it worth your while.

> A: And wear those expensive gold heels.

And that sealed the deal.

17

SO GODDAMN PRETTY

TAKE ME AWAY BY MORGAN WADE

R emembering when I was a child, my mother insisted I wear a dress every Sunday when we had dinner at my grandparent's house, and every Sunday it was a battle. The dress wasn't the issue. It was perfectly beautiful, fit nicely, and was something I actually picked out at the store. The problem was that I was being told to wear it. If my mother had never insisted, I probably would have worn it every time, but because she did, I wanted nothing to do with it.

Standing in my closet fresh out of the shower with a towel wrapped around me, I stare at the expensive pair of three inch gold heels with the wraparound ankle clasp that Adrian held up when he was in my closet a week ago. The ones he requested I wear tonight, which is why I grab a pair of comfortable sneakers instead.

Pairing them with shorts and a sleeveless shirt, I pull open my cosmetics drawer, seeing the extravagant lotion Noelle begged me to get when we were on vacation in L.A. I have a closet full of expensive shoes and nice dresses, but nothing makes me feel more like a lady than a pair of delicate lace panties, a great stick of lip gloss, and the smell of expensive lotion.

Smoothing the cream over my neck and chest, I notice how the gold flecks make my skin shine. Even though I don't want to admit it, I wonder if Adrian will like it.

An hour later, I'm standing in front of the *Tap Room* again, except this time, there's the absence of wind to lift the edges of my shirt or rain to wash away the nerves. I'm a grown woman, and yet I'm here to stand on the sidelines to watch a guy play like a fucking groupie. The sweltering summer night starts to eat away at my hesitation. Wiping my sweaty palms against my shorts, I contemplate turning on my heel and going back to my car, but then the door opens letting out the music that had been trapped inside, and that's when I hear his voice beckoning me to dare to come inside.

Passing the bouncer once again, he looks me over, not bothering to ask for my ID, and I narrow my eyes at him before heading to the bar.

Needing a little bit of liquid courage I walk up to the bar, recognizing Gael who served me before. His short cropped brown hair is covered this time by a Diamondbacks ball cap.

"Putin!" he calls over the bar to me.

"I'm surprised you remembered me," I chuckle, knowing that I recognize him because I don't frequent bars, but he must see hundreds if not thousands of people in any given week.

"How could I forget?" he gestures to me with one eyebrow cocked and a smile.

Now I know he's messing with me.

"Think you can go for another?" he asks.

"Why not?" I shake my head knowing I'm going to need something strong. Leaning against the bar top, I look around the bar as I wait for my beer. It's the same bar and yet it feels different tonight, and perhaps that's because I'm not looking for anything. There are no ghosts to chase away, no past to cling to – there is only him, the man whose voice filters past the crowd and reaches out to me.

Gael slides the beer across the bar, the sound of the glass running over years' worth of scratches drowned out by the music and chatter. The glass, already sweating from the humidity, feels cool against my hand. I never thought I would enjoy dark beer, but it seems to have attached itself as part of my persona in this bar. Dropping a few bills on the counter, I take my liquid courage with me as I walk into the small, crowded music venue. The room offers no empty tables although there are a few empty seats scattered among the crowd, and I doubt people would mind sharing. Instead of finding a seat right away, I lean against the column holding my beer, the same as I did on that first night, and stare up at the man on the stage with the easy smile and charismatic attitude.

The crowd is sucked in as much as I am with how much fun he has on stage as they sing along to the chorus of an old *John Cougar Mellencamp* song. When his eyes meet mine, a smile spreads over his face and travels into his eyes, as he pushes away from the mic, strumming the short guitar solo between verses. His black graphic t-shirt rises above the waistband of his jeans, revealing a sliver of smooth tanned skin, hinting at his six pack as his body flexes with exertion.

Following me as I move around the room, I pick a table close to the stage, sharing it with a group of people that seem to be open to making a new friend. The table is sticky with spilled beer and hours of forgotten fried food grease, but I don't mind. The group at the table tell stories as if they are all old friends and even bring me into their confidence with a crude story that would never be tolerated at Zentech – unless it happened on the golf course amongst the good ole boys club. I couldn't tell you what the story was about or what their names were when they introduced themselves, because my attention has been diverted the entire time to the man on the stage who has been eye fucking me the entire time.

When the set is finally over and the hour is late, Adrian lays his guitar gently in its case to the side of the stage. The live music has been replaced by music coming from the speakers in the corners of the room, and most of the crowd has gone home or moved to the arcade. Exiting the stage, he wastes no time making his way over to me with a purposeful stride. Hair sticks to his face, and I find myself wanting to dive my fingers into it, pushing the stray pieces behind his ears.

There's a war going on in my stomach, equal parts dread and excitement that I can't seem to shake because I keep replaying everything in my mind, from that first moment I saw him to the shock of him showing up at my sister's wedding where he turned out to be Laura's little brother. The look on my sister's face when she said, *he's ten years younger than you.*

Maybe I should stay away, putting my sister first, but I want this too much.

When someone tells me I can't have something, it only makes me want it more. It's what makes me a good businesswoman but sometimes a poor human being. I remind myself of our arrangement – no expectations, just fun, and nobody gets hurt. I can repeat that over and over in my head, but my heart knows just how dangerous this is, and that might be part of the thrill.

Looking up at Adrian as he approaches, I find myself wanting to be swept up in his energy, treated coarsely, and have any doubt fucked out of me.

His eyes sweep over me and there's no doubt he can feel the nervous energy emanating off me like a tidal wave. It's probably why he doesn't give me a chance to speak; instead he pulls me from the chair with a kiss. In his arms I'm like a rag doll, helpless to stop myself from snaking my arms around his shoulders and sinking my fingers into his hair. The room melts away like the burning of a candle until only the flame remains.

"I like it when you smile," he says against my lips, and I hadn't realized I was smiling. His expression darkens and his voice becomes low when he says, "Just make sure I'm the only one to cause it."

"Jealous of my new friends?" I ask, raising an eyebrow.

"I have never been a jealous man," he says, looking down, brown eyes fixated on me, "Until you," he finishes, sending an ache to travel straight to the sensitive nub between my thighs.

Forming in my brain are the words, this is lie number… whatever, but either I've lost count or I just don't care anymore.

Catcalls from the table indicate we're making quite a display, and the room comes back into focus.

"Your friends?" Adrian gestures to the table, letting me down so my sneakered feet touch the floor.

Looking over my shoulder, the young group at the table whistle jokingly while packing up their things. They're a reminder of the easy way I'd been when I was in college; the easy way I can still be.

Adrian pulls my attention back to him with the touch of his finger to my chin. I'm struck by his youthfulness, especially at thirty-one, and he doesn't even know what's in store for him. With his finger still on my chin, he *tsks*, tilting his head to look at my gym shoes with a raised eyebrow.

I smile, running my finger along his jaw and down his neck. "Maybe next time tell me *not* to wear them," I say.

Adrian laughs deeply, his chest shaking under the palm of my hand.

"We're heading out," one of Adrian's bandmates calls from behind him, carrying a guitar case.

"Finlay," Adrian waves him over while the other guys wave, leaving through the back.

"Adrian," I warn, not knowing if he's someone who should know we're seeing each other, but Adrian gives me a comforting smile. "Don't worry," he says.

"Finlay, this is Lake," Adrian says as the band's bass player approaches.

His shaggy blonde hair is like a halo around his head as he extends a polite hand toward me.

"This is Lake," Finlay says, his eyes sliding to Adrian. "Now I get it," he smiles.

"Get what?" I ask cautiously.

"You're a MILF," Finlay says appreciatively, and even though I know he's joking, I don't like it.

Stepping forward slightly, Adrian's hand reaches out and holds me back gently. "I know you think that's a compliment," I look Finlay up and down assessing him, "but never call me that again." I narrow my eyes on him.

Finlay clears his throat while looking at Adrian who chuckles softly. "Noted."

Very aware of Adrian standing beside me, his finger runs up the back of my leg and plays with the edge of my shorts. "Have you been playing together for long?" I ask, trying to change the subject.

"Since we were kids," Finlay answers, somewhat out of breath, lifting the strap of his guitar over his shoulder.

"Finlay was the fifth child," Adrian jokes, and the two of them share a look. I can tell they have a lot of history just by the way they interact on stage – and just now.

Heat spreads over my body as Adrian's finger slips under my shorts and plays with the edge of my panties, the wall behind us hiding his actions. I feel a sweat break out across my chest and I lift my shirt away fanning myself. "Is it hot in here?" I ask as Adrian chuckles.

"I gotta head out," Finlay says. "See you tomorrow." He points to Adrian and then turns his attention to me. "Nice to meet you, Lake."

"Want me to take yours?" Finlay points to Adrian's guitar case and he nods.

I watch as Finlay weaves through the tables towards the exit.

"Tomorrow?" I ask.

"We have a job tomorrow," Adrian says.

"You work together?" I ask as my back presses against the wall.

He nods, leaning in. "I want to take you to bed," Adrian whispers in my ear, his breath causing shivers to run down my heated body. His finger slips in between my thighs and he sucks in a breath when he feels how wet he's already made me.

"Bathroom's closer," I whisper teasingly.

He's staring down at me with hooded eyes, making promises that I intend to make him keep.

"Nuh-uh." He shakes his head. "I want to fuck you properly, Lake. Bent over my couch," his breath tickles my ear before pressing a kiss to my neck. "Against my wall," he whispers as his lips trail kisses down to my jaw. "In my bed, with your legs wrapped around my shoulders," he groans deeply causing me to shiver, and I can feel his cock growing hard as it presses against his jeans.

A sly smile spreads on my face as I press a palm to his chest, feeling the muscles flex underneath. "Any other man that talked to me that way would get his face slapped," I say, with my fingers playing at the edge of his shirt, itching to dig my fingernails into his skin. "But not you," I finish saying.

"Is that right?" he smirks causing the dimples to appear more prominently on his cheeks.

"Because I want you to do those things to me," I whisper in his ear, working past my vulnerability.

He kisses me while gathering my hair in his fist and breathing me in. I can't help but like the possessive way he handles me, as if I belong to him. "I want you to know how much I want you," he says back.

Remembering the dirty texts he sent me the other day, I push my hand against his chest and then smack him playfully. "That's for disrupting my Board meeting." I smack him again and his chest shakes with laughter.

"Did I distract you?" he asks smiling smugly, and I either want to kiss him or slap him.

"That was not funny," I say angrily, pushing at him playfully until he wraps an arm under my ass, hoisting me over his shoulder effortlessly.

"Adrian!" I yell as I'm being carried out of the bar like a spoiled child while customers stare after me, seemingly enjoying the entertainment. "You put me down right now!"

Feeling his body shake with laughter, it just angers me even more. I kick my legs until we're on the sidewalk and he sets me down. Stumbling backwards and smoothing out my hair, trying to regain my dignity.

"I am an adult!" I declare and stomp my foot on the concrete.

"I am well aware of that." Adrian rubs at his chin while watching me make even more of a spectacle on the sidewalk.

"For God's sake," I grumble, making sure my shirt is smoothed out.

"Are you done?" Adrian asks and I narrow my eyes at him, my body instantly betraying me because if he can pick me up that easily, fucking me against the wall of his apartment is definitely something I do not want to miss out on.

We stand on the sidewalk staring at each other until he reaches out for my hand that I reluctantly let him have, and we walk towards his apartment.

"Just so you know, I'm not a fucking groupie," I say, shaking out my hair and tossing the part to the side haughtily.

Crazy by Aerosmith

Knowing exactly why I came here tonight, nervous energy swirls between us and drips off me like sweat. By the time we get to his apartment complex, I can feel my shirt already sticking to my body.

The buildings open to a walkway that leads to the dark pool that's closed for the night. I stare at the water wondering what it would be like to jump in and cool my heated skin. Adrian stops in front of the gate, his thumb brushing over my taut nipple, causing a shiver to run down my body. The complex is quiet, the only sound coming from cars passing on the nearby street and the kick of an a/c unit turning on.

"Next time," Adrian says, looking at the water as he takes my hand again, leading me towards his apartment.

"How did you know what I was thinking?" I ask once we get to his door and I lean against the wall.

"I'm very observant," he says, pulling the keys from his pocket and unlocking the door.

We slip inside and the cool air from the a/c is a welcomed reprieve from the sweltering night air. Feeling the sweat drip between my breasts from the walk over, I wish I'd brought something to freshen up with. Adrian flicks on the light, and this time I take my time looking around his apartment. The same colorful print hangs in the hallway over the side table where Adrian tosses his keys into a glass bowl.

I don't know what it is about this print that moves me so much. Maybe it's the colors or the context of falling feathers turning black once they hit the ground, feeling as if it's a metaphor for something I'm not privy to yet, but seems so very familiar. It's as if I was once that colorful and vibrant, but with every passing year, I lost a feather, and they all hit the ground until there was nothing left of me.

Walking further into his apartment, Adrian excuses himself, exiting into the bedroom while I make my way over to his bookshelves on the far wall, sliding my fingers over the album sleeves and smiling while I pluck one from its place and set it on the record player. The needle skips, emanating a scratching sound through the speakers before settling into the opening chords to Crazy by *Aerosmith*. At the patio doors, I open the blinds to look out at the star littered sky.

Through the glass, I see his reflection as he approaches; bare feet against the wood planks, ripped jeans sitting low on his waist, and no shirt showing off that deliciously cut V. My body, already anticipating his touch, hums like the engine of a car. When he reaches me, his knuckles start at the top between my shoulder blades and slowly make their way to the small of my back where he gathers my shirt in his hands and lifts it from my body. As he does this, Steven Tyler's voice becomes background noise. Reaching behind me, I lean my head against his shoulder, sinking my fingers into his lush hair.

"You have great taste in music," he groans, unhooking my bra and letting it fall to the floor at my feet. He presses a kiss below my earlobe while his hands cup my breasts and make their way down my body.

Leaning forward, I press my palms to the glass as one of his hands slides beneath the waistband of my shorts, sliding over my panties. I feel like I'm underwater fighting against a current, and I get a moment where I can fill my lungs with air before his finger slips inside me and I'm pushed back under. Riveted by our reflection in the glass, I'm mesmerized by his hooded eyes, the way his nostrils flare, and the way his lips part the moment his finger dips inside of me. All this time I thought I was the one who couldn't get enough, that the mere thought of him could bring me to a place of no return, but I was wrong. Watching him in the glass, I see the reflection of a man who is drunk on me, and it is the most powerful – and the most dangerous – feeling in the world.

Tilting my head towards him, I seek out his mouth needing more of him. Our breaths mingle and I reach back again to push my fingers through his hair, holding his mouth to mine. My body goes weak while his fingers run through my slickness, circling my clit in the most tantalizing way.

Pulling away, I open my eyes to him as he tries to capture my lips again, but I stay out of reach just wanting to watch him. His brown eyes flare when he can't have what he wants, and his fingers work me harder. My eyes flutter, threatening to shut. Once again, he tries to capture my lips, but I hold him back from kissing me. I want to feel everything, not drown out the world around me with his kiss. Most of all, I want him to know what it feels like to not get what he wants so easily.

Moving out of his grasp, I turn around, pressing my back against the glass and I watch as he stands before me with hooded eyes that flick down to watch as I unzip my shorts, pushing them past my hips and letting them fall down my legs. They rake over my stomach to the lacy white underwear I so carefully selected for tonight. The material barely covers my front and even less of my ass.

"Jesus," he whispers, taking me in before dipping his head to my breast, gently swiping his tongue over the erect nub before pulling it into his mouth. Arching my back I urge him to take more, and greedily he does. I've never had a man get off on my pleasure before. It makes me feel beautiful and reckless.

"I thought you were going to take me to your bed," I remind him as he grabs hold of each side of my panties and slides them down my thighs while his knuckles trail goosebumps in their wake. "Or are you going to bend me over the couch?" I tease breathlessly.

He nips at my thigh, and I squeal in pleasure. "I don't care where I fuck you, just as long as I fuck you," he groans, placing my leg over his shoulder, but I grab onto his hair before his mouth reaches me. The way he looks at me... I feel a wave of energy run through my body, something I have never felt before. Men have looked at the way my blouse gaps during a reach or the length of my skirt when I cross my legs, but nothing has ever made me feel this wanted – like I am something *more*.

Rocking back on his knees while he looks up at me helplessly through thick black lashes, I dare to make him wait, to be the one in charge, to make him *beg*. He watches with rapt attention as I pull my finger into my mouth, wetting it, as if I even need to, before dragging it through my slickness. His nostrils flare and a whoosh of breath escapes his lips as they part while his fingers dig a little deeper into my skin.

His tongue runs over his bottom lip. "Jesus fucking Christ," he rasps before trying to taste me, but once again I stop him. All I have to do is move out of his reach, even if it's just an inch, barely noticeable.

"Lake," his voice is a harsh, warning of how bad he wants it, stirring something inside me, making me weak, but I can't stop now.

His dark expression is hazy as my finger dips inside, dragging the wetness forward to circle my clit, bringing myself close to the edge. It's intoxicating to watch as arousal completely takes him over.

His body moves involuntarily, rocking imperceptibly to the cadence of my finger moving back and forth, in and out. I've never felt so much power and vulnerability all at once, warring inside of me, but the longer I make him wait, the sweeter the high.

Looking down at him with my other hand locked in his hair as I tease him causes my breath to hitch and my nipples to pebble. His eyes flick up to mine, the word *please*, lingering on his lips in a drunken haze. I can feel his hands shake as he digs his fingers deeper into my hips like I'm his life preserver, and if he were to let go, he would sink helplessly. His mouth hovers so close that I can feel his breath against my wet and throbbing pussy making me shiver.

"Please," he begs, barely audible, the words sinking into my skin and making me lightheaded. "Let me have it," he pauses before he begs again, "please." His words break open a levee inside of me. I simply let go of his hair and his mouth is on me in a feverish daze, causing my back to hit the glass. It rattles with the force and sounds like thunder.

"Oh, fuck," I yell, shaking, my legs barely able to hold me up. The back of my hands hit the glass, trying to keep my balance as he spreads me with his fingers, sliding his tongue along my slit and then grabbing onto my ass to bring me further into him.

Rocking against him, I fuck his mouth unabashedly, a woman on fire chasing the high like the addict I am. It's him that makes me lose all decorum, causes me to forget there is a world going on around me, and lose all sense of time. With him, I am who I was always meant to be, someone reckless and wild. With each thrust of my hips, his fingers dig deeper into the tender skin of my ass cheeks that will leave evidence of my indiscretion. The cadence of my moans accelerates as his mouth latches onto my clit. Everything tenses like the stretch of a rubber band, and my eyes pop open feeling the snap.

"Adrian!" I scream, bucking against him as I fall apart like the dust being washed away by the rain.

I hear the zipper of his jeans right before they hit the floor. The familiar rip of a condom wrapper breaks the silence before he pins me to the glass, lifting my legs around his waist as he thrusts into me with such force it threatens to break the glass. He doesn't let up, fucking me with all of his pent-up frustration and elongating my orgasm so much that I can't tell when one ends and another begins. I've never been fucked with such destruction before that my breaths come in short snaps of air matching each thrust. The burn rips through me without an ounce of care, and the sound of his groans and swift intakes of air only fuel me further.

It's unlikely that anyone would be out walking the grounds of the apartment complex this time of night, but if they were, they'd get a great view of my ass being pounded into the glass door. Right now, I couldn't care less if someone were watching; I only care about him and what he does to me.

Coming to my senses enough to kiss him, I grip his face, pressing my lips to his in a slow and tantalizing way, the opposite of the storm raging inside of me. While he groans against my lips, I feel his cock pulse inside of me, his thrusts slowing while he rides out his own orgasm. His chest thunders against mine as if he's just run a marathon while he runs his hands through my hair, resting his forehead against mine to catch his breath, smiling. "I will never be able to listen to another *Aerosmith* song without thinking of your sweet fucking pussy," he says out of breath, accentuating each word with his deep and rough voice.

Laughing against his lips, I kiss him again, pulling on his bottom lip as I let go, and feeling this ache inside of me that has nothing to do with his cock. He slides out of me, placing my feet gently on the ground and holding me up. My legs feel like Jell-O, barely able to hold my own weight, and I slump against him. His brown hair is a mess, pieces sticking to his forehead and falling into his eyes. I gingerly brush them away so I can see his face, my hand resting against the rough patch of hair on his jaw.

"You're fucking killing me, Lake," he groans, still out of breath, "in the best possible way."

Does he know what his words do to me? How they burn through me like wildfire, lift me up like a gust of wind, only reminding me how easily I could crash to the ground.

The dim light from the hall creates a halo around his body. Standing in front of me, his chest heaving while I run my hands over the tight muscles of his shoulder, tracing the black ink and down his torso to the flat of his stomach where his cock, still hard, rests against his soft skin. I don't think I have ever admired a man's body this much before. I now have a better view of his tattoo and realize it wasn't scales or feathers but a compass surrounded by the desert. Drinking him in, I want to memorize every inch so that one day when I'm in another boring meeting, I can touch my fingers to my lips, close my eyes, and see him as clearly as I do now.

As I circle him, my fingers glide over his back and down to the curve of his ass cheek, admiring how nice and firm it is while his head tilts in my direction. There is no doubt he keeps himself in shape, but it's more than that. It's the protection of youth covering him like a fine mist as his body glistens with sweat.

"What?" he whispers with a slight chuckle, finally able to look at me as I stand in front of him, snaking my arms around his neck and pressing my breasts into his bare chest.

Meeting his eyes, I run my hand up the back of his head and grip his hair. "You're just so goddamn pretty," I say, causing him to laugh. Without warning, he scoops me up and throws me over his shoulder for the second time tonight.

"Adrian!" I scream while he carries me into the bedroom, and I can't help but laugh.

18

TOO OLD FOR NICKNAMES

Strong Enough by Sheryl Crow

Hooking my bra and securing my breasts back in the cups, I slip my arms through the straps adjusting them on my shoulders. As I'm bending down to grab my shirt, Adrian pads into the living room wearing only a pair of shorts, his chest bare, as he leans against the back of the couch watching me.

"Trying to sneak out again?" he asks, rubbing his chin.

Slipping my shirt over my head, I button my shorts as I admire him. "I have to get home," I say, but I don't finish the sentence with *to my daughter*. For some reason, mentioning her here, in his apartment, especially after he made good on his promise to fuck me thoroughly in his bed, feels wrong. Like uttering her name taints her with whatever I believe this to be, no matter how good it is.

Adrian nods, satisfied with my excuse. As I pass by, he stops me by touching my arm. His thumb skims over my wrist and I pull away. The tender gesture feels too personal, and it sounds silly in my head after what we just did, but I can't explain how it makes me feel *too much*.

"Adrian?" I start to say but he cuts me off as if he knows what I'm going to say.

"Admit that was fun," he says, causing me to smile, the meaning not lost on me.

All of this will end when *it's not fun anymore.*

He pulls me against his body as I kiss him goodbye, still tasting myself on his tongue and it makes me ache.

"You should definitely leave," he whispers against my lips before kissing me again, using my own words against me.

His fingers find their way into my already messy hair that I didn't even bother to try and comb out in his bathroom. If I had looked at myself in the mirror, I don't know if I would like what I see.

"Please leave," he says, smiling smugly.

I push at his chest teasingly. "Don't be a fucking asshole, Corvin."

The smile on his face could melt ice. "Hold on," he says, jogging into his bedroom and then coming out with his shirt on, sliding his feet into his shoes by the door.

"What are you doing?" I ask.

"I'm not letting you walk all the way back to your car alone," he explains while grabbing his keys from the glass bowl in the hallway.

"I'm a big girl," I say. "Besides, I got back to my car just fine the first time."

"That's only because you snuck out," he says, narrowing his eyes at me.

It's not that the neighborhood is bad. In fact, it's a pretty nice area of Tempe, but the bars are nearby. Alcohol and society in general don't mix, even in nice neighborhoods.

That's why I concede, letting him walk me out of his apartment and down to the parking lot where I stand in front of a motorcycle. Correction, in front of something that looks like a rocket on wheels.

"Where's your truck?" I ask, looking around the dark lot.

"It's at my shop. I ride my bike to and from work," Adrian explains.

"Well, I'm not getting on that." I point to the bike sitting in the parking spot in front of us.

"What's wrong with my bike?" Adrian laughs, leaning against it.

I must admit he looks pretty damn good next to that bike, but he's high if he thinks I'm getting on the back of it.

"Where do I even begin?" I shake my head looking at the small leather seat. "Can two people fit on that?" I scoff. "No, just no," I protest.

Adrian pushes off from the bike and takes my hand. "Then I'll walk you to your car."

"You'll have to walk back home alone, you know," I tell him, as he holds my hand while we walk through the apartment complex and out onto the sidewalk of the nearly deserted street.

"I'm a big boy, despite what you think," he winks.

"It's fine if you walk home alone but I can't walk to my car by myself?"

"I'm a man."

"You realize how sexist that sounds?" I ask, annoyed.

"I do, even though I have no doubt you can scare the shit out of some unsuspecting mugger."

I sniff, tilting my chin in the air as we continue to walk down the block towards my car.

"You like to argue," he says while keeping his eyes on the street ahead of us.

"Do you have a problem with that?" I stop us.

"No," Adrian chuckles. "I like it."

Smiling, we continue to walk in the late evening's still warm air. We're already into September and the heat is persistent with no relief in sight. There will be no change in colors of the leaves to look forward to, or chilly nights anytime soon. Phoenix has an endless summer, and normally I look forward to a little reprieve, but as I look over at Adrian, the curve of his lips, the strong jaw covered in stubble, and hair that touches his shoulders, I don't want summer to end.

When we pass by the record store on Southern, my eyes linger a little longer, thinking how it was only a few weeks ago that Adrian pulled me into that alcove away from the rain. It's funny how so much can change in such a short amount of time. I find myself in a situation I never thought I would be in, letting a man walk me to my car while holding my hand. Such an intimate gesture, and yet I still hardly know him.

The *Tap Room* is still going strong, and music filters onto the street as we pass.

"I like watching you play," I say, turning back to him, my voice slicing through the silence between us. "Your band is really good."

He sniffs in response as if he's embarrassed by my compliment.

"I mean it," I say, stopping at the corner. Taking a moment to articulate my words properly, I admit, "You have so much fun on stage and the crowd loves it." Thinking about it causes goosebumps to cover my skin. I can't help but think about the confession he made at my house – that he wasn't holding out hope of playing professionally.

We cross the intersection when the light turns green. "It's amazing what *not* caring does for you," he says, confusing me. Tilting my head, I urge him to continue.

"When you stop caring what people think or stop waiting to be discovered, it's freeing," he explains.

"So you wanted to be a rock star?" I ask, stopping just before we get to my car.

Adrian's laugh doesn't quite reach his eyes. If I didn't know how much music means to him by watching him on stage, I know it now. "I wrote my first song when I was fifteen years old, spent years playing in every bar that would have me, uploaded my music everywhere you could think of." He turns to me, not with melancholy eyes, but the eyes of a man who is satisfied with his outcome. "It wasn't for lack of trying, but when it didn't happen, I had to accept that it wasn't meant to be."

"You're annoyingly well adjusted," I joke, shaking my head and eliciting a genuine laugh from him.

"And you're not?"

"When my mom died, she took the well-adjusted parts of me with her," I pass it off as a joke even though it feels like the truth.

Adrian's expression darkens, his brown irises soaking up the night and extracting truths from me I don't mean to divulge. People who are having fun don't talk about things that hurt, so I distract myself by pulling my keys from my purse and hitting the button to unlock my car. My Porsche beeps a few feet away, echoing against the low concrete wall that divides the parking lot from the street.

Adrian turns his attention in the direction of my car. "Fuck, Lake," he whistles low, admiring my car as we walk closer to it.

Leaning against the shiny silver quarter panel, he nestles himself between my legs, wrapping his arms around my waist. He makes me not want the night to end.

"Are you intimidated by a successful woman, Adrian?" I ask coyly, raising an eyebrow while I drape my arms over his shoulders lazily.

"Not intimidated, *Aerosmith*," he calls me. "Definitely turned on, but not intimidated," he says, capturing my lips before I can protest. My body softens like candle wax after being warmed by a flame. All the gooey parts of me melt into him so easily.

Pulling away I gain my senses and look up at him as he pushes the hair from my eyes. "I'm too old for nicknames," I say lazily against his lips.

The corner of his mouth lifts into a half smile; as if he finds me amusing but lets me continue.

"Nicknames are for young girls who need validation from their boyfriends," I continue. "You're not my boyfriend," I pause, "and I'm not a young girl; and I definitely don't need validation."

He stares down at me, lifting a mocking eyebrow while his hands circle my waist, his thumbs brushing across my ribcage threatening to tickle me.

"How about I just call you…" a wicked grin lights up his face, "Mine?" He doesn't wait for me to answer before effectively silencing me with another kiss.

To him, it seems, we are not in a parking lot in the middle of the night, as he lazily kisses me on the hood of my Porsche. His words swirl around in my head landing right between my thighs and making me dizzy, so I pull back to search his eyes, wondering where the fuck he came from.

To minimize the noise, I wait until the overhead garage door completely closes before opening the inside door to the house. The minute I walk in the house, *Vitale* filters down the hall from Noelle's bedroom, permeating the walls and sinking into my skin. Kicking off my shoes by the entrance, I pad into the kitchen and lay my purse on the island.

I'd texted earlier to let her know I'd be home late. It's well past midnight, and I'm not upset that she's awake at this hour, but that she's awake waiting for *me*. Not knowing how to navigate this strange new world with my almost grown daughter, I grab a bottle of water and take it with me down the hall. Passing by her room on my way to the master, I stop to peer in, seeing her in her pajamas, long brown hair piled on top of her head in a messy bun, with her violin bow raised defiantly high. When she notices me, she lowers the bow, her lips pressed together as she peers back at me, the violin still resting against her chin. The silence between us could fill the Grand Canyon and neither of us knows what to say.

Aware of how I must look I know I should explain, but I don't want to. Noelle's bright blue eyes assess me. Whether she's looking for signs that I'm broken or mistreated I don't know, but she must get her answer when she lifts the bow once more, sliding it against the strings with the flick of her wrist.

The low whine of her violin starts again as I turn the corner into my bedroom and try to drown out the noise by turning the shower on. Leaving the light off, I strip out of my clothes and stand under the spray, closing my eyes. It's not thoughts of Adrian that fill my mind, but thoughts of Steven, Noelle's Dad, assault every vulnerable crevice and dark corner of my body. Sometimes I don't know what triggers these feelings, and it doesn't have to be anything bad that happens.

I can't help but look at Noelle and feel guilty that I've denied her of something she deserves because I chose the wrong person to have a kid with. Steven has been out of our lives for twelve years, but every insult, judgmental look, accusation, and broken promise is always just under the surface, waiting for small moments of vulnerability to come lurking out of the dark.

Emotional damage is harder to see because it sits below the surface and embeds itself into your DNA. I am not the person I should be because of it. Bruises heal, but words, especially the hurtful ones, stay with you forever.

Steam fills the bathroom, fogging up the glass doors of the shower. My body shudders as I place a palm to the glass and sink against the tiled stall. I sit hunched over my knees, letting the water wash over me until it turns cold, giving myself a moment to feel… but like I do every day, once it passes, I pick myself back up again.

Before I sink into bed, I notice the violin has stopped and the house is eerily quiet. If I stand still enough, I can hear her breathing heavily in her room, fast asleep. It's a sound that has always comforted me.

On the bed next to me, where I tossed it earlier, my phone lights up with a missed message. There are only two people who would text me in the middle of the night, but my breath catches at the thought of only one. Hesitating, I grab it off the bed and look at the text.

> A: Definitely don't call me tomorrow.

Sinking deeper into the pillow, I fail at suppressing a smile. Holding the phone to my chest, I close my eyes to the darkened ceiling.

Fucking asshole, I think while smiling.

Bird by Billie Marten

The hot morning sun filters through the shutters, thanks to me for forgetting to close them before I fell asleep last night. Yanking the lever closed does little to shut out the light, so I resolve to stay awake and make my way down the hall towards the kitchen.

Noelle sits at the island with a steaming mug in front of her. Mindful of the broken tile, which my toe has slowly recovered from since the last time I stubbed it, I avoid it. Noelle looks up from her phone, her big blue eyes peering at me through the steam.

"There's coffee," she says, pointing to the pot next to the sink.

"Thanks," I say, grabbing a cup from the shelf and pouring some.

Sitting on the island is the *Phoenix New Times*, still wrapped up with a rubber band.

"You grabbed the paper?" I ask, surprised.

"I went for a walk early this morning," she says.

"I hope you wore gym shoes," I remind her while opening the paper and fanning it out in front of me. "Rattlesnakes are out."

"I did."

Taking a sip of the coffee, my mouth puckers in disgust. "Did you use the whole bag of beans?" I ask, pushing the cup away from me.

"I like it strong," she says with a defiant look – that unfortunately she gets from me.

"Since when?" I ask, pouring out my cup in the sink.

"Since always," she says, but I notice her cup is still full as she hops down from the barstool. The awkwardness between us has to come to an end at some point.

"Do you want to go to *Berdena's* for some French toast?" I ask, hopeful. "It won't take me long to change." I start to move towards the hall but she stops me.

"I can't. I'm going to the mall with Grayson." She tosses the contents of her cup in the sink and sets the mug next to the pot of coffee I fully intend to discard. "And then we're gonna work on our history project together."

"Oh," I say, disappointed, making my way back to the kitchen island. Noelle and her boyfriend, Grayson, have been dating since last year. I want to know what's going through her mind, but I'm not going to force her to open up to me. I'm not sure right now is the time to talk to her about it. This is uncharted territory, and right now the waters are choppy. I'm afraid I don't know how to navigate because I've never had to.

Before I can broach the subject, Noelle is already down the hall towards her room out of earshot.

Turning back to the island, I flatten the paper with the palm of my hand when I hear her flip flops smack against the tile behind me.

There's an uneasiness in my stomach because I don't like the distance between us this morning.

Spinning around in my chair, I say, "Noelle, I want…"

"I'm gonna be late," she cuts me off, grabbing her keys from the hook on the wall.

There are times when you have to pick your battles, and by allowing her to leave, I've chosen to fight another day. The slamming door echoes through the empty house. Only the sound of the air conditioning kicking on fills the space. Taking the pot of coffee, I dump it down the drain while shaking my head.

My phone vibrates against the newspaper I never got a chance to read. When I pick it up, it's a text from Adrian.

> A: I thought you weren't going to call me?

His reverse psychology is charming and brings a smile to my face, but I flip my phone over anyway, running a hand through my hair anxiously. When I walk away, I hear it vibrate again and back track to grab it.

> A: When I said don't call me, you know I was being cheeky, right?

I laugh out loud, palming my face.

> L: OK, Rock Star. Cheeky is not something I ever thought would come out of your mouth.

> A: I thought we were too old for nicknames?

> L: I said I'm too old for nicknames.

> A: You can call me whatever you want.

The ellipsis flicker as he types another reply and I grip my phone anticipating whatever smartass comment he has next.

> A: As long as you call me.

Feeling the heat rise to my cheeks, I would be embarrassed at how easily he gets a rise out of me, but there is no one around to witness it. This is a taste of what I've been missing all these years, and Adrian is the perfect person to scratch that itch, no matter how fleeting it may be. Either he'll get bored of me or it'll cease to be fun anymore and it will end. For now, I'll enjoy my spoils and take full advantage of the fact that Adrian likes a good chase.

Intent on leaving his text unanswered, I abandon my phone on the kitchen island and walk into the living room, past the precarious pile of DVDs next to the couch and out to the backyard. Running my hands through my hair, I let the shoulder length brown locks fall to the side as I tilt my head away from the sun. Biting my lip I think about last night, the look in Adrian's eyes as he begged makes me clench my thighs.

I should feel guilty, letting him dominate my thoughts and my time, but I don't.

The sun on my shoulders feels good for the first five minutes until it feels like I'm being baked in an oven. The clear water of the pool glitters as the sun bounces off the surface. The only neighbors behind me are the prying eyes of coyotes that blend in with the brown and tan hues of McDowell Mountain, but even they are most likely napping under thick patches of sage bushes. On either side of me are one story homes like mine, flat adobe style roofs and spread far enough apart to make you feel as though you don't have neighbors.

This seclusion is what prompts me to do something I've never done since I've moved here. Stripping off my tank top and pulling down my shorts, taking my underwear with them, I stand at the edge of the pool completely naked, looking down at the cool water – and then I jump.

19

STILL HAVING FUN?

GIVEN THE DOG A BONE BY AC/DC

A large, burly man I have never met enters my home wearing carpenter boots, jeans, and a white t-shirt with the logo *Corvin & Son* printed on the chest. Immediately he starts taping clear plastic over the kitchen cabinets, sealing them off.

"You won't be able to use your stove until we're done breaking up all the tile," he says, just as Adrian passes by giving me a judgmental smirk.

"That won't be a problem," Adrian teases as he carries in what looks like a large jackhammer with a flat shovel-like end.

I narrow my eyes at him, fists at my hips while he laughs. *Asshole.*

"I'm Moe," the large man now covering my entire island with plastic, introduces himself.

"Lake," I say, while Finlay, Adrian's bandmate, enters my home from the garage, a hammer resting at his hip.

He gives me a cautious smile as he passes by, intent on his mission to rip apart my home. The living room furniture has already been moved to one side of the room while Finlay starts pulling baseboards from the wall. The sound is jarring, as if the house is being torn apart.

He works his way around the room with expertise, and I realize he must have been working for Adrian for a long time. The entire living room is now devoid of baseboards in a matter of minutes.

Spinning around in the kitchen, I'm impressed at how fast everything is being prepped for the demolition of my tile.

"We'll do the kitchen and hallway today, and leave the bedrooms and your office for tomorrow," Adrian says with a business-like tone. "I can have the guys move your stuff once the flooring is laid in here."

"Wait, you're doing all of this flooring today?" I ask confused, because when I did get around to calling places, I was quoted that it would be at least a couple of weeks.

"I'm sure you were hoping to see me work up a sweat in your home for at least a week," he pauses with a cocky smirk on his face, "but when you actually have someone who knows what they're doing, it's amazing how fast you can get the job done." He raises a brow and I feel heat prickle at my neck, just as a bead of sweat drips between my breasts.

"That's funny, because I thought it wasn't how fast you could do it but how well," I smirk back at him. "It's kind of like that jack hammer you got there," I point to the tool in Adrian's hand. "It's not the size, but how you use it."

Adrian's eyes lower to my lips, but Finlay knocks into him playfully, probably on purpose to get him back to work as he walks by, pulling his attention away from me.

"I'll be working in my office," I say, hooking my thumb over my shoulder down the hallway.

Once inside my office, I pull open my laptop and log in, checking my calendar. Immediately an instant message window pops up from Miles, asking if I'm in the hospital with the swine flu. It's funny and tragic that he thinks I'd still be working even if I was in the hospital, but the truth is, he's probably right.

Everything I need is in my office now. The mini fridge Beth got me last year for Christmas comes in handy since I can't access anything from *my* kitchen.

Minutes later I'm on our Monday morning senior officer meeting when the jack hammering starts.

"What is that?" someone asks, and before I have a chance to speak, music blares, drowning out the jack hammering.

"Is that *AC/DC*?" Lewis asks.

An instant message pops up from Miles,

> M: I'm equally disgusted and impressed he knows who AC/DC is.

His message causes me to chuckle out loud that I try to suppress with my hand over my mouth.

"Sorry, I'm having new flooring put in," I explain.

"What kind of people did you hire, Lake?" Lewis says haughtily with his irritating voice.

"Apparently, people who have good taste in music," I say. "Let me put you on mute for a few moments." I message Miles to take notes as I get up from my desk and make my way down the short hallway before I'm cut off but by plastic blocking the exit. Not knowing how to get past it, I stand there as if I'm trapped in a bubble with no way out.

The kitchen is filled with white dust as Adrian chips away at the tile using the jack hammer. His whole body vibrates with the tool, forearm muscles tight, biceps stretching the sleeves of his t-shirt and a sheen of white dust covering his olive toned skin. As if he senses me watching him, he looks up from his task and switches off the machine, peering at me through clear goggles.

Adrian makes his way over, gently removing the tape holding the plastic to the wall from his side. It's only then that I realize if I wanted to get out, I would have had to rip it.

"Are you hosting a fucking *AC/DC* concert in here or ripping out my tile?" I ask, annoyed.

Even though his mouth is covered by a mask, I can tell he's smiling by the crinkle of his eyes. He turns toward Moe who is scooping up the broken tile and throwing it in a garbage bin that's been rolled into the house, making the universal sign to cut off the music. Moe makes a sad face but turns it down to a normal level and Adrian pulls down the mask, his lush lips pulled into a smirk.

"Do you speak that way to all the men who work for you?" he asks, completely unfazed by my irritated attitude.

He shifts his weight, placing his hand against the wall above me. Opening my mouth to tell him off, he effectively cuts me off by saying, "I bet when you do, they're thinking about bending you over their desk and fucking that attitude right of you," he pauses to rake his eyes over me, "just like I am right now." His eyes darken as he snaps the mask back over those defiant lips.

My mouth opens and closes in shock at his dirty words, but there's a part of me that wants him to haul me into my office right now, bend me over my desk, and fuck me so hard I scream his name for the whole senior management to hear.

He steps forward an inch and my body tenses, nerves firing at his nearness. Just as I think he might actually pick me up and haul me into my office, he grabs the edge of his shirt and lifts it to wipe the sweat off his forehead, and my eyes drop to his hard flat stomach, the tattoo snaking around his rib cage.

Licking my lips while sweat drips down the small of my back, Adrian clears his throat and my eyes flick back up to his, revealing an amused smirk. Adrian being in my home is very dangerous.

Wondering what Finlay and Moe think of our exchange, I glance in their direction and both turn their heads away guiltily and busy themselves with broken tile and baseboards. I cross my arms over my chest and jut out my hip as I slide my eyes back to Adrian, his heated gaze mirroring my own. I'm becoming increasingly aware of how much I like being in his company, and how his persistence is slowly chipping away at all my reservations.

I'm having fun.

"Just try to keep it down," I say with a smirk playing on my lips as I turn around and head back to my office.

Slipping my headphone back on, I prop my feet up on the edge of my desk using a loose piece of paper to fan myself and listen to the last ten minutes of the meeting.

Paula Dombrowiak

Thrills by Donna Missal

Admittedly I like working from home because I don't have to wear uncomfortable heels, pencil skirts, or stifling pant suits. I can prop my bare feet on the desk while wearing shorts and one of my cheesy gas station t-shirts that Noelle and I picked up on a trip. My hair can be in a bun and there's no need for makeup. It's surprisingly more efficient working from home because I don't have to take time to get ready in the morning and fight traffic. Even though the noise of my house being destroyed is distracting, I've gotten a lot done this morning.

Pushing my chair back with my foot propped on the edge of the desk, I chew on my pen as I take a break. Going through all the org charts of both companies has been draining, and I need to get a proposal to Glen by the end of the week. Having Wyatt has been a lot of help, but the sensitive nature of this particular project is something I have to do on my own.

Biting down on the pen cap, I hear someone clear their throat from the doorway. I swivel around in my chair to see Adrian leaning against the frame, a cocky grin on his pretty face as he watches me.

Lowering my eyeglasses, I remove my feet from the desk and lean back in my chair to take in the view.

"You should keep them on, they're sexy," he says, motioning to my glasses now resting on the keyboard of my laptop.

"Can I help you?" I ask.

As per usual, he doesn't take offense to my sometimes-direct nature and simply says, "The guys are taking off soon and I need to drop some of this waste off at the shop."

Checking the time on my laptop, I realize the workday is almost over. "Oh, I was so busy I didn't realize how late it was."

Down the hall I can hear Moe's portable radio playing *Iron Maiden* at a respectable level. Adrian steps further into my office and I watch him intently as he stands in front of my desk. He leans forward, resting his palms on the wood as he peers at me with his soft brown eyes.

I bet they're thinking about bending you over their desk and fucking that attitude right of you, just like I am right now.

Images of him thrusting into me while my cheek presses against the dark wood of my desk causes a rush of heat to flood directly to my core. The ache is so deep that I have to rub my thighs together.

"Rough day?" he asks, looking at the papers spread out on my desk.

Not understanding why those two words affect me so much, I sigh, not realizing how tense my body was until I let my shoulders fall back and my body relaxes.

"Yeah," I answer honestly, but he doesn't press for more.

"Have you eaten at all today?" he asks. "And don't lie, because I know you can't get to your kitchen."

"Yeah." I roll my eyes as I gesture to the packages of chips and cookies I found in my desk that I hate to admit might have been expired.

"Come on." Adrian straightens up and motions for me to follow him.

Reluctantly, I get up from my desk, but admittedly, I'm curious as to what he's up to.

Out in my living room, I have the chance to fully inspect the gravity of my living situation. I knew it would be messy, but I wasn't prepared for everything to be covered in white dust, even though it's wrapped in plastic.

The look on my face must be telling because Finlay tries to explain. "We used the vacuum while breaking up the tile, but the dust is so fine we can't get everything," he explains sympathetically. "But at least the plastic saves you from having to clean other surfaces."

All of the tile has been removed, exposing the concrete floor underneath. The living room carpet has been fully removed, and the furniture is still piled up in the corner.

"We'll be able to lay the flooring tomorrow," Adrian confirms.

"I thought you said you would be able to do it today?"

"I might have overshot just a little bit," Adrian says, gesturing with his fingers pinched together, "but I didn't think you'd want us here until eight o'clock at night, either."

"Not happening," Finlay pipes up. "I got a life, even if you don't," Finlay teases Adrian, which I find confusing. For someone his age and who looks like him, I would think his calendar is full. "No offense," he adds, looking at me.

I laugh, nodding my head.

"I'm gonna leave everything in the garage," Moe says as he steps into the hallway addressing Adrian, who looks to me for confirmation.

I just keep telling myself it will all be worth it once this mess is done, and I'll never be updating flooring again.

"And you wonder why I've never updated the flooring until now," I explain to Adrian as he chuckles softly. "My house looks like a fucking disaster."

Moe grabs the last of the tile, scooping it into the trash bin while Finlay cleans up the tools lying haphazardly on the floor. They both head into the garage and Adrian leans in close to my ear, the music now silent. "I've been thinking about you all day." He moves my hand to cup the growing bulge in his pants, and there's nothing I can do about the ache that pulses between my legs.

"You need me to go to the shop with you, boss?" Moe pokes his head through the garage door and Adrian moves away, my hand releasing his cock.

"No," Adrian says rather dismissively, causing Moe to look between us before he disappears.

Once he hears the garage door close, he turns to me and says, "Come with me?"

"Come with you to dump off my old carpet?" I laugh. "That sounds riveting."

"I'll make it worth your while," he says with raised eyebrows and lust filled eyes.

"I need a shower," I protest. "I feel like I have a layer of century old tile on my skin."

"You can take a shower at my place," Adrian counters, and I narrow my eyes at him.

"You have an answer for everything, don't you?"

"Am I taking you away from something else?" he asks hesitantly without mentioning my daughter, but I follow his gaze down the hall to where her room is.

"She has orchestra practice after school." Looking at my kitchen, I make a note to text her to eat at Sofia's tonight.

"Seeing as how my house is destroyed and the kitchen is useless…" I don't finish my sentence.

"Let's be honest, your kitchen was useless before," Adrian teases, tilting his head at me boyishly.

"I'll have you know that I have heated up many excellent take-out meals in that microwave." I point to the kitchen. "Not to mention all the pots of coffee I've brewed." I place my hands on my hips, daring him to contradict me.

Adrian's chest shakes while he laughs.

"You're making fun of me," I pout and stomp my foot.

"Are you coming? Or do I need to lift you over my shoulder again? Because you're running out of excuses, Lake," he says wickedly, causing my pulse to race.

Leaving him standing in the middle of my destroyed living room, I head back into my office and shut down my laptop. In my bedroom, I change into a new t-shirt and freshen up in my bathroom. Running a brush through my shoulder length hair, I part it to the side, letting the wavy strands sweep across my face. A thin layer of black eyeliner makes my blue eyes stand out against my dark hair. Dabbing a bit of perfume on my wrists and neck before leaving my room, I'm ready to leave.

Adrian waits in my living room with his phone to his ear. I watch as he runs a hand through his thick hair, removing the bandana that kept most of the dust from coating his dark locks. He smiles and switches from Romanian to English effortlessly, realizing he's speaking with his dad.

Drinking in the sight of him, dirty and sweaty from the day's work, he has never looked more mouthwatering. He turns, catching me raking my eyes over him and grins before pocketing his phone.

Fully out of my trance, I clutch my purse under my arm and follow him out to the garage where I lock up.

Parked on the curb is his work truck, my old carpeting rolled up and secured in the back. Hesitating, I think about Noelle and what she will think if she sees me being dropped off by Adrian. She knows who he is, but she doesn't know who he is to *me*. I will have to cross that bridge when it comes.

Sensing I might be apprehensive, he gives me a comforting smile and opens the door. Sliding onto the ripped vinyl seat, my thighs burn because the truck has been parked in the afternoon sun all day. Lifting my thighs off the seat, I try and yank my shorts down further to cover more skin when Adrian removes his shirt, spreading it over the seat next to him, giving me and any neighbor that happens to be peering out their window an eyeful of all those hard muscles. He motions for me to move over so I can sit without burning my legs. The gesture causes my stomach to tighten and my chest to expand.

After he hops in the driver's seat and cranks over the engine, loud music blares from the speakers and he reaches over to turn it down.

"You just wanted an opportunity to take your shirt off," I tease, and he laughs.

The old Chevy's middle console is pushed up, and I slide next to him using the middle seat belt to buckle in. He chuckles while pulling out of my neighborhood, and I turn the volume back up on the radio.

Sneaking looks at him while he drives I study his profile, the way he grips the steering wheel, and how his hair flutters with the a/c. Being near him, I can't help but want to touch him, to feel him touch me. By the time we hop on the loop 101 headed towards Tempe, his hand ghosts up my leg and casually rests on my thigh. I like the way he can't help but touch me when he's around me.

Cold air blasts through the vents cooling the cab of the truck, but it does nothing to cool my heated skin as his fingers skirt along the edge of my shorts. Closing my eyes, I let the feeling take over as *Bad Company* blares through the speakers.

Kicking off my flip flops, I prop a foot on the dash spreading my thighs, and Adrian shifts in his seat. It's so easy to forget about work when I'm sitting in Adrian's truck watching the mountains blur by and the sky turning different shades of pink and orange. It's like stepping into a different person's mind, one where I don't have to worry about deadlines and people's jobs.

Adrian leans forward grabbing a pair of sunglasses sitting on the dash and hands them to me. Slipping them on, I use the rearview mirror to check them out.

"I look like a state trooper," I laugh, and Adrian slides his eyes to me, smiling. I notice how much he likes it when I smile or laugh. His eyes light up and crinkle at the sides.

"You love it when I smile," I tease.

"No," he says, shaking his head. "I *like it* when you smile." He momentarily turns to me with a wicked glint in his eyes. "I *love it* when you come."

His words cause heat to flood to my core as his fingers once again trail against my skin and slip under my shorts. As the truck speeds down the freeway, I grip the vinyl seat while his fingers find the edge of my panties, slowly moving back and forth over my sensitive skin. Looking around at the cars speeding past us, I tense while staring at him in wonder.

Does he mean to make me come while driving eighty down the freeway? By the answering look in his eye and his fingers inching their way closer to my wet core, I believe he intends to do just that.

My eyes slide towards him as he stares straight ahead focused on the road. There's a tick in his jaw as I spread my legs further, giving him greater access, which causes him to swallow hard. It's the only indication of a reaction as his finger lazily moves through my slickness. How easily he renders me submissive, especially in a vehicle hurtling down the freeway, and I realize just how much I need this. My eyes flutter closed while his finger circles my already sensitive clit, and I suck in a breath, feeling the truck slow as traffic thickens.

Breathing heavy, thighs parted, I open my eyes to see the vehicles surrounding us as a moan escapes my mouth and my fingers grip the edge of the seat. He keeps me on edge, moving his finger in circles and then down my slit to slide in and out again.

Pressing my bare foot to the dash I arch my back, pushing against him and tip my head back against the headrest. I don't care about the cars next to us wondering what they see when their eyes slide in our direction. Pressing my face into his shoulder gives me an anchor as his finger pumps in and out of me. He removes my hand from his crotch that I didn't even know was there, making a *tsk* sound.

"You're going to cause an accident if you do that," he groans, shifting in his seat as the music blares through the cab.

As my moans grow more insistent, his finger moves faster over my clit, the build exquisite, and the ache intense. Lifting my hips to meet his fingers, I roll with the motion of the truck. I feel every crack and bump in the road. A whoosh of air escapes my lungs as my arms reach overhead, slamming my palms to the roof as he causes me to fall over the edge. With my mouth open, no sound comes out, and my chest expands, gasping for air. I roll to the side, Adrian's fingers still inside me, and sink my teeth into his arm to stifle the broken cry that races through me.

When I open my eyes, Adrian is staring back at me intensely. His heated gaze locks on me until he captures my mouth in a passionate kiss. Only when the car behind us honks does he let go, hitting the gas once again, propelling us through the light before turning down a side street.

"When did we exit the freeway?" I ask, finally noticing my surroundings as I try to adjust my panties that had been pushed aside.

"I had to exit early or I was going to get into a fucking accident watching you come." Adrian grips the steering wheel as he pulls into a parking lot, stopping in front of a large brick warehouse.

Without another word he exits the vehicle, leaving me inside to watch in confusion as he punches in a code, causing the bay door to open. Inside the large industrial space are rolls of carpeting and shelves stacked with boxes that I can only imagine are filled with tile. Adrian gets back into the truck, slamming the door as he pulls inside the darkened space.

As soon as he turns the ignition off, he pulls me into his lap facing him, cupping my breasts with his palms.

"You made me come in my pants, Lake," he groans into my mouth while kissing me, and it's then that I feel the wetness seep through his jeans, and it makes me roll my hips on him. Feeling his cock grow under me fuels this need I have to get closer to him, to show him just how good he makes me feel. "I haven't come in my pants since I was a fucking teenager," he rasps.

Grinding against him, I take his lower lip between my teeth before sipping my tongue inside. His hands move up my back, pressing me further into him. Before I can even protest, he dips his hand into my shirt, pulling my breast from my bra and clamping down greedily on my nipple.

Tipping my head back, I let out a loud moan and press my palm to the ceiling of the cab as my back hits the steering wheel, sounding off the horn.

My eyes snap open and I laugh while looking around, but there's no one here but us. He wastes no time tossing me onto all fours on the passenger seat while he yanks down my shorts. I wait impatiently as he undoes his jeans before he pulls me towards him, his hard cock sliding easily through my still-wet center. He fists his hard cock in his hand, lining it up to my entrance before slamming into me. Gripping my hips and holding me in place, he says hoarsely, "This is what you fucking do to me, Lake." He slams harder into me, and I'm lost in his desperate need for me.

Punishing thrusts rattle the cab of the truck, and my broken cries echo in the large empty space of the warehouse. When he leans forward and bites my neck, an orgasm rips through my veins threatening to burn me alive. His heart hammers against my back, and I feel his cock jerk inside of me while he grips my hips. While we both breathe heavily in cadence with one another, I turn around, collapsing against the bench seat while a hysterical laugh escapes my lips. Adrian's head tips back, laughing while tucking himself back into his jeans. I push the hair from my face and reach for my shorts that had been discarded on the floor of the truck.

"Still having fun?" he asks, still breathing heavy.

I nod my head. "Yes."

"Good." He grabs me by the back of the neck and pulls me to him for a kiss.

If I could bottle this moment I would, because never have I ever been this high off a person in my life.

20

I REMEMBER EVERYTHING

You Put a Spell On Me by Austin Giorgio

F licking through a few of his shirts, I see some button downs, but mostly t-shirts lining the small walk-in closet. Opting for a soft, weathered t-shirt, I pull it off its hanger and slip it over my head. It's just the right length to cover my ass.

Pulling the material up to my nose I inhale his scent, even though it's been washed. The whole closet smells like him, masculine and sweet like bourbon.

"You like?" Adrian says from behind me. He leans against the doorframe with his hair wet and water droplets running down his chest, disappearing below the towel wrapped at his waist.

"It smells like you," I admit reaching for him, but he grabs my wrist before it reaches his towel.

"Dinner's waiting," he says, pulling me with him out of the bedroom and into the living room.

The *Black Crowes* plays softly on Adrian's record player. The food smells amazing, and my stomach growls.

"I'll be right back. I need to change." He smiles while I pout, watching as he walks back down the hall and disappearing into his bedroom.

While I wait for him, I pour a glass of wine and hop up on the counter next to the stove where the food stays warm. Taking a sip of my wine, I realize Adrian has great taste. I pull the bottle towards me reading the label; a local Riesling made in Tucson. Looking at the glass I raise an eyebrow, not realizing they even had wineries in Tucson. Whatever Adrian made is covered, staying warm on the stove, and I can't help but take a peek. Looking around for utensils, I lean down and pull the drawer open between my legs, taking out a fork. Before I can even lift a piece of it to my mouth, Adrian pulls the fork from my hand and shakes his finger at me.

I jut out my bottom lip. There are so many things to pout about this evening – one, that I'm hungry, and two, Adrian now has a shirt on.

"You are very impatient tonight," he says, standing between my legs, his hair towel-dried but still inky black from the water.

"I'm hungry," I protest. "What is this?" I point to what looks like a tiny egg roll, but the wrap is thinner and has a layer of sauce on it.

"*Sarmale*," he says, with a thick Romanian accent.

I raise an eyebrow as he laughs.

"It's basically cabbage rolls," he explains.

"I don't eat meat."

"I know, that's why I only used tofu and vegetables."

"You remembered?" I ask while taking a bite, still a little bit shocked because the one and only time I mentioned that I don't eat meat was at my sister's rehearsal dinner.

"I remember everything."

As I reach for the fork, he pulls it away. "Very impatient," he says, shaking his head.

"Gimme," I say laughing, and he holds the fork between us, extending the food to my lips, intent on feeding me.

"You look good in my shirt," he says, eyes roaming over my body. I could blame the warmth in my belly on the wine, but I'd be lying.

Eyeing him speculatively, I can't help but wonder what in the hell he sees in me. I'm a forty-three-year-old woman with a teenage daughter and an attitude that I have no intention of changing, and yet here is this man who finds pleasure in giving me orgasms and feeding me.

While shaking my head, he asks, "What?"

"Where did you learn to cook?" I ask, taking a sip of my wine, my belly feeling nice and full.

"My mother," he explains, and I raise an eyebrow at him.

"How did I know you were a mama's boy?" I tease.

He smiles while taking the wine glass and setting it down on the counter next to me. Snaking my arms around his neck, he brings another forkful to my lips, and I eat it gleefully.

"I've never eaten a meal on someone's kitchen counter before, but I think I like it." I raise my eyebrows.

"Well, that's a shame, because it's the best way to have dinner."

I see Adrian in a different light. He's not just the young, cocky musician with the dirty mouth, but a businessman who is good with his hands – in more ways than one.

He takes a bite for himself. "Before I was big enough to help my dad, I spent a lot of time in the kitchen with my mom," he explains.

"Holding the apron strings," I finish, making him laugh.

"See," he says, pointing an accusatory fork at me, "You think you're making fun of me," his hands firmly grip my hips, "but I am very secure in my masculinity."

Closing the distance, I kiss him lightly. "I think it's very sweet."

"I was never interested in learning to cook," I say. "My sister was always in the kitchen with our mom."

"She makes very good brownies," Adrian admits, and it throws me off. My sister makes brownies for him.

"Does that bother you?" he asks, noticing my apprehension.

"No, it's just odd to think of you having a relationship with my sister." I pinch my brows together.

"You don't have a good relationship with her," he says, putting the top on the leftover *Sarmale*.

Moving my hands down his arms to circle his waist, I press my cheek to his chest.

"I have this very clear memory of being outside with my dad, handing him tools while he fixed my bicycle. I could see my mom and sister through the kitchen window. They were making brownies probably; I can't remember, but they were laughing, and my mom left a fingerprint of flour on the tip of Beth's nose." I press my head further into his chest. "God, I was so jealous of that fingerprint."

Adrian touches the back of my head, smoothing down my hair. I pull away, feeling embarrassed about bringing up that memory, but I feel it's necessary for him to understand the history between Beth and me.

"Laura was always the one helping my dad in the shop," Adrian says, breaking the silence. "She's the oldest, and I was always jealous when my dad would take her instead of me. He'd kneel down to my height and tell me when I got this tall," Adrian motions to the height of the counter, "I could go with him."

He shakes his head, smiling at the memory.

"You like working with him," I say.

"He taught me everything I know," Adrian says, and I can see the pride in his eyes at the thought of his dad. "He left everything he knew back in Romania and came to America with hardly anything," Adrian explains. "But he started this business when my mom was pregnant with Laura because he wanted to give us a good life and a good future."

"I admire that so much," I say, pressing a palm to his face.

"Now Laura works in the office for my dad, and I'm the one that gets to go out on jobs with him, but he doesn't do a lot of the installing now that he's older." Adrian settles back between my legs after rinsing out the utensils in the sink next to me.

"So your sister could have seen us in the warehouse?" I smack him, embarrassed.

Adrian chuckles. "I knew she wasn't going to be there."

"You planned that?" I ask, curious.

"I know better than to plan anything around you."

"And why is that?"

"Because you continue to surprise the shit out of me," he says, grinning.

I've surprised myself lately; doing things I never thought I would do. My cheeks get hot at just the thought.

"I haven't always been…" I search for the right words and decide to switch gears. "I've worked for everything I have." There's this need inside of me to explain things to Adrian, to gain his approval somehow, because I don't want him to think I'm a spoiled brat who doesn't appreciate what she has.

"I know I can come across as abrasive sometimes, but it's only because…" I'm at a loss for words because I don't think there is an explanation good enough.

"You owe me no explanation, Lake." He tilts his head, the dim lights in the kitchen casting shadows across his face, but I can see his eyes, the soft browns that have only ever looked at me with mischief and lust. Right now they are looking right down into me, extracting truths I never thought I would confess to him. The fact that he doesn't think I need to explain anything to him is exactly the reason I should.

"I'm not used to things being like…" I pause, running my hand up his arm nervously and trying to think of the right words. "This."

Adrian presses his forehead to mine and breathes in heavily while his hands slip into my hair. "That is a goddamned shame."

Closing my eyes, I reach forward and press my lips to his. He tastes like tofu and wine.

"Thank you," I say, opening my eyes.

"For what?" he smiles.

"For feeding me and for listening." I stroke the stubble along his jaw; the fine hairs feel like a soft blanket against the pads of my fingers.

"You are very welcome." He holds my face while looking right into my eyes, and I feel the pull to him so clearly. It swirls like a monsoon between us, and goosebumps line my arms.

Wrapping my legs around his waist, I hold him close to me. I've never *needed* a man to make me feel safe or make me feel good about myself, but there's something so comforting in knowing that someone does.

Kissing him slowly, I relish in the soft, lush feel of his lips, and his arms wrapped around me.

I had him in his truck on the way over here, and again in the shower when we were supposed to be getting cleaned up. He's like a drug I keep needing another hit of, and no matter how much I have, I can't seem to get enough.

I know it's not the wine because I've barely even had a glass, but my cheeks feel flushed and my belly is warm. As my hands slip into his thick hair, I pull away enough to say, "When will I ever get enough of you?" I'm not sure if I meant to vocalize it or not, but it sits between us, a question that doesn't need an answer, but he does anyway

"I hope never," he says recklessly.

ADRIAN'S TRUCK idles in front of my house. The lights are on, and Noelle is home. Even if she hadn't texted me earlier to say she made it home okay, I would still be able to feel her presence. It's awkward to be dropped off at my house by – I don't even know what to call him. Labels are not something I prescribe to.

Even though the air blasts out of the vents, the cab of the truck feels hot as if it somehow became smaller. It's different than it was earlier while his hand was in my shorts as the truck hurdled down the freeway towards his shop. Being in front of my house is sobering, as if reality is pressing down on me. My earlier fears are coming back, knowing that she would be home and possibly see Adrian drop me off.

Things between us have been awkward at best since that night I came home late, looking like I'd been thoroughly fucked by the man staring at me right now. Noelle is not naïve and we have an open relationship, but it's because I care so much about what she thinks of me that gives me pause about this situation. The guilt I harbor is like a dark cloud over me.

His brown eyes try their hardest to look past the wall I erected the minute we entered my neighborhood and fortified as soon as we stopped in front of my house. Ever observant, I know he can feel the shift in me because I can see it in his eyes as he drapes his arm over the seat, shifting his body towards me.

"You haven't told her about us."

"There's no reason to," I explain, bringing up our arrangement that somehow has started to break loose from the confines I put us in.

His jaw ticks as he stares me down and I can tell he doesn't like it, but he has no argument for it.

Shifting uncomfortably, the back of my thighs sticks to the vinyl seat because there's no t-shirt this time to protect them. "I don't bring men home to meet my daughter, so don't think you're being singled out for any reason," I say, reaching for the door handle but he stops me.

His face is etched with concern. "I haven't asked you about Noelle's dad because it's none of my business. I just figured you would tell me when you were ready." The mention of Steven raises the hairs on the back of my neck.

My silence is his answer. I'm not giving in easily, and he knows it.

"I'm asking you now." His eyes pierce into me. Even in the darkened cab I can feel them on me, but I stay silent.

"You don't want that part of me," I warn him.

Everything inside of me is reaching for that door, to escape to the comfort of my closet where I can sink between the racks of clothes and hide from the world. It's been my safe space ever since Noelle was a toddler. Mothers don't cry in front of their daughters; we do it in private, in the middle of the night, while our kids are fast asleep, safe in their beds across the hall.

"I haven't asked you for anything," he says frustrated, and my eyes snap up to meet his.

"Haven't you?" I ask, facing him. He looks at me confused, tilting his head so that his brown locks fall into his face.

"You've asked for my time," I explain, pinching my brows together. "Time that belongs to my daughter." I gesture towards the house. "Every moment I spend with you is a moment that I don't with her. You might think that's dramatic, but you don't have a kid," I say.

He opens his mouth, but I cut him off. "Before you get offended, just know that being an uncle doesn't even come close to what it means to be a father."

"Lake," he says my name softly, aware of his error too late. When he moves his hand to touch mine, I pull it away because I can't bear to have his hands on me.

"Being a father is watching your daughter being born with awe in your eyes because nothing will ever compare to it, and then holding her in your arms with nothing but pure, untainted love."

Adrian's face blurs as my eyes fill with tears.

"It is *not* refusing to sign her birth certificate because you accuse the woman who *just gave birth* of cheating on you. It is *not* making the mother of your child feel anything less than a fucking goddess for literally giving you a life to hold in your hands. And you don't walk away when your daughter is two years old, and then blame everyone else but yourself."

Memories of Steven Whitaker, Noelle's father – the man I chose to have a baby with, altering Noelle's life in so many negative ways – come flooding to the surface with the force of a train. I'm angry and sad, and the small cab of Adrian's truck is not equipped to handle twenty years of anger and regret. Maybe I'm overreacting, but my emotions are at war with what I know is rational.

"You want to know about Noelle's father?" I ask, rhetorically. "Here's your answer. He's gone, so you have no reason to be curious, or jealous, or even worry about how to fucking compete with him."

Maybe my anger is wrongly directed at Adrian, but he's the only target within reach.

"That's not why I asked." He runs a hand through his hair. "Jesus, Lake. I just…" he hesitates, frustration coming off him in waves. "I just wanted to know where my place was."

He reaches for me, and I bat him away. "Your place?" I rear back.

He runs a hand through his hair. "That was the wrong choice of words," he admits.

Before I slam the door to his truck, I hear one last whispered plea. I'm not being fair, but I slam it anyway and don't look back. Before I open the front door, I wipe away the tears and suck in a breath, trying to settle my nerves. Inside the house, a demanding and haunting melody comes from Noelle's room, and it sets me on high alert. Her violin has always been an extension of her emotions.

Pressing my back to the door, I reach behind and flip the lock, hearing Adrian's truck finally change gears and drive away.

Everything has an expiration.

Even something good.

I forgot how destroyed my house is now until I step further in and see the exposed concrete where my tile used to be. All my furniture is piled up at one end of the living room, and everything is covered in plastic. Flicking the light on, I stand in the middle of the chaos, feeling as though I am right at home with the raging emotions swirling around in my body at the moment. Taking a deep breath, I notice Noelle step out from the hallway.

Her long hair falls in waves around her shoulders and her blue eyes are red rimmed as if she's been crying. Once she steps forward, she doesn't stop until she's in my arms, her shoulders shaking, and I forget everything that just happened.

"What's wrong?" I ask, smoothing her hair and pulling her face away from my chest so I can look at her, worried she might be hurt or damaged.

She wipes the tears from her eyes and I can feel a shift in her, something telling me it's permanent. When she looks up at me through tear-stained lashes, I know.

"I didn't go to Sofia's after practice," she admits.

My hands cup her shoulders, holding her out in front of me as she makes her confession. Soothingly, I tuck her hair behind her ear.

"It wasn't planned," she says, shaking her head. "It just happened," she shrugs. "I did everything you told me to do, make sure it was with someone I trusted, use protection…" her words die on her lips, and she wets them with her tongue. "I just didn't think I would feel this way after." A tear falls down her cheek and I capture it with my finger.

Taking a deep breath and hugging her to my side, I walk her into the kitchen. "I'd say this calls for some ice cream," I state, forgetting momentarily that everything is wrapped in plastic. "Shit," I say and both Noelle and I laugh.

"You know what?" I say, walking over to the refrigerator. "Fuck it." I rip into the plastic.

"I THINK this is the best ice cream I've ever had," Noelle says, digging into the Chunky Monkey and plopping a heaping spoonful in her mouth.

"Ice cream tastes better after a heartbreak," I tell her.

Noelle sighs. "I lost my virginity, I didn't get my heart broken," she says plainly, pushing the knife into my heart just a little bit further.

I know I'm supposed to be the cool single mom whose daughter is her best friend who can tell her anything – and I may very well be those things – but it doesn't make it sting any less to know that your daughter is growing and changing in ways that make her more adult than kid. I'm reluctant to give up those parts that make her a kid, because even though she will be an adult soon, she will forever be *my* kid.

"Same thing," I say, licking my spoon. "You're saying goodbye to something that is never coming back. And before you tell me it's sexist and outdated, it's the same for boys, only they've been taught their whole lives to celebrate it instead of mourning it." I touch her nose with the tip of my spoon, leaving a mark of ice cream, and I can't help but think about the confession I made to Adrian about being jealous of the flour marks I'd witnessed my own mom give Beth. "It's okay to mourn it."

We sit in silence for a few moments, backs pressed against the plastic covered refrigerator eating ice cream.

"You should have warned me," Noelle says, and I turn towards her, titling my head in question. "That our house looked like a scene from *Independence Day*," she smirks at me.

"I make you watch too many nineties' movies." I turn back to the ice cream, feeling full but unable to stop myself.

Noelle laughs. "Yes, you do." She takes the container from me and scrapes the sides.

"So, you and Gray?" I ask about her boyfriend, hesitantly. "Are you both good?" I didn't ask before because I didn't want to press her.

Noelle sighs, setting the spoon back into the near empty container. "Yeah."

"I'm sensing a 'but' in there somewhere."

"He's nice," she says, turning to me, "but," she pauses, choosing her words carefully. "He was *too* nice. Is that weird?" she asks.

"No," I laugh softly, leaning my head back against the refrigerator, but inside there's a dread that she inherited too much of me. "It's not weird at all."

"He didn't push me at all," she explains. "It was my idea, and I should be glad that he was," she pauses, "gentle," she all but cringes, "I don't know." She leaves her thoughts hanging in the air.

"It was your first time. It's not supposed to be good," I explain to her, licking my spoon and dropping it in the container along with hers.

"That's not what I mean," she says, tipping her head back and staring up at the ceiling. "I wanted to feel *more*."

Setting the container of ice cream to the side, I swivel around, crossing my legs in front of her. I shouldn't expect anything less from my daughter who I underestimated in the most egregious way when she told me she lost her virginity.

"It's okay to want something more," I whisper, placing my hands on her knees.

"I saw who dropped you off." She switches gears.

My mouth forms an O and I relax my back, letting it curve. "I thought you didn't want to know."

"Kinda hard not to now." She blinks her blue eyes at me. "Do Aunt Beth and Laura know?" she asks.

"No," I sigh, bringing my knees up and resting my chin against my forearms. Unsure of how to explain what Adrian and I are to each other, I use a cop-out explanation. "It's just not a good idea. I don't want to mess things up for her."

"That's not fair to you," Noelle replies and furrows her brows.

"It's complicated," I say with a sigh.

She looks down at her hands fidgeting in her lap and then looks back up at me. "Do you want to be with him?" She tilts her head to the side in a very adolescent way.

I want to say no. It's on the tip of my tongue, but I've never lied to Noelle and I'm not about to start now.

"Yes." The word exhales from my mouth as if expelling it from my lungs will free me of him, but it doesn't.

"Then don't use me or Aunt Beth as an excuse to push him away."

I flick my eyes back to her, struck by her words. "You're not an excuse, you're a reason, there's a difference," I say, reaching towards her to twirl a piece of hair between my fingers.

"You were crying when you came home," she states, and sometimes I hate how observant she is.

"Like I said, it's complicated." I let go of her hair.

"Can I say something that you're not going to like?" Noelle asks innocently.

"I'm not sure what could top you telling me you had sex, but go for it," I grumble.

"I think you use me as an excuse not to get close to anyone." I start to protest but she stops me. "But the real excuse is Steven." She's never called him Dad, because he never was one to her.

"Noelle," I start to explain, but she doesn't let me finish.

"You can say I'm naïve because I've never been in love, but I do know that being scared holds you back. If I had let my stage fright stop me from performing, then I would have never known how alive I felt doing it." She opens her bright blue eyes, more full of wisdom than I give her credit for in her seventeen years, and I don't feel so frightened of letting her go, because like Georgie said, she is magnificent.

"I don't even know what this is yet," I admit.

The only thing I am certain of is how being around him fills this void in me that nothing ever has. But I also knew the minute I met him I would get my heart broken, no matter what. The stakes are high, and I'm too old to play games with *my* heart – or my daughters.

"Then find out," she says. "I trust you."

Pulling her into a hug, I feel this immense privilege to have been the one to raise her, because I know she is who she is because of me, and me alone. Maybe she trusts me, but I'm not sure I have the same faith. I've messed up before, I could do it again.

When she breaks our hug, she looks at me with a serious expression, and says, "I'm going to break up with Grayson."

21

TURN IT UP

Kashmir by Samvel Ayrapetyan

"Mom!" I hear Noelle's voice through the fog of sleep. "Get up," she hisses, and that's when I hear the knocking on the front door.

"Shit," I curse and fling myself out of bed, hurrying into my closet to throw on some clothes.

Racing down the hallway past Noelle, I slide into home plate right in front of the front door. On the other side stands Adrian, who I wasn't sure would show up today to finish my flooring, but I should have known better than to underestimate his professionalism.

Running my fingers through my hair before opening the door, he stands, feet apart, bandana pulling his dark hair back, a few pieces sticking out over his ears, brown eyes that I have been accustomed to staring at me with such intensity that my stomach drops, tan carpenter boots, and jeans so weighted down with his utility belt that it makes them sit low on his hips. He's too fucking pretty not to stare at, and I'm a stupid woman if I ever thought I could kick him out of my bed, but I can't think for the life of me what he sees in the mess of a woman standing in front of him.

Stepping aside without a word, I let him through. Flying past him is a toddler with blonde hair pulled into pigtails on either side of her head, and my eyes fly over to Adrian who is setting his equipment down on my kitchen island. Finlay follows quickly behind and scoops her up in his arms while she dissolves into giggles as he carries her by me. I think my stomach just leaped into my chest and is now slowly making its way back into place.

"Sorry about that." He holds her upside down as she swats at his stomach. "Adrian said it would be okay if I brought her with me." He looks between Adrian and me, sensing some tension. "Emma's coming to take her to daycare in a few," Finlay confirms.

"Oh," is all I can say while I try to wipe the surprise off my face. I never pictured Finlay with a daughter. He seems so young, but then again, I was twenty-six when I had Noelle. Shaking my head to clear the fog, I answer, "Yeah, that's fine."

"Ready for some flooring today, Lake?" Adrian's question interrupts while Finlay wrangles his daughter out the door. The way he says my name, deep and low, stirs things inside of me.

I can't speak when he's staring at me that way. Crossing my arms across my chest, I ask him, "Why are you looking at me like that?"

Adrian readjusts the bandana on his head and runs his hand over the hairs on his chin.

"Because you're so fucking beautiful," he says.

Not expecting that, I can't help but be flustered. Staring down at my bare feet, I remember I had just rolled out of bed, threw on an old t-shirt and a pair of shorts without so much as running a brush through my hair. I have no makeup on, and I can't remember if I brushed my teeth.

"I'm a mess," I admit exasperatedly, trying to settle down the rogue curls in my hair.

He laughs, looking at me as if I said something funny and it irritates me.

"What is so fucking funny?" I hiss.

Adrian settles down, rubbing his chin while I narrow my eyes at him.

He dips his head so he can look me in the eye while he smiles. "Just the way I like it."

The distance between us slowly retreats, and it's impossible not to melt under that smile.

Distracting me, Moe loudly carries in large boxes of flooring and drops them in the center of the room, oblivious to the staring contest going on between Adrian and me.

"That better be the right flooring," I say, pointing at the boxes, "Because I'm not living like this for another day."

Adrian chuckles, his smile spreading across his face and into his eyes. He makes his way over to the boxes, noticing the torn plastic on the refrigerator and tilts his head in question at me.

"I wanted some fucking ice cream. Is that a crime?" I ask, placing my hands on my hips, challenging him to give me shit about it.

"Finlay," he bellows, and Finlay pokes his head out of the garage door. "Grab some more plastic from the truck," he orders.

Moments later, Finlay runs into the house, out of breath, his blonde hair flopping over his eyes as he carries in a tube of plastic. While he gets to work on re-covering the refrigerator, Moe continues to carry in boxes of flooring.

Adrian takes a box cutter from his tool belt and slices one open, holding the flap so I can see inside to the beautiful gray wood flooring. I run my hand over the wood planks. Looking around the empty space, I can finally picture it in my home. Maybe it doesn't have memories of Noelle rolling skating over it, or the time she decided it would make a great canvas for her paints, but sometimes it's good to have a fresh start.

"I told you I'm a professional," Adrian says from behind me, his breath hitting the back of my neck.

Turning to look at him, there's an understanding in his eyes that I don't deserve.

"I didn't know if you were going to come back," I admit. "The rooms aren't ready." I point down the hall to the bedrooms.

Adrian steps forward, closing the distance between us. He's hesitant to touch me, aware that we are in my home with my daughter in the next room.

"I'm not going anywhere," he says with a deep voice that rattles my bones – whether I like it or not.

When I make my way down the hall, Noelle is furiously trying to pick up all of her things from the floor. My room is mostly clean, but Noelle's usually looks like a hurricane hit it. She piles all of her clothes into a basket and sets it on her bed.

Stopping to assess the rest of the stuff in her room, she asks, "What should I do with my recording equipment?"

Looking around for a place to put them I'm at a loss, because all of the furniture will be moved to pull up carpeting, and the rest of the tile has to be broken up.

"You can put it in the bathroom. We're not touching that space right now," Adrian says from behind me.

She looks between Adrian and I as we both peer into her room. "Cool," Noelle says, starting to pack everything up.

"Is that a MIDI keyboard?" Adrian asks, but then he looks at me with questioning eyes as if he's asking for permission to speak with her.

"Noelle composes her own music," I say, with a prideful smile on my face.

"You're Laura's brother," she says. "I remember you from the wedding. You're pretty good on the guitar."

Adrian laughs, shifting his weight. "Yeah, I play alright."

"I like string instruments because there's so much range," she explains, picking up her violin. "You can basically bend them to do whatever you want." She plucks at the strings. It's interesting to see Adrian interact with her, being a musician himself. My family has been to many recitals and concerts for school, but they don't have the same appreciation for it.

Moe cranks up his portable radio, blaring *Led Zeppelin*, and Adrian shakes his head at the intrusion. At least it's not ear-splitting level, but Adrian sticks his head down the hallway telling him to shut it down.

The music abruptly cuts off, but Noelle picks up where the song leaves off, demonstrating the range with her bow, the unmistakable chords of the last verse of the song.

"Did you just play *Kashmir* by ear?" Adrian asks, astonished.

"To be fair, I've heard it once before," she says. "My mom likes to subject me to *her* classics on occasion in the car," Noelle laughs.

"Hmm." Adrian pokes his head around the corner and yells down the hall to Moe. "Turn that back up." Moe does as he's told, but now the song has changed to *Pink Floyd, Wish You Were Here*.

Noelle holds the violin under her chin, her ear trained in the direction of Moe's boom box. Her fingers twitch as if she's memorizing the placement of her fingers against the strings, and as soon as Adrian tells Moe to cut the volume Noelle slides the bow across the violin, playing the song as if she's practiced for hours.

Adrian laughs as Noelle confirms the first time wasn't a fluke.

"Jesus." He brings his hand to cover his mouth and then rubs at his chin.

Noelle places her violin back in its case, tilting her head at Adrian innocently before starting to move her equipment to the bathroom.

"Do you have any idea how extraordinary that is," Adrian begins, "to play a song from memory after only hearing it once?"

"I do."

The minute she picked up a violin for the first time I knew she was special.

"I've been playing for a long time, and even I have to practice for hours to learn the songs we cover," Adrian admits, following me into the living room. "There're only a handful of musicians who can do that, and Paul McCartney is fucking one of them." He continues talking, gesturing with his hands excitedly.

Laughing, I place my hand on his arm. "Are you fangirling over my daughter?" I tease him.

"Yes," he says. "Yes, I fucking am," he states plainly.

Noelle bounds down the hallway, her backpack hoisted over her shoulder. "I'm gonna be late," she says, kissing me on the cheek before she stops to look between Adrian and me. "We should play together sometime. I might be able to show you a few tricks." She smiles and runs out the door.

Adrian shakes his head, laughing as she leaves. My head and my heart are conflicting with each other; I don't know how to feel about the exchange. I can't help but look at Adrian and see my confession from last night in his eyes, but he doesn't look at me with anything other than respect.

Finlay starts the vacuum, the loud noise jarring me from my thoughts. I turn back to Adrian. "I'm sorry," I confess, thinking about my behavior last night, "for overreacting. It's just been me and Noelle all these years, and I've never…" I start to say.

"You don't ever have to be sorry," Adrian says, cutting me off, his soft brown eyes always able to look right into me and see things that I can't hide. "Not for that, not to me, and not ever."

I furrow my brows at him. "You're way too nice to me."

He shifts his weight. "You frustrate the fuck out of me sometimes, how's that?" he jests, lightening the moment and causing me to laugh.

Moe turns the music back on, and Adrian pinches his forehead in frustration. "Moe, what did I just say?"

"It's fine, I moved all my meetings today," I explain. "Since my office is going to be torn up, I took the day off." Taking a day off is something I haven't done in a really long time. Even Miles threatened to come over and check on me.

"Makes me wish I didn't have to work," Adrian admits and lifts his eyebrows.

Narrowing my eyes at him, I playfully instruct, "Just finish my fucking flooring."

He gives me a salute with a sexy smile before turning to Moe. "Turn it up!" he yells and Moe smiles, cranking up the volume and bringing my home back to life.

Heat Waves by Glass Animals

"When you asked if I wanted enjoy the day in the water, I thought you were talking about a pool party at your apartment complex or the lazy river at a resort, not a fucking river," I say, staring at the long line of people waiting to get on the bus to take us to the top of the Salt River.

The line consists of bikini-clad girls twenty years younger than me, and boys with coolers modified to hold waterproof portable radios, board shorts, and more six packs than I can handle.

"Rivers have diseases," I continue to complain as the line starts to move up. "And fish!" The revelation shocks me even if it was my own.

In my mind, I mentally formulate a plan of how to keep my feet from touching the water.

"There are rapids in this river," I remind him. "You better have a rope or something to tie us together because if we get separated…"

Adrian pulls me into him. "Shut the fuck up, Lake," he murmurs into my mouth before kissing me.

I pull away, looking shocked. "Did you just tell me to shut the fuck up?"

"Yes, I fucking did," he says, capturing my mouth again, making my body go limp.

"You're lucky you're a good kisser." I push my palm to his chest and gather his shirt into my fist.

"Get a room!" the kid behind us yells, and I notice the line has started boarding the bus.

"Get a better fucking attitude," I say while Adrian picks me up, my feet dangling off the hot pavement, and sets me down on the first step of the bus.

"You fucking scare me sometimes," Adrian says as we find an empty seat, thankful the bus has air conditioning. "I never know if I'm going to have to get into a fight with someone when I'm with you."

Peering around him, I give that kid behind us a dirty look while assessing him. "You can take him. He's like, what," I peer a little closer, "A hundred pounds soaking wet?" I smirk.

Adrian laughs, swinging his arm around my shoulders. "The heat makes you ornery," he says. "Sometimes you're like a bull in a China shop."

"Well, I've never been known to be subtle," I say, digging through my beach bag for some lotion.

Handing it to Adrian, I ask, "Will you put some on my back?" while pulling my shirt over my head, revealing the swimsuit I agonized over putting on this morning. In my own backyard I'd wear a bikini because no one's looking at me, but then the one piece made me look like I was an Olympic swim coach. I settled for a tankini that Noelle had me buy on one of our vacations last year. It's black because I didn't know I'd be sweltering in the hot sun all day traveling down the Salt River in a tube.

Adrian's hands spread lotion over my back while I smooth some over my arms. He massages the lotion into my shoulders, and I begin to relax.

"I promise you will have a good time," Adrian whispers as he presses a kiss to my neck.

Turning around I search his face, seeing the little flecks of green in his eyes, his long black lashes, and dimples on his cheeks as he smiles back at me.

"Should I be worried?" he asks.

"No." I shake my head and pull him in for a kiss.

As I do, there's a commotion on the bus as someone yells, party!

Laughing against his lips, I notice someone sits down next to us, pushing Adrian further into me. I'm about to curse whoever it is out, but when I turn around, I see its Finlay with his daughter on his lap; blonde hair pulled into her signature pigtails, chubby legs poking out from under a sundress, with flip flops dangling off her feet. Adrian reaches over and tickles Layla's ribs which she protests – loudly.

Across the aisle, his girlfriend, who I didn't get a chance to meet last week, takes a seat, leaning over to adjust the little girl's sundress. "Finlay, leave them alone," she chastises.

I look at Adrian as he shrugs. "Figured we'd make a day of it," he says.

"Corvin," Finlay greets, smacking his shoulder. "I haven't been tubing in years."

Peering around Adrian, I look at Finlay.

"You met Layla," Finlay gestures to his daughter who turns up her nose at me. "She's in a mood today," he apologizes.

"Something the two of you have in common," Adrian teases.

"This is Emma." Finlay motions to his girlfriend across the aisle, who has blonde hair just like Layla's, tied up in a messy bun.

"Nice to meet you," Emma smiles brightly. "I hope we're not intruding," she says sweetly.

"Not at all."

The bus lurches forward, jarring me further into Adrian as Finlay takes Layla across the aisle to sit next to Emma. We climb further into the White Mountains and the scenery is breathtaking, but the bus ride is bumpy.

"This bus smells," I can't help but complain.

Adrian chuckles. "Layla complains less than you." He points to Finlay's lap where Layla is draped half on Finlay and half on Emma, her eyes softly closed.

"That's because she's asleep." I shake my head at him.

It takes about twenty minutes to get to the top. Adrian takes my hand and leads me off the bus where we grab our tubes and carry them to the riverbank. Finlay secures a life jacket on Layla and then ties our tubes together. I'm glad I wore water shoes because I'm certain I would have lost a flip flop in the rocky banks with the river flowing steadily.

Adrian places the cooler and our dry bags in the extra tube.

"How long does it take to get back to the bottom?" I ask as Adrian pushes my sunglasses further up my nose.

"Just shut up and have fun." He kisses my nose and I smack him.

Emma places a squirming Layla in her lap as we both get in our tubes while Adrian and Finlay walk us into the water. I have to raise my butt in the shallow river until we get a little further out, and even then, it's not much deeper but it's enough to make us float. Once the slow current takes over, Adrian and Finlay jump into their tubes, letting the water guide us.

The sun beats down from a cloudless sky and I'm glad I put on sunscreen or I'd be a tomato by the time we get to the bottom. Music blares in the distance and combines with the sound of rushing water as we pass under a bridge. On either side are trucks lined up, people fishing, and little kids playing in the water.

The terrain on either side of the river is beautiful. The river is nestled in a canyon of varying colors of browns and reds. The terracotta colors are muted from little rain this summer, but sparse green bushes and large, century-old Saguaro's stand tall, dotting the mountains. The current is slow and lazy as I dangle my feet in the water, forgetting all about the possibility of the fish. It's impossibly cold but feels so good on my heated skin.

Adrian's fingers draw patterns on my leg and I close my eyes, tipping my head back. Finlay and Emma chat nearby, pointing out pieces of the landscape to Layla who sucks on a Capri Sun. Turning my head to look at Adrian, I see his shirt is off, and I admire his tanned, smooth skin, and muscular arms draping over the tube, so relaxed.

He shouldn't be able to see my eyes trained on him behind my sunglasses, but he senses me. "What are you thinking about?" he asks, tipping his head towards me.

Behind his dark sunglasses, I know his eyes are trained on me.

"I wasn't thinking about anything," I say, which isn't the whole truth. It's as if everything in the world has faded to the background, and all that's left is the cool water, the sun, and him.

He slides his glasses down his nose to look at me. "You're beautiful when you get all worked up," Adrian says, "but you're fucking gorgeous when you're relaxed." He brushes his fingers over my sun-kissed arm, and I dare in the heat to get goosebumps.

"Thanks to you." I drop my leg over his lap.

"As much as I would like to be the cause of it, no, baby, that's all you." He pushes the sunglasses back up his nose, covering his eyes, and tips his head back to the sun.

The use of the word *baby* settles over me, and I decide I like it as little butterflies flutter around inside my stomach. Adrian has me feeling like a high school girl with her first crush, and that's not a bad feeling to have.

Up ahead, clusters of tubes start to move closer together as the rapids pick up and the canyon narrows.

"So how long have you and Finlay been together?" I ask Emma, making conversation.

"We've known each other since high school. Dated off and on, and then got pregnant with Layla." She looks down at Layla, adjusting her hat.

"She's very cute." I peek under the hat and Layla narrows her eyes at me. "Kids don't like me," I say.

"She's crabby because she got woken up from her nap early and then fell asleep on the bus," Emma sighs.

After a moment, Emma turns to me while Adrian and Finlay are paddling us away from some overhanging trees. "I've known Adrian since high school and he's always been annoyingly happy, but with you, he seems," she pauses, and I'm not sure how I'll feel about what she says next. Looking back at Adrian and Finlay who stand nearby in the water while holding the rope to the tubes, she finishes. "Satisfied."

Nodding, I think I can accept that assessment. Both Emma and Finlay are good friends to him, but I can tell they aren't really sure of me, and to be honest, I'm not really sure of me. Finlay jumps back in the tube and Adrian follows. Layla reaches for Finlay and he grabs her under her chubby arms, pulling her into his lap.

"But just for the record," Emma adds, grabbing my attention and looking between Adrian and me. "The two of you would make beautiful babies." She smiles and raises her eyebrows.

I choke on my water, trying hard to catch my breath and feeling the water burn in my nose. Adrian laughs as if it's some kind of inside joke while trying to pat me on the back. "Have I missed something?" he asks while laughing.

"That's not even remotely funny, Adrian," I snipe, wiping my mouth with the back of my hand.

AFTER ABOUT AN HOUR traveling down the river, the scenery changes from canyons to rolling hills, and finally to flat, rocky shores. The mountains are always present, looming in the distance.

"I've seen more boobs today than I have in my lifetime, and that's counting my own," I say, flicking water at Adrian's bare chest to make sure he's awake.

"I'm not complaining," Finlay says.

"Don't be a pig," Emma chastises.

"I still can't believe you've never been," Adrian says, turning his attention to me.

"I was preoccupied by other things," I say, grabbing a branch as we pass under a few mesquite trees that stretch over the river like giant tunnels. Our tubes temporarily stop, but as soon as I let go of the branch, the current takes us again. "I worked through school, and then I had Noelle..." I trail off.

Adrian grabs onto a bigger branch and pushes us off, angling the tubes toward the middle of the river that opens wider in this section, and I can tell the water is deep.

"I wish I would have known you back then," he says.

"I was much nicer, so you probably wouldn't have liked me," I tease, but Adrian looks at me solemnly as if he can see right through my tough exterior to all the reasons why I'm jaded. The truth is, Adrian deserves the younger me, the girl with an open heart, but that's not who I am anymore.

"I like you just the way you are."

I lean towards him, pulling myself onto his lap.

"In your bed?" I whisper, kissing his cheek. "Against the door?" I ask, capturing his mouth. "In the cab of your truck?" I tease against his lips.

Adrian pauses but then cups the back of my head, pulling me further into him, kissing me deep and slow.

"I think you need to cool off," he says, and before I can protest, he flips the tube, dropping us both into the water.

"Adrian!" I yell grabbing onto the side of the tube, but Adrian pulls me to him and kisses me, muffling my protests.

The water is deep and I can't feel the bottom, but he holds me up, one arm around me and the other secured around the rope that's tied to the tubes.

We barely move in this stagnant, deep water, and Adrian kicks his feet to push us further down the river.

Dunking my head back into the water, I get over the shock of the cold. "This feels so good," I say, hooking my arms around his neck.

"Me or the water? Adrian asks.

"Both," I answer.

"You're not worried about fish nibbling your toes anymore?" Adrian reminds me.

"Shut up," I say and kiss him while running my fingers through his wet hair.

Layla giggles as Finlay dips her feet in the cool water but he hands her back to Emma so he can roll off the tube and into the water. When he reaches up to grab hold of Layla, she protests.

"I won't let go," he tells her, and finally Layla kicks away from Emma and into Finlay's arms. I made a lot of assumptions about Finlay without even knowing him, and now I see him in a different light. Sliding my eyes back to Adrian, I tilt my head, assessing him, knowing I made the worst kind of assumptions about him too.

The day seems long but I've stopped counting the hours. I feel lighter, and not just because Adrian is holding me up in the water.

"Where did you come from?" I whisper, watching the water drip from his hair and down his face, feeling as if I'm drunk but I've only been drinking water.

"I've always been here," he says against my lips. Safely behind the tubes, hidden away from Emma and Finlay, I tip my head back into the water while holding onto Adrian's neck as an anchor knowing that he won't let go, just like Finlay promised Layla, making her feel safe to take that risk and jump into the water. It's enough to create a lump in my throat, and I close my eyes, not just to block out the sun but to block out everything from coming to the surface.

The river seems to go on forever, but Adrian says we're almost to the end. Safely back in the tubes, I watch as water droplets on my legs are burned away by the sun.

"Look," Adrian says, rousing me from a groggy state, and I follow the direction he's pointing to the riverbed some distance ahead. Sitting up in my tube, I shield my eyes further from the sun, staring in awe at the horses bending their heads to take a drink of the cool water.

"Oh my God," I whisper as if my voice would scare them away.

"Look, Layla," I hear Emma say.

"Horsies!" Layla's high pitch squeal mirrors the feeling inside of me.

"They're so fucking beautiful," I say, and Adrian laughs at my choice of words, but I can't think of any other way to describe them.

We float closer, entering the bottleneck of other tubes filled with people stopping to look at them. The horses paw at the rocks, their necks stretching down, touching their mouths to the cool water as if they are oblivious to our presence. I've never seen anything so majestic in my life, and I can only describe it as that; majestic. The sight moves through me, embeds itself in my memory, and I don't even think to pull my phone from the dry bag to take a picture.

"Did you know they're believed to be descendants of the horses brought over by Spanish missionaries in the 1600's?" Adrian speaks for the first time, and I realize I've been gripping his arm so tight that I've left half-moon indents from my fingernails.

"They are unbranded, wild, and free," he says nostalgically, and I watch, entranced, as more than twenty wild horses use the Salt River to take a break from the brutal summer sun. I've heard about them, of course, but I always thought they were a myth, hard to glimpse – like ghosts.

"I didn't think there were any wild horses left," I say, craning my neck as we pass by.

"The federal government wanted to remove them, called them stray livestock."

"What a joke," Finlay pipes up.

"But they're still free, right?" Emma asks, holding a squirming Layla in her arms.

"There was so much public outrage it made national news, and the governor signed into law to protect them. Now people from all over the country come here just to see the wild horses, and all it costs is an $8 day pass to the Tonto National Forest," Adrian continues, smiling at me.

"How do you know all this?" I ask, turning back to the horses, taking one last look as the river takes us farther away.

There are so many things I don't know about Adrian, and what a tragedy that is.

He runs a hand through his hair, turning to me and drenching me with his gaze he replies, "I pay attention."

THE SAGUAROS in the surrounding preserve start to look like shadowy figures against the purple and pink sky, but not in an ominous way; more like standing guard as I press a bare foot to Adrian's chest in the cab of his truck.

I'm still on a high from seeing the wild horses on the riverbank. Being in the sun all day has made me lazy, and I didn't bother putting my swim top back on, letting my bare breasts lay heavy against my chest. Stretching my body along the length of the bench seat, all I have on are my shorts. There's no one around except the coyotes and jackrabbits, and of course the Saguaros standing ever vigilant in the distance.

Adrian covers my bare foot with the palm of his hand, rubbing the top with his thumb. The radio is on, filling the cab with music, and all I can do is smile at him while plucking another grape from the vine and popping it in my mouth.

"Thank you again for today," I say, mouth full of grapes and pushing my toes further into his bare chest.

His elbow hangs out the window, and I can feel a soft breeze filter in.

"Which part?" he asks, raising an eyebrow.

"All of it," I answer excitedly. "I can't tell you the last time I felt this relaxed." Looking out the front windshield at the darkening sky, everything feels so much more like a dream. "It's like there's no tomorrow, only right now." I turn back to see him watching me.

Propping my head up with my hand, I sink back against the door, letting my other leg rest on his lap.

"I like being the one to make you happy, Lake." His mouth tilts into a genuine smile.

"Do you come out here often?" This is part of the McDowell Mountains I'd never been to before. It's past the trailhead for the Sonoran

Preserve, and has a beautiful view of the city below. We'd parted ways with Finlay and Emma in the parking lot. Layla was already fast asleep in Emma's arms, her pudgy cheeks reddened from the excitement and the sun. Adrian drove past the exit to my house and brought me up here so we could enjoy the rest of the food he'd packed that I didn't get a chance to eat while we were on the river.

When he shut off the engine, I slide onto his lap, letting my hair shield our faces while I kissed him. My swimsuit had already dried by the time we got here. I didn't want to put it back on after he'd taken it off, feeling uninhibited in this part of the desert.

"My dad took me up here four wheeling a bunch of times," Adrian sighs, looking out at the preserve.

"My dad took me to the Frank Lloyd Wright house a bunch of times," I say, digging my foot into his ribs to try and make him laugh.

"It's a very nice house," he says, grabbing my foot and running a finger under the bottom, causing me to jerk my foot away from him, laughing.

"My dad was an engineer. He liked to know how things worked." I settle back down, letting my foot rest in his lap again.

Adrian nods, making a sound of agreement deep in his throat.

"And you?" he asks.

I think on that for a minute, because I don't really know what I am.

"I like it when things make sense." I nod. "Numbers never lie."

"And people do," he says definitively while seeming to look right into me at the catalog of lies I've tallied since we met.

"Yes."

"Even me." There's a slight tick in his jaw when he says it.

"Yes."

"That's fair." He rubs his chin and then looks at me. "Everyone lies, Lake. Sometimes we lie to ourselves."

Swallowing hard I look away, letting my hair fall into my face because he's right. I have lied. I'm lying right now in the cab of this truck when I look at him and try to tell myself that this is just a summer fling.

When I look back at him he's staring at me intently, and not at my bare breasts but at my face, right into my eyes. Sitting up, I pull my legs from him and straddle his lap, holding his face between my hands.

"You're starting to grow on me, Corvin," I say, smiling against his lips.

His palms slide up my back and fist my hair. A low groan vibrates in his chest, and I can feel my nipples pebble against him. When I open my eyes, I expect him to be staring back at me, but his eyes are closed as he breathes me in.

"*Nu te îndrăgosti de mine,*" he whispers in Romanian.

I'm caught up in the smell of him and the feel of him, unaware that the world around has faded to black.

"Are you going to tell me what you just said?" I ask, running my nose along his jaw, feeling his hands tighten in my hair.

"No."

"I'll just look it up later," I tease him, pulling away so I can look into his eyes.

"I hope you do."

22

ANNUAL POTLUCK

IMMORTALE (FEAT. VEGAS JONES) BY MÅNESKIN

"Don't be mad," Miles says, falling in step with me and handing over a cup of coffee while balancing his tablet in the other hand.

"That's not how you should start a conversation if you don't want me to be mad," I explain to Miles as we make our way towards my office.

"I booked a cruise!" Miles squeals.

"Why would I be mad about that?" I ask, confused.

"I got it at a great price," he gushes, "and Edmund and I have never been to the Caribbean. I think it was a good deal because it's right at the end of hurricane season, but I'm sure it'll be fine," he laughs nervously.

"Again, why would I be mad?" I ask more sternly.

Miles interlaces his fingers nervously. "It leaves next week." He scrunches up his face which makes me laugh.

"It's fine, Miles. God, you make me sound like the Wicked Witch of the West." I continue towards my office.

"Last year when I didn't give at least two weeks' notice before I flew back East to spend Thanksgiving with Edmunds family, you nearly had a conniption." Miles follows me into my office where I place my bag on the table next to my desk.

"First of all, I did not have a conniption or whatever that means, and the only reason I was slightly," I look at him pointedly, "upset, is because you left me to host the annual company potluck."

Miles purses his lips and then gives me a toothy smile. Looking at my calendar, I ask, "When exactly are you leaving?"

Miles starts to back out of my office when he says through a nervous smile, "The eighteenth."

I look back at the calendar and realize that is the day before this year's potluck. When I look back up, Miles is standing outside of my door and Wyatt crashes into him.

"Sorry, sorry." She apologizes, and stops Miles from hitting the doorframe.

"I wouldn't go in there if I were you," he tells Wyatt while backing away, leaving her staring after him in confusion.

"Lake?" Wyatt enters my office, a grave look on her face.

"What did I tell you about barging..." I pull the glasses from my face.

"I found something you're going to want to see," she interrupts.

"*Please* don't tell me something that's going to put me in a *bad* mood." I pinch my forehead, looking at her expectantly. I had every intention of coming into work today ready to save the world, but alas, the universe just wants to strike me down.

"Well, that depends on your perspective." Wyatt widens her eyes, and there is a hint of malice which piques my interest.

Motioning for her to join me on my side of the desk, I grumble, "Whatever it is, it can't be worse than hosting the company potluck by myself."

Momentarily, Wyatt looks at me clearly confused, but then she sets her laptop in front of me, opening a file. "I requested a sample of invoices from Waterman's and checked them against orders. Everything was fine, but then there was one where the date didn't match, and I thought it must have been a flubbed number, so I started looking at the incoming payment."

Wyatt continues but she doesn't need to; I see it plain as day. The addresses are fictitious. I look up at Wyatt, glee beginning to run through me. She was right that it's about perspective as a smile spreads on my face.

"Have you shown this to anyone else?" I close her laptop.

"Of course not," she says flustered. "I wanted you to look at it first because I just couldn't believe it, but I checked everything three, four times."

"I need to speak with Lewis," I say, standing up from my desk.

"Do you want me to go with you?" Wyatt asks as she follows me into the hallway.

"No," I say abruptly, stopping in the hall which causes Wyatt to almost crash into me. "Not because I don't trust you," I confirm, "but because Lewis can't speak in front of you." Wyatt's expression softens. "I'll take it from here." I give her a reassuring smile.

She nods and I leave her standing outside my office as I make my way a few doors down. Lewis looks up from his desk ready to say something sarcastic when he must see the look on my face and closes his mouth.

"Lewis, we need to talk," I begin and close the door behind me.

I'M RUNNING LATE as usual, and grab a solid copper colored dress that's belted at the waist from the hook and slip it over my head. Leaving the collar unbuttoned to the third one down, I look at myself in the mirror when I hear Noelle enter my room, her friend Sofia not far behind.

"Are you decent?" she yells before she enters.

"That depends, but if you're asking if I'm dressed, then the answer is yes," I yell back smiling.

Both girls enter my closet and Noelle immediately jumps up on the island like she used to when she was little. Sofia twirls around, getting a look at everything all at once.

"My mom never talks to me like that," she says, running her hand over one of my gowns.

"Like what?" I ask, fixing the belt on my dress.

"You know, joking, having fun," she says absently, as if she realizes it's a problem but she doesn't care enough to be sad about it. I often wondered if I was too much a friend to Noelle and not enough of a mother, but I love the relationship we have so I don't really care.

"Aren't you supposed to be at practice?" I ask.

"We finish early on Fridays," she says. "Sofia and I are going to the movies." Hopping off the island, she stands behind me. "That's pretty." She motions to the dress.

"You look hot," Sofia says, draping herself over the island. "Do you have a date?" She wiggles her eyebrows while her light blonde hair fans out over the wood top.

I look at Noelle before I answer, "Something like that," but then quickly change the subject. "What movie are you seeing?" Turning around, I look between the two of them. "More importantly, who are you seeing it with?"

Sofia dissolves into girlish giggles, so much higher strung than Noelle, reminding me a little bit of Georgie and myself. Sometimes the differences in people are what bring them together. Noelle has always been a little shy and reserved, and Sofia is the one that brings her out of her shell. On more than one occasion, Noelle's sensible nature has stopped Sofia from getting into too much trouble. They complement each other.

"Sofia's boyfriend has a friend, and I said I would go with."

"You make it sound like a chore." Sofia playfully smacks her on the arm and then turns to me. "Nathan is really cute, and he's nice too."

"He plays soccer," Noelle says, as if it's something heinous.

"We deplore any kind of sport," I explain cheekily to Sofia.

"Hating the sport is one thing, but liking the players because they're hot is something else entirely," Sofia teases, reaching up to pluck a hat off the rack.

"This is cute." She places the brown, wide brimmed fedora on her head. "Can I borrow this?" She looks at me expectantly and I nod.

"Thanks!" she squeals. "Come on we're gonna be late," she turns to Noelle, tugging on her arm.

"I'll meet you out front," Noelle says, turning back to me.

Checking my dress one last time, Noelle places her chin on my shoulder, looking at our reflections in the mirror. We have never looked more alike than we do now, and it's not just our blue eyes the shape of almonds, or our brown hair and high cheekbones. "You look happy."

"You look beautiful." I smile at her.

"Are you going to see him?" she asks plainly, removing her chin from my shoulder.

"Yes."

"What's it like?" she asks, backing up and resting her elbows on the island.

I'm not supposed to know what she means, but innately, I do.

"Do you remember when you were eight years old, and we went to Disneyland?" I ask. Noelle nods her head.

"You wanted to go on the Pirates of The Caribbean ride, but you were afraid."

"I remember." A smile spreads on her face at the memory as it does mine.

"When you finally got on the ride and we made it to the dark tunnel, you held onto my hand and screamed as we plummeted into what felt like nothingness, but when the ride was over, you wanted to do it again."

Noelle laughs, the sound filling the space of the closet, the same closet that holds all my secrets.

"It's just like that," I whisper.

My Friday nights are consumed with loud music, sticky floors, and Russian beers. It's an acquired taste, much like cigars, but the longer you do it, the more likely you are to become addicted.

The sun sets earlier in the evening, providing relief from its relenting rays as I walk down the sidewalk from my parked car. The weather has shifted only imperceptibly, the air just a bit thinner and easier to move through. Waking up from its summer slumber, the city is alive. Even the trees are starting to look taller, their branches bending towards the sky, and the terracotta landscape of the surrounding mountains are shedding their muted colors and becoming darker shades of amber and laurel.

As soon as I enter the bar, Gael spots me, a bright smile stretching across his face as he makes drinks behind the bar. When I push my way through the crowd, there's a dark beer waiting on the counter for me.

"Am I that predictable?" I tilt my head and slide the beer closer to me.

"You're the only woman man enough to drink the Russian beer," Gael jests, but I know that's not true. He just likes to tease me.

"I'll take that as a compliment," I wink, hearing Gael's easy laugh in the background as I turn towards the crowd.

Taking a sip of the beer, I hear the band start up after what must have been a break because it's already late in the evening.

Adrian's voice fills the noisy bar, cutting through all the chatter, chairs scraping against the hardwood, and the flapping of the double doors to the kitchen. It's a velvety growl with guttural undertones that seeps under my skin. Just another acquired taste I have developed over the last two months, like the taste of dark beer, the smell of bourbon, an appetite for late nights, and long hair.

Walking away from the bar, I head into the packed venue where a sweat-soaked Adrian presses his lips to the mic while strumming his guitar, a sight that never gets old, no matter how many times I see it.

A two-top near the side of the stage is empty, and as I near it, I notice the reserved sign sitting on the top. Catching Adrian's eye on stage, he smiles, nodding towards the table for me to sit. As many times as I've come to see him play, I deserve my own damn table.

Taking a seat, I cross my legs in the direction of the stage. Adrian's eyes travel from my face, down my leg, and settle on my gold heels that reflect the lights from the stage. Pushing back the dark hair from his face, he can't keep his eyes off me, and I drown in his attention.

As he finishes the last half of his set, he tries to focus on the crowd, but his eyes always end up on mine. My favorite part about watching him play is how the veins in his forearms become much more prominent while he strums the guitar. I've traced those veins and the tattoos covering his arm with my fingers, memorizing each one.

Looking around at the crowd, I see how much they love him, the energy he presents on stage, the fun he has with Finlay, and I am almost jealous that I must share him with them. When he transitions into *Crazy* by *Aerosmith*, the way he looks at me, I feel like the only person in the room. The weight of his stare lays heavy across my body, pressing on my chest and causing heat to bloom outward. Within those soft brown eyes are promises he intends to keep.

Almost embarrassed at taking up all his attention, I look back towards the crowded tables surrounding the room. A few people are on the dance floor, holding hands, bodies pressed together. Across the room at the table directly opposite mine, I lock eyes with Taylor.

23

SO, YOU'RE THE REASON

Starfire by Caitlyn Smith

The same Taylor I met at my sister's bridal shower, who used to be Adrian's girlfriend, is standing in front of me.

Used to, *until me.*

Fuck.

The blood rushes from my face and the Russian beer threatens to work its way up my throat. Somewhere nearby a waitress drops a plate, the noise cutting through the blood rushing in my ears, and everyone claps. That's when I get up from the table and rush into the bathroom.

Reality has crashed down on me, hard, and everything feels like it's unraveling like a loose thread on a sweater, one little tug and the whole sweater comes apart. Admittedly I was enjoying my secret world, the one where I got to be someone else, where no one knew the real me.

Taylor saw me, and I'm certain she remembered who I was. Of course, I could be just another patron enjoying a night out with friends listening to music, except no one would believe that by the way Adrian and I were looking at each other. After washing my hands I grab for a towel, and see that stupid heart with mine and Steven's initials – the heart that should have been erased or drawn over a long time ago. Frustrated, I give it the middle finger for no other reason than to make myself feel better, but when I turn around, there stands Taylor.

Momentarily, I'm thrown off kilter, the three-inch heels nearly breaking my ankle, but Taylor manages to catch me before I make an even bigger spectacle.

"Shit!" I yelp and then adjust the strap on my shoe. "Thank you. I'm usually not that clumsy."

"You're Lake, Beth's sister." She doesn't say it as a question but rather a statement.

"And you're Taylor," I pause hesitating to say Adrian's girlfriend, which is how she introduced herself to me initially, but instead I say, "Laura's friend."

By the look on her face, this feels like a standoff in the girl's bathroom in high school and I am too old for this.

"It was nice to see you again." I try to exit the bathroom, but Taylor stops me.

"So you're the reason Adrian and I aren't together," she says from behind me.

Slowly turning back around, I notice her jet black hair falling over her shoulder in waves, dark brown eyes partially hidden behind beautiful long black eyelashes, which I'm sure are fake. She's recognizably beautiful, and as I narrow my eyes at her, I still see the same person who was kind to me at the bridal shower, the girl who had no idea that I fucked her 'boyfriend' the night before.

Adrian and I haven't talked much about Taylor since the night of the rehearsal dinner, partially because I haven't asked, and because I didn't think I had anything to worry about.

Shoving my hands in the pockets of my shirt dress, I ask, "Then why are you here tonight?" She knows that I'm with him, and it's beneath me to deny it.

"Same reason you are," she says.

"I suppose you're right." I give her a tight smile.

She will tell Laura what she saw tonight, there's no denying that. I have lulled myself into this fantasy that I could have my cake and eat it too. Nobody would have to know, and nobody would get hurt – least of all me. This is a stark reminder that I'm past my expiration date.

When I walk out of the bathroom I don't even look at the stage and head right for the exit. I only make it to the street when I hear Adrian call after me.

"Hey!" The familiar voice has less impact than it did the first time. In fact, I want to un-hear it. I want to erase it from my memory.

I don't want to turn around and see him standing on the street, this man whom I'd given more to than I'd allowed myself with anyone else. Now I feel stupid for letting my guard down, thinking this could be my reality.

"You're just going to leave?" Adrian says angrily and I finally turn around.

"Why is she here?" I turn around pointing to the bar.

"You're upset about Taylor?" he asks, frustrated.

"Of course I'm fucking upset about Taylor." I look at him flabbergasted, because how can he not see what a problem this is for me and for him?

"There's no need to be jealous of her," he says innocently, and I know he doesn't mean it as an insult, but it still irritates me.

Walking towards him, I close the gap. "Do I look like the kind of woman who would be jealous over some girl?" I ask coldly.

"I don't know, Lake. You stormed out of the bar. You tell me." He flaps his arms to his sides with frustration.

"She will tell Laura." I point towards the entrance of the bar, and when Adrian doesn't acknowledge the gravity of the situation, I continue, "And my sister will know about us."

"Maybe this is a good thing, Lake. I didn't want to lie to them in the first place," he raises his voice.

"A good thing? You think having my sister find out I've been fucking her brother-in-law is a good thing?" A nervous laugh escapes while I back away from him. A flicker of guilt passes over his face.

"What is this?" This is far from where we started, and I lost myself somewhere along the way.

Adrian closes the distance between us in two strides.

"I have *always* known what this is." He reaches for me but I pull away, and I can see the hurt in his eyes.

"How do you know?" I challenge, furrowing my brows at him.

"The problem here is that you refuse to acknowledge what we are. It's not just fucking, Lake. It never was for me." He shakes his head. "*You* wanted casual. *You* wanted no expectations," he raises his voice, pointing at me in frustration.

"And you agreed to it!" I yell.

"I agreed," a laugh escapes his lips, "because I just wanted *you*."

Adrian is the type of man to wear his emotions on his sleeve. That's why he's such a good musician; because he doesn't hold back. The crowd gets to experience the music through him, and that's what connects them.

I am not wired that way.

It is just one of the many differences between us.

Pedestrians passing by stare, and I'm too angry to care. That is until Taylor steps out of the bar and onto the sidewalk looking between the two of us. At least there's a touch of remorse in her eyes, not realizing we were out here arguing over her.

"Jesus Christ," I hiss, turning away from them both, running my fingers through my hair. I start to walk away when Adrian grabs onto my wrist. When I whirl around, the look on my face is enough to make him think twice. His fingers let go but his hand remains suspended in the air while I let my arm fall to my side.

Panic rips through me as fight or flight takes over.

I'm done fighting.

It's so much easier to walk away.

That's what I do.

24

MORAL COMPASS

Tell Me When It's Over by Sheryl Crow and Chris Stapleton

"Honey, if you wanted a moral compass," Georgie pauses dramatically with a forkful of French toast halfway to her mouth, "you picked the wrong gal." She shoves the food in her mouth and washes it down with orange juice.

Holding up the glass and looking at me pointedly, she says, "You don't even have the decency to take me to a place that has mimosas."

Hiding my laughter behind the back of my hand, I motion with the other for the waitress to refill my coffee.

"I needed to be sober." I take a sip, crossing my legs under the table as we sit on the patio of *Berdena's*. The morning is perfect, and the waterfront is teeming with joggers and people enjoying the cooler weather.

Georgie leans forward. "Honey, nobody needs to be sober when they find out you've been fucking their little brother." She tilts her head innocently while demurely placing another forkful of French toast in her mouth.

"Fuck," I mutter, palming my face. "I hate family. I just wish…" I stop, looking up at the sky as if some divine knowledge is going to strike me on the spot.

"You don't mean that," Georgie says. "You and Beth are sisters, and while I don't know all the history, I do know you care about her very much. I mean who else would threaten her ex-husband to swim with the fishes?" She wiggles her eyebrows.

"I did not say that," I laugh.

"Oh, Lake, I was being nice." Georgie takes a sip of her orange juice, puckering her lips with distaste and setting it down before she finishes. "If memory serves, you told him you would cut off his dick and shove it up his ass during their divorce."

"Well, I mean," rolling my eyes, "he was being unnecessarily nasty." Taking a sip of my coffee, I peer at Georgie through the steam, seeing her smile back at me.

"You feel guilty and that's understandable, but Beth doesn't even know how you feel about Adrian. You never gave her a chance," Georgie pleads. "Does she even know half the stuff you've told me about Steven?" Georgie adds.

"It's a little late for that. Besides, it doesn't matter."

"If she knew, maybe she'd have wanted to protect you, too." Georgie looks at me with wide eyes. "I think she'd have a better understanding about where you're coming from."

Slumping back in my chair, I know Georgie is right. I should have told Beth the truth about Adrian the minute I continued to see him after the wedding. I had plenty of time to do that.

"I just," looking down at my lap, I search for the words. "Never thought…"

"That you would fall in love with him?" Georgie finishes for me, one eyebrow cocked.

"Don't be absurd, Georgie." I cross my arms over my chest and look away.

"Don't bullshit a bullshitter," Georgie says, and I flick my eyes back to her, narrowing them. She's petite, but her attitude makes up for it.

"I don't need all this drama." I wave my hand in the air like I can erase it from my life.

"Think of all the orgasm's you'll miss," she counters.

"I have a lot going on at work. I haven't even told you the worst of it."

"Do not underestimate how scary you can be" She points at me. "You'll kick ass like you always do, and besides, all that bullshit with the Waterman merger is temporary."

"He's younger than me," I say but don't get to finish my sentence when Georgie silences me.

"I fail to see the problem here. Next!" she says, loudly.

"I'm in a different place in life than him, Georgie," I say sternly. "God," I hesitate to even say it out loud because it sounds absurd in my head. "I'm past the point of wanting to have another baby," I say sadly, because I wanted Noelle to have a sibling. I wanted to have a baby with someone who would love them with every fiber of their being like I did. Someone like Adrian, and it made me realize this the minute I saw him with his nieces and Layla because I know in my heart he would be a good dad. "I don't want to take that away from someone."

"Have you even talked to him about this?"

"No, Georgie." I look at her crossly. "I neglected to ask him if he wants a baby in between dirty texts and multiple orgasms."

"Multiple?" Georgie raises an eyebrow.

I roll my eyes at her.

"Then there's Noelle," I continue before she derails the conversation further. "I don't stop being a mother when she turns eighteen. I've been preoccupied lately, and I wasn't there for her when she needed me." I stop, choosing my words carefully, thinking about that night in front of the refrigerator eating ice cream. "She's not a little girl anymore," I grit my teeth.

"Oh yeah, because she had sex." Georgie pushes a piece of French toast through the syrup on her plate casually.

"How do *you* know?" I ask, astonished.

"She texted me." Georgie places her elbows on the table. "I told her it's probably good he had a small dick, because you know, first time and all, but yeesh," she rears back, smiling tightly. "Don't want to keep that around forever." Georgie shakes her head and refocuses her attention on her plate.

"Tell me you didn't actually say that to her?" I stare her down, disbelievingly.

Georgie looks up from her plate, mouth full, and syrup dripping down her chin. "What? That's how kids talk these days; they're unnaturally honest and open. It's weird." She shakes her head and wipes the syrup from her chin.

Slapping my forehead, I groan loudly. "This is another reason I need to be around more." Looking pointedly at her, I explain, "So I can monitor who she's talking to."

"Oh stop. You want your daughter to be stuck with her high school boyfriend, *unsatisfied*, thinking what he's packing is normal?" She looks at me as if I'm the one who's being unreasonable.

"Why would she text you about that anyway?" I cringe.

"Because I'm the cool aunt." Georgie smiles proudly.

Motioning to the waitress to get our check, Georgie pushes the empty plate away from her.

"Lake," Georgie looks at me seriously. "Stop making excuses for why you can't be with him."

"They're not excuses, they're reasons," I hand the waitress my card, "and there are a lot of them." I remind her.

"Beth will understand."

"Beth is the least of my worries."

SITTING IN MY CAR, I take a few moments to gather myself by checking my reflection in the visor mirror. I refresh the coral lip gloss, watching as it shines on my lips from the sun that filters in through the windshield.

"Why the fuck am I worrying about my lip gloss?" I mutter to myself, flipping the visor back up, angry with myself.

Slamming the car door shut, I walk up the stone steps to Beth's front door when I feel my phone vibrate.

> A: This is not over.

And then another message.

> A: If you won't talk to me, I will be forced to come to you.

I shove my phone back in my pocket. I've wanted to text him back the last twenty messages, but I couldn't... at least not yet. I needed to see Beth first.

Beth isn't expecting me, but I chose today to visit her because I know this is Eric's weekend with Ashley. I also know that Beth likes to hike Thunderbird Mountain on the weekends, and it takes forty-five minutes to get from the bottom to the top and back. While Beth hikes, Laura visits her mom. Checking the time on my phone, I know she should be home.

When I knock on the door I know she will answer, and that's why I'm shocked when Laura stands in front of me. She has always been welcoming, trying her best to make me feel like part of the family, even when my sister has not, and that's why it hurts me to see her looking at me like I've betrayed her. It's as if she'd given me something, and instead of taking care of it, I've broken it.

I don't even care how she knows, just that she knows. At this point, Taylor is inconsequential.

"Laura, I..."

She puts her hand up to stop me. "When I was in college and my brother was in high school, that's when I started to notice how my friends looked at him." She gives a weak smile, "Especially when he started to play the guitar."

She's being way too nice to me, something I probably don't deserve, but I'll take it.

"It used to make me uncomfortable because Addy is my little brother. He's kind and sweet, and I didn't want anyone to hurt him," she sighs. "But when Taylor and Addy started dating, it was like the best of both worlds – until it started to impact our friendship." Laura shakes her head, her blonde hair tumbling around her shoulders. "They were never on the same page. She wanted to settle down, he was chasing a dream, and then when he wanted to settle down, she was chasing her career."

"Why are you telling me this?" I ask.

"Because I don't want him to get hurt again."

"I know what you think of me," I explain, looking her in the eye. "It was never my intention to come between anyone."

"But you lied, and you had my brother lie to me." Her disappointment washes over me.

From the side, I see Beth peer into the doorway as Laura steps aside.

"I'm sorry." I try to say as sincerely as I can.

She takes one look at me and turns back into the house, but I follow her.

"Beth, just let me explain." I trail after her.

"I asked you to stay away from him," she says, turning around to face me.

"That wasn't fair of you," I say angrily.

"Fair? You want to talk about fair? Don't you have enough, Lake?" she spits. "You got the family name, you got the college degree, the fancy job, the fancy car…" she points towards my car parked at the curb.

"I worked for all of that, Beth! No one stopped you from having it, too!"

"You don't understand." She shakes her head as she walks into the kitchen, the same kitchen I was in months earlier, celebrating her marriage to Laura. The same kitchen where Ianna made me feel so welcome, and Florina shoved food in my hands to take home. "Lake, you filled a room with your presence, you sucked up all the oxygen, and I used to admire you, be in awe of you when we were growing up, until…" she pauses, "there wasn't anything left for me." She shakes her head sadly. "And then mom died and you just shut down, and I was alone."

It feels like all the oxygen has been sucked out of the room now, and none of it is by my doing.

"Well, you have it now, don't you? The family you always wanted," I say, gesturing around the house.

"Do you have any idea what it was like being married to Eric and feeling so alone?" Beth asks.

"Are you asking if I know what it feels like to be alone?" I scoff. "I've been alone for a long time."

"It's not the same, Lake. You chose to be alone!" Beth states.

I'm honestly taken aback. How could she think I wanted this?

"Steven was…" I pause, thinking of my conversation with Georgie, because there are things I never really told Beth. "He made me feel like I was always in the wrong, that I wasn't good enough. He manipulated the truth so that I always blamed myself when things went wrong. He said Noelle wasn't his, accused me of cheating!" A rock forms in my throat and tears threaten to spill over onto my cheeks. "So yeah, I chose to be alone rather than be with someone like him."

Beth's face is full of shock, slowly dissolving into sadness. I've never felt our differences as much as I do right now. Maybe we want the same things, but we have vastly different ways of getting it.

"You didn't know that, did you?" I ask.

Beth's eyes widen as she stands on the opposite side of the island, her palms pressed to the granite.

"You never wanted anyone to know you, Lake," Beth says, frustrated. It feels like an insult, but it's true.

"Because I didn't want you to look at me like you are now, like I'm a weak," I say, swallowing hard. I'm not as tough as everyone believes me to be. All those insecurities are tucked away deep down inside of me, because I don't want anyone to see them.

"And now we're right back to where we started, where everything is about you," Beth says quietly. "What did you expect would happen after you pushed me away all these years? I'm finally happy, and Laura's family is so wonderful," Beth pauses. "Adrian is not someone you use to have fun with or live out some fantasy."

"That's not what I was doing!" I say, stunned.

"Then what was it, Lake? Because I'd really like to know."

I want to tell her how Adrian made me feel like I was more than just someone's mother, someone's sister, or someone's boss. That he made me happy, even if it was short lived.

But I can't tell her any of that. I definitely can't tell her that somewhere in between meeting him at the bar that night and now, I think I fell in love with him. What scares me is that I don't really know, and Adrian deserves someone who does know.

"Does it really even matter now?" I ask, because for me, I already know it's over.

Beth stares at me as if she's contemplating whether she really wants to know. There have been so many confessions today, truths dug up that don't belong in this kitchen. So when she nods yes, I've already decided I'm done.

"It's nothing, Beth," I say, feeling as if I'm deflating by the minute because when I deny it, I know exactly why I do it. It's because I feel foolish for doing the very thing I told myself not to. "Just like you said, a sad older woman living out her fantasy." I stare at her as if I'm daring her to counter this, and when she doesn't, I turn around and leave.

25

EXPIRATION DATE

Lie to Me by Jonny Lang

Knowing there was always an expiration date, I just didn't think it would hurt this bad.

If I don't go to him, he will come to me. He made that abundantly clear in the multiple text messages he's sent since that night at the bar. When my boots tap against the wood flooring, I can't help but think about him and realize the fresh start I thought I would have in my home will be nothing but a reminder of him. Grabbing my purse on the kitchen island, I pass the spot where I'd stubbed my toe multiple times on the broken tile that's no longer there. I don't miss it, I would never miss it, but I will always remember it was there.

Wrapping a jacket around my shoulders, I head into the garage. A half hour later I'm parking in front of Adrian's warehouse. Faded white letters on the brick above the open bay doors read *Corvin & Son*. The air is crisp as it whips around the brick building, lifting my hair from the collar of my jacket. Taking a few steps inside, I look around. The fluorescent lights above illuminate the open space surrounded by industrial shelving stacked with boxes. In the back is a small office with a Plexiglas window that looks into the warehouse.

Stopping in front of the wooden playhouse Adrian had been building for his nieces, I think of how much they will love it. When I'd first seen it months ago, it was only framed, but now the roof is on, false shutters flank the window, and the once exposed wood is now painted pink. When I peer inside, I notice the flooring is complete, a dark brown that looks sturdy enough to withstand muddy feet and dolls being dragged across it.

Smiling, I remember the one Noelle had as a child, except it was made of plastic and took me all weekend to build by myself. The door never closed right and there was a gap in the roof so that when it rained, the inside would be wet, but she didn't care. She stayed outside for hours with her dolls and stuffed animals inside that playhouse until I made her come in to eat.

"I'm going to take it over to Ianna's this weekend." Adrian's raspy voice cuts through my memories.

Turning around to look at him, I see he's wearing his *Corvin & Son* gray weathered t-shirt that stretches across his chest, faded jeans, and tan carpenter boots. He's just gotten done with a job and he's cleaning up for the night, and here I am to ruin it.

I miss the easy smile on his face that lights up his eyes, the relaxed way he always held himself, so calming. Right now his body is tense as he shoves his hands in his pockets, looking at me with trepidation. I hate being the one to make him feel this way, but it's necessary as I stare back at him, stone-faced, trying so hard not to look at him like I once did, like he was the reason for turning on the light inside of me. It takes willpower not to reach up and touch his face, to feel the fine hairs lining his jaw that I know are soft and soothing.

"Her girls will love it." I look back at the playhouse and wish that I had a do-over. Everything in my life seems to happen too late. My timing is perpetually off.

"You came here to say goodbye," he confirms with a tick in his jaw, a sign of his frustration.

Turning back around, I look him in the eye when I say, "It's not fun anymore."

Adrian takes three strides to close the gap between us and places his hands in my hair, his face so close I can feel his breath against my lips. Closing my eyes I grip his wrists, and allow myself to be intoxicated by him this one last time. That's exactly what he is, a human being capable of rendering me drunk, able to slip under my skin and travel like bourbon in my bloodstream.

"Don't say that," he whispers a plea.

"We both know it was never meant to last," I say, opening my eyes and seeing him stare back at me with his beautiful brown eyes. When he lets go of me, it's as if the fog has been lifted and we are left on opposite sides of a river.

"Why do you have to be so goddamn difficult?" His hands fall to his sides, balled into fists. "Is this about your sister? Or Taylor?" he asks, as if there is a simple answer and a simple solution... but there isn't.

"No," I explain. "It's about us." Narrowing my eyes sympathetically, I wonder why he can't see this for what it is. "That was only the catalyst for the inevitable," I say.

Nothing feels this good for the rest of your life. There is always a fall, one that makes your stomach drop and disorients you. I thought I was ready for it, but I'm not.

"You and I are in two different places in life," I try my hardest to explain.

"This is you using my age as a weapon again." I can see the frustration and anger in his eyes as clear as I can see the mountain range falling under darkness behind him.

"It's not a weapon, it's a fact. I'm forty-three years old, for Christ's sake. I have an almost grown daughter, and I don't want to start all over again. I don't have the energy or the patience," I say sadly. As much as I might have wanted it before, that is just another example of bad timing. "We want different things."

"Do not pretend to know what I want when you've never asked me!" His anger surprises me, but it's the truth.

"I've never asked because we were never supposed to be anything more than temporary," I reply while biting my lip.

"The minute I saw you in the bar, Lake, I knew you weren't temporary," he says with such conviction, and I wonder how he could be so sure... because here I am, breaking his heart.

"I don't want to ask you to give up something for me," I explain, trying to make him see the bigger picture.

"You have no idea what I would give up for *you*." He pulls the bandana from his head in obvious frustration, and steps closer as if he's ready to swallow me up along with the space between us.

"Why?" I ask, shaking my head in disbelief. "I'm broken." I place a palm to my chest feeling each broken heart beat.

"We're all broken, Lake." Adrian shakes his head and holds onto my arms. "And we will break a million more times before this life is over."

"We're victims of bad timing," I plead, raising my arms in the air causing Adrian to release me. "I never wanted permanent. I made that clear from the start. You changed the rules," I accuse him.

"There are no rules. No one gets to decide who you love; not Laura, not Beth, and not even you, as much as you fucking try," he says with such certainty that I almost believe him. "They didn't like being lied to, but they'll get over it. Everything else we'll figure out because that's what you do when you love someone. You figure it out," he says angrily.

The word *love* swirls in the air between us like vapor. He'd said it to me before, using my reverse psychology.

Nu te îndrăgosti de mine, don't fall in love with me.

But I didn't listen, didn't heed the warning, and now I'm paying the price.

"Don't pretend that everything you have said to me was true because it's not," I say tilting my head memorizing him as if I even needed to. I've already done so countless times.

He shakes his head in disbelief. "How is it so easy for you to believe that everything I've said is a lie?" he asks, looking at me with such sadness, as if he feels sorry for me.

"Because that's what men do, Adrian, whether they know it or not," I explain, shoving my hands in the pockets of my jacket, feeling the chill of a Fall Phoenix evening.

I've cataloged them all in my mind and now they've come crawling back from the dark corners were I'd tucked them.

I've never done this…

You are the sexiest woman I have ever met...
I usually last a lot longer than that, but fuck, you...
Because I sure as fuck have been thinking about you...
You have a great ass...
I've never fucked anyone in a bathroom before...
I would never make a fool of you...
It's the best pussy I've ever had...

"You're scared," he says plainly.

"Of course I'm fucking scared, Adrian!" I raise my voice.

"It's okay," Adrian offers while shaking his head.

"I don't trust myself!" I yell and feel the tears clawing their way up my throat. "I don't trust myself," I say quietly, making peace with my admission.

Adrian rubs his chin and I can see the anger creeping up his neck, causing his eyes to burn brighter, the soft brown blazing under the fluorescent lights from above.

"I'm not him, Lake!" He raises his voice as his eyes plead with me. I can feel him reaching for me through the space, trying to get me to see what's right in front of me, but my eyes are clouded by the past.

"You're punishing me because of what someone else did to you, and it's not fair." He tries to approach me but I back away, warning him off with my eyes. One touch would be the end of both of us.

"I hate to break it to you, but your dick isn't magic. You can't fuck him out of me," I say angrily and I can tell that my words hit their target by the hurt look on his face. "No matter how good it was." I shrug.

"So I was just a good fuck to you?" He stands with his feet apart and his arms crossed over his chest waiting for my answer.

I have the audacity to flinch but quickly regain my composure. "We both got what we wanted."

He steps forward lowering his arms, and he's close enough for me to smell his cologne. It fills the space between us. "I will never get enough of you, Lake. If you let me love you, I will give you *every-fucking-thing* you have been missing before me." The air becomes heavy like an impending storm, and I have to pull at the collar of my jacket just to get some air. "Tell me you don't feel the same," he dares me.

Swallowing hard, I fight through the emotions as I shake my head no, not able to trust the words inching their way up my throat. I'm too stubborn, or too weak – a character flaw that will cost me everything. I can't put myself in a position again to be hopeful because I won't survive it when it collapses in on me.

"You can tell yourself all the beautiful lies you want." He shakes his head as if he feels sorry for me which is even more heartbreaking. "But I think we both know the truth."

26

PLAYING DIRTY

WORLD ON FIRE BY SARAH MCLACHLAN

The auditorium is packed with nearly every seat taken as families filter in, getting ready for the winter concert, proud and excited smiles on their faces mirroring my own. Decorations of snowflakes hang from the rafters, something of a novelty in a town that has never seen snow.

I wish I'd gotten here earlier, I would have been in the front row, but now I'm stuck somewhere in the middle. Crossing my legs I crane my neck, looking over the heads in front of me, searching the door as I nervously fold the program in my hand.

My purse still sits on the empty chair next to me, saving his place.

"He'll be here," Georgie says from my left.

Turning to her, I smile weakly. Knowing better, I didn't save a place for Beth or Laura. We haven't talked since that day at her house even though dad pleaded with us to put things behind us, forgive each other. Beth and I share the same stubborn streak, something we inherited from our mother.

"Yeah," I say, rolling up the program once more and focusing on the stage that is now dimming under the stage lights.

The excited voices die down to a whisper, and the shuffling of bodies becomes louder as everyone gets into their seats, preparing for the show to start. I've been to many concerts over the years, and each one has exceeded my expectations. It's a melancholy feeling to know that this will be one of the last I will see.

Someone cursing a few chairs down draws my attention, and I watch my dad shuffle over legs and feet, stepping on a few on his way to the empty seat I saved for him.

"Excuse me, sorry, pardon me," he says, making a scene as he finally reaches the seat.

"So sorry I'm late," he says as I remove my purse from the seat so he can sit down.

"Always making a grand entrance, I see," Georgie says, poking her head from around me.

"Fashionably late," Dad says proudly.

"Bridge game run over?" I ask.

"No, Lake," he says sternly. "If you must know, Alba McKinnely brought over cookies just as I was leaving, and I didn't want to be rude and rush her."

"Alba, huh?" Georgie says, raising her eyebrows. "Is she cute?"

"Georgie!" I scold.

"Cute is not an adjective I would use to describe someone in their seventies," Dad counters back, sitting with his back stiff against the auditorium seats.

Georgie makes a disbelieving noise in the back of her throat.

"She still has all her own teeth and doesn't need a walker," he clarifies.

"So, she's cute," Georgie says.

My dad rolls his eyes, peering around me to meet Georgie's eyes. "Yes." He smiles.

I sigh audibly while Georgie snickers.

"Benjamin has a girlfriend," Georgie teases.

"Shhhhhh," someone says from behind us, and Georgie turns abruptly to scowl at them.

"Anyway," she says, pushing the hair off her shoulder.

"I do not have a girlfriend!" Dad denies.

"Okay, the show is about to start. We can discuss this Alba later." I eye my dad speculatively.

The lights flicker as last-minute arrivals come through the door.

"You didn't save a seat for your sister and Laura," my dad whispers, if you can call it that.

"Dad let's not get into this now," I say, annoyed.

"Noelle's her niece," he counters, as if I don't know that. "She should be here."

I groan.

"I don't understand the two of you," he sighs, shaking his head. "Your mother would disapprove." He shifts in his chair.

"Playing dirty," I mutter.

"I do what I want," he leans over and whispers.

Out of the corner of my eye, I see Beth appear at the entrance of the auditorium, followed by Laura, and then Ashley. For a moment I'm elated because I don't get to spend a lot of time with Ashley, and I know Noelle will be excited that she's here, but quickly that elation falls off into the abyss to be replaced with anxiety.

"Tell me you did not invite them," I scowl at my dad.

"He really does play dirty," Georgie says next to me.

"It came out. What was I supposed to do?" He shrugs but then stands, waving at Beth and making a spectacle.

"Do you mind moving down?" he says to the family sitting next to us.

"Oh my God." I cup my hand to my face in embarrassment.

"Just over a couple more if you don't mind," he directs them. The family shuffles over, more confused than angry. The auditorium fills with our voices, shuffling feet, and annoyed sighs.

As Beth makes her way through the aisle, I catch a glimpse of Ianna, whom I didn't notice was with them at first. She gives me an excited smile and I remember how she'd asked me about Noelle's music all those months ago at the bridal shower.

My dad stands up, offering his seat to Beth and I give him a dirty look to which he shrugs at. Ignoring Georgie snickering next to me, I give Beth a tight smile and she gives one back.

"Sorry I'm late," she offers, shifting in her seat uncomfortably while

Laura takes the seat next to her, and then my dad makes room for Ianna.

Noelle will be happy she has family in the audience, and I'm glad that after everything, Beth is here. I want to tell her how much I appreciate it, but before I can say anything, the director taps the mic, piercing our ears with loud feedback that's quickly corrected. While the announcements of tonight's lineup are given, I tilt my head towards Beth in the dim auditorium, offering her a genuine smile which she seems to recognize as an olive branch. Peering down the row I mouth a hello to Ashley who waves excitedly. My dad pokes his head down the line, sitting at the end next to Ianna, and I narrow my eyes at him.

"Benjamin is a character," Georgie whispers.

"Yeah, a real character," I mumble as the show begins.

The curtain opens to the main orchestra, and Noelle is near the front wearing her black dress with a white collar, violin at her chin, her brow furrowed looking out to the crowd, as excited murmurs travel down our row.

Georgie smacks my arm excitedly with pride making me laugh. When the piece is over, the auditorium is filled with clapping. The night is filled with cello and piano solos, but none are as great as when it's your own kid on stage, playing a piece she composed herself. When the last chord echoes through the auditorium, I shoot out of my seat clapping loudly, the sound amplified like thunder when our whole row jumps out of their seats, clapping. I'm not just swelling in pride for Noelle, but for the pride *they* have for her.

"I had no idea she was so talented," Ianna says, and she's the first one to hug me, crushing the flowers I'd brought to my chest after the concert. Everyone stands near the exit to the parking lot, gathered around the stage doors waiting for our kids to pile out.

"Thank you," I say, hugging her back. She looks different without her kids, less harried, and more relaxed.

Her phone buzzes in her hands and she lifts a finger as a way of saying hang on, while she answers. "She can only have one," I hear her say as she moves away from the crowd. "I told her before I left. She's playing you, Andy," she says to her husband on the phone.

"It was wonderful. I felt like I was at a real concert," Laura gushes. "Didn't you think so?" Laura asks as she turns to Beth.

We exchange glances and polite smiles, but I wonder how she really feels about being here, about seeing me in particular.

"You should be really proud. She's just..." Beth pauses, presumably trying to find the right words.

"Magnificent!" Georgie cuts in, and Beth laughs a little tightly. I find I like the sound of it.

My attention is diverted the minute I see Noelle emerge from the auditorium exit. The look on her face is pure shock at seeing her Aunt Beth and the rest of the family.

Holding the flowers in my hand, I wait my turn while the rest of the family bombards her with praise and hugs. The minute the crowd parts, she tilts her head at me with a beautiful smile, walking right into my arms.

"I'm so proud of you, kid," I say, kissing the top of her head.

She takes the flowers, smelling the bouquet of white roses, lavender lilies, and carnations. "These are so beautiful."

Before I get another chance to tell her how wonderful the show was, she grabs Ashley and whisks her away to see her friends, all wanting to share in the excitement.

"Should we go to *Maggiano's*?" Dad asks. "I'm hungry."

"Oh," I say, clearly not having thought that far yet. Beth looks at Laura uncomfortably.

Our dad stands looking between us, seeing the obvious tension. "You need to get over this nonsense," he scolds us. "So what if Lake boinked your brother-in-law?" He shrugs and I feel the heat creep up my neck and into my cheeks.

"Dad!" Beth shrieks.

"Have you been drinking?" I ask, pinching my forehead with embarrassment.

"What?" he holds his hands up innocently. "I'm just saying, it's not the end of the world."

Laura begins to laugh, holding her hand over her mouth, and Ianna gives me a comforting smile as she chuckles.

"For the record," she whispers. "I was always rooting for you," she winks, and I furrow my brows wondering if she knew the whole time. Maybe she takes after her brother, being very observant, or maybe he confided in her. Either way, I'm glad Ianna's not mad at me.

"Noelle?" Dad waves her over to us. "You'd like to go to *Maggiano's*, wouldn't you?" He puts an arm around her shoulders.

"Sure, Grandpa," she agrees, looking between all of us, probably wondering what's so amusing.

"Then it's settled," he says, satisfied, leading us out the door and towards the parking lot.

Trying to avoid an awkward dinner, I pull Beth to the side before we veer off to our cars.

"Look, Beth, I'm…"

"No," she interrupts me. "Lake, I was awful to you," she says, surprising me. "I was just shocked, and I didn't handle it well."

It's true, she could have handled it better, but it's not going to do any of us good to rehash that now. What's done is done.

"I think we both could have handled it better," I admit instead.

Beth toes the ground before she speaks. "How did we grow so far apart that I didn't know what was happening with you?" she asks, bringing up Steven without saying it directly.

"I thought I could handle things on my own," I shrug. "You know how cocky I am." I try to make a joke, but Beth doesn't let me pass it off as something inconsequential.

"You really went to bat for me during the divorce with Eric," she reminds me.

"You would have threatened to cut off Steven's dick and shove it up his ass too," I say, shrugging.

"I can't pull off scary the same way you do," she laughs.

"Well, I mean, that is true." I raise my eyebrows proudly.

Beth's expression becomes serious as she looks at me. Whether I like it or not, she knows me well enough to know when I'm using a joke to deflect from the seriousness of the situation.

"Did you love him?" she asks, shoving her hands in the pockets of her jacket. "Adrian," she clarifies.

Blowing out a breath, I'm not sure how to respond. There is a part of me that loves him deeply, and another part that doesn't really know what love is. I feel like there are things I need to face about myself to be able to answer that honestly.

"That's not an easy question to answer," I answer honestly. Having spent years not trusting people, or myself, I closed myself off to the possibility. It was so easy for me to believe that everything Adrian said to me was a lie when I should have been holding those truths close to my heart. His words have come back to haunt me many times over these last couple of months.

You can tell yourself all the beautiful lies you want, but I think we both know the truth.

I won't ask about him though, because I don't deserve to know. Not after the way we left things. Right now, I need to focus on what's in front of me and what's inside of me, however long that takes.

"He's a great guy, Lake. I hope you know that."

Nodding, I know she's telling me exactly what I'm missing.

"I really just want you to be happy," she says, squeezing my arm.

"I promise I won't make family get-togethers awkward." I smile back at her.

Beth laughs. "That's an issue for another night. Right now, I'm starving."

Linking my arm with hers, we continue walking through the packed parking lot, seeing our dad waiting by the car with a satisfied expression.

"The real issue is what are we going to do about dad and this Alba woman?" I ask, narrowing my eyes at him.

27

BIG SHOES TO FILL

Sex & Stardust by ZZ Ward

Miles reopens the door to my office and stands at the entrance, his bowtie askew but tablet firmly clutched against his chest. There is only so much information I can give Miles at this time, and the little bit that I could has him rattled. He's been my assistant for a long time and has been privy to confidential information before, but nothing like this.

"Anything I can do?" he asks, again.

"You should start that monthly birthday celebration again," I say. "Everyone seemed to like that."

"Okay," he nods, "but I meant for you," he clarifies.

Closing my laptop, I hold it close to my chest. I shouldn't be smiling at a time like this, but I can't help it. Adrenaline has already started coursing through my body and it makes me fidgety.

"I have everything I need."

Miles steps out of the way as I walk down the long hallway, past reception, to the board rooms on the other side of the building. Glen called an emergency Board meeting after yesterday's events. Before entering the room, I check to make sure there are no wrinkles in my skirt and check my blouse. The third button has come loose, most likely from my laptop pulling at the fabric. Reaching to refasten it, I stop myself, thinking that if there were ever a time to leave it unbuttoned, now would be it. So I leave it open and push the board room doors open confidently.

The chatter stops as they watch me walk in, but I pay no attention to them. They know exactly why they're here. The only one who doesn't know the nature of the meeting is sitting at the far end of the table looking annoyed, no doubt upset that his tee time had to be canceled.

Asa Waterman.

If he's not happy about that, he will definitely not be happy about the announcement I'm about to make.

The room quiets as I place my laptop on the table. I don't take a seat; instead I stand at the head next to Glen. His tight smile and nod by way of greeting lets me know I'm free to begin whenever I'm ready.

"What's this all about?" Asa pipes up from the other end of the table. His casual golf shirt and khakis confirm my suspicion.

"Welcome, Mr. Waterman," I say with a slight smile, and watch as his eyes travel from my face to that strategically unfastened third button. My conversation with Glen all those months back comes to mind.

While men like Asa Waterman are distracted by that third button, they never see me coming.

"Let's get to the point, I'm missing my tee time," he grumbles. Looking at the other stone faces around the table he sits back in his chair, and I can tell he's worried.

I address the Board and tell them what they already know. "It has been made clear that your company is overvalued," I explain, addressing Waterman directly.

He has the nerve to laugh, but I expected as much. "I assure you the company is valued correctly, unless you're trying to get a deal. In that case, this isn't Bargain Hunters," he says sarcastically hoping to get a laugh, but no one in the room finds him funny.

"There's a problem with your Accounts Receivable, Mr. Waterman."

"You called a meeting just for that?" Asa demands, annoyed. "Grant Weatherly, my CFO, will look into it." He waves it off as if it's no big deal, but it is.

"We've already looked into it," I clarify.

"Are you accusing me of something, Ms. Kennedy?" Asa stands up, looking directly at me with challenging eyes. Maybe he thinks I'm bluffing or just plain dumb, but I am neither of those things. From all my years in finance, I am certain of one thing – Financial Statements don't lie, unless someone makes a liar out of them.

"You've falsified your financials," I pause to look him in the eye, "so no, I'm not accusing you of anything, Mr. Waterman. I'm here to remove you from your title."

Asa slaps his palms to the table, rattling my laptop and several cups of coffee. The gentlemen in the room stiffen, and I bristle. "I don't know what you are playing at, little girl," he says, venomous eyes fixed on me, "But the only one losing their title here will be you." He points an angry finger at me.

I can't help but laugh just a little because it's like watching a cornered rat trying to find its way out, but it can't. Asa does what rat's do when they're cornered – bite.

"Glen, are you going to stand here and listen to this garbage?" Asa demands, and then turns his attention to Lewis looking for an ally, but Lewis stares back at him stone-faced.

Glen stands, placing his fingertips against the polished wood.

"The evidence doesn't lie," Glen says, angrily.

"The shareholders are going to hear about this." He pushes his chair back so hard that it hits the wall behind him. Several of the Board members shift in their chairs, presumably getting ready to either move out of the way, or to block him from leaving.

"Asa," Glen says, calmly, "they already have."

"I won't stand for this!" Asa bellows, his face red with anger. "The deal is off!" He slices a hand through the air.

"You're right," I interrupt, placing my hands on the table in front of me. "The deal *is* off."

Asa looks at me, clearly confused. "You don't get to decide. You have no authority here!" he spits.

"You *would* be right about that, except I've already contacted your shareholders, and by proxy, Zentech now owns the majority stock of Waterman's. And I'm afraid there are *management* changes." I smile wickedly, only because I can't help but love seeing a man like Waterman being taken down. I don't relish the fact that his company was taken right out from under him, because it's not just him that is losing a job; unfortunately, others will too. That was always a fact.

"They wouldn't do that," he says, disbelievingly. "That's illegal!" He looks to Lewis for confirmation, but gets none.

Lewis stands, looking at me before addressing Asa. "I assure you, it's completely legal."

"You bitch!" Asa yells as he starts to round the table, but Lewis cuts him off. For a moment I'm afraid he'll crawl over the table to get to me, but when the other Board members stand, Asa gathers control of himself.

"I think you need to leave." Glen holds the door open, where two security guards are waiting by the entrance. We knew Asa wouldn't take it well and had taken precautions in case something like this happened.

"I will see you in court!" Asa threatens, shaking off one of the security guards as they try to escort him out of the room.

Watching through the glass doors as he leaves, I steady my legs by gripping onto the back of the chair. Employees poke their heads over the cubicle walls to see what the commotion is about. Glen has already crafted an email to send out about recent events, wanting to get ahead of any rumors or falsifications filed by Waterman. This isn't over, and we both know it.

Lewis looks across the table at me with sympathetic eyes, and I nod letting him know I'm alright. Inside, my nerves are at war with my pride because I don't want to let a man like Asa rattle me, but I am human.

After giving Lewis a thankful smile, he takes a seat adjusting his tie.

"Lake," Glen reaches over and touches my shoulder. "You did what you had to do," he reassures me.

None of us wanted it to come to this, least of all Glen, but in the end, he got what he wanted. Nodding, I take my seat, glad for the reprieve. There were many ways to go about handling Waterman's deliberate falsifications, but only one I knew I would enjoy.

Glen's office is just down the hall from the board room, behind wooden double doors. His secretary, Doris, who has been here longer than me, guards his office. Her large, horn-rimmed glasses make her look less than intimidating, but the steely eyes behind them could stop any man in their tracks.

Momentarily, she looks up from her computer as I enter.

"Today is your lucky day, Doris," I smile at her cryptically.

"Take a seat. He'll be with you in a minute," she says, not looking back up at me as I saunter over to the couch opposite her desk.

Before I can even sit down, Glen pops his head from behind the door. "I've been calling your line," Glen says, clearly annoyed.

Doris doesn't look over at him when she says, "I've been busy."

Glen sighs in frustration when he notices me standing in the middle of the waiting area, and then a smile spreads on his face. "Lake, come in." He waves me through.

Shutting the door behind me, I take a seat in front of his large old school desk.

"I finished the proposal and wanted to review it with you before we bring it to the Board for a vote." I slide the stack of documents towards him. "The summary is on top, but if you flip to the next page, you'll see the recommendations for reduction of the department heads," I explain, watching nervously as Glen puts his glasses on to look through the papers. His finger stops on one particular spot, and then he looks across the desk at me, lowering his glasses.

"Lake?" he questions me, looking back at the paper as if there must be some mistake. "You can't," he doesn't finish his sentence.

Standing up, I reach across the table to shake his hand. "It has been a pleasure," I say, feeling a lump form in my throat.

"But, why?" Glen asks, taking my hand in a firm handshake.

"It's time for me to move on, Glen." My life has been full of certainty for far too long, and I can't keep using my job as a crutch anymore. I need to find something that gives me purpose and fills me with joy instead of stress. This year has taught me that much.

"And you're sure about this?" He stands up while I nod. "Are you leaving us for a competitor?" he jokes.

"Of course not, nothing like that. I'm going to take some time off," I reassure him, "and then figure out what I want to do next."

"Things won't be the same here without you," Glen says, retracting his hand.

"I provided you with some recommendations for my replacement on the last page." I point to the deck sitting in front of him.

Glen quickly reviews the slide. Looking up at me with amusement, he says, "Grant Weatherly?"

"I know Waterman's CFO is probably an odd choice for my replacement, given the circumstances, but I assure you he'd be a good fit."

"He'll have some pretty big shoes to fill," Glen says, smiling at me.

***

"I still can't believe you're leaving," Miles says while I pack up my desk.

He was the first person to know of my departure – even before Glen. We've worked together for such a long time, I couldn't blindside him. He'd become like extended family.

"I've been here most of my career, and I let it consume my life," I say, shutting down my laptop and closing it for the last time. "It's time for me to find out what's next."

His expression is sullen as he clutches his tablet to his chest.

"What will you do now?" Miles asks.

Taking a deep breath, I level my eyes on him. "I don't know." It's the most honest answer I can give. Not because I haven't thought about it, but I just needed time to breathe before I did. If I learned anything this past year it's that I need to do things for myself, and I need time to find out what I want. Autopilot is a dangerous switch to turn on because you can lose yourself so quickly, and it's hard to turn off.

"What if I don't like my new boss?" Miles whines with a hint of panic.

Leaning my hip against the desk, I remind him, "You didn't like *me* at first, either."

"That's because you were rude," Miles says, rolling his eyes.

"Have I changed since the day we met?" I ask.

Miles looks up at the ceiling while he contemplates his answer. "Not really."

Smiling, I push off from the desk and finish placing my personal items in a box Miles brought from the copy room.

"You grew on me," he finally says, while I finish placing the last remaining items into the box.

"Change is bad for my complexion," he huffs. "Besides," Miles reaches over the box and touches my arm, "no one could ever replace *you*."

Leaving is bittersweet, because although I won't miss the constant stress, I will miss *most* of the people.

"I doubt Grant Weatherly will have you schedule bikini waxes," I tease.

"Is he hot, ya know, works out, but like not too much, because I don't like a lot of bulk, that scares me." Miles follows me out of the office.

"What happened to Edmund?" I ask, curiously.

"We moved in together but that doesn't mean I can't look," Miles says, trotting alongside me as I walk down the row of offices.

"Um, congrats, I think."

When I pass Lewis's office, the phone is to his ear and he's leaning back in his chair. Stopping momentarily, I give him a goodbye salute and he nods back at me. He became an unlikely ally, but I always knew I could count on Lewis when the chips were down.

"Lunch Friday?" Miles points at me while the elevator doors open.

"Of course."

"Don't just say you're going to keep in touch and then don't," he accuses.

"I won't."

"Okay, good." Miles sighs as Wyatt rushes forward, grabbing the door and jumping on before it closes.

The elevator jars back into motion, and she turns to me. "Thank you," she says.

"For what?" I ask, balancing the box on my knee to get a better grip.

"I got hired on permanently," she beams. "I know it was you who gave me such a wonderful performance review, so thank you," she nods.

"I don't know what you're talking about," I say with a wink, knowing performance reviews are confidential, but what are they going to do, fire me?

Wyatt clears her throat. "I won't let you down," she says.

The elevator door opens and I step off, but Wyatt stays on, holding the door.

"Have your career, Wyatt, because you deserve it, but don't forget to have a life too." Wyatt tilts her head in question. "Eat the birthday cake, take that trip, sleep with the guy in IT," I nod, causing her smile to widen.

"By the way," I pull my laptop out of the box and hand it to her. "Can you give this to Mark in IT for me?"

She nods, letting the elevator doors close. Outside the building, I feel the spring heat against my skin, it takes a moment before I feel the weight lift off my shoulders. I thought the panic would hit me by now, but it doesn't. I just feel free for the first time in my life, and that is entirely because of me, and not because of someone else.

There's a nice breeze on the riverfront, and I walk along the path towards a small cafe called *Breakfast Club*. Waiting for me outside at a table is Georgie. Setting down my box on the table unceremoniously, Georgie greets me with a hug.

"How do you feel?" she asks, still holding onto my arms.

"Nervous, but good," I say, honestly.

Taking a seat, the waitress drops off water and I order a coffee and a muffin.

"There's an opening at the clinic for a receptionist, but there's room to grow. Our current office manager is a mess, but I think I can convince Dr. Stickuphisass to fire her." Georgie talks a mile a minute and I feel out of breath just listening to her.

"Slow down there, tornado." I hold my hand up.

Georgie takes a sip of her water. "First of all, I'm not looking for a new job just yet. Second, you know I can't work around animals because I'll want to take them all home, and third," I pause, looking at Georgie suspiciously, "why would Dr. Stickuphisass fire someone for *you*? I thought he didn't like you?"

"Where's my coffee?" She looks around for our waitress, obviously trying to avoid me.

"Georgie!" I demand, leaning over the table. "Please tell me you are not sleeping with your boss."

"Okay, I will *not* tell you that I am sleeping with my boss," she says robotically.

I lean back in my chair, stunned.

"Just once, and it was an accident..." she talks with her hands.

"How do you *accidentally* sleep with your boss?" I roll my eyes.

Georgie shrugs. "I don't really know, but it kinda felt like an accident." She gives me a tight smile. "I dropped a tray of instruments, and one minute he was yelling at me, and the next I was naked on the examining table."

28

WINGMAN
FIVE MONTHS LATER

Stars by The Cranberries

"Why do you have to be on the third floor again?" I ask out of breath, thighs burning, but also thankful that reinforcements are supposed to be coming soon.

"I don't get a choice," Noelle says, annoyed.

"I really don't know how you can fit all this shit in that tiny room either," I say, dropping the laundry basket full of clothes.

"I like choices," Noelle huffs, pushing the propped open door further with her hip.

Two girls sit on one of the empty beds, both of them turning at the ruckus we're making as we enter the room. I kick the laundry basket through the door, my arms ready to give out, and this is only the first trip.

"You must be Noelle." The blonde girl hops off the bed to greet her. "I'm Michelle," she introduces herself. "I'm your roommate."

"I'm Lake, Noelle's mother," I introduce myself, looking past Michelle to the dark-haired girl on the floor glaring at us.

"Oh, that's Stevie," Michelle says. "She's from New York." She waves her off as if that explains everything.

Noelle sets the box on her bed while I finish kicking her laundry basket to her side of the room.

"There's rolling baskets to fit all your stuff in down at drop off," Michelle offers.

"Oh, I know, we're just waiting for reinforcements," I say.

With perfect timing, Georgie bursts through the door with a plant in one hand and what looks like a bottle of champagne in the other.

"Jesus, did they remodel? Because it was way shittier when I went here," Georgie huffs as she looks around the room, assessing the tiny space. "No fair."

"Seriously, Mom?" Noelle looks at the bottle in Georgie's hand and then back at me clearly annoyed.

"So we can celebrate." Georgie holds it up, looking at us innocently.

"I'm pretty sure you're not allowed to bring alcohol into the dorm," I say, raising an eyebrow.

"Relax, it's sparkling cider." Georgie lifts her brows at Noelle and then leans close to me, discreetly opening her purse, which looks more like an overnight bag, showing me the flask hidden inside with a wink. "For the adults, because I have a feeling, you're gonna need it."

"I'm fine," I say, rolling my eyes. "I've been fine." I look to Noelle for confirmation.

"Who's the emo girl on the floor?" Georgie hooks her thumb in Stevie's direction.

"There are boys on this floor?" My dad grouses as he stumbles into the room.

"Ben, good to see you," Georgie greets him.

"Is that champagne?" Dad asks, and points to her bottle.

"Sparkling cider," Georgie says in a disappointed tone. "But the good stuff is…"

"Okay, Georgie," I interrupt them and take the bottle from her, setting it on the desk. "We need to go back downstairs so we can load all her stuff in the basket."

"You mean I gotta go back down those stairs?" Dad asks.

"There's an elevator," Michelle offers.

"I'm good here," he says, taking a seat on the bed opposite Stevie, who eyes him suspiciously.

"I'll watch Ben," Georgie gestures to my dad.

"I don't need a babysitter," Dad protests.

"Someone has to keep the college girls from fawning over you," Georgie explains to him, and my dad scoffs dismissively.

"Come on," I gesture to Noelle and put my arm around her while we walk down the hall, dodging students and parents carrying garbage bags and baskets full of belongings.

After waiting twenty minutes for an empty elevator, we make it back downstairs to the lobby and walk another ten minutes just to get to the car and start loading her things in the basket.

"I'm sorry," I say, leaning against the trunk of Noelle's little VW bug, since nothing was going to fit in my Porsche. The early August sun is relentless, and I mentally curse the state for having school start when the weather is like living in Satan's armpit.

"It's fine," Noelle laughs.

My eyes start to get misty, and Noelle scolds me. "Don't start," she says, pointing at me as sweat drips down my back.

I hold my hands up. "I'm not starting." I blink them away and get back to work unloading everything.

GEORGIE PULLS the pizza box towards her and grabs another piece.

"Do you have a hollow leg?" Noelle asks her.

"I worked up an appetite," Georgie scoffs.

"You don't work up an appetite by directing everyone where to put my stuff," Noelle argues and rolls her eyes.

"Supervision is hard work," she protests.

Stevie tosses her dark locks behind her shoulder rolling her eyes as she pushes her plate away. "You call this pizza?" she asks no one in particular.

"You're welcome," I say, wondering where her parents are since Michelle's stopped in before heading back to California.

"I think I should get going," my dad says, getting up from the chair positioned at the desk.

"Are you gonna be able to find your way back to the car?" I ask, knowing he had to park several blocks over because of all the traffic with students moving in.

"I'll walk back with you," Georgie suggests as she gets up from the floor, dusting off her shorts.

"I don't need an escort," Dad argues with her.

"Don't get your boxers in a twist, Ben," Georgie says, shaking her head. "Maybe I need help to get to *my* car." She places her hands on her hips, but my dad is not buying it.

"Hmm," he grunts.

"But don't walk too close to me because I don't want you to cock block me if some hot college boys walk by," Georgie says.

Noelle chokes on her sparkling cider.

Georgie gives Noelle a big hug. "Proud of you, honey," she says and then gives me a wink.

"Don't be a stranger," Dad says as he gives Noelle a hug. "Sunday is pot roast day in the dining hall. If you get hungry, I can sneak you some."

"Dad, she'll be fine. She's on a meal plan, and she can come home anytime she wants to eat for free."

Noelle cocks an eyebrow in my direction.

Placing a hand on my hip, I say, "I can order take out."

"Come on, Ben, maybe we can hit up a few bars on the way to our cars. You can be my wingman," Georgie grabs onto his arm as my dad harrumphs while they exit into the still chaotic hallway.

Dumping a few napkins in the trash bin, I look around.

"These boxes aren't going to fit in your trash," I say, realizing the trash can is way too small.

"There's a dumpster downstairs," Michelle directs.

"I'll help you," Noelle offers and grabs the rest of the pizza boxes.

The elevator ride to the lobby is quiet, and I already dread leaving. It's not like she's far away, but the thought of not waking up to the sound of her violin or the patter of her feet on the floor fills me with an emptiness I always knew would come but refused to prepare for.

Noelle tosses the boxes into the dumpster after I hand her mine. The lid shuts with a loud clunk that echoes off the building walls. The air is thick and tumultuous, as is the street filled with cars and college students exploring their new surroundings.

It's too hot to sit outside, so we take a seat on the lobby couch adjacent to the mailboxes.

"Your roommates seem nice, even that Stevie. She came around when the pizza got delivered," I chuckle.

Noelle laughs, playing with the frayed end of her shorts and knocking her high-top vans together.

"I should be excited," she says, continuing to look down at her dust covered shoes.

She rests her head against my shoulder. "You'll be excited tomorrow when you wake up in your dorm room for the first time and realize you're all grown up."

I can feel all her fears, trepidations, excitement, and guilt. It comes off her in waves with just that simple touch of her head to my shoulder.

"I've been selfish," she says, and before I can interject, she stops me. "I've had you all to myself these past eighteen years." Her voice breaks. "I never stopped to think that maybe you needed more than just me, because all *I* needed was you."

"Noelle, I already told you…"

"I know what you told me, that it was your choice not to bring someone else into our lives, but I think you were just using me as an excuse, because in reality, you were scared."

I open my mouth to protest.

"I don't blame you for being scared because of what you went through with Steven." She turns to face me, determination in her blue eyes. "I've always looked up to you because you're such a strong woman, someone I hope to be someday, but right now, I just feel sorry for you," she says.

I open my mouth in shock. "Noelle?"

"I feel sorry for you because you're letting your fears cloud your judgment," Noelle says with conviction. "Adrian made you happy. I saw it; something I didn't know was missing in you because I never saw it before. But once I did, it gave me a whole new perspective because it's the first time I saw you as a person and not just my mom."

"Noelle, I... I don't know what to say." I grab onto her hand because I have this overwhelming need to touch her, to help her understand she is the only person I will ever need.

"Say that you'll go to him," Noelle says. "You've been miserable these past months."

I shake my head. "You don't understand."

"I might be young and naïve about certain things, but I know you, and I know that he made you happy." Noelle squeezes my hand as she pleads. "Don't worry about me or our relationship, because I'm old enough to know that nothing will change what you and I have. I just have to learn to be mature enough to share you," she says, her eyes glistening with tears, and my own are ready to spill over.

"Go to him," she says, looking at me with the same intense blue eyes as my own. "I'm okay. You did your job."

Feeling the tears threatening to spill over, I pull her into a hug.

"It's too late," I whisper.

I've never stopped thinking about him, and even once drove past the *Tap Room* to see if I could hear him play, but the rushing traffic drowned out the opportunity. I've managed to avoid him at family gatherings which is something I know Laura hates. Either Adrian would conveniently be too busy to come to a birthday party or I'd be out of town for a holiday. No one talked about him, and I didn't ask.

"It's never too late, and you won't know unless you try," Noelle says.

Taking a big breath I pull away, still holding onto her, one hand smoothing down her hair and the other wiping away the tears staining her cheeks.

Pushing the hair from her face, I tuck it behind her ear. "Friday night, *Sixteen Candles*. I'll order pizza and you can pick up popcorn on your way." I poke her in the arm playfully.

Noelle rolls her eyes. "You do realize how misogynistic that movie is, right?"

I feign being offended, holding my hand over my heart. "It was the eighties, and speaking ill of John Hughes is a punishable offense," I say, putting my arm over her shoulder and leading her to the elevator bank. "Besides, it's my birthday and I get to pick, so there."

Noelle laughs as I press the button.

"Okay, but next time I get to pick the movie," Noelle says, turning her back to the elevator.

"Deal," I agree, just as the doors open and a group of girls pile out.

Holding the door for her, she gets on. "Remember everything I told you. No going out alone, always watch your drink, use condoms..."

"Moooom!" she whines.

"And call me," I say, looking at my beautiful girl. "Call me, and I will always pick up."

Her face softens and the gravity of these elevator doors closing weighs on us. We both know that she is always a phone call and a thirty-minute drive away, but once these doors close, a new chapter begins for both of us.

The doors bang against my arm, and I slowly let go, but Noelle moves forward, crashing into me. "You're gonna do great things," I say into her hair and kiss the top of her head before letting go.

As I walk back to my car, I feel tiny drops of rain hit my skin with the force of a train, because each one reminds me of Adrian.

Go to him.

If only it were that simple.

When I get to my car, Georgie is leaning against it.

"Have you been waiting here the whole time?" I ask, walking into her waiting hug.

"Your dad is a terrible wingman. I was holding out for you," she winks.

The rain is only a slight drizzle, not enough to cool anything off, but enough to draw the humidity even tighter around you.

"I don't think I'm much better," I say, laughing at my best friend.

"I thought maybe you'd need a drink." She throws her arm around my shoulder although the height difference makes it hard, but she manages to steer me down the street towards a pub.

We settle into a booth, and Georgie orders us a bottle of wine.

"How's our girl?" she asks, nodding her head in the direction of the dorm building.

"Way too fucking smart for her own good," I say shrugging, and then smiling at the waitress as she pours a glass for each of us.

"That girl is all you, sweetheart. You can take all the credit because you did it *alone*." Georgie raises her eyebrows, along with her glass.

Letting out a breath, I feel as though a weight has been lifted off my shoulders. "For eighteen years that girl has been your life and you poured every ounce of yourself into her, and it shows," Georgie says, her green eyes pinning me. "Now it's your turn."

"I'm going to be forty-four-years-old, Georgie." I place my forearms on the table and lean over them.

"Fuck your forty-four years old, Lake," she says pointedly. "And fuck every negative thought in that gorgeous, brilliant head of yours." She slaps her palm flat on the table between us.

"The truth is, it wasn't my age, it wasn't Beth, and it wasn't Noelle either that sabotaged my relationship with Adrian." Noelle was right, I've been the one holding myself back because I'm scared. I didn't want to fall because landing meant opening myself up to a future I couldn't predict. It was so much easier to walk away than to stand in front of him and confess that I'd fallen in love with him. Being in love meant being vulnerable, and I had spent years avoiding vulnerability.

My confession comes not as a shock or a revelation, but a release, like letting go of something that has weighed me down for too long.

"It was me."

29

GRACELAND

Pain of Love by Whissell

Hearing Noelle's car pull into the driveway, I race to the door and fling it open. She drags a large garbage bag out of her backseat and shrugs at me as I narrow my eyes at her.
Laundry.

"Have you become a shut-in?" she asks, bending down to pick up the papers.

"Just leave them," I yell to her but she doesn't listen, gathering them in her arms while dragging the massive bag of laundry.

When she reaches the door, she drops the bag and hands me the papers.

"I haven't been a shut-in," I protest, snatching the papers from her and dropping them on the coffee table.

"Happy birthday," she says, giving me a sweet smile.

The doorbell sounds and I jump up from the couch.

"Pizza," I tell Noelle, wiggling my eyebrows, but when I get to the door, I can tell it's not the delivery man.

When I open the door, I'm shocked to find Beth on my porch, along with Laura and Ianna.

"What are you guys doing here?" I ask, shocked, and look back at Noelle to confirm if she arranged this, but she just smiles.

Ianna's three girls run into the house as if they own the place, running straight for the patio door, faces pushed into the glass while they stare longingly at the pool.

"Surprise!" Beth says, holding her hands out like she's in a jazz show.

"I hope you don't mind that I brought the girls," Ianna apologizes while she runs through the living room, trying to wrangle them up.

Watching the girls excitedly jump up and down makes me realize what this house was missing: family.

"Happy birthday!" Laura says, giving me a hug, one that feels warm and inviting and so needed.

Trying to shut the door behind them, it's stopped by a hand and a shout. When I pull it open, Georgie stands on the doorstep, juggling a bottle of wine and a couple of pizza boxes.

"A little help here," she says, frazzled.

Grabbing the pizza, I open the door wider for her and then lock it behind her.

"Did you commandeer the pizza before he even got to my house?" I ask, setting everything down on the kitchen island.

Georgie makes herself at home, pulling glasses and plates down from the cabinets.

"Can we go in the pool?!" The girls ask, snubbing their noses at pizza if it means they get to go swimming.

"I brought suits," Ianna says bashfully, "just in case."

"I don't mind at all," I say truthfully.

Taking the pizza outside, I turn on the misters and the water feature in the pool for the girls. I hand out spare swimsuits to anyone that can fit in them, and those that can't, improvise.

Dangling my feet in the water, I sit on the edge of the pool, my belly full of the pizza and warmed by the wine I watch as the girls kick and scream in the shallow end.

Having everyone here with me, this just might be the best birthday I've had in a very long time.

Laura joins me on the edge, kicking water with her feet as we watch everyone enjoy the now darkening sky, a spectacular sunset cresting behind the mountains, turning the sky brilliant shades of pink, purple, and orange. If I had to pick one thing about Arizona that is remarkable, it wouldn't be the Grand Canyon or the world class golf courses; it would be the sunsets. They are unearthly when the sky is filled with clouds, stretching endlessly over the mountains, and you feel as if you could die a happy person for having seen it.

"You can ask me about him," Laura says quietly.

"I know," I sigh.

Sensing she wants to say more but she's hesitating, I turn my head slightly in her direction, meeting her eyes. They are the same color as Adrian's.

"I wish I would have known the two of you together," she says, and I don't miss the slightly sad undertone, as if she's mourning something. "Addy is the baby of the family," she explains. "As much as he liked to think he was looking out for his sisters, most of the time it was us protecting him."

"I used to do the same for Beth," I say. "Being the oldest, it was my job to make Beth's life a living hell," I laugh, "but God help anyone else that messed with her." I tilt my head, giving Laura a devilish smile. An image of her ex-husband, Eric, comes to mind.

Laura laughs heartily. "I'm not surprised."

Lightning flashes in the distance meaning the pool party will have to come to an end soon.

"I promised I wouldn't get in the middle," Laura says, and I feel myself holding in a breath, as if all the air has been sucked out of the space between us. She didn't say she promised *him*, she just said she promised.

"And I'm only saying this because I want you both to be happy." One of the beach balls flies in our direction, and Laura tosses it back in. "But he almost passed up on a once in a lifetime opportunity because he was waiting," she pauses, "for you."

Taken aback, I know my cheeks are flushed, and not just because of the summer heat.

Opportunity?

"What do you mean?" I ask, swiveling my body towards her.

"It's in the Phoenix New Times," she laughs nervously, and then looks around for Beth who's gathering up her nieces and drying them off. The impending storm gets closer as lightning shatters the darkened sky and thunder rumbles close behind. "Beth said you have a subscription."

I push myself up from the pool's edge and grab a towel, remembering the pile of papers Noelle brought in. Leaving Laura outside, I push open the patio door and rush into the living room. On the coffee table is the pile of papers, and I tear the rubber bands off, one by one, until I see the article mentioned on the cover.

Local band gets their start at the Yucca Tap Room, Tempe's oldest live music venue.

Flipping through the pages, I stop when I see a picture of Adrian on stage. His dark hair covers his eyes as he sings into the microphone. Scanning through the article, it provides some background information on Adrian, and then my finger stops on the words *signed with Stonewall Records*.

Long time music journalist, Erin Langford, who is married to rock legend Jack O'Donnell, was in town covering a charity golf event hosted by Alice Cooper and stopped in at the Yucca Tap Room. With an ear for music and responsible for discovering rising band, No Cover, Langford used her connections to sign Adrian Corvin with Stonewall records, owned by Wade Kernish and Adam Grant. Adrian Corvin and band will be giving a farewell concert at the Yucca Tap Room on Friday night before joining the last half of the Summerfest Tour.

Flipping the paper over to look on the front, I check the date. This was from last week. "Beth!" I yell, spotting her tiptoeing through my kitchen with a towel wrapped around her lower half, still dripping water from her hair.

I show her the paper. "Is the concert tonight? Did I miss it?"

Not waiting for an answer, I grab my phone from the side table and check the time. I can't believe how late it is. We'd lost track of time in the pool, but I just might make it to Tempe before the show is over.

"Why aren't you guys there?" I ask suddenly, realizing if this is the last time he's playing at the *Tap Room*, wouldn't they want to be there for him?

"We wanted to be here with you," Beth says, as if it's obvious.

"Yeah, but," I stammer, trying to figure out what to do. If this is a sign, some kind of fate, I should take the chance.

"Lake," Beth interrupts my chaotic thoughts, "go," she says sternly. "Go tell him how you feel."

Nodding, I feel out of breath but then I stop, looking at everyone in my house, and I can't just leave. Catching Noelle's eye as she tightens the towel around her chest, shivering from the sudden shock of cool air compared to outside, I hold up the paper.

"What have you been waiting for?" she asks.

"I can't just leave everyone here," I say, scanning the room.

"I've been waiting for someone to knock some sense into you," Georgie says, smiling. "Go, I'll watch these hooligans and make sure no one steals anything." Georgie gives Ianna's middle daughter the *I'm watching you* sign with her fingers, to which she sticks her tongue out. "This one looks like she's going to be stamping license plates when she gets older," Georgie teases, scooping her up and tickling her.

There's a sense of urgency that rushes through my body like adrenaline. I almost forget that I'm wearing a bathing suit as I grab my purse to rush out the door, so I run into my bedroom to change. There's no time to fix my hair so I leave it air dried and curly, shoving my feet into a pair of tennis shoes, grabbing a t-shirt off the hanger, realize it's from *Graceland*, but not having the time to care. This is how I rush down the hallway, wearing an *I've been to Graceland* shirt with Elvis's face on it.

Modern technology affords me many other options besides running across town, but I owe him a grand gesture to make him see that I'm finally ready. I can't let him go on tour without telling him that I love him.

AFTER RACING TO GET HERE, the monsoon had gotten the better of me. Not only is my hair plastered to my face from the rain, so is the *Graceland* shirt I made the mistake of not changing before I left the house.

I thought it was a cosmic sign, the rain telling me I was meant to be here, that I would make it in time. But when I look up at the stage, Adrian's not here. In his place is Finlay, and he doesn't look happy to see me.

Finlay narrows his eyes at me as he closes the guitar case. His posture is stiff and weary as he picks it up by the handle and walks towards me.

I'm too late.

Adrian is already gone.

"You look like someone threw you in the river," Finlay says.

"Nice to see you too," I say, jutting out my hip defiantly.

"He's not here." Finlay tries to squeeze by me, but I don't move, and his guitar case is too big to fit by.

Cocking my head to the side, I ask, "Why aren't you with him?" when I realize Finlay's here and Adrian is not.

His features start to soften, and the carefree Finlay I used to know starts to emerge. Maybe he doesn't hate me after all.

"Layla," he scratches his head, "and Emma."

They're the reason for his smile, and the melting of his heart towards me.

"I didn't want to leave them," he shrugs.

"How did he take it?" I venture to ask.

"He understands."

Of course he would.

"Do you have time for a beer?" I ask, expectantly.

To my surprise, Finlay nods. "Why not?" he smiles.

"Don't go anywhere," I say. "Stay right here, I'll be right back," I plead, and Finlay nods with a confused smile.

As I make my way to the bathrooms, I snag a butter knife off one of the tables and take it with me. At the sink next to the towels is the sharpie heart with mine and Steven's initials, a twenty-year-old reminder of a person that no longer has a place in the dark corners of my mind. I'd let him have too much power over me for far too long. So I take the knife and chisel away at the five layers of paint and plaster on the wall.

A woman emerges from one of the stalls and she sidles up next to me to wash her hands, looking curiously as I stab at the wall with my butter knife. "Good for you, honey," she says as she tosses the paper towel in the bin before leaving.

Stepping back, I look at my handy work. Only half the heart remains with my initials. I don't want to erase the person I'd once been; I want to embrace her, and leave her intact. Satisfied, I leave the bathroom, excited that Finlay is still waiting for me.

When we step up to the counter, Gael meets my gaze from the other end of the bar. A smile spreads on his face and he sets to work pouring me a Russian beer. He doesn't acknowledge that he hasn't seen me in a long time, and instead just slides the beer to me as if I'd never been gone. He places a blueberry ale in front of Finlay.

"Really, Gael?" Finlay complains, looking at the beer with disgust.

"We both know you can't handle anything stronger," Gael teases, laughing.

"Of course, I can," Finlay grumbles.

Gael looks down his nose at Finlay skeptically. "A guy throws up once," Finlay holds a finger in the air at Gael, "on the pinball machine, and he's labeled for life."

"Once was enough, Finlay," Gael says, and then saunters back down to the other end of the bar.

Finlay and I are left alone at the bar to stare at our beers. It's been a while since I've had a beer.

My lips pucker with the bitter taste, but after a few sips, it's like riding a bike. That's when the memories start to come, and I can't help but smile no matter how hard it hurts.

"How have you been?" Finlay asks, twirling the glass between his fingers.

Letting out a breath, I'm not sure where to start. "I quit my job," I blurt out, raising an eyebrow.

"Wow, that's a switch," he whistles.

"I started doing some non-profit work for the Salt River Wild Horse Management Group," I admit, knowing Finlay will recognize the significance of the group. "I thought I could help with fundraising, a little accounting, but now I'm basically running their back office." I take another sip of my beer.

Finlay turns towards me. "You surprised me, Lake."

"I'm gonna take that as a good thing?" I venture.

Finlay runs his thumb along the edge of the glass. "I mean, when Adrian first told me he was seeing an older woman, I thought," he pauses, and I narrow my eyes at him remembering how he called me a MILF, "this woman is going to eat him alive," Finlay chuckles, and I can't help but laugh, placing my hand over my mouth to contain the laughter.

"And then I met you," he continues, and I laugh even harder.

"Did I exceed your expectations?" I say between fits of laughter.

Finlay shakes his head, scoffing. "Sure fucking did." He slams his beer back down on the bar top after taking a swig. "I fucking hate blueberries," he mutters, giving Gael a scowl.

Propping my elbow on the counter, I palm my cheek. Feeling a little sorry for myself, I run a finger down the side of my glass.

"I was really pissed at you," he admits.

"Get in line, Finlay," I say, truthfully.

"But then I thought maybe it's a good thing you broke his heart, because I don't know if he would have left if the two of you were still together," Finlay admits and tilts his head towards me.

Sitting up straighter, I say, "I wouldn't have let him pass that up."

"He almost didn't leave, but I told him," Finlay shrugs, "I'd handle the business."

"How did Marius take it?" I ask, noticing my beer is almost gone, Finlay's too. We'd been sitting here a while, the time escaping me.

Finlay does his best Marius impression. "Play guitar, come back, lay floor, all good."

I double over laughing. "That's pretty good."

When I take the last sip of my beer, I set it back down slowly as if it will afford me some extra time. Turning towards Finlay, who drains the last of his glass, I boldly ask, "Am I too late?"

30

SINCE YOU ASKED NICELY

Lovesick by BANKS

"I thought when you quit your job I would get to see you more," Georgie huffs on the other end of the phone.

"There's a fundraiser coming up and I'm working to get all the details finalized," I say, cradling the phone to my ear while I shuffle through the refrigerator, looking for something to eat. There's a box with last night's pizza I'd forgotten about. Flipping open the box, I grab a piece and bite off the end, kicking the door closed with my foot.

"We'll do yoga tomorrow, I promise." Taking a seat at the kitchen island, I grab a paper towel to set my pizza on and take a sip of my coffee. "And we'll get coffee and donuts after so you can show me wedding venues."

"I still can't believe I'm getting married," Georgie says, a softness to her tone that only started to appear the day she told me she'd gotten engaged.

"Who knew Dr. Stickuphisass would be the one to finally get Georgie De Rossi to settle down," I tease before taking another bite of my cold pizza.

Georgie laughs into the phone. "Georgie Whitman," she clears her throat.

"I'm happy for you," I say sincerely.

"How are you doing?" she asks.

It's been a week since my birthday, and a week since my anticlimactic grand gesture of racing off, only to find that Adrian had already left. I've kept myself busy, too busy according to Georgie. In the evenings when everything is quiet and there's no more work to do, I think about him, especially when it rains.

"I'm really good actually," which is the truth. "I miss Noelle, but she comes home often to do her laundry so it's like she never left," I joke.

"That kid," Georgie laughs. "And don't you cancel on me tomorrow. I need a yoga wingman, uh, woman, you know what I mean. I can't be the only one in there cracking bones and falling on my ass," she says.

"I will be there cracking right along with you."

Hanging up the phone, I place it on top of the Phoenix New Times paper, the one I can't seem to throw away. I've read the article about Adrian over and over, so excited that it finally happened for him. Once again, I'm reminded of my awful timing in life. Scanning the latest issue, I pull the pages open thinking about how Noelle makes fun of me for reading an actual paper instead of reading it online like the rest of the world, or so she says. I like the feel of the paper in my hand, and the way it smells. It wouldn't be the same if I were sitting in front of a computer.

While I'm reading an article about another local venue closing, my phone vibrates. I pick it up expecting some silly yoga video from Georgie. When I see it's from Adrian, I nearly drop it. Not one text since I broke it off with him, but every time I got a notification, my heart would skip a beat that it might be from him.

> A: I bet you're eating leftover pizza for breakfast.

There's a jolt of electricity that travels through my body at the shock of seeing his text, but then I sit up straighter in my chair and look around while holding the cold pizza in my hand.

Impossible.

He can't see me, he's just busting my balls about my bad eating habits so I play along, hoping to hear more from him. I'm like an addict who needs just one more hit to get me through the day.

> L: You think you know me so well.

Testing the waters, I try to calm the beating of my heart.

> A: I know that you can't cook, that you like to sit at your kitchen island, reading the paper, and drink your coffee with a little bit of cream, but when you run out, you'll drink it black. I know that you love the rain, and Aerosmith is your favorite band.

The phone wobbles in my hand as I laugh because he knows me, really knows me.

> L: And how do you know all that? I tease.

> A: I pay attention.

His words bring a smile to my face. I wonder where he is, if he's sitting on the tour bus traveling down the highway or texting me just before doing a sound check. No matter where he is, I'm giddy at just the mental image of him and being able to talk to him. Finlay must have told him I came looking for him. It's the only explanation for the contact.

> L: I know you like spicy food, but you cook things bland because you know I don't. I know that you like to be barefoot because the minute you get home, you kick off your boots. I also know you love the desert, being in the middle of nowhere with no one around but the coyotes and Saguaros, and that music is what makes your soul happy.

Saying all this, I want him to know that I've paid attention too, that I've seen him and I know him, even when he thought I didn't.

> A: You got one thing wrong.

Pinching my eyebrows together, I watch the ellipsis as he types.

> A: I'd rather be in the middle of nowhere with you.

How can one stupid sentence make me blush? Smiling, I hold the phone in my hand and stare at it, wishing I could reach through and touch him, brush my fingers along the fine hairs of his jaw and look into his soulful eyes.

> L: I would rather be anywhere right now as long as it was with you.

> A: Is that so?

> L: Yes.

> A: Even if it was outside your house?

Dropping my phone, I race to the door and open it without hesitation because I know he's out there. He wouldn't tease me like that. He's standing at the curb, the phone raised before him, and then his eyes flick to mine, a slow smile spreading on his face. He's wearing those ripped jeans that I love so much, a hand tucked into the pocket, pushing his jeans further down his hips, and his tan carpenter boots, one foot casually crossed over the other.

He's leaning against that piece of metal on wheels. In my bare feet, I race down the steps, instantly regretting it because the pavement burns my feet, but there's no way I'm turning around now. So I do the only thing I can, jump into his arms and wrap my legs around his waist.

There's a whoosh of air as I slam into him.

"I can't believe you're here," I say, patting him down, and then finally settling my palms against his face. The sun brightens his brown eyes, making the green flecks more prominent. I've missed those eyes raking over me and settling on my face, pulling out all my secrets.

"You kept me waiting *far* too long, baby," he says, with a raspy voice.

"I told you I don't like nicknames," I tease, pushing my hands into his hair and breathing him in.

"What should I call you then?" he asks, playing along.

"Just call me yours," I whisper before kissing him.

Melting against him, I don't think a kiss has ever tasted sweeter. My hands sink further into his hair as he kisses me back, and I don't care if it's a hundred-and-ten out, I'll stay out here all day kissing him if I could.

Peeking over his shoulder at the motorcycle, I smile. "If you think I'm getting on the back of that bike, you're crazy," I say against his lips as he walks towards the house with me still wrapped around him.

"I am crazy," he says, palming my ass and kissing me again. "You're gonna put some shoes on and then your sweet ass is getting on the back of my bike."

"Well, since you asked so nicely," I laugh.

I<small>F</small> Y<small>OU</small> W<small>ERE</small> H<small>ERE</small> <small>BY</small> T<small>HOMPSON</small> T<small>WINS</small>

P<small>ULLING</small> up outside of his apartment a short while later, I'm glad he gave me his leather jacket to keep the sun from burning me. The ride wasn't so bad either, especially because I could wrap my arms around Adrian's waist. Although leaning my cheek against his warm shoulder would have been ideal, the helmet he made me wear prevented it.

Pulling off the helmet, I shake out my hair and catch him watching me. God, I've missed his eyes on me.

We walk past the swimming pool and stop at the stairs leading up to his apartment. The first time I met him, I stood on this first step with trepidation about going into a stranger's apartment. He looks at me, just as he did that night, giving me a sign that everything will be alright. I didn't know it then, but he would turn out to be my Jake Ryan. When he takes my hand and rubs his thumb along the top, I let him lead me up the stairs.

"I have something for you," he says, while digging in his pockets for the key.

Lifting my eyebrows at him, I wrap my hand around his waist, feeling his heated skin from the ride over. "Oh, yeah?" I ask, imagining what he has in store for me.

He grins with those lush lips curved into a smile as he unlocks the door and pushes it open with his hip. When I step inside, I notice most of the furniture is gone and boxes are stacked up along an empty wall.

"Are you moving?" I ask, feeling a nervous flutter of my heart. He's a touring artist now, and what that means for us I don't know.

"I'm gonna be on tour, and my lease is up next month," he explains as I walk in further, seeing how different his apartment looks without his bookcase full of records and the old record player I'd dropped an *Aerosmith* album on all those months ago. The graffiti poster with the colorful feathers is gone, and so are the pictures above the fireplace. There's no soft gray couch in the middle of the room either.

As I twirl around, taking in the emptiness and what this really means, I finally notice the birthday cake with white frosting and pink roses sitting on the kitchen counter as Adrian lights the last candle. The flames flicker, casting shadows on the empty walls, and I'm transfixed as I try to count the number of candles. "There better not be forty-four candles on there. You'll set this place on fire," I joke.

With a smile, he lifts me on the counter and then takes his place opposite me, crossing his legs in front of the cake.

"Make a wish, Lake," he says with a deep voice, the only sound to be heard over the beating of my heart.

"*Sixteen Candles*?" I ask, looking across the cake at him. "How did you…" I start to ask, trying to figure out how he could possibly know that *Sixteen Candles* is my favorite movie, but then I remember when he came to measure my house for new flooring. He'd picked up the DVD from the pile next to my couch.

"I told you," he gifts me with a cunning smile. "I pay attention," he says, "especially when it comes to you."

I tilt my head to get a better look at him. A great head of hair, perfect smile, broad shoulders – he might not have a Porsche, but he's about as close to Jake Ryan as they come.

Looking at the cake, I try to think of something to wish for... but I'm at a loss. There's nothing left I want – nothing left to wish for.

"When do you have to go back on tour?"

"Tomorrow," he says. "I wanted to get here sooner after Finlay told me you were at the *Tap Room* looking for me, but this was the first break we had," he explains, reaching over to hold my hand, the flames fluttering between us.

Closing my eyes, I know what I want to wish for now. Sucking in a deep breath, I blow out hard, trying to get each candle. It takes me a second try to get them all, and even then I need Adrian's help.

Swiping a finger through the frosting, I bring it to my mouth and lick my finger clean. "Mmmm," I moan because it's whipped cream frosting, light and sweet – my favorite.

When I look over at Adrian, he's staring at me intently with heated eyes. "Do that again," he groans, and I comply, except this time, I place the frosting to his lips.

"I suppose all your utensils are packed away?" I raise an eyebrow.

Nodding, he says, "We're just going to have to eat the cake with our hands."

Shrugging, I dig in, pulling off a small piece while Adrian laughs. The inside is vanilla with strawberry filling. I hold it out for Adrian to take a bite, but before he's able to, I push some of the frosting on his nose and cheek.

"You're going to have to lick that off," he says with a smirk.

"Well, in that case..." I take the remaining cake in my hand, lift his shirt up and spread it on his chest.

He grabs hold of my wrists before I can do more damage, and I lean further across the cake so I can kiss him. Looking down between us, Adrian cocks his head to the side, smiling as I notice I've got frosting all over the front of my shorts.

Lifting my eyebrows, I say, "Your rules, Corvin." I shake my head. "You're going to have to lick it off."

Adrian grabs hold of my hips and pulls me against him as I laugh hysterically, the cake smashed between us. Trying to undo my shorts on top of the counter proves to be more difficult than I imagined, so he hops off, pulling me with him and tossing me over his shoulder.

"Adrian!" I scream. The frosting smeared all over my shorts mars his chest as he carries me out of the kitchen. "Put me down right now!" I demand halfheartedly.

It takes only a few strides for him to carry me into the bedroom where he throws me on the bed. Pulling the frosting covered shirt over his head, he crawls across the bed, grabbing onto my hips and yanking me towards him. It's been way too fucking long, and I ache just looking at him.

Taking him in, I feel the familiar burn in the center of my chest. I feel the need to say it even though I know he can see it written all over my face. He's always known it, even before I did myself.

Taking his face in my hands, I look him in the eyes when I say, "I love you, Adrian Corvin."

His smile brightens up the dimly lit space and he presses his forehead to mine. "I need you to say it again," he orders me.

I press a kiss to his lips. "I love you."

"Happy birthday, Lake," he says with his deep, raspy voice, right before yanking my shorts down.

EPILOGUE

Never Loved a Girl by Aerosmith

Weaving in between tents and RV's, I make my way through this small, temporary city that has been erected by people camping out for the past three days. The music festival has some pretty big names on the lineup, attracting thousands of people from all over the place.

Adrian was invited for the first time last summer, playing the smaller stage with earlier times in the day that didn't yield such large crowds.

This year is entirely different.

As I pass by the tents, I see some people are reading tarot cards, a few are playing music, and some are selling homemade jewelry. Stopping at one of the stalls, I pick up a beautiful turquoise bracelet for Noelle.

She's been traveling with her college roommates and her new boyfriend over the summer. International service has been sketchy the last couple of weeks and we haven't been able to talk much, but she comes home tomorrow. Adrian and I will meet her back in Phoenix for a much needed break from touring.

Slipping the bracelet on my wrist, I pay the girl and continue through the crowd, looking at the time and realizing how late it is. Adrian goes on soon, and I like to watch from the VIP area at the side of the stage.

When I get to the gate, I flash my badge at security, but he makes me wait.

"What's the problem?" I ask, annoyed.

I don't know how many times I've been through these gates during the past few days, but you would think they know me by now.

"You're going to have to wait," the security guard says, holding me back. I cross my arms over my chest in anger.

"I need to get back there before the show starts," I protest.

"We have to clear the area for a few minutes," the security guard, a large man, wearing a black t-shirt with white lettering, SECURITY, states as he turns his back to me.

"I have a pass," I declare, tapping him on his shoulder and shoving it in his face.

"So do a lot of people," he says in a bored tone, turning back around as a group of people walk through the blocked off VIP area.

"My boyfriend is about to go on and I'm gonna be late." The minute I say it I internally cringe because I know how that sounds. "I'm in a fucking hurry."

"Jack O'Donnell is coming through," the security guard explains.

"Oh," I say mockingly, "Jack O'Donnell is coming through." I motion with my hand. "Are we not allowed to make eye contact too?" I ask in a snotty tone, which elicits a snort from the security guard.

"I'm just doing my job, ma'am," he makes the mistake of saying.

"Do I look like a fucking ma'am to you?" I ask, haughtily.

He turns around to assess me, white sneakers, jean shorts, and an *Adrian Corvin Band* t-shirt – the one with cool sun graphic and cactus outline. My brown hair is down in messy beach waves, and I pull my sunglasses down further on my nose to get a better look at this guy.

Just then, Jack O'Donnell and his entourage walks by security like a fucking circus, and I shake my head. Security closes in tightly, and I tap my foot impatiently while they walk by as if they have all the time in the world. Meanwhile, I'm going to miss Adrian's show.

The security guard turns back towards me, flips the lock on the gate and opens it for me. "About fucking time," I say, shaking my head, and then make my way through the VIP area.

Backstage is chaotic with roadies moving equipment, guitar techs racing around, and other artists gathering together in groups before their show starts.

Racing through the crowds, I finally see Adrian. He's wearing a bandana to keep his hair out of his face, tight jeans, and a graphic t-shirt that stretches tight over his biceps while he chats with one of the engineers.

Racing through the crowd to get to him, he sees me coming and turns his attention towards me. Wrapping my arms around his neck, I reach up for a kiss, and the backstage noise becomes background static. His hand wraps around my waist, holding me tight to him.

"You kept me waiting," he rasps in my ear, and I can feel his smile against my cheek.

"Blame it on Jack O'Donnell and his big fucking ego blocking off the VIP area so he *walk* through." I use air quotes. "Who does he think he is? The fucking President?" I complain.

Feeling a tap on my shoulder, I look up at Adrian's eyes to see he's looking past me with a smirk on his face.

"If that is Jack O'Donnell standing behind me," I don't finish my sentence as I shake my head, trying to gain my composure.

When I turn around, I am met with piercing blue eyes, a jaw that could cut glass, and a presence that sucks all the air from the space between us.

"Is this your girl?" Jack asks Adrian who has an arm wrapped around me. He's either trying to keep me from lunging at Jack, or he's possessively making sure that Jack knows who I belong to.

"Excuse me?" I narrow my eyes at him, "am I fucking invisible?" I feel Adrian's arm tighten around me.

Jack turns his gaze back on me, a smile spreading on his handsome face. "What's your name?" he asks.

"Lake Kennedy," I reply pointedly.

Jack levels his gaze on me, and I try not to let it show that his piercing blue eyes affect me. He could probably have me kicked out of the VIP area and then what would I do? Adrian will be disappointed, and I'll be kicking myself that I couldn't keep my mouth in check.

"I'll be sure to let security know to let you through next time." He nods in Adrian's direction. "Enjoyed your show at the *Rhythm Room* last week," Jack says.

Adrian moves me to his side. "Thanks, man."

Jack smiles at me before turning and walking away.

"Fucking wild cat," Adrian mutters as he pulls me into him, and before I can protest, he kisses me.

Smiling against his lips, I ask, "Are you trying to shut me up with a kiss?"

Adrian nods, a chuckle making his chest shake. "Stay out of trouble, will ya?"

"Adrian!" one of the producers calls, motioning with his hand for Adrian to get ready.

"I have a spot for you up front." He motions to the crowd at the front of the stage.

"But I like watching from the side of the stage. You know I don't like being around all those people," I protest.

"I want to be able to see you."

"Let's go!" one of the guys yells, tapping Adrian on the shoulder and handing him a guitar.

He gives me a kiss and points to the front of the stage. One of the security guards helps me through the crowd to the front of the stage where there's an area blocked off just for me.

It's louder on the field but I have a great view of the stage, and I watch with a smile on my face as Adrian walks out. It never gets old watching him play and seeing how the crowd responds to him. He's so natural with the way he connects with people, and the way he looks so at ease up there.

"Tonight I have a special guest," Adrian says to the crowd, surprising me. He never mentioned he'd be playing with someone tonight. "I hope you will indulge me because she is amazing." Adrian looks to the side of the stage.

She.

Who the fuck is she?

I crane my neck to see who the fuck he's talking about when I see Noelle walk across the stage, violin in hand.

What the fuck?!

"This is Noelle Kennedy," he introduces her as he drapes an arm over her shoulders, giving her a comforting hug. "She is going to be accompanying me on her violin for a special song."

Adrian looks down to the front of the stage locking eyes with me as I look back, confused and in shock.

"Lake, this one's for you, baby."

Noelle raises the violin to her chin and pulls the bow across the strings, and I recognize the melody right away. Adrian joins in with his guitar, and the rest of the band follows suit as he starts to sing the lyrics of the song *Crazy*, by *Aerosmith*.

Our song.

Watching the two people I love most on stage playing together is an experience I don't think I will ever get over. Noelle is absolutely brilliant as she walks across the stage, joining Adrian in the middle who turns to her, strumming the guitar and smiling at her proudly. She's never played before a huge crowd like this before, but you would never know it. As the song progresses she gets more at ease, walking to the front, connecting with the crowd who is losing their shit for my daughter.

Hopping on the balls of my feet, I can't help but cheer as I watch them. Over the past year I've watched them become closer, music connecting them in a way that I can't relate to. It makes me happy that Noelle loves him, because who wouldn't?

He's Adrian Corvin.

When the song ends, I want to crawl over the security line and climb up on stage, but Adrian's voice stops me.

"Let's have a big hand for Noelle Kennedy!" Adrian says into the mic, and the crowd erupts.

"I invited her because not only is she an amazing musician and composer, but she's a very important part of my life. I wanted her to be here when I ask her mother to marry me."

My heart literally stops and all the breath whooshes out of my lungs. It feels like time stops, and all the noise disappears except for his voice. I watch as he walks to the front of the stage, gets down on one knee, and stretches his hand towards me.

"Lake Kennedy, will you marry me?" he asks, producing a ring from his pocket.

Looking at Noelle, who stands to the side with tears in her eyes, she nods at me, gripping her violin tight to her chest. I look back at Adrian, and our life over the past two years flashes before my eyes. From the night we met at the *Tap Room*, all of our secret kisses, hushed promises, fights, and adventures. My heart skips a beat as I nod enthusiastically, and the air fills my chest again. Taking his hand, he pulls me up on stage.

"Yes," I say. "Yes!" I scream, while he slips the ring on my finger that I barely register. Wrapping my arms around his neck and sinking my fingers into his hair, the bandana slipping to the ground while I kiss him in front of a thousand cheering people.

Momentarily pulling away, I lock eyes with Noelle who's standing nearby. I never dreamed of having someone in our lives. In fact, I was dead set against it. That was before I knew how wonderful it could be. That was before I saw how well Adrian and my daughter got along. That was before I realized that she needed someone like him in her life. That's when the tears spill over onto my cheeks, and I curse at myself for being so emotional in front of all these people.

Noelle walks into my waiting embrace, mouthing the words, *I love you*.

"I can't believe you kept this a secret from me!" I yell over the noise of the crowd, imagining the two of them conspiring together to make this moment happen.

Noelle shrugs, looking over at Adrian with a secret smile.

"And you!" I train my gaze on him while jabbing a finger at his chest. His expression causes my heart to slow, the adrenaline to dissipate, and I forget why I'm mad. "Fucking asshole," I grumble before kissing him again.

. . .

Paula Dombrowiak

NOT ready to leave Paula's angsty world of romance? Read on for the blurb and an exclusive excerpt of King of Nothing, book one in the Kingmaker trilogy; a steamy marriage of convenience, billionaire romance with plenty of political scandal.

KING OF NOTHING BLURB

**I'm not the sort of girl you take home to meet your parents.
But our marriage of convenience is the perfect revenge.**

I find Darren Walker drowning himself in expensive whiskey. Young, handsome, and educated, he's the playboy son of a U.S. Senator, and his father's sudden death has hit him harder than expected.

When he offers me millions of dollars to marry him, I want to tell him that I can't be bought.

But of course, that's not true, and Darren is prepared to play dirty.

He's made it his life's mission to squander his potential in order to avoid living in his father's shadow. But if he wants to see even one cent of his trust fund, he needs a wife. And not just any wife will do.

Ours will purely be a marriage of convenience, and I'm going to be his final, perfect revenge.

My name is Evangeline Bowen, and I'm an escort to the rich and powerful. But soon I'll be the wife of a Senator's son, who thinks he knows all my dark secrets.

All of them, except for one…

King of Nothing is the first book in The Kingmaker trilogy, a steamy marriage of convenience romance full of political scandal. The books must be read in order for the best reader experience.

King of Nothing is available on all storefronts. Read on for an excerpt from King of Nothing.

KING OF NOTHING EXCERPT

If anyone has the power to make my cock limp, it's Rausch.

I'm surprised to see a few wrinkles in his normally perfectly pressed dress shirt. To my right, his security man stands in front of the door, blocking my exit – not that I would while still being naked. I notice Alistair stand from his perch on the couch, still in his boxers, a solemn look on his face as if he's a child waiting out his punishment.

"Your parents are dead, and you trash a hotel room." His blue eyes look past me as he adds on, "And apparently fuck hookers."

I follow his gaze to see Evangeline coming from the bedroom, her hair still wet and dripping onto her shoulders while she holds her shoes.

"What makes you think I'm a hooker?" she asks as she slips on her heels.

Rausch assesses her carefully, his mouth pressed firmly in a tight line. "An educated guess."

"Don't talk to her like that, Rausch," I tell him angrily after seeing her shocked expression.

"Touching," he says in an annoyed tone, turning his gaze back to me.

I give Evangeline an apologetic look.

"Jesus Christ, Darren. Do you know how much this will cost to fix?" Rausch gestures dramatically to the trashed room. I notice the TV mounted on the wall is cracked, and I just now remember that I hit it on my way out of the room last night, looking down at my knuckles to notice the bruises only just now.

"Just have the hotel send me the bill."

"Money is not going to fix this," Rausch yells, "especially when you don't have any."

"You're not making any sense."

Alistair straightens. "Can we just calm down?"

"I don't think either of you fuckups really understand the gravity of the situation," Rausch spits, pinching his eyebrows as if he's talking to two disorderly students instead of two grown men. "Your parents are dead, and not only is that a difficult situation for Congress, but it also means your money – your *parent's* money," he makes a point to say, "is tied up in probate."

"Can you – just stop saying that?" I throw my hands up.

"That your parents are dead? No, because the sooner you wake up and join reality, the better."

"What do you mean, there's no money?"

"The money is locked up in probate."

I look up from the floor to meet Rausch's satisfied gaze, and in a matter of a second, I upturn the coffee table, the contents scattering across the room. The security man makes his way over, but stops when Rausch raises his hand.

"What the fuck do you mean, probate?" I question, staring at Rausch with my chest heaving.

"You went to law school; did they not teach you about probate law?" Rausch doesn't rattle easily, that's why he got the reputation he has. Unbreakable, formidable, and effective – *The Kingmaker*.

Of course I know about probate law, and that means my parents money could be frozen anywhere from six months to two years.

I'm mad at Rausch for being the only one I have right now. I'm mad at myself for being such a fuckup. I'm mad at the pilot for crashing the helicopter. I'm mad that I feel *anything*.

"Is that what you think I'm worried about?" I ask him.

"You have worried about no one else but yourself, *Darren*, your whole life," Rausch lectures. "What do you think your mother would say if she saw you right now?" His eyes travel south, and then over to Evangeline, who is still standing next to me, eyeing the exit that is still blocked by the security guard.

If I want to drink and fuck myself into oblivion, that's my choice, but it's a low blow to use my mother to get a reaction out of me. As much as I want to think that I'm invincible, there is a chink in my armor—my mother—and Rausch knows it.

"Jesus, Dare." Alistair hands me a pair of shorts, even though it's too late for modesty and any sort of decorum.

"This is what I'm talking about." Rausch points to the overturned table. "It's exactly why your parents put stipulations in their wills."

I pull on the shorts and toss my hair out of my eyes. "Stipulations?" I ask, cautiously.

"Yes, Darren. If you weren't being such a fucking child, you would listen to me," Rausch continues, and he's right. I don't want to listen to him, but he has me in a stranglehold right now, like a boa constrictor around my neck. Worse yet, he knows it.

My father rarely discussed business with me, and he certainly didn't make me privy to his will or his wishes, should something happen to him. He certainly wasn't anticipating dying in a helicopter crash with my mom and leaving me alone to figure things out.

When I look at Rausch I take that back, because my father did anticipate such things, he just put Rausch in charge—not me. He never would have trusted me to handle his estate. Right now, I'm at Rausch's mercy, so I keep my mouth shut while the anger burns through me.

"You don't get any money until you're thirty years old," Rausch says, and then after a dramatic pause, adds, "or married."

Jesus fuck!

He'll make me beg, give me condescending lectures, and torture me for the next three fucking years. My heart sinks into my stomach, and Rausch can see it all on my face – the realization that he owns me. A satisfied smirk appears on his mouth.

Perhaps if I had been the good son, stayed out of trouble, listened to him more, prayed at the altar of Emerson, who he loved so fucking much, maybe then he wouldn't have put Rausch in charge of his affairs.

I narrow my eyes at Rausch because I've never been known to back down from a fight, and I still have skin in this game. It's an impulsive move, but dire situations require dire action. I grab Evangeline, pulling her to my side. "Well, isn't it convenient that my fiancée is right here?"

She looks at me with shock on her face. I lean in with a pleading look to kiss the side of her neck and whisper, *"I'll pay you extra."* Whether that has any weight with her or not after what she just heard, I don't know, but I slip my arm around her waist and tug her closer.

"Are you fucking serious?" Rausch laughs.

"Very." I narrow my eyes at him in challenge, because I am done fucking around.

"You wouldn't dare." His demeanor changes as he realizes that I am *very* serious, because I have a lot to lose.

I fix my gaze on Rausch, glaring back at him. "Try me."

Alistair makes a strangled noise behind me that I ignore.

"Isn't it convenient that we're in Las Vegas," I taunt him. "We could get married today, right baby?" I dig my fingers into her side, and she returns the favor by digging her heel into the top of my bare foot.

Fuck!

Rausch's eyes narrow. "This is beneath you, Darren. All these years I thought *he's gonna wake up one day, figure his shit out.* Especially now, with your parents gone." I can see the deep lines in his brow, his grief hidden somewhere behind his anger towards me.

"This is me figuring my shit out." I gesture toward Evangeline.

Rausch runs a hand over his jaw and down his chin, looking between Evangeline and me.

"I would say that the two of you deserve each other, but then I'd feel sorry for her." His eyes roam over Evangeline.

I feel her straighten next to me. "You don't have to feel sorry for me," she speaks up. "Darren here is a great lay, and from what I gather, he's loaded – or at least he's gonna be. What's not to like?"

The look on Rausch's face makes me want to die with laughter, and I have to press a fist to my mouth in order to contain it.

"I'm not *fucking* around anymore, Darren. I want *you* at the airport in an hour! And I want *you* to go back to whatever street corner you came from."

"You shouldn't talk to the future mother of my children that way!" I call after him as the elevator doors close with him in it.

Evangeline shakes me loose, and I lift my foot to inspect it. "Jesus, is there a fucking hole?"

She stands with her arms crossed over her chest and a haughty expression gracing her face. "If there is one, you deserved it. What the fuck is wrong with you?"

I narrow my eyes at her, but then I hear Alistair's muffled laughter from behind me and I whirl around.

"I was going to say I'm sorry I threw you out last night, but…"

"I deserved it."

"Where did you sleep?" I ask sheepishly.

"On the bench outside the elevator banks, until Rausch found me," he explains. "Not something I recommend waking up to." He gives a half smile, and I imagine that to be true.

With Rausch gone, I feel like I can finally breathe.

"This is all very touching, but I should get going," Evangeline interrupts, heading towards the elevator.

"I propose, and you're leaving?" I ask, half teasing.

She turns to face me, and I can see her nipples through the thin material of her dress. But that's not what threatens to get me hard again – it's that defiant little smirk of hers. "You must still be drunk," she says and then forcefully hits the button to the elevator.

"But you said I was a great fuck, and baby, that was with a hell of a hangover. Just imagine when I'm at my full potential." I wink and she rolls her eyes at me.

"Darren."

"Yes, dear?"

She scoffs. "Good luck with everything."

"Just let her leave. You heard what Rausch said," Alistair says from behind me.

"I heard exactly what he said." I grit my teeth and then turn back to Evangeline. I can't let her leave, she's my contingency plan. I will not let Rausch win, even if it means I have to play dirty. "And you're not going anywhere."

"You got what you paid for," she says. "Why would I stick around?"

"Because someone as exquisite as you would most certainly work for an agency," I explain. "Despite my reputation, paying for pussy isn't something I have a ton of experience with. Alistair, on the other hand, is more versed in the art of hiring escorts."

"I'm not sure that's a compliment," Alistair interjects.

"Any ideas which agency she's with?"

Alistair gives Evangeline a careful once over as if there's a price tag with the agency's name written on it.

"There's only a few reputable high-end places here in Vegas."

"Give me your phone," I demand and hold out my hand.

"What happened to yours?"

"It's probably on its way to a landfill by now."

"Here." He shakes his head and hands me the phone reluctantly.

Evangeline watches as I scroll through the phone. Finding the number I need, I hit dial and hold the phone to my ear.

"Hello," someone answers. "Yes, can you tell me if Ellen is available?" I watch as her eyes go wide, and the little pulse in her neck thrums like the beating of a hummingbird's wings.

"Oh, that's too bad because I personally wanted to thank her for sending over Holly—or is it Evangeline—I never know what the protocol is," I tell the woman on the line when she says Ellen is indisposed.

Evangeline makes her way across the suite to me. The expression on her face looks like she's ready to commit malice.

"We met in a bar last night, and she was worth *every* penny," I smile.

"What did you do?" she asks in horror, trying to grab the phone away from me, but it doesn't matter, the damage is already done.

"Consider it an insurance policy. I need a wife, and now you need the money."

"Is that why you insisted on transferring money to my account?" she accuses.

"Do you think I'm a fucking fortune teller?" I counter back angrily, seeing how her expression changes. "Is that why you wanted so badly to just take the cash, so there wouldn't be a trail?"

Her eyes narrow. "You're a prick!"

"Not the first time I've heard that."

"I knew I shouldn't have come here." She checks her purse, presumably to make sure she hasn't left anything behind.

"Don't forget, you need me."

"We'll see about that!" she shouts, visibly shaking with anger. She turns on her heel and walks back to the elevator. I feel sorry for the button as she jabs it, but better the elevator than me.

Before the doors close, I say, "I need an answer tonight."

King of Nothing is available on all storefronts, Paula's direct shop and borrow at your digital library.

ALSO BY PAULA DOMBROWIAK

THE BLOOD & BONE SERIES

BLOOD AND BONE (BOOK 1)

Two days. One Interview. Twenty-five years of Rock 'n Roll. Telling his story might just repair past relationships and ignite new ones.

BREATH TO BEAR (BOOK 2)

These chains that weigh me down, my guilt I wear like a crown, SHE is my Breath to Bear

BONDS WE BREAK (BOOK 3)

To have and to hold from this day forward - to love and to cherish, till death do us part - and these are the bonds we break.

BOUND TO BURN (BOOK 4)

Love has a way of blazing through you like poison, leaving you breathless but still wanting more.

BLOOD & BONE BOXSET PLUS BONUS NOVELLA

ALL FOUR BOOKS IN THE BLOOD & BONE SERIES PLUS A BONUS NOVELLA.

Blood & Bone legacy, bonus novella, gives you a glimpse twenty years in the future through the eyes of their children.

This is their legacy.

Already read the series but just want the bonus novella?

Grab it exclusively on my SHOP at www.payhip.com/pauladombrowiakbooks

BLOOD & BONE LEGACY, A BONUS NOVELLA

KINGMAKER SERIES

A Steamy, Marriage of Convenience, Political Romance Trilogy

Check out all the details at www.pauladombrowiak.com/kingmaker-trilogy

King of Nothing, Book 1

Queen of Ruin, Book 2

State of Union, Book 3

ABOUT THE AUTHOR

Paula Dombrowiak grew up in the suburbs of Chicago, Illinois but currently lives in Arizona. She is the author of Blood and Bone, her first adult romance novel which combines her love of music and imperfect relationships. Paula is a lifelong music junkie, whose wardrobe consists of band T-shirts and leggings which are perpetually covered in pet hair. She is a sucker for a redeemable villain, bad boys and the tragically flawed. Music is what inspires her storytelling.

If you would like a place to discuss only my books, you can join my Facebook Reader Group **Paula's Rock Stars Reader Group**

You can always find out more information about me and my books on my website

PAULADOMBROWIAK.COM

ACKNOWLEDGMENTS

I could not have written this book without the support of my family. Thank you so much for always being there for me, and for allowing me the space to create.

To my incredible friends Marybeth and Linda, for always supporting me, providing lots of laughs that usually involve wine and bruschetta. There are little pieces of both of you in Georgie. She has Marybeth's sass and Linda's unyielding loyalty.

To my beautiful alpha reader's, Nattie (a.k.a. Poopsie) and Mishie, this book would not be possible without your support and incredible feedback. I'm not sure how I got so lucky to call you both friends but you're stuck with me for life.

To my wonderful beta reader Kelly, thank you so much for reading this on such short notice and providing your feedback to make this story the best it could be.

To my lovely editor, Katy Nielsen, I owe you a pound of the finest chocolate. This book took much longer than I expected to write and I think I knocked a couple years off your life on this one but we pulled it off! Thank you for your partnership and your friendship.

To my street team, the Rockettes (although we should rename it to the Jaxson Human fan club), you know who you are. Thank you for sharing all my teasers on your social media because it makes a huge difference for this little indie author. I love you girls!!!

To all the Bookstagrammers, Bloggers, and Booktokers out there who have supported me, shared my posts, reviewed my books, and reached out to me, thank you, thank you, thank you! Word of mouth is huge! Your love of books astounds me, and I am so grateful to be a part of such a wonderful book community.

To my ARC readers, thank you from the bottom of my heart for reading and providing your honest review. Reviews are so important - especially for us little indie authors.

Last, but certainly not least, to my readers!!! I can't tell you how much you mean to me. In my heart I've always been a writer, but you make it real. I am always touched when readers reach out to me to say how much they connected with my characters. I strive to write from the heart, create characters that are real and flawed, and portray them in the most sensitive way possible. I hope you continue on this journey with me. Thank you for your support!

Printed in Great Britain
by Amazon